THE SLIP

A Novel

Lucas Schaefer

SIMON & SCHUSTER
New York Amsterdam/Antwerp London
Toronto Sydney New Delhi

Simon & Schuster
1230 Avenue of the Americas
New York, NY 10020

This book is a work of fiction. Any references to historical events, real people, or real places are used fictitiously. Other names, characters, places, and events are products of the author's imagination, and any resemblance to actual events or places or persons, living or dead, is entirely coincidental.

First Simon & Schuster hardcover edition June 2025

For information about special discounts for bulk purchases, please contact Simon & Schuster Special Sales at 1-866-506-1949 or business@simonandschuster.com.

The Simon & Schuster Speakers Bureau can bring authors to your live event. For more information or to book an event, contact the Simon & Schuster Speakers Bureau at 1-866-248-3049 or visit our website at www.simonspeakers.com.

Interior design by Lewelin Polanco

Manufactured in the United States of America

1 3 5 7 9 10 8 6 4 2

Library of Congress Cataloging-in-Publication Data has been applied for.

ISBN 978-1-6680-3070-7
ISBN 978-1-6680-3072-1 (ebook)

For Greg and Oscar

Ten Years Later, Still No Sign of Missing Teen

by Dan Kennedy, *Austin American-Statesman*

August 8, 2008

This week marks ten years since the disappearance of a Massachusetts teenager visiting Austin. Nathaniel Rothstein, then sixteen, was living with his uncle and aunt for the summer when he vanished from their North Campus home in August 1998.

Family remember Rothstein's love of fantasy novels and his commitment to the theater. In Austin, he volunteered at a local assisted living facility and had begun to develop an interest in boxing.

Rothstein's uncle, Robert "Bob" Alexander, says the family continues to search for him. "What would I want to tell my nephew if he sees this? I'd tell him what anyone in this situation would tell their missing kid. Come home."

Still No Sign of Missing Teen

TUESDAY

THE MORNING AFTER ED Hooley saw a coyote in the supply closet, Bob Alexander declared something smelled rotten inside Terry Tucker's Boxing Gym.

This was at six a.m. on a Tuesday, midway through abs and stretching. Inside the ring, the eleven members of the First Thing crew sprawled out on foam mats as Terry Tucker, fifty-four, led them through an arduous medley of scissor kicks and side-to-sides, knees-to-your-ears and upside-down bicycle. It was August in Austin, the average age inside the ring was forty-nine, and though it would be hours before a single speck of perspiration would appear on Terry's left temple, his charges were sopping.

Sopping except for Bob Alexander. Bob was lanky and spry, a semi-affable curmudgeon. At sixty-eight, he was the oldest of the First Thingers and among the fittest, too, though on this morning he was only going through the motions. Preoccupying Bob was the anonymous note that had been placed under the windshield wiper of his Audi sometime the night before.

It had been a decade since his nephew had disappeared, and things like this still happened on occasion. A lead to nowhere, a tip to nothing. A psychic in New Braunfels who'd experienced a vision. "Sounds promising," Bob had told the detective who'd called with that gem. A few days before, a short article on the tenth anniversary of the disappearance had run in the *Statesman*, so of course the kooks and grifters were coming out of the woodwork now.

No one had ever shown up at his house before, though, and it was this, combined with the note's puzzling content, which meant that as soon as Bob left the gym, he would take the folded paper, stowed in his glove compartment, to Austin Police headquarters, a time-suck in building form, where, if he had to guess, he'd rehash the story of his missing nephew, Nathaniel Rothstein, without coming any closer to finding him.

Bob had never figured out how to talk about it all. It was strange to lose a nephew. Lose a son, well, that's awful. A tragedy. But a *nephew*? Who even *liked* their nephew? Nephews were always conspiring against patriarchs, trying to kill the king. And why shouldn't they? Uncles were worse. Bob liked to joke it was amazing he was never a suspect given the reputation of that breed. "You want to end pedophilia?" Bob had told the *Statesman* reporter. "*Ban uncles*."

"That is off the record and he's kidding," Bob's wife, Marlene, had been quick to add. "He's a professor," she'd said, by way of explanation. "That's why he's so . . . voluble."

"I'm more voluble than a professor," said Bob, recently retired. "*Professor emeritus*."

Even with his friends here, at the gym, Bob rarely brought it up. Most of them had known Nathaniel, too. The kid had spent hours hitting the heavy bag that weird summer of 1998. But there were parts of the story the First Thingers didn't know, parts Bob didn't want them to know. Besides, with them it was easy to ignore the subject. People "disappeared" from this place all the time. It was the nature of the business, the nature of a gym.

That was where Bob's mind was on this seemingly typical Tuesday morning at Terry Tucker's, when, halfway through two-minute planks, he let out a sigh signaling he could no longer remain balanced on his forearms and slumped facedown onto his mat. There, his nose an inch above the canvas, Bob smelled The Smell for the first time and, surveying the rest of his cohort—flush and grimacing but all, much to his annoyance, still in position—said, "Who laid an egg in here? It smells like a colostomy bag."

It should be noted that except for Bob Alexander, none of the First Thingers smelled anything unusual. No matter. This was exactly the sort of scandal they lived for, the reason they showed up each morning before scooting off to garages downtown or office parks along 360, the only evidence of their pre-dawn lives stashed in gym bags or tossed into hampers. Among the regulars were a money manager, multiple realtors, a district court judge. Turned out hitting inanimate objects for an hour before work made office life more tolerable. Turned out no one was making poop jokes with the guy one elliptical over at Planet Fitness.

And so, despite the fact that the only foreign odor emanating from their surroundings was the breakfast sausage that Ed Hooley—the gym's "squatter-in-residence"—had been heating on a hot plate in his small room at the back, still scrawny Judge Ulbrecht said, "How you know it's a solid?" and Bob replied, "Is that an admission of guilt, Your Honor?" to which Jocelyn Carter, self-described as the biggest butch in this band of weenies, countered, "Doesn't shit usually come out of an *asshole*, Bob?" The others yowled in approval. "Not bad," said Bob, his mood improving. "Not bad."

Were Ed Hooley present for this exchange, he would have known for certain that the coyote he thought he saw at 12:54 that morning was not a figment of his imagination, nor was the stool sample he found inside the ring at 3:01, two sheepish grins curled one atop the other. For almost twenty minutes, he'd scrubbed the stain with Oxi-Clean wipes, then covered it with three strips of duct tape, as he'd seen Terry do with rips in the canvas. After, he'd sprayed citrus-scented Febreze over the offending area and laid a foam mat on top, which, three hours later, Bob Alexander would appropriate for abs and stretching. But Ed was in his room finishing breakfast, and by the time he came out to sweep, the First Thingers had descended the boxing ring's shaky metal steps, passed through the garage doors that faced the gravel lot, and begun their morning run.

Please let her be real. This was what Ed told himself as he gathered the dust bunnies that had somehow collected in the eight hours since he'd last swept. It had *looked* like a coyote. Mangy and matted, like someone had taken a dog and beaten out the cuteness.

Ed ran his broom along the wall, pausing in front of the supply closet. He'd never liked that musty sliver of a storeroom, shelves of cobwebbed fight trophies and mismatched gloves. But Terry always told him his main responsibility was to "keep an eye on the place," which was why, when Ed heard that rustling just before one a.m., he'd risen from his cot, walked through the darkened weight room, past the cluster of sleeping heavy bags, and to the closet door across from the ring. There the noise intensified: claws on cardboard, a low growl. *It's only in your head*, his identical twin, Larry, always told him. For fifty-two years, this had accounted for most of Ed's problems. He took a deep breath.

The coyote had been pawing through a box of unspooled hand wraps. She craned her neck to observe the figure in the doorway, squat and ruddy-faced. Her chary yellow eyes locked with Ed's, wide and watery, and in that moment, Ed did what anyone might do whose fate relied on knowing the real from the imaginary and whose track record in this knowing was not good: he shut the door and, left eye twitching, returned to his room, where he lay awake, tapping his socked foot against the floor.

And now, at 6:13 a.m., five hours after the sighting, three hours after he'd worked up the courage to return, only to discover those devilish droppings but no beast, he was ready to try again.

Ed ran a finger over the scar along his neck, a crude rendering of the number two, carved into him many years before. He touched the doorknob gingerly.

Please let her be real.

Ed's residency at the gym, he knew, was predicated not only on his "keeping an eye on the place," but also on his ability to "stay sane-ish," and as peculiar as it would be for a coyote to be hiding in the supply closet, it was significantly less peculiar than the alternative: that the only place that hungry coyote existed was in Ed Hooley's mind.

Ed didn't find her in the supply closet. Nor was the coyote hiding against the deceased pommel horse underneath the ring; behind the cracked toilet in the bathroom; nor below any of the torn barber's chairs from which, starting at two p.m. daily, old-timers debated who would win fights that never happened, the sound of leather on flesh and the smell of sweat and Vaseline doing as much to keep them alive as any diet or doctor, or so understood their wives, whose own mental health depended on those afternoons alone.

The coyote wasn't in the gravel lot, either, which was where Ed was searching when the First Thingers began to trickle back from their run. "Hey, Ed," they called, slapping his shoulder as they made their way into the gym. "Hey," twanged Ed, nodding to the passing herd. He prayed they hadn't seen him moments earlier, crawling around their cars.

Ed felt a special loyalty to the First Thingers. It was they who'd outfitted his room when he'd shown up three years before. Jocelyn Carter had spearheaded the campaign, securing a spare cot from the nurse's office at Burnet Middle School, where she taught biology. Soon, others followed. Ed inherited a ten-speed bicycle, the hot plate. Items destined for Goodwill ended up with him instead: a deck of well-used Uno cards, a lava lamp. One day, Bob Alexander showed up with an entire garbage bag of supplies.

This was in the winter of 2005, seven years after his nephew Nathaniel's disappearance. By then, enough time had passed that the missing boy rarely came up in gym conversation; only those who'd been around at the time knew the details. Nathaniel had come by way of Newton, Mass., the troubled, taciturn son of Bob's harried sister, no dad in sight. In Austin, he'd loosened up, started coming to the gym. Then one day, poof, gone. Never to be seen again.

In the days after the vanishing, Bob had batted away any attempted condolences with a confident "He'll be back." As the months passed and the kid stayed gone, Bob found other ways to say, *Let's not go there*: "Don't feel sorry for me. I'm not missing." Or: "Everyone's got something, right?" To Bob's gym friends, it seemed like he couldn't acknowledge the weight of what happened, or just wanted to forget it.

So it was a bit of a surprise when Bob appeared with a garbage bag of the kid's stuff, which his friends assumed he'd long ago sent back to Boston, or thrown away. Bob had made this move without consulting his wife or benefiting from her curational abilities. Inside were the sloppy seconds of a nineties-era high school boy: a bottle of Acqua di Gio cologne, the liquid turned a sickly yellow; a leather Dopp kit, complete with dried-out Clearasil pads and half a tube of Colgate; the baggy novelty tees of a pudgy kid desperate for his peers to focus on shirts silkscreened with Bart or Beavis and not on the body beneath them. "Thanks for taking this stuff off my hands," he'd told Ed.

Ever since, Ed had kept the small cash allowance Terry paid him in an electric-blue Velcro wallet, which still housed an age-softened reminder card from Newton Centre Orthodontics for an appointment scheduled a decade before. Ed's boxing gloves were the missing boy's, as was the gym bag he kept them in. On cold days, it wasn't atypical to find Ed Hooley in an oversized Patriots hoodie and matching beanie. Practically a sin in Texas.

Bob had never told Ed the story of his nephew; Ed had picked that up from the others. But like a transplant recipient in the presence of his dead donor's kin, Ed felt a quiet reverence for Bob Alexander.

Now, at 6:41 a.m. in the gravel lot outside the gym, Ed watched the old professor trot toward him, the last of the First Thingers to return from their run.

"Heya, Bob," said Ed hopefully.

Bob raised his bushy eyebrows in acknowledgment, continued into the gym.

Ed wanted to tell him about the coyote, but he knew that level of honesty wouldn't lead anywhere good. Instead, he followed Bob inside, screwing up his mouth like his twin brother had once taught him, to keep the words from tumbling out into the world.

For the next three hours, Ed completed his chores as usual. He deposited a case of plastic water bottles into the refrigerator near the gym's entrance, leaving the crinkled dollar bills in the Tupperware on the top shelf untouched. In the weight room, he Windexed the mirror-covered walls, hoping the coyote might appear in the spritz and smears. By ten, Ed was changing the dimming bulb in the bathroom, so tired from his restless sleep that he resolved to take a short nap.

That resolve weakened when he emerged from the bathroom. There he saw Terry Tucker kneeling in the ring, cutting duct tape with his teeth and laying it over the spot Ed swore he'd already covered. "What you doing?" Ed asked, frozen next to a double-end bag.

"Fixing a tear in the canvas," said Terry, smoothing out a strip. "Nothing to see here."

To another man in another profession, what Terry Tucker saw that Tuesday morning might've elicited a wince or a grimace, some evidence that his facial muscles remained intact. But for thirty-five years, Terry had walked the narrow isthmus between the seas of sport and criminality, and on that crooked strip of land called Boxing, this sort of aggravation seemed, if not typical, plausible enough.

Terry had spent the morning on the phone, trying to lock down an inaugural opponent for twenty-one-year-old Alexis Cepeda, his latest fighter to turn pro. Cepeda had been runner-up at regional Golden Gloves in San Antonio, but recently he'd seemed unsure of himself in the ring. Much to Terry's irritation, he'd also begun showing up late, as was the case this morning.

Terry's own career as a trainer had never taken off as he'd imagined. Fights had yielded modest paydays, but most of his income came from the gym. He'd opened the place in '84, in what had been Ming's Automotive, the building's past life evident in the garage doors and in a rusty old gas pump that still stood near the entrance to the gravel lot. Terry had once believed success would mean finding a fighter to go all the way with. Over the years, he'd learned that the one he'd be going all the way with was Terry Tucker's Boxing Gym.

People came and went, the gym remained. It didn't stay the same, exactly. Year after year it became ever more itself. Inside, the walls were covered in tattered fight posters over which Terry was forever stapling fresh ones, fights at the Alamodome, fights at Austin Coliseum, so many fights it seemed one could drain the walls of cement and insulation and the building would stand on the strength of those posters alone. Many listed days and months but no years, Alvarez–Barrowman from the previous December already sun-bleached, edges fraying, its age indistinguishable from Hopkins–De La Hoya, from Hagler–Hearns.

Expect nothing from no one, Terry had learned, but be open to everyone, because you never knew. Who would stick with it, who would burn out. For years he'd tried to force his patrons to enter the gym through his cramped front office rather than via the garage doors; he liked to have eyes on all who passed, every newcomer a potential investment. As his dreams of discovering the next x, y, or z dimmed (and this was boxing almost a decade into the twenty-first century: most people didn't know who x, y, or z was in the first place), he loosened up on that particular rule. Still: you never knew.

Would Alexis Cepeda make it? All Terry knew for sure was that if the kid could gain some confidence back, maybe he had an outside chance.

This chance was why, at 9:55 a.m., Terry Tucker, stacking the foam mats still laid out from that morning's class, cradled his portable phone on his shoulder and listened to the nasal whir of Lemuel Pugh, on a scratchy line from across town, try to sell him on "a fellow with a very mild palsy," for Lemuel, ninety-one, made a living promoting surefire losers for up-and-comers to KO.

"You gonna deny a boy his dream on account of a little shaky-shake?" Lemuel was saying when Terry noticed it: a greenish brown crust around the rims of three new strips of duct tape, just above the spot where Bob Alexander's nose had hovered four hours prior.

"Seems like it," said Terry, squatting down to get a closer look. He pulled the tape back, the crust expanding into a damp mass of putridity.

"OK, try this on your noggin, then: I got an old boy, one win, *thirty-nine* losses . . ."

The smell wafted up, through Terry's nostrils and to his brain, where an image formed of a grapefruit in sunglasses reading the newspaper on the toilet.

It wasn't the stain itself that caused Terry to itch at his thick salt-and-pepper goatee (consolation, he called it, for all he'd lost on top), to stop listening to Lemuel's interminable nattering. It wasn't even that someone had indeed laid an egg in his ring, a serious crime for which he could already name several suspects.

What bothered Terry was that he could envision, with startling accuracy, what happened after Ed Hooley discovered the specimen at 3:01 that morning. He knew Ed wasn't the perpetrator. He knew, too, that this was the sort of incident that could lead to a Hooley meltdown: Ed's left eye spasming as he stammered and wept and begged to stay.

Terry had learned a few things since Ed walked through the garage doors three years before, a stocky man in a stinking sleeveless shirt, his limp brown hair combed inexplicably forward. Between bouts of soft conversation with himself, Ed had claimed his twin brother would be back for him in an hour.

"One night only," Terry had told the vagrant at closing time, the alleged twin nowhere to be found. The next day Terry showed up to find Ed had stayed awake cleaning, not a bang-up job but more than the gym owner usually mustered. "Two nights only," said Terry.

Now, peering down at the canvas, Terry told Lemuel he'd call him back. Ed had been right to cover the stain, but he'd only used three strips of duct tape when no less than double that would do. Terry jumped down from the ring, grabbed the roll off his desk.

He tried to move quickly, lest Ed catch him in the act. But just as he was laying down a sixth and final strip, Ed came out of the bathroom.

"What you doing?" Ed asked, and Terry could see the panic in his eyes.

If only he'd known what was going through that Hooley mind. Someone shit in the ring, he would've said, *it happened*, let's continue with our lives! But everything in Terry's experience suggested candor wasn't the best policy here, which was why he said, "Fixing a tear in the canvas. Nothing to see here," and smoothed an already perfectly laid strip of duct tape, and stared at it until he thought Ed was gone.

Ed was still there, however, holding on to the tether of a double-end bag, his left eye twitching, so Terry resorted to his only option left. "Wrap up," he called. Sometimes the only way to get Ed out of his head was to make him move his feet.

Eleven minutes later, at 10:13, Ed Hooley, hands carefully wrapped, clambered up the metal steps and met Terry Tucker in the center of the ring.

At the very moment Ed's right glove hit Terry's left focus mitt, the coyote, curled inside a truck tire lying flat on the weight room floor, awoke to the whoosh of a jump rope swinging so fast that the cable never once smacked against the rubber flooring. Had Miriam Lopez, twenty-two, been paying attention to her skipping reflection in the mirrored wall, she might've noticed two pointed ears poking out from the truck tire six feet behind her. But Miriam—the gym's only patron at that dead late-morning hour—wasn't watching Miriam. She was watching Ed, through the doorway separating weight room from ring room, lumber around the canvas.

It was hard to look away. There was slight and nimble Terry calling out, "Jab jab jab," and there was Ed, red and wheezing, smashing his gloved fist again and again into Terry's covered hand. He was a hesitant fighter, Ed Hooley, eyeing the mitts suspiciously, as if at any moment they might grow little leather arms and hit back. When he got tired, he'd bite his lower lip, snap his head against his shoulder.

"One two!" Terry called, and Ed threw his left, then his right. "One two hook two!" Jab cross hook cross.

Miriam swung the rope twice before allowing her feet to touch the ground, then three times, causing it to whistle. She'd found the boxing gym at the start of field training. "You're about to embark on eleven weeks working overnights with *me*," her field training officer had told her on day one, pleasantly suppressing a belch. "So you may want to find a way to blow off steam." This morning, before Miriam arrived at the gym, they'd dropped off a robbery suspect at APD headquarters, her final act as an apprentice. Tomorrow, Probationary Police Officer Miriam Lopez would set out on her own.

She knew she wasn't ready. The rap on PPO Lopez was that she lacked, in the words of her training officer, a certain "Jew no say qua," that ineffable *Do not even think about fucking with me* quality that cops exuded. Their first night together, Miriam had watched the officer break up a college party inside a packed apartment on Riverside Drive. "PSA if you'd like to avoid a repeat visit from yours truly," he'd told the crowd, "you can either smoke this much pot or play your music this loud, but you cannot do both." Before he'd finished, it seemed to Miriam as if the apartment had emptied, the fog of smoke lifted.

Whatever *that* was, Miriam didn't have it. "Perps don't respond to passivity," he'd told her another time, after she'd allowed a drunk to back-talk her.

"I guess I'm more of a doer," Miriam said to her shoes.

"*Do with your mouth*," he'd instructed.

Why was she like this? Miriam couldn't even bring herself to tell Ed Hooley to quit staring at her, a habit of his if he wasn't otherwise occupied.

In the ring, Terry stabbed a mitt into Ed's belly, his sign for *done good*, then extended his arms, mitts facing the canvas. "Five six five!" Terry called. Ed squatted low, uppercutting the pads.

The coyote yawned from her tire, buried her face in her paws.

The guy was weird around women, Miriam knew. He'd sing their names to tunes he'd invented, offer strange gifts, like swans he'd made from old candy wrappers that never quite turned out. Miriam had watched others refuse Ed's bad origami, tell him to buzz off with ease. She could never access that part of herself.

It wasn't that she was scared of Ed physically. Miriam had scored well on the APD fitness test, still held the Lanier High record in the 1500 meters. Hell, she could shoot him in the head if she had to. It was never the *doing* that paralyzed Miriam Lopez, only the forever in between.

"You got one more round in you?" Terry asked Ed as Miriam moved into the ring room, taking a spot under one of the speed bags.

"Lopez," barked Terry. She turned, raised her wrapped hand to say hello. From the ring, Terry nodded to her, asked Ed for a one-two.

Miriam started in on the speed bag. Maybe her real problem with Ed Hooley was that he reminded her a little too much of being on the clock. She ran into a lot of Eds in a night, Eds at their lowest. This Ed, safe inside the gym, was probably the best version on offer. Being a cop was kind of like being a social worker, Miriam had come to realize. Problem was, she wasn't social.

That's what she'd told Bob Alexander, at least, when she'd run into him seventy minutes prior, in front of APD headquarters. Miriam had been headed out the revolving door, still trying to get the burglar's rank odor out of her nostrils, just as Bob had stepped in it. He spotted her mid-revolution, kept on revolving until it spat him out next to her, at the top of the steps to the building. "You," Bob had said, pointing a long finger at her. "I know you."

He was still in the sweat-splotched ensemble she assumed he'd worn to the gym: a pocket T-shirt and high white socks. Miriam had seen Bob there only a couple of times, him leaving late or her coming early. She liked those old, yapping morning people, with whom she couldn't get a word in even if she'd wanted.

Outside police headquarters, Bob had insisted on buying Miriam a coffee from the vendor across the street. "Anything to not go into that building."

Until then, she'd never heard about Bob's nephew's disappearance, didn't know what to make of the folded note Bob pulled from the pocket of his tennis shorts. On it, someone had written his nephew's birthdate in a childlike scrawl. *10/27/81*.

"That's all they wrote?" Miriam had asked him.

"Pretty weird," said Bob. "But people are weird. I have to say: I would not have suspected you were a police officer." He'd dealt with many a cop since his nephew disappeared. "I know they're trying to help, but I've never been down for the big swinging dick stuff. Have you?"

"You talk a lot on this job," said Miriam. "A lot more than I thought when I signed up." That's when she'd confessed to Bob that she wasn't social.

"Better than some of your colleagues," said Bob. "They're *antisocial*."

It had occurred to Miriam then that it might be wise to change the subject from the big swinging dicks of her antisocial colleagues, many of whom were in the building right across from them. "So, you have any idea what happened to him, your nephew?"

"I had my theories back in the day," said Bob. "When something terrible happens, it's easy to let the mind go wild. You get to be my age you realize the answers are never that interesting. Some BS note on my car?" A theatrical shrug. "Just another Tuesday."

Miriam thanked him for the coffee.

"*Nathaniel Rothstein*," he said, by way of signing off. The name of his nephew. "You ever hear anything about his case, maybe you'll let me know."

"Hey, Bob, if you don't mind my asking . . ." said Miriam, as the old man turned to go. "If I don't seem like a cop, what do I seem like?"

Bob considered this a moment, then raised his coffee cup in a toast. "*A normal person*," he said, and continued across the street.

At Terry Tucker's Boxing Gym, Miriam attacked the speed bag with alternating fists, embarrassed at the memory. Bob had told her about what must've been the worst thing that ever happened to him, and *that's* how she'd responded? She glanced back at Ed Hooley.

In only eleven weeks, Miriam had learned that her city contained a limitless supply of limited people, enough undesirables loitering on the margins that were they to choose a single spot to congregate, they could form a city of their own. The cops Miriam worked with were so at ease patrolling those sordid fringes. Not PPO Lopez. She was too unsure of herself to meld with the rest of that mordant lot, whose personalities, on the job, seemed to become one personality: *Police*. She didn't even *think* like a cop. Why hadn't she asked Bob more questions about that creepy note? Miriam was too preoccupied searching for clues to a more pressing mystery: the mystery of herself.

Had Miriam been less inside her head, she might've sensed a nearby rustling, might've glanced not at Ed Hooley but through the doorway to the weight room, where she would've seen the coyote standing tentatively on quivering legs, head bobbing slightly.

If Miriam had then walked closer, she would've understood that the animal wasn't drifting off, but rather was staring at the mirrored wall, mesmerized by the sight of the saddest creature the coyote had ever seen.

The coyote took a wobbly step forward. The mirror creature did the same. *This is not good*, thought the coyote, and, unnerved, headed toward Miriam. But there was too much noise coming from over there, so the coyote circled the other way, past her tire, under benches, between dumbbells, and toward the only door in sight, nudging it open with her snout. In the far corner of this new room, an unmade bedsheet hung over the side of a cot. She struggled under the narrow bed, relieved to find a secure hiding space.

The round ended at 10:43. Terry returned to his office, determined to track down Alexis Cepeda, his (potentially) promising young fighter whose tardy had stretched into an unexcused absence. In the ring, Ed pulled off his gloves, then started toward his room as a new round began. Miriam Lopez didn't turn when he passed but knew once he was no longer there. She thwacked at the speed bag harder than before.

He'd want to say hello (he liked that girl, liked how her short ponytail poked out the back of her ball cap), but the day had been too much for Ed Hooley. Exhausted, from the mitts and the all-nighter, exhausted of himself, he kicked off his sneakers and lay down without bothering to unwrap his hands.

In the years before his brother dropped him here, Ed sometimes used to bathe in nearby Shoal Creek. He knew coyotes lived in the woods surrounding those murky waters, had listened to them howl late at night. The way Ed saw it, back then, he'd invaded their home. He wondered if one was now returning the favor.

Ed could hear his other half scoffing at the notion. *No coyote's comin' for you, brother.* Ed and Larry hadn't lived together since childhood, their reunions always brief before Larry was off again on his next adventure. Yet no matter how long they were apart, Larry's low voice was always with his twin. He offered Ed firm if abstruse advice, the proud architect of a language of which he was the only fluent speaker. *Now imbibe some air and shut them peepers.* "You're right, Larry," said Ed, trying to get comfortable. "You're right."

Thirty-three minutes later, calmed by the thrum of Ed Hooley's snores, the coyote excused herself from underneath the cot. There was food in this room, she knew, not any of her favorites (oh, blessed rat!) but something, and she sensed it was trapped underneath two coils atop the hot plate on the floor. The coyote licked at the coils, stuck her tongue low between them.

No rat, but it would do.

At 2:15 p.m. on Tuesday, August 12, 2008, as the napping Ed Hooley approached his fourth hour of unconsciousness, a different scene was playing out on a mattress five miles south of Terry Tucker's Boxing Gym.

In a messy condominium on South Congress Avenue, twenty-one-year-old Alexis Cepeda, only three minutes awake, was pulling owl-print bedsheets this way and that in hopes of finding his boxer shorts when he noticed a note scrawled in Sharpie across his left leg: *PROPERTY OF B.S.!!! ☺☺ Door locks itself!!*

For her part, B.S., a.k.a. Bethanny Simons, a first-year associate at the law firm of Elkins and Meriwether LLP, was already in the fifth hour of a continuing legal education course deep inside the Sheraton Downtown, in the most frigid of their conference spaces, the cavernous Ballroom C. This particular seminar, A Guide to the Texas Franchise Tax, was sponsored by the Texas Society of Certified Public Accountants, and if one was curious as to why B.S. had decided, the previous night, to bed a twenty-one-year-old (!) boxer (!!) from Mexico (!!!), one needn't look further than either side of the poor girl now. To her left: a sallow wretch, a dribble of chicken salad from the complimentary boxed lunch hanging precariously from the edge of his mouth. To her right: a woman who looked alarmingly like Bethanny might twenty years from now if she wasn't careful—hips swollen, thighs thickened, those wild apricot curls tamed into a sullen flop. *Your life is so fun now, isn't it?* this beaten-down version of Bethanny seemed to be signaling to Actual Bethanny through heavy eyes. *Just wait two decades, bitch.*

At lunch, against her better judgment, Bethanny had called Alexis's phone ("Just wanted to make sure you made it out OK!" she planned) but no one answered. She phoned again at the 2:30 break, curious if Alexis's recollection of their night together was the same as hers. By then, Alexis's phone was dead, and all Bethanny got was an automated message telling her the voicemail was full.

As it turned out, Alexis's memory of the evening was hideously intact, which was why, when B.S. called that second time, at 2:30, her young one-night stand, due at the gym five hours earlier, was instead bent naked before the sink top in the pastel blast of empty lotion bottles that constituted Bethanny's bathroom, madly scrubbing at his Sharpied leg with a worn lime loofah.

"Best way to get your big head straight is to get your little head straight," Carlos Ortega had told him the afternoon before. Carlos, forty-one, was an ex-fighter known for working everyone at the gym to their last nerve. Six hours prior to Alexis meeting Bethanny, Carlos had watched the lightweight shuffle sluggishly around the heavy bag. "You get worse every day," grumbled Carlos, who didn't speak so much as cough up words. "You ask me," he added, raising a finger, "too much pussy."

Carlos Ortega said this hopefully, because too much pussy was his way of saying, not enough pussy, *tell me about pussy*. Later, on the hood of Carlos's 1982 Cimarron, Alexis explained his problem: Three weeks before, he'd told his girlfriend that he was going pro and she'd burst into tears. "You in six-inch heels, me coming out to Akon . . . are you seriously not smiling right now?" he'd said, holding her close. The way Izzy Escobedo looked at him then, he knew there was someone else.

To Alexis's family, it was shocking he'd lasted this long. Sure, he was cute (tight fade, *Who me?* grin, even the fist-flattened nose had its charms). Izzy Escobedo, though? She was *serious*. National Honor Society; a Scholastic Art Award; Marian the Librarian in the Travis High production of *The Music Man*.

"Hold on to that one," Alexis's tía Lola had been saying for years, never quite believing that her goofball nephew might actually pull this off.

He would have, too, if Izzy hadn't enrolled at Texas State, if her T.A. in organic chemistry hadn't been Augustine Benavides.

"Prince Augustine," Alexis sneered from the hood of Carlos's car.

"I was you, I'd fuck him up," offered Carlos.

Problem was, Alexis needed to fuck up guys much tougher than Augustine. Carlos was right: he *was* getting worse. No focus, sloppy footwork. Since the summer he'd met Izzy when he was thirteen, Alexis's entire life had revolved around her and boxing, and without one, the other suffered, and without both, well . . .

"Best way to get over pussy is more pussy," Carlos advised/imagined, which was how Alexis ended up downing shots at Wild Bill's on Dirty Sixth, why he'd sidled up to that boozy redhead alone at the bar.

She was a chatty girl whose exuberance didn't quite mask her general ungainliness, twenty-five and dressed like she'd raided an older woman's closet for executive wear that didn't settle on her like it should.

Bethanny had come post-work, just one drink after a long day, but then one drink became two drinks and two drinks became Alexis Cepeda.

Their flirtation was concise. He told her she had the most freckles of anyone he'd ever seen. She said he was almost short enough to be a jockey.

"What's with the bling?" he asked, touching her thumbnail, which was painted azalea pink. She'd bejeweled it with a sparkly heart the week before, after a thirteen-hour day poring over regulation commentary resulted in a Yellowtail-fueled shopping binge, including forty impulsive minutes scouring nail art on the web.

"My boss told me it's *inappropriate*," she told Alexis, four shots in.

"Fuck your boss," he said smoothly, motioned for another round.

"I kind of want to put you in my pocket," she confided.

"I'm gonna be the champion of the world," he slurred.

The sex lasted thirty-nine minutes. This was about twenty-nine minutes longer than either of them wanted, but every time Alexis got close to finishing, the detached head of Prince Augustine Benavides, pulled from MySpace, would float across the bed and multiply, settling on the girl's face, her nipples, the owls on her bedspread, until there were five bobbling Augustine heads, ten of them, taunting him to finish. "Almost there," he kept saying, as if repeating it enough might will it to be so.

"Like *twenty minutes in* I grab his butt," Bethanny told her best friend, Justine, over the phone the next day from the Sheraton, after Alexis didn't answer during the 2:30 break. She could feel the eyes of Beaten Down Bethanny upon her as about a dozen of them made unnecessary phone calls in the hotel driveway, anything to escape the conference room air-conditioning, and each other.

"Jesus," said Justine. "Your vagina must be a hellscape right now." Justine sold muffins part-time out of a trailer called the New Cupcake on Barton Springs Road and at twenty-seven seemed primed for a career as the receptionist to a hard-drinking detective in a pulp novel. "Pistol wouldn't shoot?"

"Pistol?" said Bethanny. "Try submachine gun."

"A regular John Dillinger."

"Is a submachine gun actually *long*?" asked Bethanny. "My point is I'm rubbing that little butt and you can tell he *likes* it. And I like it. Obviously. I mean, a *boxer*? And as I'm doing it he's thrusting harder, all"—here she lowered her voice—"'Yeah baby,' and he's moaning in Spanish, and I'm thinking, *yes!*, I've figured out the code to getting this dude off." Bethanny made sure to say this last part loud enough for her beaten-down double to hear. "Except he's still *going and going*, and I can, like, feel the UTI developing inside of me . . ." She turned back toward the hotel, satisfied to see her fat future-self galumphing through the Sheraton's automatic door. "So finally I just stuck my thumb up his ass."

Ding ding ding. It was as if Bethanny had pushed straight through Alexis Cepeda: his insides the roads of colonial Mexico, her thumb Miguel Hidalgo leading the revolution. He finished with a shudder, rolled off her in a daze. By the time Bethanny had peed and brushed her teeth, Alexis was fast asleep.

"Do you want to see him again?" asked Justine.

Bethanny scrunched her face, perplexed. "I really do."

In the bathroom, Alexis set the loofah on the sink top, his leg no less markered than when he'd started scrubbing twelve minutes before. It wasn't so much that it happened that bothered him, only that it felt so *good*.

Alexis turned away from the mirror and twisted his head around, straining to get a decent view of his backside. *Looks right*, he thought, hoping for some sign that everything was as it should be. Alexis massaged his neck. *But how would I even know it looks right if I never seen my own ass before? <u>Have I seen my own ass before?</u>* He spread himself open. *Interesting . . .*

If he'd explored more deeply, he might've seen something else of interest, but one look was enough for Alexis Cepeda, and it wasn't until a few minutes later, when Bethanny returned to Ballroom C, that she thought to glance down at her thumb, painted azalea pink except for a patch of unpolished nail in the shape of a clumsy heart.

At 4:58 p.m. outside Terry Tucker's Boxing Gym, the gravel lot had begun to fill.

For much of its life, the gym had been sandwiched between a Burger King and a U-Haul rental on this practical stretch of North Lamar Boulevard. At the start of summer, word spread that a developer had bought the U-Haul lot. A high fence now surrounded that property, the stubby building where renters would check in leveled, the fleet of trucks vanquished. On the other side, cars snaked around the Burger King drive-thru.

In the gravel lot, patrons pulled workout bags from trunks or backseats, then started toward the garage doors. Pros and amateurs and none-of-the-aboves. A stumpy State Farm agent; a bone-thin muralist. Fifty-six-year-old Barbara-Ann Jaffee, a gabby market researcher in a tunic-like Jazzercise tee, her good-natured golden retriever, Frisco, as always at her side.

This was Ed Hooley's favorite time of day. He trundled about the weight room, bumping fists and saying hey, still in the hand wraps he'd put on seven hours before. Ed had slept longer than he'd intended, hopeful that the four-legged shadow of uncertainty that had trailed him that morning would canter off as he made his late-afternoon rounds.

If that had been his fate, then Ed's story, our story, would've ended now, at 4:58 on this outwardly ordinary Tuesday at Terry Tucker's Boxing Gym, except that, just as Ed entered the main room, Frisco, the golden retriever, charged through the garage doors, straight at him.

The creature, barking wildly, lifted himself high on hind legs, gave Ed's chest a rough high five with his front paws, then turned and sprinted toward the ring, darting from one corner to the next without ever venturing under the cloth siding.

"Frisco Jaffee, *absolutely* not," yelled Barbara-Ann, rushing in after her unleashed pup. She caught the dog by his collar, squatted in front of him. "Is this who you are, Frisco?" she said as Ed watched, dumbfounded.

Barbara-Ann had to use both hands to drag Frisco toward the weight room. "This is not how I raised him," she told onlookers as Frisco barked in the direction of the ring. Barbara-Ann grabbed a jump rope and used it to leash the dog to the leg of a weight bench. "What can I say? He's nuts," she told the crowd. "You're *nuts*," she told Frisco.

But Frisco, Ed suspected, wasn't nuts. There was only one reason that normally agreeable animal would be losing it like that. There was something underneath the ring. A living thing. If Ed were to get over this whole messy day, he'd need to see it for himself.

He knew that crawling underneath the ring in view of fifty-some people would lead to too many questions. Ed could wait until eight thirty, closing time, but he could already feel his left eye pulsing.

A solution emerged in the unlikely form of Alexis Cepeda, who arrived at the gym at 6:02, a remarkable eight hours and seventeen minutes after he told Terry he'd be there.

Since he'd left the apartment of Bethanny Simons, Alexis had gone for a run around Town Lake and, over the course of three listless miles, determined it was time for a change.

Of course his girlfriend had left him. He was a loser, a shrimpy kid who'd barely eked out a high school diploma. He couldn't even screw right anymore, not without a stranger's thumb up his butt. *A professional boxer?*

Why hadn't Alexis kept his ambitions more manageable? Terry had warned him that turning pro would present challenges outside the physical. In his early teens, Alexis had crossed the border on foot from Reynosa, his only documentation someone else's now long-expired ID. At twenty-one, he couldn't get on an airplane, and if he ever left the country, he'd have no way to return. What kind of boxer fought only within driving distance of where he lived? Alexis worked a few nights a week under the table as a busser at a Brazilian steakhouse. He could probably double his hours if he asked. It was time, he knew, to get his shit together.

"What's with the leg?" asked Carlos Ortega, skulking outside the gym when Alexis appeared in the gravel lot. Alexis was still Sharpied, Bethanny's message melted into an illegible smear.

Alexis shrugged. "This is it, man. Last day," he said. "Fuck this, y'know?"

"Yeah, man," said Carlos. "Fuck this."

Inside, Alexis wrapped his hands on the bench across from the ring, nodding at the fighters who passed him, otherwise keeping his head down. Next to him sat Ed Hooley. To Alexis he looked vaguely crazed: knees bouncing, eyes watering. Alexis had always been a little skeptical of the guy, though he couldn't say why. Just a feeling.

"You OK, Hooley?" Alexis asked.

"Just having a sit-down," Ed said uncertainly.

Alexis reached under the bench for his gym bag, pulled out his gloves. "You mind lacing me up?" He wanted to hurry into bag work before Terry could read him the riot act for no-showing.

Grateful for the distraction, Ed took the left glove and pulled it over Alexis's hand, did the same on the right, then tied them both forcefully.

Alexis tapped him in the gut—a thank-you—and went off to work the bags.

In the coming weeks and months, Alexis would claim he'd never fight, never spar even, without first soft-punching Ed Hooley in the belly, a tradition that began that Tuesday in August 2008. "He's my lucky charm," he'd tell a local news reporter for a segment on the up-and-comer six months later. KXAN would feature B-roll of Alexis working out, along with a somewhat self-conscious shot of the two men engaging in their pre-fight ritual.

It was true that Alexis did tap Ed Hooley's stomach before every fight at the start of his professional career. But it wasn't for good luck.

This was only a cover, a feel-good way to explain how he'd broken out of his slump. The real reason was not one he would share with KXAN or anyone else until a few years after retiring from boxing, when, polishing off a nightcap at the Adolphus in Dallas, he'd look across the bar to find a forty-something Bethanny Simons sipping a martini.

Alexis would be in town for the opening of a new Toyota dealership, the sort of quick-buck promotional event available to former professional athletes of regional renown. Bethanny had transitioned to litigation, was trying a case at the courthouse down the street. "Are you who I think you are?" he would ask.

"Wow," she'd say, startled. "Wow. Yikes. Wow."

"Uh-oh. Yikes?"

"Not yikes you. Yikes me. Yikes *twenties*."

On that day many years after Ed Hooley saw the coyote in the supply closet, Bethanny Simons would invite Alexis Cepeda to join her for a drink. They would offer each other glosses on their professional trajectories, their respective divorces. At last call, unsure why he was revealing this information but revealing it nonetheless, Alexis would explain that the evening after their encounter, he'd stood in front of the heavy bag at Terry Tucker's, sure it would be his last workout before Real Life began.

He tapped his gloves together, threw a jab. Then another. He threw a cross, and as the bag began to swing, he started to work around it, still thinking about the events of the previous night. He replayed the sex in his mind, and for every "Almost there" he'd moaned, he hit harder.

The thumb appeared with forty seconds left on the clock. "Jesus, I did that?" Bethanny would ask, unspearing a martini olive with her teeth. "And it was a real thumb? I mean, the one you saw?"

"I'm telling you: I see it, like, out the corner of my eye as I'm working the bag. A lady's thumb. Pink nail polish. *Your* thumb. But huge. Person-sized."

"Did it have feet?"

"Do thumbs have feet? Like wobbling over or whatever. I shouldn't be telling you this."

"You *have* to tell me this!"

Alexis kept going: one two one! Harder and harder. "And as I'm punching, I see the thumb coming closer and closer, faster and faster, and I start to move around the bag away from it. One two! And then, just as the clock's winding down, it catches up to me. Stops right behind me. Bends at the joint."

"Were you like, What's going on?"

"I'm *terrified*. And then the thumb, it's like . . ."—and here Alexis would look around to make sure no one was listening—"The thumb, it's like, *inside of me*."

Alexis moved around the bag like he'd never moved before, throwing shots at a clip he'd never imagined. When the fight clock beeped, signaling the end of the round, he ignored it, kept throwing. "There's this guy a few feet away at the double-end bag," he would tell Bethanny. "You ever hit a double-end bag? It's a bitch, pardon my language. And it's his first day. He's sick of hitting this thing, and I'm going all out at this point, so he comes over to watch."

Soon other spectators followed. People turned from speed bags, stopped skipping rope. Another three-minute round ended, and the boxer was nowhere close to slowing down. None of the assembled realized that a giant thumb was two feet up Alexis, propelling him around the bag.

Terry Tucker was watching, too. He'd been in his office when he heard a commotion, came out to find twenty people gathered around his newest fighter to turn pro. Terry always said it was impossible to know a boxer's worth until you watched him in the ring. Still, even he had to admit he was seeing a different Alexis Cepeda.

Another three-minute round, another minute in between, another three minutes: Alexis never stopped. And suddenly, though Terry tried not to admit it, he could envision, in the future, a different Terry Tucker, too. By the fifth round, Terry was back on the phone with Lemuel Pugh, trying to find the kid a suitable opponent. By the sixth, he'd scheduled Alexis Cepeda's professional debut for Waco in the fall.

"If this story isn't true," Bethanny would tell Alexis all those years later, "it's the weirdest way to pick a girl up."

"Am I picking you up?" Alexis would ask, feigning uncertainty.

"Are you?" Bethanny would disingenuously counter.

By the eighth round, folks were streaming in from the weight room, standing on top of benches.

By the ninth, all fifty-four people inside Terry Tucker's Boxing Gym had crowded around Alexis Cepeda, focused on nothing but the most exhilarating workout they would ever witness in their lives.

All fifty-four people except for Ed Hooley, who'd scrambled underneath the vacant boxing ring unnoticed, now face-to-face with the coyote he thought he'd seen eighteen hours before.

She was grislier than Ed remembered.

He found the coyote between the legs of the overturned pommel horse, curled into herself and trembling. A smattering of bald patches along her back revealed fingerprint-sized islands of pink-white flesh. Her legs were hairless and scabby, a yellow crust had formed around the rims of her eyes. Most agitating to Ed was her size. She was minuscule, pathetic.

Ed poked at her belly. When she didn't wake, he poked again, harder. The second time, she opened her eyes and let out a soft whimper, chin resting against her paws. "What are you, anyway?" Ed could feel eighteen hours' worth of anxiety coursing through him.

"What are you, huh?" said Ed. The coyote looked away. "Look at me," he said, swatting his hand just in front of the animal's face. "Look at me." He swatted again. "What you gonna do about it?" Ed's left eye twitched. The coyote burrowed her snout under her paws. "What you gonna do?"

He swatted once more, and this time he made contact. It was more graze than slap, his longish fingernails just catching her ear, but it was enough to awaken the coyote.

She scrambled up on those skeletal legs, shaken and delirious, bared her fangs, and, using whatever bit of muscle was left in her, lunged at Ed, sinking her teeth through the wrap on his right hand.

He yelped when she did it, a yelp he hoped no one in the gym would hear, and then scampered backward, eyes fixed on the coyote, who'd retreated to the pommel horse, scared of what Ed might do.

Ed unwrapped his hand and examined the bite mark, two bloody holes the size of nail heads in the soft tissue between his thumb and index finger. In the coming weeks, as the wound healed, he would keep his hand wrapped in front of other people, but that wouldn't stop him from retreating to his room every few hours to examine the damage and shake with relief. This, finally, was his proof.

From nearby, the sound of cheers and, soon after, feet on metal steps, the creak of floorboards as fighters re-entered the ring.

Ed and the coyote rested on their backs, his hand on her stomach, moving with her shallow breath. They stayed that way until he could make out the last of the cars pulling out of the gravel lot, and the clang of dumbbells being set back on their racks in the weight room.

"Where you been?" asked Terry when Ed appeared in the weight room doorway looking dusty.

"Been around."

"Mm-hmm," said Terry. "You finish closing up?"

Later, after he'd locked the garage doors, Ed scoured his room for a dollar, depositing loose change in the Tupperware in the fridge and taking a plastic water bottle in exchange. Back under the ring, he held the bottle above the coyote's mouth and, when she wouldn't drink that way, he cupped one hand and poured water into it. When she finished, he brought her a link of breakfast sausage and, after she held that down, another. Ed tried to wipe a damp washcloth on the coyote's front legs, but she whimpered and hid her paws under herself, so he opted for the Febreze instead, then wrapped the nakedest parts with used hand wraps from the supply closet.

By eleven, the coyote was asleep again. Ed would watch her for many hours, knowing when she woke what he would need to do.

At 5:41 on Wednesday morning, some twenty-three and a half hours after he smelled something rotten inside Terry Tucker's Boxing Gym, Bob Alexander was cruising along North Lamar Boulevard, headed to his workout as usual. He'd just turned up the radio, Jethro Tull at full crank, when he passed Ed Hooley swiveling down the road on the ten-speed bicycle he'd been given three years before. Around his neck, Ed wore an animal like a stole.

"What the—" said Bob, Ed and his bicycle already fading in the rearview mirror.

So peculiar was the sight that Bob didn't mention it during abs and stretching, sure the other First Thingers would think the old man had finally lost it. Bob might've thought he *had* lost it if, coming back from his morning run, he hadn't found Ed in the gravel lot, same as the day before. On Ed's sleeveless shirt: a smudge of dried mud. In that Rorschach-like print, Bob Alexander saw a paw.

He wasn't about to ask Ed for details. The man's relationship with reality was too fragile, the circumstances too bizarre. Instead, Bob raised his bushy eyebrows, his usual hello, and jogged back into the gym.

Whatever happened, he was unexpectedly relieved to see Ed back. Bob would never say it, but he was proud of the fact Ed had found a safe place in this world. Proud of the small part he'd played in making it happen. Ten years before, Bob had failed at that task. It felt good to get this minor do-over.

Sometimes, Bob still imagined his nephew Nathaniel out there. Maybe there were some folks keeping half an eye out for him, like the First Thingers did for Ed. Maybe he'd found a boxing gym of his own. It was a nice thought.

Bob had learned the hard way that nice thoughts brought limited returns. Imagining, he knew, didn't get you far.

He was reminded of this fact that Wednesday afternoon, when he received an automated message from the Austin Police Department that the evidence he'd submitted the day before—the anonymous note left on his windshield—had been processed. Should there be developments, someone would get in touch. If past were prologue, Bob knew no one ever would.

In the months to come, the memory of Ed Hooley and the coyote, like that anonymous note, would fade from the retired professor's mind. Life went on, full of its small joys and disappointments.

Still, every so often, at moments he didn't expect—at the end of two-minute planks, say, his nose an inch above the canvas—Bob would remember what he saw that Wednesday morning. It would come to him all at once and disappear as quickly, as it had in real time.

At 5:41, after Ed Hooley passed on his bicycle, Bob turned back, only for a second. When he did, the coyote craned her neck to reveal herself to him. She looked at him and he at her, and then she howled: a wild bay that even with the music and the motor, Bob was certain he could hear.

PART ONE

Tomato Can

LET ME TELL YOU something," said David Dalice, twenty-seven years in Texas from "the baddest shanty in all of Haiti" and Director of Hospitality at the Shoal Creek Rehabilitation Center. "To get to your woman's heart, you get down between those legs, stick your tongue in deep deep deep, and get as close to that pulsing organ as you possibly can."

David offered this lesson as he led his newest trainee on morning rounds. It was a standard part of the How to Please Your Woman seminar he'd been presenting to his teenage male underlings for decades. The year was 1998, the city Austin, the floor Assisted Living. The trainee was Nathaniel Rothstein, and this was his first day on the job.

The job, a volunteer position, was to assist David in making Shoal Creek—a "luxury eldercare community," according to the brochure—feel like home to its residents. As Director of Hospitality, David was responsible for the happiness of all of them—from the still-with-it here on the first floor, to the losing-it on the second, to the lost-it on top—and walking these long halls was the bread-and-butter of his every day. He'd remind passersby of the 10 a.m. calisthenics class in the multipurpose room, poke his head into the games parlor to visit with the ladies playing bridge. ("Arthritis acting up? On a young thing like you? Madam, you don't look a day over nineteen!")

David had worked at Shoal Creek since immigrating to the Texas capital back when he was twenty. Now forty-seven, he'd become, over the years, a star in this place, and he strode the floral-carpeted corridors with the low-key bonhomie of a man sure of his position.

"And hello to Dr. Abruzzi!" David said as a stout and whiskered woman walkered past. Dr. Gloria Abruzzi was David's favorite resident: a retired psychologist whose sharp tongue belied her increasingly foggy memory.

"A most beautiful purple on that shirt," David told her now.

"Matches my varicose veins," said Dr. Abruzzi, winking at David, then grimacing as she passed his newest charge.

Nathaniel Rothstein raised a hand, then stuffed it back into the pocket of his oversized Patriots hoodie. He was the sort of pudgy, sullen sluggard who slunk into Shoal Creek each June from the torpid swamp that was the high school volunteer pool: baby face smattered in freckles, with a puff of coarse brown hair and a blank expression that suggested he might be filled with a simmering rage, or else nothing at all.

Since arriving at Shoal Creek at sunup, the boy had been almost silent, lagging a few paces behind David like an adolescent Igor, nodding slightly whenever advice was offered, but otherwise uninterested to the point of near invisibility. Few of the residents seemed to notice him.

Only during David's sexual digressions did Nathaniel show signs of life, glancing up from his grubby Vans to examine his new mentor. David was soft and strong, like a snowman in scrubs. He wore a thin mustache, parted in the center, and often sported the sort of authoritative grin that would've gone well with a crown and scepter. Each time he caught Nathaniel looking at him, he looked back, and the speed with which Nathaniel then turned away made David Dalice feel powerful as the sun.

"Comrade, I'm signing you up for community service," the boy's uncle, Bob Alexander, had told David three weeks prior. This was at Terry Tucker's Boxing Gym, where David's Saturday morning workouts had evolved, in middle age, from exercise with a side of gossip to the other way around. Bob was among his favorite conversationalists, a fifty-eight-year-old history professor and David's most consistent source of weed.

Bob had explained the situation as they collapsed into two worn barber's chairs along Old-Timers' Row after their workout. He needed to find a volunteer gig for his sixteen-year-old nephew, who'd be spending the summer with the Alexanders as a favor to Bob's younger sister "back east." Days before, Nathaniel—"a schlemiel of the first order"—had gotten into a fight with "some lemon" at school. "Big deal, right? High school stuff. Except . . ." Here Bob leaned into David. "My guy snaps. Breaks the other kid's jaw! Police and everything."

"Your sister didn't think, 'Man, this boy can defend himself'?"

"My sister's tired," said Bob. "Single mother, raising some gloomy kid? And now he's suspended for the rest of the year? She wanted them to toss him into juvie for a couple days! Scare him straight. I said, 'Linda, he's a white kid from Newton, Massachusetts . . .'"

David let out a guttural laugh. "If I was a white boy from that rich place, you know the first thing I'd do?"

"If you were smart, rob a bank." Bob pulled a dime bag from the pocket of his tiny tennis shorts, tossed it David's way. "I told her, 'Linda, they'll do it all right, but only after they find your body!'"

David had assured Bob Alexander they'd be fine. He'd worked at Shoal Creek close to three decades, and for many of those years had taken under his wing a summer volunteer. Usually these were wayward high school boys who the other department heads didn't want to deal with: the crater-faced grandsons of wealthy donors, the burger-breathed spawn of longtime trustees.

Indeed, David had learned long ago that among the various do-gooders who populated the place, he derived the most pleasure from the ones who did the least good. The rosy gerontology majors who speed-walked onto the scene straight from College Station? It was never any fun with those competent souls, their small, tasteful gold crucifixes and toothy grins making David feel each of his forty-seven years. Stoners, slackers, cultural Wiccans: these were his people.

David snapped his neck, indicating Nathaniel should follow. He usually saved his most lurid commentary for the locked Special Care Unit—best to keep it clean around the sentient—but this was not a man who countered silence with more of the same.

"Tell me this," said David, in a voice so low only the boy could hear. "When was the last time you think I ate some pussy?"

Nathaniel winced in disgust. "How should I know?"

David let a heavy silence fall between them. In these situations, David knew, patience was key, and it didn't take long for the boy to surrender.

"Last week?" said Nathaniel.

David let out a high-pitched *Oh!* "You think that low of me? Last week? Last night I ate the finest, wettest pussy on all of Highway 290." Then, at normal volume: "And a good morning to you, Mrs. King!"

At the service elevator, David pressed the up arrow, then gave the boy a friendly elbow. "She called herself Juanita Boggs." The elevator dinged. "Juanita Boggs of Elgin, Texas."

"Cool," said Nathaniel, trying to sound indifferent.

"And how about you?" David asked, after they were both inside. They stared straight ahead as the doors closed in front of them. "When did this young stallion last lick the sweetness?"

Eight hours later, David pulled into the gravel lot outside Terry Tucker's Boxing Gym.

He'd been coming to the gym since it opened, to little fanfare, in 1984. In the time since, he'd watched it become an Austin institution: pros and amateurs jab-jab-jabbing alongside clean-cut Dell executives and retired hippies, a jumble of humanity all sweating it out as one.

This was not his usual gym-ing hour. In recent years, David had fallen in with an irascible assemblage of men in their late-thirties and forties (plus Bob Alexander) who gathered early in the mornings, though David's work schedule allowed him to join only on Saturdays. These were a chatty band of boomers, but for David all white and all dads, but for David all men for whom sartorial and hygienic considerations no longer factored into their pre-gym preparation. Who cared if the thick band of Stan Hart's jockstrap was somehow always visible over the waist of his shorts, or if Lee Gorbinski, the runner of the bunch, wore smelly athletic shirts with globular stains at chest level from where he'd Vaselined his nipples? Not Stan Hart, not Lee Gorbinski. David suspected Bob, holder of an endowed chair in American history at the state's flagship university, rolled in each Saturday without having so much as brushed his teeth.

David scanned the lot for Terry's truck, considered driving away. It had been years since David visited the gym on a weekday afternoon, when the real fighters outnumbered the laity, and while he craved the relief a workout would provide, he knew he'd probably be the heaviest and oldest guy training.

He would've preferred his normal after-work routine: a trip to Central Market, Dutch oven simmering and a cool glass of pinot gris at the ready by the time his wife stepped through the door. But Ramona Stew, chief nursing officer at Brackenridge Hospital, had a dinner meeting, which meant that if David—who was prone to introspection but tried hard not to be—went home, he'd be left alone to consider what he'd made of his forty-seven years on this planet.

How was it that a man who'd climbed the ranks at Shoal Creek, from orderly to chief orderly, social services to activities, all the way to administration, a man who now lived among the UT professoriate in leafy Hyde Park, how was it that this man found himself, summer after summer, regaling sulky skater boys and teenage Dungeon Masters with stories of invented sex partners, when he still had an actual sex partner with whom he had actual sex?

They'd been married nearly thirty years, David and Ramona. Despite his creaky knees and her lousy back, he even still licked the sweetness on occasion, though he wouldn't phrase it that way in front of his wife, for Ramona was the sort of earthy Austin woman who felt strongly that if you're too squeamish to call a body part by its proper name you probably shouldn't stick your tongue in it, either.

What would Ramona say if she ever learned about her husband's "lessons"? He'd continued with them all that morning, into the afternoon. Had Nathaniel ever taken two women at once? Taken three? Did he wash himself properly ahead of the act? "Before you fill the cavity," the teacher had told his pupil, "you always clean the drill."

David got out of the car.

Time to punch it out, he told himself. Every now and then, David managed to truly let go at the boxing gym, to get so lost in a workout he could channel another version of himself—a better version. *Nothing like smacking the shit out of a heavy bag to get your head on straight*. The problem he'd created for himself was, objectively, a silly one, but David knew that like a scrape resulting in sepsis, silly could turn serious if left untreated.

In the shower before his shift that morning, David had vowed, once and for all, to forsake the filthy talk. He'd made this commitment before, but always, till then, in the gloom of the just-after: no easier time to swear off drinking than once he'd emptied the bottle. Today—Monday, June 1—was supposed to be different. 1998 was different. That winter, only a month after the Drudge Report published the name Monica Lewinsky for the first time, a sexual harassment allegation had led to the ouster of a custodian at Shoal Creek.

Now text-heavy posters outlining the Federal Sexual Harassment Policy adorned the walls of the staff locker room, and HR had instituted a mandatory half-day training on the subject for all employees. If any summer was the summer for Professor Dalice to go on sabbatical, it was this one, especially since his latest student was the nephew of an actual friend. David knew he *needed* to, and he *intended* to, right up until the moment he saw that dumpy boy.

"Dalice," grunted Terry Tucker from behind the desk in his small front office. Terry was sorting crumpled cash into piles, didn't look up as he spoke.

"Terry Tucker motherfucker," sang David. "How's business?"

"Be better if you ever paid." Terry was a small and muscular white guy with a brown goatee and, at the moment, rectangular readers halfway down his nose. His first real job had been working under David, who was three years older, as an assistant housekeeper at Shoal Creek. In the quarter century since, the men had maintained an uneasy friendship. David had seen what Terry had been like as a young man—talk about a lemon—and his unlikely rise both annoyed and fascinated David, Terry the canker sore he could never stop licking.

"You like my new fencing?" said Terry.

David had noticed it as soon as he'd parked: two metal bike racks that Terry had installed in front of the open garage doors that faced the gravel lot, his latest innovation to force all patrons to enter through his office. "I like to make my debtors look me in the eye," said Terry, still sorting. "Don't forget to sign in."

David looked down at the sign-in sheet affixed to a clipboard on the edge of the desk. "Sure thing, boss," he said, and, ignoring Terry, went down the step that led into the gym proper.

4 p.m. on a weekday: no errant jockstrap waistbands here. The current inhabitants of Terry Tucker's were mostly Black and Mexican, big guys in track pants and slim guys in A-shirts, guys who slung over their shoulders not the tidy athletic bags popular among the just-for-fun crowd but the heavy duffels of actual athletes.

David lowered himself onto the bench across from the ring, setting his own tidy gym bag next to him. Soon the after-work crowd would start to accumulate. For now, there was still room to spread out, the heavy bags unoccupied. Gloves came last for the real fighters. Most worked jobs that started early—construction, UPS—and now they were at the beginning of their gym routines, Terry Tucker's just starting to come to life. A buzz-cut blond dude—fat biceps, tank top already dirty with sweat—sent a speed bag ricocheting between the drum and his sideways fists. On the apron of the canvas, a wiry Black woman sat entranced—headphones on, long legs dangling—returning to her body after what, David assumed, had been a long day. He'd been there before.

In the ring, Felix Barrowman, twenty-four, pummeled an invisible opponent, letting out a *pa! pa! pa!* each time he unleashed a combination. Felix was a sinewy Black guy, a "green-eyed Casanova" in the estimation of Ramona, and the most promising fighter Terry Tucker's Boxing Gym had ever seen.

"Looking like a future middleweight champion of the world!" called David as the fight clock beeped, signaling the end of the round. "Sak pase?" David could never resist testing Felix with the Creole greeting he'd taught the boxer.

"Na-boo-lay," said Felix, breathing heavy but grinning, his accent wholly American. The year before, Felix had knocked out a Brazilian up-and-comer on HBO's *Boxing After Dark*, and in the process had turned himself into the one who was up-and-coming. Word was if Felix played his cards right, he could set himself and Terry up for a chance at a title.

"Get me four, five more KOs, Tuck thinks I got a shot," said Felix.

"That is what I like to hear," said David. From his bag, he took out his neatly coiled hand wraps, unfurled them.

The fight clock beeped, sending Felix back to the center of the canvas. David began to slowly wrap his hands. He had to give Terry credit: the man was a savvy operator. Terry's amateurs frequently made it deep into Texas State Golden Gloves, and each year one or two turned pro. None had the earning potential of Felix, but that didn't matter. The bulk of Terry's earnings came from monthly membership fees, and the presence of these "real" boxers, who by and large looked one way, gave the gym a legitimacy that attracted the much larger pool of hobbyists—the Bob Alexander set—who by and large looked another.

It was the same reason these nonfighters thrilled at the lack of air-conditioning, why they took pleasure in the mostly harmless riffraff who lurked around the edges of the place.

A couple years before, the *Statesman* had run a story on the gym, "Not Your Trendy, High-Priced Fitness Club: Everyone Welcome at Terry Tucker's," and it was true: everyone *was* welcome. Octavio Gonzalez had twice been deported, twice found his way back. The first time Josue Mendoza showed up at the gym he was living out of his car. At least a half dozen of Terry's guys had, at one point or another, done time.

It was real, this place, in a way the big box gyms weren't. And though many of the nonfighters were drawn to Terry Tucker's, at least in part, out of that weird, white-collar obsession with "authenticity," it was this crossing of worlds that also gave the gym its magic. David had to admit it appealed to him, too.

Alone in the thicket of heavy bags, David swung his arms in a half-hearted shoulder stretch, regarded his world-weary competitor. At Terry Tucker's, duct tape cured everything—a permanent Band-Aid for any rip or tear—and the gym owner had taken his love of the stuff to an extreme on David's favored heavy bag, now mummified from head to toe.

David got into fight position. A few Christmases ago, Ramona had gotten him a pair of black Everlast gloves that Velcroed at the wrists to replace his battered lace-ups. They still looked new. David pushed the bag to make it swing. He jabbed softly, jabbed again.

This was the silliest part of David's silly problem: none of his stories were true. He didn't even *want* them to be true. Never unfaithful or much tempted was David Dalice, yet get him alone with a concupiscent Trekkie and he'd launch into the most prick-tingling of sexual soliloquies without so much as bothering to remove his wedding band. Worse still, he liked it, liked the thrill of dangling the bait and reeling in his charges.

David had a well-established timeline: each summer, a new volunteer began work the first week of June, and each summer, by Independence Day, David would have him in his thrall, so much so that even the most sheepish of his subordinates wouldn't dare so much as smile at the hemp-scented, devil-stick-wielding temptress who invariably worked at their favored Spencer Gifts location without first consulting the Magical Pussy Whisperer of Shoal Creek Rehab.

His sheltered white underlings had such particular notions of Black sexuality that David as Don Juan wasn't exactly a difficult sell. "Is it true what they say about Black guys *down there*?" more than one acolyte had asked him over the years, always in the chummy, conspiratorial tone that meant August had arrived. Here his answers were so off the wall that no person who'd seen a penis, let alone possessed one, could've possibly taken David Dalice at his word.

Nevertheless, Wayne Devereaux, summer volunteer class of 1989, still believed his old boss was a Guinness World Record holder in this regard, and would even, on a golf outing to Palm Springs as a sales associate for IBM, claim he saw it once: an uncut phallus so colossal that, like the fingernails featured in those same record books, it had begun to coil. ("And this new DB2 Universal Database . . ." he'd add, setting up to hit the drive. "Trust me boys: it's gonna make your schlongs just as hard.")

Why did David do this? There was little in his history to suggest it was a good idea. After all, there were few demographic groups who needed, for their own survival, to master the social mores of an exotic culture more quickly than six-foot-three, two-hundred-pound Haitian men in suburban Texas nursing homes circa 1970. That was the year he started at Shoal Creek, the year he turned twenty. To the residents then, he was less David than Black Goliath, his brawny body not yet softened into a more palatable pudge, his short Afro a sign of . . . well, who knew exactly, but nothing good.

Change or die, the saying goes, and the Shoal Creek citizenry of the first Nixon administration had chosen the latter. This was where Austin's moneyed liberals hid their most embarrassing relations: Red Scared grand-thises and sodomy-fixated great-thats and slobbering uncles who'd lost control of their tongues but not their checkbooks, lest they miss their monthly three dollars to the John Birch Society. Yes, this was where the good folk of Austin stowed away those doddering olds, and at a discount, too, for what was then called Shoal Creek Home for the Aged was the most budget of extended-care facilities: dank and fetid, the common room a semicircle of the semiconscious, each as static as the fuzz emanating from the broken TV they huddled around.

It hadn't occurred to him then that he'd be there long. He was like a lot of twenty-year-olds: living his life as if it weren't his life, as if life were something that would start at some later date. *Monsieur Sans Souci* his father called him, Mr. Carefree. David had been born into Haiti's sliver of a middle class, to civil servants, both small and bookish. The family joke had always been that he'd been mixed up with someone else's child at birth, leaving Rose and Samuel Dalice with an easygoing jock who would grow to tower over them.

He didn't lack ambition. David imagined a big future for himself—in business, maybe, even law—but he was young. What was wrong with a year spent lifting weights, taking a class or two to "get back into it" before committing to a career? "Bonne idée" was his father's take, which translated loosely into "I've heard about a scholarship for Caribbean students at a Black college in Texas and will be covertly applying on your behalf."

It was a bad match from the start. He found sleepy Austin eerily staid compared with the go-go-go of his old neighborhood. Years later, he'd see *The Wizard of Oz* and think back to his early time stateside as much the opposite, a denizen of bustling Emerald City blown away to live out his days with farm folk in black and white.

He felt especially out of sorts in the dorm. David was mortified to spend his first night stuck on the toilet in the communal bathroom, his gut not yet acclimated to cafeteria chicken à la king.

His English was passable, but not good enough for what was expected of him. His class-clown persona didn't jibe with his classmates' studiousness, for these were young people raised with that twice-as-good ethos, who knew what it would take to succeed Black in Texas and intended to make it happen. At home he could rein in his more impish tendencies, but here his self-consciousness got the better of him: he'd come late to class and couldn't sit still once he got there.

David had another problem, too. His scholarship covered only tuition and housing. Mr. Carefree needed a job.

"I always say you haven't lived till you've scraped the gunk off another man's pecker," Shoal Creek's grizzled chief orderly told him as he showed David how to prepare a patient for a bed bath on his first day. He tossed David a washcloth, made for the door. "So live, kid. *Live.*"

It wasn't sexy, but unlike English Comp I, it felt possible. A month in Texas and a building's worth of almost-dead Texans was something of a relief.

David kept his head down in the beginning, barely spoke a word for a week. It didn't matter. On his first Tuesday, a man accused him of stealing his wife's Galmor rose gold wristwatch, despite the fact that it had been buried with her fourteen years prior. An unhappy couple, married six decades and each bent on outlasting the other, both privately inquired about David's spell-casting abilities. And then there was the poor United Daughter of the Confederacy, who arose on Christmas 1965 to find she'd forgotten who she was but would see David ambling down the hall five years later and suddenly remember. Otherwise in a permanent hypnagogic state, she'd dissolve into what can only be described as a *Psycho*-style screaming fit whenever she saw him, until the danger passed and she could return to her forgetful slumber.

For some, it was too much, and each year a handful of Black employees—spit on or cussed at or called "mammy" or "alligator bait" one time too many—would walk off the job. But David Dalice had an advantage in dealing with the dying of Shoal Creek: they weren't his people. At least that's what he told himself. Not my people, not my country. Who cared what they called him? This was acting, more or less. And so, he learned to act the part: to smile broadly, to laugh jollily, to let the people know he came in peace.

Was David Dalice good at this? Oh, was he good. (It felt good to be good.) When he entered a resident's room, he knocked three times, announced himself, and once inside, spoke with his palms extended, as if he were dealing with an anxious pet. He remembered names, birthdays. Put people at ease.

An accomplished flirt, he started dating Ramona, then a nurse, not to mention a white woman ten years his senior. Later, they'd tell people that after David flunked out his second semester, they had to marry or else he'd be sent home. They weren't exactly forced into it. Ramona was a nurse's nurse, the sort of plainspoken DIYer whose flinty competence (and, alas, heterosexuality) meant she always assumed she'd die alone. Here she'd finally met a man who appreciated her droll candor. As for David, alone with Ramona he could let down the mask. He vented about schoolwork, about politics back home. Being with an older woman turned him on.

As the snarling bigotry of one dying generation gave way to more cloying forms of white supremacy, David's stock only rose. By '73, he was chief orderly. By '75, employee of the year. His annual performance reviews were glowing. *A breath of fresh air!* (1977) *David, you're unshakable!* (1979) "You asking if I'm Haitian?" he'd tell residents skittish about HIV in the mid-1980s. "Don't worry, young lady: I'm just a Cuban with a tan."

If, at times, he wanted to pick up cranky Hank Foster and shake him, throw fussy Mrs. Bowers's wig down the laundry chute, if he'd fought with Ramona or was just in a bad mood, the residents would never know, because at Shoal Creek he wasn't David Dalice but "David Dalice," happy warrior. And as the years passed, as "David" became as indispensable to the people there as the grab bars in the showers, he spent so much time in character that *David* David revealed himself not in days or in hours but in moments: a goodbye kiss as his wife went off to a meeting, a few whales on the heavy bag after a dumb day at work.

Now when items went "missing" at Shoal Creek, residents came to David for help. They proffered baked goods on his birthday, introduced him proudly to their visiting kids. He was Director of Hospitality. An American success story. And yet . . .

What was David—real David—really?

Despite his ascendance to administration, he knew he was little more than a glorified activities director. The new title had come after ElderPlus Inc. took over in '88, turning humble Shoal Creek Home for the Aged into high-end Shoal Creek Rehabilitation Center ("The great enemy of clear language is insincerity," was Ramona's/George Orwell's take). New faux-marble flooring in the lobby; new "studio spaces" for yoga and art; same $26,000 a year.

Not peanuts, but his was not the salary that had moved them from a rickety apartment on West Sixth to a condo in Clarksville to the three-bedroom bungalow they now called home.

It's not like Ramona kept him there. Ramona Stew, 1998: skin like a rattlesnake from all those summers topless at Barton Springs and bottomless at Hippie Hollow, butt-length hair now a regal white in the style of a wizard. She'd moved to public hospital work years before, had long thought her "*over*qualified, *under*appreciated, hot-as-*hell* husband" was too good to be "stuck on some Carnival cruise down the River Styx."

What even Ramona didn't know was that five months earlier, at the start of the spring '98 term, David had enrolled in night classes at Austin Community College. He was a people person, she always said. Why not try for a degree in social work? Become a therapist?

A therapist. It sounded modest enough to be possible: he could do it in five, six years if he buckled down. There was respectability in therapy, some money, even. Real conversations with real people. Besides, his old academic woes seemed so distant all this time later. "You'll reduce to part-time," Ramona suggested. "We have the money."

Still, he had his doubts, so off to poker night, he told Ramona. Off to poker night with the menfolk and if all went well, surprise!, guess where I really was, my Wizardess?

It was a surprise all right. This time around, he was fifteen years older than his next-youngest classmate. He felt enormous, cartoonishly so, and couldn't face forward but had to angle sideways, the manufacturers of individual classroom desks apparently unversed in the bellies of middle-aged men. Worse, though he knew a pronoun was different from a noun, when the instructor, who looked fresh out of college herself, asked him for a definition, he felt himself lapsing into garrulous "David" mode, unable somehow to say in his own voice that he just wasn't sure.

"I believe the answer is 'A thing'?" he tried with a too-big grin.

If she'd said, "That's a noun, not a pronoun," or given the correct answer, he might've stayed, but instead the instructor offered a dramatic wince and snapped her fingers. "So close!" she'd said, as one might address a first grader. "So close!" she'd said, in a way that made David know he wasn't close at all.

Why couldn't he have just done what every other man did when they realized they hadn't become the person they had set out to be? Watch too much porn or start running marathons, marinate steak while downing a vodka tonic, pour another and ruminate over the grill?

That might've been David Dalice's fate, if not for one thing . . . That gang of gofers, that wretched rafter of turkeys. Why did they obsess him so, those sorry white boys, one assigned to him each summer, whose lives, he'd learned over three decades, never turned out quite as he imagined?

Consider the case of Wayne Devereaux, the Guinness Book true believer. At seventeen he'd arrived at Shoal Creek tanned and towheaded, in seemingly excellent health, but tasked with so much as wheeling a resident from one end of a corridor to another and he took on the bearing of the chronically fatigued, maundering down the hall like the dazed survivor of a terrorist attack.

Yet somehow this same Wayne Devereaux, 2.4 GPA, a cool 1120 on the SAT, would go on to Texas A&M University, on to the business school there, and then to IBM.

It wasn't just Wayne, either. Over the years, it seemed all of David's laziest disciples had scaled heights staggeringly disproportionate to their own nonexistent ambitions. The most vacuous went on to found an ad agency. The biggest drunk was in oil and gas. Last summer's tutee, now a freshman at Dartmouth, would in time become a senior executive at National Instruments, but not before gaining notoriety in Hanover for his frequent (and admittedly epic) contributions to a website called RateMyPoop. "You taught me how to #2," he'd written to David in an email, with a link to his most-lauded specimen.

Some men in David's position might've tried to live vicariously through their overprivileged toadies—trading *Hustler*s in the men's room, smoking up together in the woods behind the staff lot. But David had no interest in such foolishness. Real power was making them live vicariously through him.

No booze or cars or real women need apply. Only stories of three-ways in Fredericksburg and gang bangs in Pflugerville, of spit-roasting Miss Abilene 1987 with—who could possibly believe this?—Mr. T.

And who could blame him, really?

How many marriages might've been saved, how many midlife nipple piercings or ill-advised hair bleachings avoided, if only all men had an everlasting coterie of horny teenage boys hanging on their every word?

And so, summer after summer, day after day, he'd taught his silly lessons, for David Dalice was an addict, and those children, those profound mediocrities who would one day rule the world, those children were his drugs.

At Terry Tucker's Boxing Gym, the after-work influx had begun. Now other sounds subsumed the staccato smack of the speed bag, the *pa! pa! pa!*s Felix Barrowman let loose in the ring. The rowdy salaams of bros reunited, the slightly unhinged chatter of the deskbound finally unleashed. In the weight room, civilians commandeered the ancient machines the boxers never bothered with, setting off the ventilator hum of Terry's Reagan-era StairMaster, the tumble-dry drone from the dusty blades of the air bike.

The boxers did not mind these intrusions. They fed off the manic energy of the newcomers, knew that even if they'd been feeling lethargic all afternoon, they were the hot shots now, and they responded accordingly, nothing more invigorating than being watched.

They smacked harder, *pa!*-ed louder, and David did, too, his slow and steady rotation around the bag gaining steam. Jabs and crosses yielded to more intricate combinations, the final thirty seconds of each round a nonstop barrage.

Terry was up now, too, politicking. He buzzed about, welcoming passing gymgoers with jabs to their guts or bits of clipped instruction. The boxers he called Barrowman, Chavez, Dupree. For the paying customers he had nicknames: "That the Smile from Kyle? Get in here, man." "Protect your face, A-List. Those teeth don't look cheap!"

David could always hear, in Terry's glad-handing, a little too much of his own Shoal Creek self: how he used pet names to cozy up to the nurses ("Miss Down-to-Business," "The Minx of Managua"), and curried favor with the male residents by trading sobriquets of the Grand Poohbah variety ("There's the Boss Man!" "Hiya, Chief!").

It bothered David, this kind-of similarity between them, bothered him like all of their other kind-of similarities. The nicknames, the fact that Terry had his own pack of followers, even more loyal to him than the summer volunteers were to David. While some of the pros had their own people, Terry trained all the amateurs himself, and David had seen how those young men revered him. He wasn't a father figure exactly (to Terry's displeasure, most of them already had fathers, which meant that if they ever turned pro, they already had managers, too), but a trusted uncle for sure.

They called Terry "Coach" and brought their girlfriends over to his place in Bryker Woods to watch pay-per-view fights and swim in the pool, Terry's wife, Elise, always ready with aluminum trays of tortillas and taco fixings. The regulars at the gym were regulars at Terry's fight-watching parties, too, and though David often liked to tell Ramona he was "thinking about skipping this one," he always ended up deep in one of Terry's leather recliners, wishing he hadn't gone for that third Corona, hadn't praised Elise's seven-layer dip with quite such zeal.

Whenever Terry passed David now, he didn't acknowledge him,

and this only made David throw with more ferocity. Hook to the head! Hook to the body! One-two! One-two! One-two!

When was the last time he'd gone this hard?

The trouble with this place, thought David, as more and more patrons poured into the gym, was that nobody remembered anything.

Austin's population had doubled every twenty-five years since the Civil War, each generation bemoaning the changing city as if their particular cohort played no part in the change. In the popular imagination, the most Austin of Austinites were those coriaceous old hippies who seemed to have sprung from the sun-scorched Texas soil like weeds; David had spent enough years among the CNAs and orderlies of Shoal Creek to know many Black families had been around generations longer.

David's T-shirt was now thick with sweat. The heavy bags hung from chains affixed to the ceiling, and when David looked up he could see they were all jangling. Around him, fraternity boys and those boys' future selves—insurance brokers, engineers, CPAs—swung wildly. Next to David, two middle-aged women in long T-shirts from vacations past worked opposite ends of a bag, all four of their sneakered feet facing it dead-on. Were David in the mood, he would've shown the men how power came not from their arms but their legs, would've corrected the ladies' stances. But David wasn't in the mood.

To the assembled, he was just another body at Terry Tucker's Boxing Gym, his own role in Terry's history unknown to them. How many of these people were even in Austin in 1973, when Terry, then nineteen, began working under David at Shoal Creek? He'd been a grungy creature, Terry had, more acne than flesh, with Muppetish brown hair and an aroma so ripe it came off him in plumes, the skunky scent of a pothead Pig-Pen.

Of the many unlikely trajectories of David's disciples, it was Terry's whose rubbed him rawest, for it seemed to David that in a parallel universe, his ex-minion's journey—from village dumbass to Austin institution—might've, *could've*, been his own. Terry Tucker motherfucker: the successful owner of a boxing gym? The same boxing gym where David now spent his Saturday mornings, mostly gossiping with Bob Alexander, for a membership fee, which he did sometimes pay, of twenty-five dollars a month?

It had started as a joke, the whole boxing thing, during David's third year on the job. Early that fall, a fight manager named Lemuel Pugh became a temporary resident at Shoal Creek, sentenced to a month of bed rest for breaking his hip. No one quite like Lem Pugh back in Port-au-Prince: dainty as a kinglet, with a voice like sand in the eyes and the stringy hair of a geriatric Jesus. ("We've returned to that Peyton Place three times since my last movement," were the first words he ever spoke to David, referring, David had to assume, to the television, its picture spinning like a slot machine, "so how 'bout a bit more prune juice in the sippy?")

Back then, Lem was the state's premier manager of tomato cans: "has-beens, coulda-beens, and never-would-bes," Lem liked to call them, whose sole purpose was to provide young fighters of actual promise with easy wins to pad their records. A few of Lem's tomato cans—called such because dropped ones leaked red—were well-past-their-prime heavyweights. Others were untrained Samsons whose ambitions outweighed—or, depending on the man, perfectly aligned with—their abilities. In the end, the only real requirement was a willingness to get in the ring.

It didn't take Lem long to realize he'd hit pay dirt with the staff at Shoal Creek: a bevy of big boys in need of extra cash. Big boys and puny Terry, who Lem would later sign to fight a woman in an ill-advised riff on the Battle of the Sexes.

It was ludicrous from the start, this cadre of orderlies and nursing assistants re-inventing themselves as professional boxers. Even before small, white Terry arrived on the scene, they were a sight, a gaggle of titanic Black men from Baytown and Barbados, Port Arthur and Port-au-Prince, whose glee at the sheer absurdity of the situation—getting paid? for *this*?—propelled them out of bed at 4:15 each morning and into the dank recesses of the Town Lake YMCA, a circus of strongmen with not a minute of fight experience among them:

Step right up to witness "One-Eyed" Ralph from Loss Prevention—eye patch covering his left socket, eyeball still intact somewhere in the high grasses of Tân An—test his dexterity while sparring with the speed bag!

See Ernest "Zaftig" Wilks, only five years away from gastric band surgery, attempt to drag a truck tire connected to a chain around the Y parking lot without going into cardiac arrest!

Even David, the strongest of the lot, had trouble finding rhythm with the double-end bag, and at least once each session had to stop to redo his hand wraps, having not wound them tight enough to begin with.

And yet—and to David this was the most curious part, and the most exhilarating—the other gymgoers seemed blind to their incompetence, accepted without question that the Shoal Creek gang of tomato cans was indeed the real deal. How credulous, these white men! Were they so focused on girth, on hue, that they couldn't see these tenderfoots had no earthly idea what they were doing?

In the locker room, buff UT kids asked after the men's records ("We undefeated," deadpanned Ernest Wilks) while stout gym rats, furry as actual rats, trolled for tips on training ("Y'all just watch and learn," said One-Eyed Ralph). "Is it true," implored a gnomish graybeard, naked as the Lorax, "that before a fight you boys *abstain*?" ("Abstain?" gasped David in mock horror. "Before a fight I require *extra* relations!" he said, to a whistle from the man and the hoots of the Shoal Creekers).

Lem threw Terry into the mix a few weeks into their training, after hearing that the state's winningest female pugilist, Holly Hendrix, was looking to fight a man. Women's boxing was still seen as a novelty act in '73. That September, Billie Jean King had trounced Bobby Riggs on the tennis court, earning the respect of skeptics. Holly hoped to follow suit.

The trouble was that no one wanted to get in the ring with her. To her male counterparts, many of them Black and Mexican, beating the shit out of a twenty-two-year-old white woman seemed like a poor career choice. Losing to her might've been worse. A tomato can was needed, preferably one who wasn't strong enough to get a lucky shot off or accidentally instigate a race riot. Shoal Creek's assistant housekeeper fit the bill.

The insertion of Terry into this strange enterprise only added to the others' burgeoning sense of legitimacy, for now there was a boxer definitively worse than they were. On Terry's first day of training, they stood in a half-moon observing him as he rain-danced around the double-end bag, his fists and feet moving in concert with neither the target nor each other. "Keep those arms up!" huffed Ernest. "Aim for the *bag*," scoffed One-Eyed Ralph. *Maybe we* are *boxers*, thought David.

They were careful to keep it light, to make clear to each other, and to themselves, that they were in on the joke and not its punch line. And so, when Lemuel Pugh suggested David adopt the fight name "RastaMasta"—a nod to the island he apparently thought his new fighter was from—David didn't say, "I've told you, man, I'm *Haitian*," didn't chuck him out the window (as Ramona had advised), but rather leaned in full bore, and entered the ring at the Austin Coliseum for his professional debut wearing the Jamaican flag as a cape, the others, even Terry, following behind in tricolor tams and bright dashikis. David lost in two rounds but didn't disgrace himself: taken down by a liver shot, he'd had the good sense to stay there.

"Not my country, baby!" he'd crowed after his first payday. This was at Happy Szechuan #2, where he'd taken Ramona for lunch the following afternoon. She'd spent the morning applying warm compresses to his swollen left eyelid and was in no mood to celebrate, but David had insisted, knowing that nothing warmed his wife's heart like strip-mall Chinese. "The best seat in the house for the pride of Kingston and his queen!" he'd told the teenage host, a shaggy-haired fount of indifference, clasping the boy's palm and slipping him a dollar. From their booth, Ramona eyed a fat tilapia floating at the top of the fish tank. "Listen, Joe Frazier," she'd said, twirling lo mein, "when this ends in chronic traumatic encephalopathy, don't come crying to me." David signaled for the lad. "Hey, bwoy," he called, making a bad attempt at Jamaican patois, "yuh got some sugga for this tea*?*" David hissed with laughter as Ramona rolled her eyes.

Yes, it was all a big joke, this boxing thing, but they kept at it. David partook in hastily arranged matches in San Angelo and Leon Springs. That December, he made it to the ninth round of a Saturday night bout in Alvarado against a hometown boy with prospects, David's near-upset upsetting enough to the natives to receive below-the-fold front-page coverage in the local paper. The next February in Double Bayou, Ernest Wilks fought all the way to a split decision. Even Terry showed vague signs of improvement, and by the spring was able to skip rope for three rounds straight, could slip and slide and pivot.

For, joke or no joke, there was no pretend training, no pretending in the ring. And as the men of Shoal Creek turned their fists sideways and found rhythm with the speed bags, as they learned to make the heavy bags swing, they felt inside themselves, despite themselves, the tug of possibility, and every smack of glove to bag, of fist to face, began to sound a little like *What if?*

Of course, it ended badly, as most jokes do. Terry lost his Battle of the Sexes, and the publicity from that debacle wasn't good for Lemuel Pugh. He closed up shop for a while, went to gambol through the forest on his sore hip with the hooch-brewing Pughs of Deep East Texas. "Good riddance," said Ramona. At the time, David had reluctantly agreed. He'd badly twisted an ankle in Smithville the month before. Best not to let this dumb joke go too far.

All these years later, it should've been a silly story to tell at cookouts or on double dates. The seventies, man! What the hell, right? Yet somehow Terry—*Terry!*—had taken this loopy episode from that muzzy era and turned it into something real. A career as a trainer? The owner of a gym?

How did he do it? How did any of them? Through hard work, maybe, some late-blooming ingenuity. But David couldn't ignore the bits and pieces he picked up each summer, which his trainees dropped as casually as cats shed fur: how one had a trust fund and another came from a long line of oilmen, how last year's helper would be the fifth in his family to go Dartmouth green.

Once, on a jog, David had asked Bob Alexander how Terry had the money to start the gym in the first place. "A small business loan," Bob had told him. "And if you're wondering what kind of fool banker would've given that hophead any money, let me teach you a favored term of the undeserved . . ." And here Bob stopped running and raised his bushy eyebrows: "*Family friend*."

In the years since receiving that lucky loan, Terry had garnered a fair amount of attention, in David's view, for the owner of a modest gym. In addition to the story in the *Statesman* about how everyone was welcome at Terry Tucker's, the gym had been featured in *Ring* magazine and even once in a *Sports Illustrated* sidebar, and was a perennial subject of documentary shorts made by undergraduate film students at UT.

David himself had been interviewed a couple times about Terry. To David's irritation, no matter how hard he tried otherwise, he always ended up going the full "David" in these conversations—jokey and jolly—fearful he'd come across as embittered if he didn't.

It wasn't as if Terry's triumphs were even that grand. The youngest child of a renowned military scholar, he'd chosen getting high over higher ed, got his act together only after taking up the sweet science. Tragically unskilled at the start, he would've fizzled if he'd only boxed a year or two, as David had, but he had the means—and was deluded enough—to stick with it.

In '76, he turned pro, amassing a three-year record of two wins and nine losses, before realizing he was always up against the ropes because he was meant to be behind them, as a trainer.

Since then, Terry had remade himself into a local celebrity of sorts, his teenage foibles, rather than hindering his future success, an essential part of his origin story, the *stoned-out-of-my-gourd* expressionlessness of his youth graduated into a face of wry imperturbability.

At forty-seven years of age, David knew there were worthier things to preoccupy himself with than the success of Terry Tucker. David wasn't exactly living on the streets himself. He knew, too, that this was a one-way rivalry, that Terry probably wasn't spending a lot of time dwelling on their shared history or thinking much about his former boss at all.

But David had never been able to shake his mild sense of aggrievement at his once-dopey ex-disciple's ascent, just as, in the time since that *Statesman* story had been published, he hadn't been able to shake the final line, a quote from Terry: "I always tell the new kids: if it's possible for me, it's possible for anybody. *Anybody*."

Now Terry Tucker's had reached its sweaty, raucous peak.

Gymgoers skipped rope in the single traffic lane of the filled gravel lot, sending pebbles pinging into wheel wells, bumpers. In the weight room, patrons lay on blue mats tossing medicine balls to their standing partners, sneakers braced on knees spandexed or bare, while a trio of skinny guys pivoted around overturned truck tires, punching in near unison. From the bench press, a muscled white boy let loose with ostentatious groans.

The wall thermometer in the main room read 81 degrees. Here, every bag slapped, swayed, quavered. The ring was awash in shadowboxers fighting air, pumping themselves up with encouragements muttered through mouthguards, the sweat-drenched patients in a psych ward for the super-fit.

David had been at it nine rounds, ten. Some ridiculous number. Even when he'd first started coming, thirty pounds lighter, he almost never went this long. He'd feel it tomorrow.

But he didn't feel it now. On those rare days like today, when he stuffed his resentments and his jealousies and his regrets into his gloves and raised his fists to his face, he forgot his iffy knees and added girth. He forgot his forty-seven-year-old self altogether.

Tomorrow, David will continue with his lessons. Ask him now and he'll say he's done. He'll believe it, too, but come morning, he'll launch in as soon as he punches in. An addiction to something preposterous is still an addiction, difficult to shake. But David knows he didn't come to the boxing gym to escape all that. Not really.

The fight clock issues its final warning, thirty seconds left in David's final round. Now it isn't about what he's throwing or how he's throwing it. The goal is keep going keep going don't stop. And as he does this he becomes, for as long as he's punching, that other version of himself.

In this moment, David is no longer the Director of Hospitality at Shoal Creek Rehabilitation. He is David the future lawyer, the one-day businessman, the someday therapist. David the maybe-not-a-tomato-can, who takes it nine rounds in Alvarado and wakes the next morning bruised but ready for more.

In this moment, he is David the fighter, who knows—who knew way back in 1973, back when he threw his first punch—that his true strength doesn't live in his arms *or* his legs, his thighs, his feet, not in any one part but in his whole self, who understands the secret hunger that makes his body move.

Around him, the denizens of Terry Tucker's Boxing Gym go at it as he goes at it. Fifteen seconds, ten seconds. They hear what he hears. The machine-gun fire of wrapped wrists against speed bag, the squeak of fight shoes pivoting on canvas, leather against leather, against flesh. They release themselves from themselves.

What if?

Like Me

I.

In the days after Nathaniel Rothstein disappeared, the police would search for his cell phone.

The phone was a Nokia 5190: "for emergencies only," according to the mother. If the police had found the phone and searched its history, they would've seen that Nathaniel had spent that summer talking to the Russian girl, sometimes as often as four times in a day. But the phone would vanish along with Nathaniel, neither to be seen nor heard from again, and of all the scenarios in which the boy should disappear—murdered, kidnapped, run away—it was hard for anyone who'd ever encountered him to believe a girl was involved. He would not have believed it, either.

Nathaniel was sixteen, with puffy brown hair and thick freckles and a *This is dumb* countenance, his clammy hands forever balled in the pouch of his Pats hoodie. He was not morbidly obese but had the misfortune of carrying his weight in his chest, and since grade school the other boys had made fun of his "double Ds," his "breasteses," his "titties."

For this reason, at the suggestion of Dr. Lichtblau, his pediatrician back east, Nathaniel completed fifty push-ups every afternoon. He'd do them on the day he went missing, and he was doing them nine weeks earlier, an hour after finishing his first shift as a summer volunteer at a local nursing facility, Shoal Creek Rehab. It was the first of June 1998, and to understand what happened with the Russian girl, what happened to Nathaniel Rothstein, it is here we must begin.

The time: 4 p.m. The location: his older cousin's bedroom floor in Austin's oak-lined North Campus neighborhood. The outfit: billowy Joe Boxers, one big smiley face.

What a relief to finally be alone, to be free of his new boss—his uncle's friend David—who'd spent the day bragging about sex acts he'd engaged in and asking the boy if he'd ever tried them.

Tell me this, young stallion: Have you ever witnessed two temptresses snowballing your fluids? Used your gonads as a tea bag? Have you ever licked the sweetness?

Up and down Nathaniel went, thirty push-ups, thirty-one, those hideous questions lodged in his brain. He found himself murmuring them each time he lowered his swollen nipples to the carpet, his answers coming not in word form but from the ferocity with which Nathaniel Rothstein thrust himself back into the air.

He'd arrived in Austin four days ago, and he still couldn't get over the unfairness of it all. Not only did he have to spend his entire break in some random city, but he had to *volunteer*? All for taking a swing at a kid who'd been asking for it?

Nathaniel had planned to spend these months in the cool wings of the Newton South High School auditorium, working stage crew for the summer Shakespeare crowd. Instead, he'd been sentenced to a "cooling-off period," as his mother put it, in a place ten times hotter than Massachusetts: his aunt Marlene and uncle Bob's house, two thousand miles southwest.

"Why's it my fault some *fag* came on to me?" he'd muttered to his mom as they'd crept along the Mass Pike toward the airport the day of his departure. The word hadn't felt right coming up, and after he'd said it he felt even more miserable than before. "That's just great," said Linda Rothstein, honking her horn as much at Nathaniel as she was at the traffic. "My son, who loves the theater and beating up homosexuals. I'm sure you'll have a very successful career."

The crazy part, in hindsight, was that old Rothstein never had it so bad. Sure, it would be another year before his man boobs flattened, before those freckled chipmunk cheeks started to dissolve. Yes, he was easily embarrassed, so prone to blushing he was more red than white, as classically Caucasian as the Kool-Aid Man. Maybe he hadn't yet found his people, for even among the stagehands he loitered on the margins, never loose enough to hang easily with those proud outcasts who'd quote *Rocky Horror* and "the Scottish play" ad nauseam, who knew their way around woodshops and fly lofts and boy oh boy each other, and had embraced their outsiderness with such verve that in the process they'd turned the outside in.

Indeed, the boy's real problem wasn't who he'd become but the fear that he'd done becoming, for somehow it hadn't occurred to him that the Nathaniel Rothstein of 1998—as ill-defined on the outside as he was on the in—wasn't the Nathaniel Rothstein of forever, that this blob of wet clay was years from the sculptor and the kiln.

It was his nebulous nature that had drawn him to theater in the first place. He thrilled at the decisiveness of it, the magic of watching one person become another, fully formed. The Newton South Stars musical that spring had been *Man of La Mancha*, a play within a play. Nathaniel had gone a little misty on opening night when floppy-haired Ben Shooman, in the lead, bent his back and administered his old-man makeup center stage, transforming from Cervantes into Don Quixote right before their eyes.

He was careful not to let anyone notice. So bottled was the boy that, back at the start of rehearsals, he'd found himself unable even to purchase the soundtrack, mortified at how the kohl-eyed salesgirl at Newbury Comics would react if he submitted so fey an offering. He'd slipped the CD into the pouch of his hoodie and bought an Oasis album instead, reasoning that if he purchased *something,* no one would suspect him of shoplifting.

The maneuver worked so well that Nathaniel repeated it multiple times that spring, keeping the unwanted CDs naked in his desk drawer, hiding the musicals under the manlier guises of Radiohead and The Prodigy. Now the naked baby of Nirvana's *Nevermind* served as a literal cover for *Little Shop of Horrors*, while Nathaniel's *40oz. to Freedom* jewel case wouldn't shut all the way, since around its plastic hub he'd forced the original cast recording of *Rent*, discs one and two.

But *La Mancha* was his favorite and, back in Newton, he'd taken to pacing his room to the soundtrack—Discman tucked in the elastic waistband of his mesh shorts, door locked—too self-conscious to mouth the words, fearful of even a single note escaping him.

All this would've been news to Linda Rothstein. Whenever his mother fished for details, Nathaniel's stock response was that the technical aspects were what led him to techie-dom. "I dunno, Mom. The light board's just, like, cool."

In truth, he'd never touched the light board, set foot in the light booth. By the time of *La Mancha* he'd ascended only to assistant prop master, a position usually held by freshmen. This suited Nathaniel fine. The pleasure was in the watching, and in the imagining born of that.

How badly he wanted to *be* somebody. To be somebody else.

Oh, Nathaniel! If only this prisoner of pubescence had the foresight to understand he hadn't been sentenced to life. That high school would end soon, that the brood of oily, wild-haired boys he'd eaten lunch with since sixth grade—boys with pet pythons, who spoke Python—wouldn't be his forever friends (were barely his friends now, their lack of cohesion such that they'd given themselves a name, the Lunch Bunch, compensation for the fact that their only true commonality was that each had nowhere else to sit).

If only someone had said, *Look into my crystal ball, will ya?*, who knows what would've become of that pumpkin of a boy. If he hadn't gotten into that stupid brawl, hadn't been exiled to Austin, the story of Nathaniel Rothstein might've been the story of many an ungainly straight boy's transformation during that exhilarating season: of fingers fiddling with bra straps in ancient Ford Tauri, of sweaty bills and (mostly aspirational) strips of Trojans presented solemnly to bored clerks at CVS.

But thanks to Uncle Bob he'd ended up at Shoal Creek in June

1998, which was why, eight hours after David Dalice asked him if he'd ever licked the sweetness, Nathaniel was halfway through that frenzied set of push-ups in nothing but those smiley boxers, an erection that seemed world-record-setting in its rigidity complicating each descent.

He wasn't gay, but there was no denying that David, the *thought* of David, had a, well . . . physiological effect.

How could it be? Some old fatso yammering on about slurping pussy? All morning, Nathaniel had wanted to escape the guy.

Yet he couldn't deny a pang of envy observing the man in his world: the elaborate handshakes he'd worked out with the orderlies, the private jokes he shared with the nurses ("David, you are bad!"). And the way he talked about sex . . . To be so *open*?

He'd first met David in the men's staff locker room at 6:55 that morning, as his uncle had instructed. At school no one actually showered in the locker room: getting naked after gym class was for eighties movies, not real life. But at Shoal Creek, many of the CNAs and orderlies used the dingy facilities for all they had to offer (especially the recent immigrants, mostly bachelors who lived with roommates and shared bathrooms without fans).

Nathaniel had been unprepared to set foot in that steamy place, ill at ease among those wide-awake men, who called out to each other through thin curtains and between stalls, and dressed not as Nathaniel would have—struggling into his boxers with one hand while keeping his towel wrapped around his waist with the other—but out in the open, free.

"Is that my newest pupil?" a voice had boomed from the sinks in the back. David was washing his hands, a big man in scrubs with a clean-shaven head and thin mustache. He was Haitian, he'd tell the boy later, his regal baritone still bearing traces of his homeland. "Come back here and present yourself, lest any of these fine gents mistake you for a peeping Tom."

Nathaniel accidentally made eye contact with the person closest to him, an older Black man in a janitor's uniform on his way out the door. "I'd get a move on if I was you." The boy felt his face go flush.

At lunch, in the staff cafeteria, it happened again, Nathaniel's ears heating up like the coils of an electric stove at the mere sight of the chef, a plump girl in catwoman glasses who was (why did this embarrass him?) not much older than he. The gatekeeper of the hot food, too, which was why Nathaniel had settled for a self-service Yoplait while David ordered a double cheeseburger, side of wings. "And one of these," David had added, plucking the tall paper chef's hat from the girl's head and putting it on his own.

"Your boss is trouble," Alejandra had chided Nathaniel, snapping her tongs at him. "Enough with this wicked chef," said David, joining Nathaniel at a table. "I'm the chef now." And though they were both talking to him, Nathaniel knew they were really talking to each other.

As he watched David flirt and fool and tease, a thought entered Nathaniel's headspace that he tried to ignore. How did Black people *do this*? No white person in his orbit ever seemed to display David's seductive swagger, his preternatural ease.

When Bob had told him he'd be volunteering for a family friend, it never occurred to Nathaniel that the friend wouldn't be white. He'd driven to Shoal Creek that morning in his uncle's spare Volvo already dreading the prospect of spending the day having to say actual words to actual people; seeing his boss was a Black guy made him even more nervous than before. None of his mom's friends or the kids who passed for his friends were Black. Black people had always seemed . . . a little intimidating?

He was pretty sure this thought wasn't racist. After all, these were *good* qualities, traits he would've killed for. At mostly white Newton South, it seemed a widely established fact that Black guys possessed a particular kind of cool. All year, "It's All About the Benjamins" had blared from the open windows of the shiny SUVs in the senior lot. Many of the most popular guys wore looks trickled down from hip-hop fashion—backwards caps and work boots—while the boys who were still more into sports than girls hadn't yet traded out the jerseys of their smooth-pitted youths: Andy Goldenberger masquerading as Ty Law, Chicago-born Eli Finkel forever #23. It wasn't just the white kids, either. Big Jared Tang, who owned his girth in a way Nathaniel never could, often lumbered the halls in baggy jeans, a gold chain over an outsized T-shirt emblazoned with a photograph of the recently deceased Notorious B.I.G.

The year before, in freshman English, dotty old Mrs. Bartlett had read the class an excerpt from *Black Like Me*. It was a true story—and, in Nathaniel's estimation, a boring one—about a white guy who'd pretended to be African American to see what it was like. Nathaniel had spaced out for the details (the 1950s? somewhere in the South?), only remembered the euphoric response from the peanut gallery each time his teacher uttered the n-word as she read aloud: "Mrs. Bartlett's gettin' jiggy wit it!" "Mrs. Bartlett's a G!"

It was funny, Nathaniel understood, because being Black meant being cool, and Mrs. Bartlett, like Nathaniel, was definitely not.

The few Black guys at South, meanwhile, *did* seem pretty cool. While all of the white teachers dressed like teachers—dowdy slacks and mustard stains—Nathaniel's one Black instructor, Mr. Bell for Algebra II, always wore tailored suits, the stale scent of institutionality that had seeped into the flesh of all who passed through the double doors to the main entrance supplanted, in this one case, with a different fragrance, woody and expensive.

As for the students, they were METCO mostly, a couple dozen kids bused in from Dorchester and Mattapan. A group of Black upperclassmen usually sat a couple tables over from the Lunch Bunch in the cafeteria; Nathaniel had always admired those guys in their color-block rugby shirts, their FUBU jeans and jackets. They had a warmth with each other, embracing and fist-bumping and yukking it up while Nathaniel could barely even look at his piteous tablemates lest he see—reflected off Bryan Hillman's Transitions lenses or in the mirrored insides of Elliott Glomb-Golden's solar-system-themed zip-up lunch bag—a little too much of himself.

Those Black guys were great with girls, too; even some *teachers* glowed in their presence. What was it, exactly? Was *slavery* the reason, Nathaniel sometimes wondered, why Miah Walker, who sat one desk over in tenth-grade English, was always getting his C+ papers back with notes to *Keep going!* while Nathaniel's C+'s earned him *Follow the directions more closely, please* or the occasional (kill me now) *See me*. Or was it simply that the gruntish greetings on offer from the Rothsteins of the world were no match for Miah's high fives, for that smooth *What's up, Ms. P?*

It must be said that Nathaniel's definition of "Black people" was not even an accurate representation of the Black people in his own life. Somehow, in calculating *how Black people did it*, he hadn't included in the equation the trio of freshmen nerds who'd sat in a cafeteria cluster of their own all year playing Magic: The Gathering; nor the two Black kids *from* Newton, neither of whom anyone would've described as self-possessed (but both of whom were mixed, the unspoken assumption among Nathaniel and his white peers being that they weren't "really" Black). Also not on Nathaniel's radar was the entire cohort of METCO girls: some fashionable, some not; some studious, some not; none, in Nathaniel's Abercrombied conception of the word, *hot*.

Nevertheless, as Nathaniel followed his new boss on his morning rounds, that was how he conceived of the question: How did Black people do it? How did David Dalice?

Nathaniel's first afternoon at Shoal Creek transpired much as the morning had. While nurse's assistants changed diapers and bedsheets, Nathaniel trailed David, who, as head of hospitality, was all about changing hearts and minds. They shepherded residents on the second floor to the common area to hear a folk singer, an aged man in a tie-dye shirt who'd gone bald up top but kept the shoulder-length tresses of his youth. On the third floor—the locked unit—they covered folding tables in butcher paper for an impending finger-painting session. The sounds on this level unsettled Nathaniel: a groaning woman begging to be put down, a damp fart exorcised. David appeared unfazed, his lewd monologue inescapable.

At 2:30, David told Nathaniel that, for the boy's final act, he'd be setting out on his own. A first-floor resident with dodgy eyesight enjoyed books but had lost the ability to make out the letters on the page; Nathaniel would be reading to her every afternoon. "She's a little peevish around new faces," David warned on their way over.

Dr. Gloria Abruzzi had managed to keep her private apartment in Assisted Living despite mounting memory issues, that not-great vision, and occasionally tetchy skin. "A woman of independent spirit," David said.

"What kind of doctor is she?" asked Nathaniel.

For the first and only time that day, the impish twinkle went out of David's eyes. "A doctor of the *mind*," he said, and added, sternly, "She worked hard for it, too, so call her by her title."

Outside Apartment 103, a three-foot plastic Santa Claus dressed as a waiter and serving dust-covered spaghetti and meatballs stood guard.

"Does she know it's *summer*?" asked Nathaniel. "Or is she, like . . ." Was there a nice word for crazy?

"*Italian*," said David. He gave Nathaniel a parting salute, continued on his way.

Finally, Nathaniel was rid of the guy. Yet inside Dr. Abruzzi's darkened living room he found that even without David, David was still with him, taunting the boy like some debauched Jiminy Cricket.

See him there: bashful Nathaniel slouched in his armchair, reading *Bridge to Terabithia* to a thickset, frowning woman in large, tinted bifocals. How was Dr. Abruzzi to know that as Nathaniel stuttered out that tragic tale his mind was not on the heartbreak of childhood, but back in the staff cafeteria, where David had concluded his lunchtime lesson on good hygiene with a reminder that "before you fill the cavity you always clean the drill."

Oh, the things he imagined as he read to the old lady! Alejandra's palms braced against the glass canopy of the buffet station . . . Nathaniel grinding into her from behind, naked but for a T-shirt and the chef's hat . . . David circling like a high school wrestling coach. "You're bad," moaned Alejandra. "Work that drill, boy," goaded David. "Hey, marble mouth," said Dr. Abruzzi. "Speak up a titch?"

And now, Uncle Bob still at the university, Aunt Marlene out with friends, up and down Nathaniel Rothstein went, forty push-ups, forty-one, knowing that when—if—he reached fifty, he would burrow under his cousin Max's bulky denim comforter, cradling his clunky "emergencies only" cell phone between shoulder and always-burning cheek.

He'd been calling the hotline since arriving in Austin. In just four days he already felt like he knew the ladies well: Natalia, Natasha, Sasha, Sabrina. "You like big-titted Estonian girl?" This was how they talked. Nathaniel couldn't imagine saying aloud the acts he envisaged during these encounters, which was fine since they asked the questions and all he had to murmur was *Yes*.

You lick me on boobie?

You slap me my buttocks?

I suckle fat balls?

Yes, yes, god yes.

He'd hang up just before letting loose, the thought of one of the girls still on the line afterward too humiliating to bear.

Nathaniel had first learned about the 1-900 number waiting for Uncle Bob to pick him up at the airport, when he'd seen an ad for it on the back page of Austin's free alternative weekly. Back in Newton, he'd never dare call a sex hotline, but here it felt permissible, as if sleeping in someone else's bed, in someone else's house, meant that someone else was dialing the number. Nathaniel had been paying from a $350 check card his grandma had given him last Hanukkah. "Spend it on something fun," she'd told him. In four days, Nathaniel had already called nine times.

He picked up his cell phone from his cousin's desk, turned it on, then grabbed his wallet from his jeans on the floor.

In bed, Nathaniel got under the covers and surveyed his surroundings. His cousin Max was twenty: gangly, confident, a rising junior at Oberlin, where he'd stayed for the summer. Nathaniel knew if the Lunch Bunch were to ask him about this room he'd call it *gay*, but privately he was envious. It was all so Max: the framed *Mrs. Doubtfire* poster hanging above the bed; the dozen different-colored Chuck Taylors in the closet, the once-white parts covered in doodles; the *Entertainment Weekly*s stacked on the toilet tank in the en suite bathroom. Nathaniel couldn't imagine what a room *so Nathaniel* would even look like.

And that would've been it, another wank in a summer of wanks, a lifetime of wanks, for it took him only a single shift under the employ of David Dalice to know once and for all that he'd never have the oomph necessary, that Natalia, Natasha, Sasha, and Sabrina were the closest he'd ever get . . .

Yes, that would've been it, if, after Nathaniel dialed the number, his arms aching from all those push-ups, the slinky Soviet on the other end of the line had offered her normal sultry salutation. If she'd recognized, as she usually did, that the caller lacked the verbal dexterity to match her light nibbles with deep licks, her spread legs with a thrusting pelvis of his own, she would've thrown him to the bed or pushed him up against a wall and done what she'd always done: all the work herself.

Except this time it wasn't "You have it out yet, big man?" or "You ready for nasty fun?" that Nathaniel heard after a single ring, but the unexpected shalom of a civilian. "Hello," she said, as if Nathaniel had called a neighbor, a friend. "Hello?" Her accent was thick as always, her tenor weirdly casual. "Is no one there?"

Nathaniel felt a familiar muteness taking hold, the same chin-to-his-chest disquiet he experienced whenever a teacher asked a question and no one raised their hand. "Hey," he said, or meant to say, the result, in reality, a husky "Heh." She said nothing back. "Uh, which one's this?" he murmured.

"This Sasha," said Sasha. It sounded like she was doing something else. "So, what you want?"

What did *he* want? The magic of the hotline was that the ladies told him what he was doing and made sure he did it right. So chatty were the usual girls that sometimes, in addition to describing themselves, they'd even tell Nathaniel what *he* looked like: shaving his head down to a buzz cut or performing a double mastectomy. What did he want? Where even to begin?

He wanted a million things, a million things he could never muster the courage to say. On the phone, Nathaniel wanted what he saw in the handful of porno clips he'd watched and rewatched on his computer back home, free previews on for-pay sites that took three minutes to load and only lasted fifteen seconds. He wanted to try all the positions, say all the things. Mostly, he wanted to make the Natalias, Natashas, Sashas, and Sabrinas of the world need him like the girls in those clips needed the guys. They were always slobbering and submissive, begging for it longer, harder. The thought of becoming the object of their salivating drove Nathaniel to an ecstasy bordering on madness.

For this reason, it was the sounds that did him in, the women's high snivels and low moans, which, for $2.99 per minute, he was allowed to pretend he provoked.

His more intricate fantasies took place in his flaccid hours. His list of crushes was monumental, ghastly, an out-and-out Breakfast Club of each and every, and he'd cycled each and every through his dream scenarios.

How he longed to hold hands under the table at the Cheesecake Factory with long-legged Ashley Pedder, whom he'd eyed all fall striding down the corridor with her field hockey stick erupting out of her backpack like Donatello's bo staff, to share a spinach and hot cheese dip with Lizzie Jacobson, whose heartfelt rendition of "One Moment in Time" at last year's a cappella show had resulted in a standing O.

What would it feel like to remove the cardigan from the delicate shoulders of Amanda Chen, the only evangelical in Semite-heavy Newton South, to unlace Irina Sokolov's Doc Martens, or wake up next to Eliza Etscovitz, leader of the cliquish yearbook girls, her tight, flared black pants on the floor below?

To lean in as they leaned in, like actors playing the mirror game, until boy and girl were lip to lip?

What did Nathaniel want?

He wanted everything and had the words for no things, which

was why instead of saying anything he pushed his boxers down to his thighs and started in.

Nathaniel made the grunting guy noises he'd gleaned from those pornos, hoping Sasha would follow suit with some ravenous girl ones.

Except she didn't. Instead, she asked again what he wanted, and when he didn't answer, asked again, and again, each time with a little more venom.

"I want—" he tried, unable to finish the sentence. "I need—"

Sasha told him she was sick of listening to weak boys hem and haw all day, tired of soft boys who didn't know how to get a girl off. "Say something," she snarled and, when he didn't, couldn't: "Pa-tet-ic."

It was new to Nathaniel, this stimulation via flagellation, the newness a turn-on in itself, so that by the time Sasha snapped, "Do you know how lucky you are to have someone like me?" he couldn't even manage "Yes, yes, god yes."

"I—" said Nathaniel.

"But you do *nothing* with it."

"Um," Nathaniel said, voice going high. He was getting close.

Every other time he'd called, by now the girl would've transitioned into a carnal vibrato, but Sasha was playing a different game, her provocations only intensifying. "Oh, you think you're such *big* man? Such *strong* man? I ask you one last time," she hissed. "*What you want?*"

He wanted to make her wail and whimper, to beg for his body, scream his name, but he could never find the words, or the guts, to say, as himself, what he desired.

Nathaniel attempted to end it—a few decisive tugs should've done the trick—but his body refused to release, and in its refusal the early thrill of being dominated gave way to a twinge of shame.

Harder and harder Nathaniel went. He tried to channel the more assured guys at school, to inhabit the flanneled lax bros on whose carpenter-jeaned laps girls were always plopping, to become floppy-haired leading man Ben Shooman, a player among South Stars players, famous for flirting via high-octane tongue-twister competition, but when Nathaniel tried to imagine what *he'd* say to Sasha, *red leather yellow leather* was all that came to mind.

Why couldn't Nathaniel be the guy who said what he wanted? Who *did* what he wanted?

Screw it, thought Nathaniel, ready to click off the phone and finish the job alone, and he would've too, if, among the junior Lotharios clogging his brain, none providing any real direction, the genuine article hadn't pushed his way to the front.

Before you fill the cavity . . .

That voice! That hateful voice!

For hours, Nathaniel had tried to banish his brash boss from his head, but here he was, back again, David mocking, David goading, and the boy, desperate to achieve the sexed-up delirium the hotline girls normally provided, found he couldn't fight him anymore.

Nathaniel Rothstein did as he was told, submitting to David's imagined orders. He spit into his palm and, aroused, spit some more. He spit directly onto himself, the wildness of the act provoking a full-body shiver, a quaking that set off something in the deepest recesses of his belly and his balls, so that when he went to whisper it was her that he wanted, it was Sasha, what came out instead was so strong and deep and nasty that it seemed impossible it was coming from him.

"I want you," Nathaniel growled through gritted teeth, shaking the bed with such fury that one wrong move and *Mrs. Doubtfire* might come crashing down. "I fucking want you."

"That's it," said Sasha. "Say it. *Say it.*"

He moaned and cussed and seethed, his voice, with each passing syllable, not just deeper but somehow richer (what was it?), until his raspy caw was as far removed from his body as was his timid Nathaniel Rothstein soul, until he was ripping off her shirt and tearing off her panties in a tone and timbre not his own, Sasha trembling, Sasha howling, Sasha doing all the things he wanted her to do, until the filthy words that had been bubbling up below his waist geysered through his insides up his gullet and out into the world.

It was only after they'd hung up that Nathaniel Rothstein realized the weirdness of what he'd done. He'd spoken in a register lower than his own, adopting a vague island lilt that made him sound princely, authoritative, a little bit . . . like David?

And then there was that other thing, how every time Nathaniel mentioned one of his own body parts—commanding Sasha to lick his this, to ride his that—he'd preceded it with a single word:

Black.

II.

It should be said upfront that in the aftermath of this expulsion, Nathaniel Rothstein vowed to never again talk dirty to Natalia, Natasha, Sasha, or Sabrina. He was not a boy who'd grown up thinking he thought much about race, but he knew enough to understand that a white teenager pretending to be a Black man while getting off on a phone sex hotline was . . . not ideal.

The fact that in concurrence with the beep of hanging up his phone he also heard Aunt Marlene's CR-V pulling into the driveway only added to Nathaniel's sense that it would probably be best just to put him out to pasture. Had he really used that *voice*? Had he really said those *words*? Was his aunt, a petite woman whose expressiveness was so pronounced she was frequently compared to a mime, really now outside his door—"Just gauging levels of interest in chicken cacciatore"—as he Kleenexed away the slick remains of his depravity?

Yes, he told himself, that would be it for Natalia, Natasha, Sasha, and Sabrina, and it might've been, too, if at one thirty that morning, and again at four, the emergencies-only cell phone, tucked under his pillow, hadn't sounded. Twice Nathaniel Rothstein stirred, twice he failed to answer, and though the boy didn't fully awaken either time, a vague dread seeped into his consciousness, and when he arose the next morning to see that it was not a Rothstein who'd called nor an Alexander, but a mysterious 512 number (wasn't 512 *Austin*?), he knew that, like a serial killer grown cocky after one too many flawless disembowelments, he'd left a fingerprint where one didn't belong.

Had he forgotten to use the check card, leading AT&T to alert his mother to his deviant ways? Was it possible that he'd neglected to shut the blinds, that the seven-year-old daughter of the across-the-street neighbors whose room looked into Nathaniel's had seen the boy writhing and wailing, a piggy in heat, and alerted Mom and Dad, who'd somehow traced the phone? The possibilities were endless and all ended nowhere good, and just as Nathaniel reconciled himself to the fact that he'd wind up in therapy, or on the sex offender registry, or (the most likely scenario) dead of humiliation-induced cardiac arrest (squeezed into a casket, rosy even in death, a scarlet J.O. affixed to the lapel of his boxy suit), just as he realized he'd made a mistake from which he'd never recover, the cell phone rang again.

One ring, two rings, 512 once more. Could Aunt Marlene hear? Could Bob? Fuck, shit, don't hit the green button . . .

"Hello?" Nathaniel said, or tried to say, only a hard H sound emerging. On second thought: say nothing. He sat up in bed. Three seconds, four . . .

"Why this heavy breathing?" A girl's voice. A woman's voice? Rich. Sultry. Soviet. "I want to hear big boy again. You have accent, like me, eh? Where you from? Jamaica maybe?"

Nine times Nathaniel had called the hotline as himself. The tenth time he'd embodied someone else, and now, somehow . . . *Was the hotline calling back?*

Nathaniel checked the clock—6:01 a.m.—peeled back the denim comforter, and snuck over to the lockless bedroom door, putting his free ear to it to make sure no one was nearby. "Uh . . ."

"There is no need for stutters and stammers," the woman continued. "We are already friends. My name is Sasha Semyonova. You know, yes?"

Natalia, Natasha, Sabrina, and Sasha Semyonova. Was this some kind of extortion racket? Had he been recorded? How much could he pay?

"I have a little secret to tell you, Papa," Sasha continued. "Want to hear it?"

Nathaniel managed a Paleolithic "Yuh."

"Yesterday," purred the Russian, "you make me come harder than I have in sixteen years."

Come harder? Come again? How was it possible? Until eleven seconds prior, it seemed inconceivable that he, Nathaniel Joshua Rothstein, assistant prop master for the Newton South High School theater department, known virgin, could make a girl come. Until eleven seconds prior, he hadn't realized girls *could* come.

"So my Jamaican prince, what say you?" said Sasha. She let out a pouty moan. "Why not be a good boy and help your woman come again?"

III.

This was what Nathaniel Rothstein did not know:

That as he and Sasha started in on round two—the boy ensconced in his cousin's comforter, a denim den of guilt and seed—David was also prone, on a lawn chair in his backyard, vowing to limit himself to a couple pre-work puffs on a joint rolled with Bob Alexander's weed.

The afternoon before, when Nathaniel was first pretending to get inside Sasha Semyonova "as" a Black man, David, an actual Black man, was actually inside Terry Tucker's Boxing Gym, vowing to quit telling made-up sex stories to his latest charge. Now, in the six a.m. quiet, David was pleasantly glazed enough to admit to himself the truth: he'd probably continue to fuck with Nathaniel Rothstein.

It was always so *easy*. Come on strong, lay off some, make the kid come skulking back. Easy and predictable.

Indeed, in the days that followed, David mellowed on the filthy talk, engaging in subtler forms of fuckery: a box of Magnums, a gag gift from his twenty-fifth work anniversary party, placed at the front of his staff locker just so; a lunchtime call from his father, now in Miami, who rang most days from his cab. "Well, hello there, young thing!" David bellowed into his mobile. He held it to his chest and nodded for Nathaniel to get back to work. "Your ears are a bit tender for what's about to transpire."

For a week, Rothstein remained Rothstein, the only foreshadowing of the coming thaw those satisfying instances when David spied the boy spying him: from a darkened corner of Shoal Creek's small yoga studio as David laid out mats, from the driver's seat of Bob's spare Volvo at day's end. *What is he thinking?* David wondered. *How tough will this nut be to crack*?

What was he thinking? Oh, David, if only you knew! (And not very tough, FYI: easy to crack a busted nut.) What was he thinking? Of pert almond nipples. Of plump Russki tuchus. He was thinking of Sasha, his Sasha, and gathering intel, for a week in Austin and this was the takeaway: there was no point in phone-schtupping as Nathaniel Rothstein if you could do it as David Dalice.

3:35 to 4:25. That was the sweet spot, the fifty-minute span after work and before one Alexander or the other returned, heralding another night of strenuously polite (Aunt Marlene) or aggressively provocative (Uncle Bob) interrogation. 3:35 to 4:25. Just enough time to scarf down a Lunchable in front of *Geraldo*, retreat to Cousin Max's bed, and wait for the call.

By 4:05, he was at the ready, one hand on his cell phone, the other summoning David's spirit, for though he'd tried to get into character unaroused—before the bathroom mirror, shower on to mask the sound—he could never talk like that soft. Like rubbing sticks to make fire, it was friction that generated David Dalice.

They hadn't used the 900 number since that first time. Now she called him, always at the stroke of 4:09. Pleasantries were not their strong suit. "Let me lick that sweetness." "Magnum? *Nyet*. You plow me bare." They got off as soon as they got off, usually about 4:13.

Did Nathaniel sound like David Dalice? Um, no. Afraid not. He didn't speak in David's animated style but low and lascivious, the Caribbean inflection usually abandoned altogether a couple cranks in. An inconsistent intonation? No biggie. Like the child ham's supporting turn in an otherwise interminable school play, Nathaniel succeeded not on talent but pure vigor, enthralling because he was, if not believable, undeniably alive.

His was a simmering, snarling show, the words coming raw and rapid-fire. Once, he growled he was going so hard he might rip his dick right from his crotch, and she made him swear if he did he'd still keep the thing shoved inside her. What liberation! To openly bask in one's unbridled randiness. To tell another, *I'm a perv!* and hear in response, *I also*. But it was the telling that exhilarated him most, the mere act of allowing himself to say these things as much a turn-on as Sasha herself was.

In those early days, neither gave up much about themselves. Sasha said she called Nathaniel for no reason other than that he got her going. Nathaniel knew enough not to question his good fortune.

At times, off the phone, doubts lingered. Was there a chance Sasha had found a way to charge him for her calls? What if she was recording their sessions?

These feelings usually came in the moments after Sasha hung up, when he was left with only a faint echo of the things he'd said and that embarrassing mess.

But doubts or no, when Sasha called, Nathaniel answered, the chance to become the version of himself he'd created for her too intoxicating to pass up.

He assured himself she knew nothing real about him anyway, his alter ego affording him not only license to talk dirty but protection, too. It wasn't like she ever asked for personal information, except his name, which she inquired about during their fifth go-round.

Nathaniel wasn't about to give his real one, and after a too-long pause managed only "Uh, David."

"Please to make your acquaintance, Uh, David," said Sasha. She didn't bring it up again.

As the tanks and Tevas of late spring dissolved into the bare skin of a heavy Austin summer, the gap between Nathaniel on the phone and off it only grew more pronounced in the boy's mind.

The hour before dinner was the worst, when Uncle Bob swam laps at Barton Springs and insisted Nathaniel at the very least hang out on the grass as he did it. The place was a city staple: a spring-fed pool with a natural rock bottom, whose uninhibited inhabitants all seemed free in ways Nathaniel didn't.

The boy had learned not to object. More than once, Bob had threatened instead to take Nathaniel to his other favorite swimming hole, the clothing-optional Hippie Hollow: "And I think you'll have no trouble imagining the option your old uncle Bob chooses."

Barton Springs it was, then, this unfortunate ritual always ending the same way: a fully dressed Nathaniel hiding under his floppy safari hat and trying to finish off whatever Skinemax-ed dragon trilogy he happened to be reading, Bob lounging next to him in nothing but an off-brand swim brief, doing his best at manly bonding.

"Now there's a looker," Bob would say, one sopping fourteen-year-old or another skittering past, snapping neon gum or unwedging the front of her one-piece.

The boy could feel his chubby cheeks inflame. "Uh-huh," he'd mumble, barely able to make himself look up.

"What is wrong with this kid?" he overheard Bob tell his aunt one night. "He's had every advantage. Caring mother, good schools. He's from Newton, for Chrissake! Everyone knows *someone* from Newton, and they're *always* successful! It's a land of success! And still: a dud. I'm telling you, Mar, I'm trying, but this kid just don't got it."

In the before times, when Nathaniel didn't got it and knew he didn't got it, he might've been able to ignore this diagnosis. But now he longed to find a way to tell the world it wasn't true, for even if everyone in his physical life believed he didn't got it, Nathaniel had learned that somewhere deep inside himself, somewhere he did . . .

Sometimes, after hanging up, he'd imagine telling the Lunch Bunch about Sasha, or even, weirdly, telling one of their moms. What would it feel like to hear, *And Nathaniel, anyone special in your life?* and to be able to respond, just once, with *Yes*?

At work, he'd begun to fantasize about telling David, too. Talking about girls, about sex, with a guy as experienced as that? It made Nathaniel's heart beat so hard in David's presence that he was sure the man could hear.

But hearing wasn't necessary, for David could see: the way Nathaniel scratched at his neck whenever David appeared, how the red boy reddened. The telltale signs. A sexual frenzy was afoot. A girl was on the scene.

So it came as little surprise when, ten days into Nathaniel's tenure at Shoal Creek, the boy's perennially parted lips parted a bit wider and apropos of nothing he blurted, "What's your favorite position?"

The season of questions had begun.

This was at the end of their morning meeting in the staff locker room. For years, David had showered here in the mornings. He preferred to leave the house in a polo and jeans instead of scrubs, as if he weren't going to work at all, or maybe had one of those jobs where he was so high up nice clothing wasn't required.

His a.m. congress with Nathaniel always began at 6:55 and lasted ten minutes—half before the 7 a.m. nursing shift began and half after—so that by the time David was announcing their tasks for the day, often with a towel draped over his bare shoulders as he finished shaving, it was just the two of them. ("Why don't you shave at home?" Nathaniel had inquired early on. "What makes you think I'm coming from home?" said David.)

"Any questions?" David always asked at meeting's end. How careful Nathaniel was never to make eye contact. He'd vomit out a No-like sound and hurry on his way. But on this day—the memory of the previous afternoon's Sasha date still wedged below his waist—vanity got the better of him and he looked not down but straight ahead, and in that moment his mirrored eyes locked with David's, and out it came.

Had he really just said it? Who talked like that? Surely the answer would be *None of your—*

"Favorite position?" said David. "A weighty inquiry." He futzed with his razor, trying to suppress a grin. "What do the words 'Sit on the Throne' mean to you?"

"Sit on the Throne . . ." repeated Nathaniel, a word cloud materializing above his head.

And off they went!

Imagine an all-star version of Telephone, the message the exact same from first lip to final ear. Dalice to Rothstein, Rothstein to Sasha Semyonova!

"Your lap is the royal seat . . ." said David.

"Put that ass on me . . ." said Nathaniel.

"Sitting, sitting!" cried Sasha. "*Bozhe moi* yes!"

They hovered and belly-flopped, wheelbarrowed and sporked. Four minutes turned to six minutes, nine. A girl from school, Nathaniel explained, when David asked how they'd met. "Things have been headed this way for a while." And: "We're doing long-distance while I'm here."

Nathaniel had hesitated to tell David this last part, worried the man might make fun of him for asking about sex stuff when the only sex happening was over the phone. He had little to fear. According to David, this made his lessons *more* necessary, these months away a chance for Nathaniel to transform for his woman, from boy into man.

Soon David's running monologue became a dialogue as he and Nathaniel set up and took down, stocked and stacked and sorted. When Nathaniel wasn't with David, he *was* David, or thinking about what he'd do *as* David, or how he'd tell David about what David had done (always careful to characterize his David, to David, as Nathaniel).

He'd never before spent so much time with someone not his mom in such short order. A stranger to bunks and to barracks, Nathaniel was new to the peculiar thrill of making friends in fast-forward. But that's what was happening, David ever generous with his advice, Nathaniel always ready to receive it.

"What kind of girl likes this slumping walk?" asked David one day, Nathaniel slouching down the hall ahead of him. He pressed his thumb into the small of the boy's back. "When you stand hard before your woman," he whispered, "the protractor should read ninety degrees." (*What the hell?* thought Bob Alexander that evening, observing his nephew stride ramrod straight through the Barton Springs parking lot. "Hey, Himmler, wait up!")

The morning meetings turned into elaborate strategy sessions on personal hygiene. "I'll be forty-eight in August," David told Nathaniel. "Do you think I look this good by doing *nothing*?" Lotion was essential. Facial cleanser key.

"How do you smell like that, anyway?" asked Nathaniel at the end of one such lesson. David produced from his locker a bottle of Acqua di Gio, gave the kid a squirt. "Only thirty-nine dollars at Barton Creek Mall . . ." ("Can I give you a suggestion, Mr. Armani?" said Bob over breakfast the next morning. "My eggs taste like Bloomingdale's. Maybe stick to one spritz?")

Did Nathaniel volunteer much information about his alleged girlfriend? She existed as a physical specimen only in relation to the adult stars of the day, Jenna's this and Nikki's that, an impossible assortment, the Mrs. Potato Head of tits and ass. As for personality, he offered only the usual pablum: great sense of humor, mature for her age. David never pressed. When dealing with characters of dubious existence, man and boy had learned, best not to get stuck in the weeds.

Instead, they focused on self-improvement. At his mentor's urging, Nathaniel grew a mustache as best he could: a downy tuft, soft as lanugo. A mid-workday trip to Target for taco night decorations also yielded a six-pack of wifebeaters ("There is no shame in prominent nipples but they must be kept in check") and—how both of their hearts raced as Nathaniel dropped these in front of the cash register!—a skimpy pair of leopard-print briefs. Twenty-pound dumbbells, long hibernating in David's closet, arose anew in his student's sticky palms.

On the third Friday in June, David took the boy to lunch at the Frisco for chili burgers and root beer floats. By meal's end a warmth had settled in their bellies and Nathaniel, who'd wondered what, exactly, his uncle had told his new friend about him, asked David if he knew about "the thing" that had landed the boy in Austin in the first place.

"Why don't you tell me?" said David, and so Nathaniel did: about the collection of unfortunates he'd sat with every day at lunch since middle school, about little Elliott Glomb-Golden, hoarse and hyperactive and always doing annoying shit just to be annoying.

On the day in question, Elliott, who sat across from Nathaniel and whose mother still packed his lunch, brought a Twinkie for dessert. "I bet Big Boy wants some of this," he'd told Nathaniel as he unwrapped the pastry, and then he'd started blowing it—"When you say blowing . . . ?" David asked, and here Nathaniel stuck his tongue into his cheek—slurping the Twinkie, moaning over the Twinkie, the breading turning slicker with each suck. "He thought it was funny, I don't know why. I asked him to stop but he wouldn't. I just, I didn't want . . ." Nathaniel hesitated.

"You didn't want to be the guy sitting at the table with the kid blowing a Twinkie?" David tried.

All he'd meant to do was slap it out of the boy's small hand. But how easy that turned out to be! His eyes followed the Twinkie as it fell to the linoleum. Then he looked back at his stunned victim. So often he'd seen, in the wide, damp eyes of his fellow Lunch Bunchers, his own reflection. But in that moment, Nathaniel sensed himself separating from the others, wanted to separate more. And as he threw himself across the table at Elliott Glomb-Golden, he felt outside himself, above himself, and with each punch propelled higher, higher, crazed as Icarus as he felt soul separating from body, the true Nathaniel Rothstein finally escaping his fleshy host.

On and on and up and up he went (it was fifteen seconds start to finish but in his memory could've been fifteen minutes, fifteen years), until something clipped the wax wings that were his untrained fists and Nathaniel Rothstein was felled via headlock, the hairless forearms of a schlubby campus Rent-a-Cop his version of the sun.

This was not, of course, how the boy related Pastry-Fellate '98 to David Dalice. He managed to say little of substance after sticking tongue to cheek, the narration in his mind failing, per usual, to translate into more than empty phrases ("It was weird," "I can't really explain it"). But David had been around enough teenage boys to understand the contours of what had transpired.

"It felt so *good*," Nathaniel finally managed, and though David didn't respond, only signaled for the waiter, in the parking lot of the Frisco he instructed the boy to be dressed and downstairs at 6:45 sharp the next morning. "If you're the reason your uncle is late, I'll never hear the end of it. And listen," he added, wiggling his fat ring finger, "the stories of Shoal Creek stay at Shoal Creek."

This was why, eighteen hours later, when Bob Alexander went to leave for his Saturday morning workout at Terry Tucker's Boxing Gym, he found his nephew sitting on the front stoop, the boy's pasty legs stuffed into a pair of Cousin Max's Umbros. "I told David I'd try it out," Nathaniel explained.

"You told David you'd try it out," said Uncle Bob, jangling his keys as the boy followed him to the car.

IV.

It was not an auspicious beginning.

Taking in the humble garage, Nathaniel felt a bit of that old bashfulness returning, his neck hot with the knowledge that he was entering this manly place with his uncle, of all people, no David yet in sight.

Inside Terry Tucker's front office, the back wall covered in clipped stories about fighters from the gym, a small man in red cotton shorts sat legs up on the desk, face obscured behind that morning's *Statesman*. "That that skinny-dicked loquacious sumbitch Bob Alexander?" he grumbled from behind the paper.

"Skinny-dicked Loquacious Sumbitch *and company*," said Bob, stooping to write their names on the sign-in sheet on the desk. Nathaniel followed Bob down a step into the gym proper without ever seeing Terry Tucker's face.

Ten minutes later, still no David, the boy slouched on the bench across from the ring as Bob and his gang of middle-aged gabbers sat on the canvas doing butterfly stretches ("keeping the old inguen supple," Bob explained, pressing his bony elbows to his knees).

Nathaniel had met this crew, the First Thingers, when they came for Bob's Wednesday night poker games: ruddy Stan Hart and scrawny Judge Ulbrecht and Lee Gorbinski, the diehard runner of the bunch ("Never have I met a man," Bob told his nephew, "whose farts smell more like actual fruit"). A mortifying congregation were these, fellows who'd apparently seen Bob's tiny swim briefs and decided to raise him: too-short shorts and pit-stained shirts, Judge Ulbrecht's sweatpants so thin Nathaniel could make out the head of his penis.

The boy kept his head bowed, desperate for David to arrive. He was grateful, at least, for his boss's warning to keep Shoal Creek at Shoal Creek: if David's stories were off-limits with this embarrassing group, at least Nathaniel's would be, too.

Bob had given Nathaniel an old pair of hand wraps, and now he struggled to follow his uncle's instructions, which the older man offered only in between clauses: "I'm telling you boys: every time they show this lady on TV, she's in a beret. A *look*, Marlene calls it. It's a look all right! She looks like Benny Hill. Other left, son, *other* left!"

"I'll let David show me," Nathaniel told Bob, the wraps a messy tangle in his lap, and soon his uncle and the others had descended from the ring, up the step and out the office door for their morning jog.

Every few seconds, more people ambled into Terry's office to pay their respects, then down the step. There were older white men, furry-eared as his uncle, and white women, too: UT coeds and a couple of ladies in Spandex leggings with the cropped, feathered hair of TV moms.

But at this early hour most of the newcomers were younger, darker: guys still groggy from sleep, who sought refuge in their headphones or sipped coffee from metal thermoses. Some stashed their duffel bags beneath the canvas, others under the bench where Nathaniel sat. He knew he should get up to make room but was paralyzed by his own awkwardness, sinewy arms reaching under and around him.

Later, Nathaniel would learn that many of the kids his age completed chores for free gym access, which was why a squad of Mexican teens was already at work, actors doubling as stagehands to bring Terry Tucker's Boxing Gym to life. Two bowl-haired boys signaled to each other from opposite ends of the room, plugging in the digital fight clocks mounted on the walls at the same time so they beeped in unison. A stocky kid with a fat mole above his lip swept, working his broomstick in short, efficient brushstrokes, while a strapping dude in a wifebeater, boasting the bushy pits of the truly post-pubescent, lifted a rusted chain to open the metal garage doors, soaking the gym in heat and light.

In the pre-David era, Nathaniel might've bolted, all of it too physical, too intimate for him to handle. Braver now, not much but not much was needed, he closed his eyes and listened—to the tentative slaps and whooshes of bags and ropes awakening alongside their handlers—until he heard that familiar baritone and saw, from out of the fog of floating dust particles, his new mentor, who'd stepped between the bike racks meant to direct patrons to the front entrance and through the garage doors instead.

"Two great fighters finally unite," said David, already breathing heavily. He plopped himself down on the bench next to Nathaniel, slid his gym bag between his legs. David wore a Terry Tucker's T-shirt and black athletic shorts, his bare knee touching his student's. For what felt like the first time since Nathaniel arrived, the boy exhaled.

Nathaniel had no natural talent for the sport, couldn't work the speed bag or remember to relax his shoulders, as David kept reminding him. None of it mattered. Standing side by side before the mirrored walls of the weight room, he tried to do as David did—jab and cross and hook and cut—and found if he kept his eyes on his teacher, as instructed, his full focus on replicating David's movements, he could keep his self-consciousness in check.

Even better, trying out these punches on the heavy bag, gloves borrowed from the supply closet, Nathaniel could feel himself relaxing, as if he were expelling his anxieties hit by hit. "It feels good to smack the shit out of things, doesn't it?" David asked. It really did.

Only when the outside world encroached did Nathaniel feel that familiar tingle of timidity burble beneath his flesh. To the regulars at Terry Tucker's Boxing Gym, Nathaniel was what all earnest newbies were: a mild affront to the cash-only grit of the place. "*You're* Bob's nephew?" scoffed a husky redhead, Jocelyn Carter, in between rounds. "Fuck me, man, wouldn'ta guessed it!" She whacked the boy hard with the side of her glove. "Guess Bob's flat ass ain't genetic!"

Later, as David chatted with friends in the weight room, Nathaniel haplessly tried to figure out the double-end bag when a skinny Mexican guy in long denim shorts approached him. "You payin' that dude?" asked the man, Carlos Ortega, his face scrunched in bafflement as Nathaniel tried to ignore him. "Don't be payin' that dude, homes! He takin' you for a *ride*, homes! You *wastin'* that money." Carlos would've kept at it had David not returned midway through the hectoring, barked, "Ortega," then flicked his wrist: *shoo*.

Even more intimidating than Carlos was Felix Barrowman: "a true contender," David explained as they watched him work over a heavy bag, letting out quick *pa! pa! pa!*s with each blow. Nathaniel felt terror at the prospect of having to say even a single word in the presence of this actual athlete. He needn't have worried. When he went to open the door to the single-occupant bathroom only to find Felix exiting at the same time, the passing boxer didn't even look at him.

But if those others didn't see much in Nathaniel, David seemed to, and the boy, still diffident in this big world, was now hungry for it, too. Watching the leisurely lope of those just-waking boxers, the grace and force of the fighters shadowboxing in the ring, he felt the same longing as he did when he observed those Black guys in the school cafeteria: to be loose and strong and easy.

He didn't fit into this place yet, no, not like David. But with the older man as his guide, why couldn't he find a way? Why couldn't he shoot the shit with the old-timers, work the double-end bag effortlessly enough to keep the naysayers at bay? What if, in this place, his past, which Nathaniel had always assumed was ominous prologue, could be, maybe, merely past? "Fuck me, man?" he imagined telling

Jocelyn Carter, as they slapped their knees and cackled maniacally into each other's faces. "Fuck *you*!"

At 8:20 a.m., shirts soaked in sweat, David and Nathaniel retired to the bench to watch Saturday sparring, which had commenced a few minutes before. In the ring, the two bowl-haired teenagers, now re-outfitted in puffy leather headgear, body cups Velcroed around their slim waists, circled each other as Terry Tucker, serving as both referee and trainer, circled them.

Terry was five foot seven and all lean muscle, a fanny pack strapped casually around his waist, a portable phone clipped to his red cotton shorts. A minute in, the phone rang and Terry cradled it under his neck, answered, "Boxing," and conducted his business, neither he nor his fighters pausing from the action.

David had never brought one of his charges to the gym before. It had been heady, really, to see Nathaniel duck when he ducked (well, almost . . .), slide when he slid (there was potential there!), to have Nathaniel listen to him as intently as the boys in the ring listened to Terry.

Even though David hated to admit it, Terry had real talent for bringing out the best in his young fighters. David had seen him work his magic before, seen how he could turn the unruliest kids into soldiers in his little army. He rewarded dedication with attention, instruction. To spar on Saturdays, Terry had to ask you first. This was the goal for many of them, to get in the ring. Raw talent was one way to nab an invite. Another was to keep coming back.

Sometimes, David still wondered if he might've crafted a life more like his old disciple's, making good money teaching boys to become men in the ring, and not meh money teaching them the difference between cowgirl and reverse cowgirl in the Alzheimer's wing of a nursing home. Today had felt like something of an answer. But now David felt a twinge of irritation as he watched Nathaniel watching Terry center stage.

"Are you, like, good friends with him?" the boy asked expectantly, as if Terry were famous.

"With Terry Tucker motherfucker?" said David, summoning a chuckle. "Do you know who that little thing used to work for?" The fight clock beeped and Terry swatted one of the bowl-haired boys on the ass as the boxers returned to their corners.

Just then, Felix Barrowman sat down next to David. "What's good with you, old man?" said Felix.

"I'm teaching my friend here a thing or two about the ways of this world," said David. He introduced Felix to Nathaniel, whose heather gray T-shirt had become, in its entirety, a full shade darker from the sweat.

The boy half-raised his wrapped hand in a bashful hello. Felix looked at him coolly, then turned his head back toward the ring. "You raising up a champion, huh?" said Felix.

David knew Felix was teasing, but try as he might to tease back, there wasn't a hint of playfulness in his tone when he found himself saying, "We'll see."

V.

And so, with his uncle's blessing, Nathaniel ditched those awkward early evening outings to Barton Springs and began meeting David at the gym instead.

They did this, they assured themselves, not out of any delusions of grandeur, but because they'd had fun the first time, and because, after, each had retreated to his respective bed, where, hungry and virile, they'd met their lovers, sheets soon a damp tangle of man and wife, of boy and phone, and after the after they'd both thought, *We should repeat this day again.*

To casual observers, theirs might've seemed like typical workouts between laypeople. To Nathaniel Rothstein, serial P.E. evader, and David Dalice, veteran of the Saturday-at-Terry's kaffeeklatsch, it felt as if they'd been transported into a movie montage: the Hoosiers clicking under Norman Dale, Miyagi sculpting his Nathaniel-san. Each saw in the other something he wanted in himself, and as David called out combinations before the mirrored walls of the weight room, as they jabbed and crossed in not-quite unison, the boy had a passing vision of the man he might become, and the man remembered what it was like to be a boy, when the future was inchoate and every punch a possibility.

In those first days, Nathaniel showed little improvement. He punched hard but not smart, unable to discern, exactly, what it meant, as David and Terry and Uncle Bob kept saying, that power came not from his arms but his legs.

His defensive skills were especially lacking. One night, David tried to teach Nathaniel how to slip punches. It was a simple-seeming maneuver: a slight shift of the head to avoid an incoming blow. Like everything in boxing, this simplicity was an illusion. The slip was a full-body movement. "When you slip you should feel a twist in your torso," David instructed. "Keep your hands up. Bend your knees."

Even with David jabbing in slow motion, Nathaniel couldn't do it. Like an amateur manipulating a marionette, he could control only one part of himself at a time.

But though Nathaniel failed to slip or roll or parry, how *good* it felt, to throw, to fight!, that and his coach's exhortations—*You got this, boy, that's what I'm talking about!*—powering him forward.

His favorite part of these workouts came at the end, when David donned ragged leather mitts and called out combinations for Nathaniel in the ring. There, Nathaniel's world narrowed to just the two of them, David, mitts held high, asking more of him with each passing round—"Jab cross hook, again!"—until he was punching with abandon.

It was that same clobbering Glomb-Golden sensation, similar to the one Nathaniel had felt back in his bedroom in Newton, where he'd transform, via Discman, into Don Quixote or Jean Valjean, similar to the out-of-body exhilaration he experienced on the phone with Sasha. Nathaniel the boxer was as foreign to the boy as those other personas—bully, hero, lover—and after round or song or call he'd always revert back to original-flavor Rothstein, the memory of not being himself what kept him going as himself in the hours in between.

One night, Uncle Bob appeared in Nathaniel's doorway with a worn UT gym bag and a pair of boxing gloves, black leather fading at the fists. "Barton Springs hasn't been the same without you," said Bob.

"Really?" said Nathaniel.

"Seemed like an avuncular thing to say." Bob handed over the gloves. "I've been meaning to get a new pair anyway. Good for you, giving this a go."

Nathaniel tried one on, fastening the Velcro strap and raising his arm to get a better look. "Thanks, Uncle Bob," he said softly, admiring his bulging hand a beat longer, he knew, than he should.

A gratifying truth: twenty-seven years at Shoal Creek Rehab and none of David's protégés had ever absorbed his wisdom with Nathaniel's spongy greed.

The boy had begun to *walk* like David, *smell* like David, even *dress* like David: after weeks of laundering hoodies perfumed in the scents of Shoal Creek, Bob's wife, Marlene, had found a medical supply store off MoPac and bought her nephew a couple pairs of scrubs. Now when Nathaniel arrived in the mornings, he changed out of his jeans and T-shirt (in a stall, of course), leaving his civvies in a locker two doors down from David's own.

He'd also taken to asking David about his unexpected foray into boxing. No one had ever shown much interest in hearing about this time in David's life; most people, even at the gym, didn't know to ask. But Nathaniel wanted to know all the details: about David's stint as a tomato can, about the time he fought so well in Alvarado, Texas, that it even made the paper there.

Back in '73, David had picked up the Alvarado *Graphic* on his way out of town. It was the first time he'd ever seen his name in print, and he'd added it to the shoebox in the bedroom closet where he kept his most important documents: his Haitian passport, a letter his mother had hidden in his suitcase before he came to the States.

In 1985, when he and Ramona moved to the Hyde Park bungalow, the shoebox, somehow, didn't move with them. At the time, David brushed it off. Who cared if his expired Haitian passport had been lost? By then he was a naturalized citizen with U.S. papers. Who needed some old letter? His mother was still very much alive in '85; she could write him new letters from Miami. David could see wanting to pass the article on to a son, maybe, but Ramona was into her forties, their window for babies closed.

"This is not worth getting worked up about," he'd told her. Ramona had raised holy hell with the moving company, weeks later was still threatening to report them to the Better Business Bureau. "Let it go," said David. "Not every thing must be a Thing."

Now, in 1998, David could admit that it might've been nice to be able to share the article with his summer volunteer. He'd have to make do showing Nathaniel the only physical evidence he had left of his fight days: a single framed photograph.

In the old condo, the photograph had lived atop his dresser. After he and Ramona moved to the bungalow, David had stashed it in the bottom drawer; displaying the artifact in what was meant to be the home they'd grow old in struck him as a little sad.

The photo had been taken in the wing of the Austin Coliseum before his first fight. David stood Superman-style, hands on hips, and wore a Jamaican flag as a cape. The rest of his crew spread around him mugging for the camera in their Rasta garb: One-Eyed Ralph pointing in faux fear at one of David's biceps; Ernest "Zaftig" Wilks giving a thumbs-up, his wink exaggerated as a pirate's; little Terry using both hands to point a finger-pistol at someone off-camera, like one of Charlie's Angels.

At morning meeting a few days before the July 4 break, Nathaniel sat on a bench by the sinks inspecting the photograph as David finished getting ready. The boy wanted to know how skinny Terry had become as toned as he was now, what became of David's opponent ("A stunt double on *CHiPS*, if you can believe it").

"Is that the Haitian flag?" Nathaniel asked.

David explained it was Jamaican, told him the story of his birth as RastaMasta. "Those people see this big Black guy, they don't know," he said, trying for nonchalance. "People want pizzazz, OK? No one is obsessing over the details."

"So you pretended to be Jamaican?" asked Nathaniel. He seemed a little confused.

"Let me see that thing," said David, joining him on the bench. "Those were fun times," he said, examining the photograph. "*Fun times*. If ever you were feeling angry? Or sad? Hit a bag. Hit a *person*! And get paid! Oh, there's nothing like it."

Nathaniel peered down at the photo. "You think I could ever, like, get good?" He could see his own reflection in the picture glass.

"Look what you did to that little gnat at school! You just have to find a way to harness your anger, you know? Find that anger and put it in your fists, in your feet . . . No one in this world knows what you are capable of but you."

This last part came out more urgently than David had intended, the air suddenly too thick with meaning for his taste. "I'll promise you this, boy," he said, returning to the exaggerated version of himself. "Train hard enough and you'll have the ladies licking their lips in your presence." He poked Nathaniel in the chest. "Train hard enough and you could be *just like me*!"

VI.

Those words were still reverberating in Nathaniel's ears hours later, when he arrived at the gym to find a white passenger van in the gravel lot. Inside, Felix Barrowman stood in the center of the ring, talking to a dozen teenage boys who sat around him, each in identical black shorts and white T-shirts. Most of the regulars had stopped what they were doing to listen.

"Juvie," whispered David when Nathaniel found him on the bench across from the ring. Every summer, a dozen kids from the city's juvenile detention center came to the boxing gym for a workout, a reward for good behavior. "This year," said David, nodding toward Felix, "they get a special guest."

"Look, guys, I know how it is," Felix was telling the group. They were mostly Black and brown boys, but otherwise, thought Nathaniel, just like he was: their guarded eyes, unable, in the boxer's presence, to conceal their curiosity, mustaches patchy as his own.

"Out there, in the world, people think they know you, right?" said Felix. "Maybe they're judging you based on how you look, right? How you dress?" Nathaniel heard a snicker. "I'm a six-foot Black man in the United States of America, y'all. Look at me. You don't think I've been there? I been there. But the thing is, in here, it's different. In here, we try to make it different."

Felix told the boys how boxing had taken him to New York and Miami, Guadalajara and Toronto. "And in every one of those cities, *every single one*, there's a place like Terry Tucker's. Every city in the country, most countries in the *world*. Places like this, it's not about what you've done in your past, or how you look, or how much money your daddy makes, or if you got a daddy at all. Places like this, it's about what you're willing to leave inside the ring. So find your boxing gym. Even if it isn't a boxing gym. Y'all hear me?"

Nathaniel knew Felix wasn't talking to him, about him. Still, it kind of *was* Nathaniel, wasn't it? Was him enough so that as the other boys, ready to try their hands at the bags, offered a respectful if let's-move-it-along "yes," Nathaniel murmured a soft one of his own.

"C'mon, guys, that all you got?"

"Yes," the others said louder, Nathaniel's arms erupting in goose bumps at the prospect that this place existed in other places, that in those other places, there might be room for him, too. *Every city in the country, most countries in the world . . .*

"Y'all ready to do this?"

"Yes," they yelled, and though Nathaniel said nothing, in his mind he was the loudest of them all.

That night, boxing still on the brain, Nathaniel logged on to his cousin Max's desktop, where he used the Ask Jeeves search engine to investigate subjects too outlandish or embarrassing to even bring to David: "can you get 6 pack from boxing workout?" "boxing gym + Newton" "becoming amateur boxer + how."

He Asked about "David Dalice," too. A man in a place called Wichita Falls had archived all of the articles about Texas boxers he'd collected in his life, including a few paragraphs from the December 9, 1973, edition of the Alvarado *Graphic* under the headline *Newcomer Rasta Dalice gives hometown hero Bandit Bengochea a run for his money!* David had lost in nine rounds in a fight he wasn't expected to make it through one.

Before Sasha, Nathaniel would've kept his nascent boxing fantasies between him and his computer. He liked the idea of sharing them with her, though, of imagining himself with a boxer's build, a boxer's swagger, as she imagined those things, too . . .

The opportunity arose the next afternoon when, after they'd finished, Sasha said she wasn't ready to hang up yet. "Let's play question game," she proposed, which, to Nathaniel's relief, seemed to involve her asking questions and Nathaniel responding in his low mumble, offering just enough syllables to encourage her to keep going.

"Heavyweight?" she asked, after he said he was a boxer. "Yeah," said Nathaniel, no idea what the other weight classes were, or which he'd be.

They decided to add a regular 6:15 a.m. call to their repertoire (he from the safety of his bathroom, shower on), a 10:18 call after Bob and Marlene had gone to bed. Soon they were lingering on the phone after each session. Nathaniel told Sasha that when he wasn't training, he had a job in "extended care." Sasha worked the drive-thru at a burger joint, talked dirty for extra cash. Each, miraculously, lived in Austin. Both claimed to be twenty-five.

"Will you dream of me, *kotik*?" Sasha took to asking before parting ways for the night. "Course," said Nathaniel, nervous to say more but unwilling, unable to hang up.

Shoal Creek Rehab and the real David, the circadian rhythms of Nathaniel Rothstein's summer life: all of this, on the phone with Sasha, was verboten. This didn't stop the boy from imagining—while sweeping the multipurpose room or helping David into his Uncle Sam costume (a July 4 tradition at Shoal Creek)—how he'd relay the day's events to Sasha.

Sometimes, after hanging up, Nathaniel would even pretend she was in bed next to him and invent whole conversations between them in his mind. In these fantasies, he spoke in his confident David voice, smoothing out the filler words that defined his speaking style, sculpting vaguely interesting moments into actual anecdotes.

Nathaniel had returned from the long weekend to find the stars-and-stripes bunting he'd stapled to the reception desk disappeared, even a scrap of patriotic paraphernalia too disorienting for some Shoal Creekers the morning after.

One person who *was* confused post-holiday: Dr. Gloria Abruzzi. When Nathaniel went to the old woman's apartment to read, she seemed unsure who he was. This happened on occasion (the real David had warned him it would). Sometimes Dr. Abruzzi was a little out of it, other times very much on. What struck Nathaniel was how quickly she could swing from one to the other.

As the boy read aloud from *Tuck Everlasting*, Dr. Abruzzi sat on her sofa in distracted silence. Nathaniel was sure she wasn't following along, but ten minutes in she said she'd had enough of this "gobbledygook" about the fountain of youth. "If I wanted to spend time with people who refuse to die when they should," said Dr. Abruzzi, "I'd go to the cafeteria."

These were the sort of stories Nathaniel imagined telling Sasha. What would it feel like, he occasionally wondered, to present her with a truer version of himself?

He did make a half-hearted attempt to confess once, early in a call. "I'm not Jamaican," Nathaniel managed, mid-stroke. But Sasha was busy describing him undressing her, so by the time she got around to asking where he *was* from, the most he could whimper was "Ha . . . Ha . . . Haiti," for by then his fingers were all the way inside her, not the stubby, freckled fingers of Nathaniel Rothstein but the embrocated digits of David Dalice.

The embrocated *Black* digits, for Nathaniel's David never went more than a few clauses without using that beguiling word. If his relationship with Sasha were a wobbly ship, David's race served as ballast. He was Black, a detail Sasha could never forget since he rarely referenced a part of his own body without prefacing it with the adjective.

Why did he do this? Shouldn't the established fact of his Blackness have rendered the descriptor unnecessary? It wasn't as if, as Sasha bounced upon him, she instructed him to slap her doily-white Russian ass.

Yet no matter what else he did or said to her, Nathaniel knew, it was this one trait that most enthralled her, provoking Sasha's wildest whinnies and most rapturous moans.

A more probing version of Nathaniel might've considered why so often his David became a beast for Sasha to ride, a stallion for her to straddle, why he spat that word with a ferociousness he didn't any other. What it said about Sasha, about Nathaniel, about the country in which they lived.

But after over a decade in proudly liberal Newton's public schools, Nathaniel had the sense that, if anything, he'd already probed *too much*. Each fall, every student was required to sign a Respect for Human Differences pledge, vowing not to prejudge any other member of the school community based on race, class, or gender; the theater department adhered to a policy of "color-blind casting," filling roles, according to a typed note forever tacked to the South Stars bulletin board, without considering an actor's race or ethnicity. And then there were the interminable classroom talk-it-outs that came in the wake of race-related tumult, be it national or, as was the case the spring of Nathaniel's freshman year, closer to home.

Every April, Newton South's seniors wrote a fifteen-page "thesis" on a historical subject of their choosing, turned in an accompanying creative project. That year, Becca Waters had researched the Ku Klux Klan, sculpted a white hood out of papier-mâché. A faithful representation, the hood was displayed in a case outside the library alongside a diorama of the Scopes Trial and a collage inspired by Elizabeth Cady Stanton. A Black parent, Wanda Peters, had seen it and demanded it be taken down, and the brouhaha that followed resulted in the hood's removal, competing guest columns in the Newton *TAB* condemning and condoning that decision, and an endless panoply of class discussions on censorship versus sensitivity, "how we're all feeling," and on and on.

(The white students were feeling all sorts of ways: sympathetic, jokey, "just so *guilty*," aggrieved. The Black students, many of whom, in any given class period, were the only Black student, stayed mostly quiet. "What was Becca supposed to do for the *creative portion*?" Linda Rothstein had asked, after Nathaniel told her about it. "Burn a cross?")

Never in any of these in-class discussions had they explored why almost all the Black kids sat at the same couple cafeteria tables, nor had they ever broached the topic of why these students, bused in from "underprivileged" areas, had ended up in those areas in the first place (nor had Linda Rothstein ever raised this, nor had Nathaniel ever asked). No one had ever pointed out, at least not publicly, that the South Stars policy was useless, since none of the METCO kids auditioned for plays anyway (their bus back to Boston left before evening rehearsals ended). Was it weird that Nathaniel didn't, until David, have a single Black friend?

For all of the well-intentioned yapping, no one talked about anything real, not really, the point that deep down we were really all the same, of course, not the color but the content, the emphasis on *diversity* both perfunctory and never-ending. Nathaniel hadn't asked those deeper questions either, hadn't ever considered why the conversations they did have were so relentlessly abstract, but he could sense, in a way only teenagers can (and with that teenage certainty), that phoniness was afoot.

It was this phoniness that allowed him, allowed many of the white students, to brush the whole enterprise off as fraudulent. "Everyone's just so *politically correct*," Nathaniel had grouched to Linda during Becca Waters–gate, parroting a line he'd heard from a Lunch Buncher, who was parroting a line from his own mother. It was a defense mechanism, this collective rolling of the eyes, and whether Nathaniel understood it or not (and he didn't, but also didn't want to), it let him off the hook this way, him and all the other white people, for if they weren't scoffing at the often hokey treatment the Newton South administration had prescribed for the "race problem," they might have to consider the discomfiting diagnosis itself.

Was there a different way?

Maybe if, in Mrs. Harrison's sophomore U.S. history class, they'd explored how the fear of revolt had birthed in the brains of white slave owners the lie of the "black savage," how white supremacists had used and sexualized that lie to justify their lynching, maybe if they'd delved into the Federal Housing Administration's refusal, in the 1930s, to lend to Blacks, redlining those supposed savages right out of the suburbs, suburbs like Nathaniel's, maybe if, as a class, they'd drawn a line from Nat Turner to Newton, from *King Kong* to today, maybe Nathaniel would've understood why playing the black brute on the phone was more than just "not P.C."

But there was no *today* in tenth-grade U.S. history, which ended, nonsensically, with the Vietnam War, nor were these the topics on offer in Nathaniel's textbook, *America: Past to Promise*, whose very title got it wrong, since history doesn't tell us where to go but how we got there, and even a child should know that the opposite of past isn't promise: it's present. If we were forever progressing, what was all the fuss about anyway?

Not a surprise then that when it came to race in America, it seemed to Nathaniel that between *To Kill a Mockingbird* and Black History Month and that universal sound of the substitute teacher—the rumble of a rolling TV cart—heralding another forty-five long minutes of *Roots*, his teachers had all laid it on a bit thick.

Was it *wrong* to pretend to be Black? Nathaniel knew it was, but he never fully registered the weight of that wrongness, made no attempt to register it, lumped the act instead with the other entries in his ever-expanding file of Things He Wasn't Supposed to Do and Was Doing with Sasha, the smashing of those taboos half the turn-on.

Had the boy's professed Blackness been less central to his relationship—or had he considered the meaning of it more—he would've reacted differently when, the Thursday after Independence Day, Sasha Semyonova called with news. Natalia, Natasha, and Sabrina had decided to take a trip to "their hometown of Odessa," which meant "the shadow of the blue moon now shines upon us": Sasha would have the apartment all to herself.

"*You all live together?*" Nathaniel blurted, so wicked a possibility he hadn't considered it.

"You're missing point," said Sasha. "*August eight.* It's a Saturday. Nine p.m. You see me in flesh, yes?"

Yes, thought Nathaniel, moving from bed to swivel chair and marking down, on a Post-it from his cousin Max's desk, the when and where of their proposed encounter. *Yes yes god yes.* And though he told himself then he'd never go through with it, though he told himself he couldn't even if he wanted to, as Sasha began to tell the boy exactly what she'd do to him in four weeks' time—August 8, 1998—Nathaniel found himself turning on his cousin's desktop and, Nokia balanced against his shoulder, typing into the Ask Jeeves search bar a question he felt certain that doughy valet had never been Asked before. Tell me Jeeves show me Jeeves help me Jeeves, please!

How do you turn from white to black?

VII.

That night—tentatively at first, for he wasn't serious, not really, this was just *out of curiosity*, he and Sasha wouldn't *really* meet anyway—Nathaniel began to search the internet for ways he might darken.

Nothing crazy: he wasn't looking to transform into an "eight-rock" like David. He'd picked up the phrase courtesy of Jeeves, for even in those early days of the World Wide Web, the British butler occasionally came through: an entire "Glossary of Harlem Slang," by one Zora Neale Hurston, complete with a "colorscale" describing the tonal gradations of African Americans.

Nathaniel found the document fascinating, spent twenty minutes scrolling through. Part of him knew the words were old-fashioned, but he liked how they sounded on his tongue—sex was *jelly*, pretty girls *frail eel*—had even heard the Black kids at school use a few of them before. "Hello, *my people*!" Miah Walker always announced when he strolled into English class. Nathaniel imagined entering the boxing gym like that. "Hello, *my people*!" he tried now, catching his reflection in the monitor.

Too much, thought Nathaniel, clicking out of the window with those luscious turns of phrase. He knew he didn't need to transform into a *righteous-ragged eight-rock* or a *tight-headed inky dink*, had a hard time imagining himself asking Dr. Lichtblau to turn him *seal brown* via intravenous injections of Melanotan II, which he discovered on a message board for bodybuilders.

No, all the boy needed was a dusting, a bronzing, enough to let him pass . . .

It seemed . . . *conceivable.* More than half a million Haitians were "mulatto" after all, a fact he'd learned while poring over the photographs in Cousin Max's *World Book*. As in, European *and* African. As in, ocher and umber and everything in between. And how far off from "high yellow" was Nathaniel to begin with? Compared to the "goyim," as his grandma Phyllis called white non-Jews, he was downright dusky, freckles so dark and dense that in some spots you couldn't see the pink underneath. That coarse hair of his was only a half-inch shy of Jew-fro already . . .

And then there was his mother. At his grandma's condo in Boca the previous Hanukkah, he'd seen a photograph of Linda Rothstein from the seventies, back when his parents would rent a summer house on Cape Cod, back when she liked to "sit out," reading Erica Jong and burning to a crisp. "Ten minutes on Megansett Beach," said Grandma Phyllis, flipping through album pages, "and this one turns into a *schvartze*!"

"Jesus, Mom!" Linda had snapped. "You can't say things like that." Nathaniel's mother did not like to dwell on her married days, but even after Phyllis excused herself from the couch ("Who knew Uncle Julius would survive Buchenwald so his grandniece could become the language police?"), her daughter had stayed on the page. "I looked *good*," marveled Linda, and though Nathaniel made a show then of getting up "to puke," he had to admit it was true.

What if, Nathaniel wondered, typing "'makeup' + 'white to black'" into the search bar, all it took was a bit of foundation the night of, a shade or two darker than his own hue? That's what they'd done for *Man of La Mancha*. Nothing over-the-top, just a little something to infuse those whey-faced Newtonites with a couple drops of Spanish blood. They'd all laughed before dress rehearsal when Alf Hartman, a ginger in real life, normally bright as glue, came out of the dressing room made up as Sancho Panza. He'd run figure-eights around the girls waiting in the wings, cried *Arriba! Arriba!* like Speedy Gonzales. It was funny not because Alf looked so different than usual but because he didn't, as if, perhaps, a single grandparent had been a Hernandez of Guanajuato and not a Hartman of Pound Ridge.

What if . . . and yet, no, cosmetics wouldn't be right, for "'makeup' + 'white to black'" did not yield links to compacts and brushes but rather to a smorgasbord of historical freakery: a 1921 "amateur's guide to minstrelsy" for sale on eBay ("YOU can use BURNT CORK to black up as Old Darky Servant!" read the yellowed pamphlet's cover. "YOU can wear the nose putty of the Ghetto Jew!"); the personal site of a collector out of Alpharetta, Georgia, who specialized in the "lost art of ethnic mimicry" (five-inch-high bow ties and double-jingle tambourines, "aboriginal hairpieces" and a bald cap garnished with a queue).

Ugh, thought Nathaniel Rothstein, though it was a bit of an obligatory ugh, truth be told, for the boy found those pages absorbing, felt the same comfortable thrill reading them as when he settled in for a *Geraldo* featuring Klansmen, the same comfortable thrill as when he saw lions at the zoo. Yes, *ugh*, thought Nathaniel, and even if it was a desultory ugh, the ugh of a boy confident his obituary would not read "eaten by lions," it *was* an ugh nonetheless, a not-racist *ugh!*, since Nathaniel admired David, felt strong *as* David, had no interest in making fun.

On the top of the third page of search results came a link to Powell's Books, and to an image of a cover that Nathaniel had, strangely, seen before. The background was a faded photograph of a round-faced white man staring sagely into the camera. In the bottom corner was a second, smaller photograph, framed in white, like a Polaroid. It was the side profile of a round-faced Black man in dark glasses. Mrs. Bartlett had projected this image in ninth-grade English. The two men, she'd told the class, were the same.

Black Like Me.

Nathaniel clicked on the Powell's summary, learning the specifics he'd spaced out for the first time around. In 1959, a white journalist named John Howard Griffin disguised himself as a Black man to understand the injustices of the Jim Crow South. For six weeks, Griffin traveled from New Orleans to Hattiesburg, Mobile to Montgomery, searching those segregated cities for work, for places to eat and sleep, all while masquerading as Black. Two years later, he published his findings to international acclaim. By the thirty-fifth anniversary, more than ten million copies had been sold.

The summary, the editorial blurbs: everything was about the meaning of the book, nothing about how Griffin had done it in the first place. Nathaniel didn't think Mrs. Bartlett had told them, either. But now he clicked and scrolled, clicked and scrolled, from Powell's to Amazon to a homemade Griffin fan page, its bright yellow Comic Sans text almost unreadable against the black background. According to the site, Griffin had darkened his skin by ingesting a large amount of a drug called methoxsalen, normally used to combat vitiligo and psoriasis, in combination with a few days under an ultraviolet lamp.

A bit extreme, thought Nathaniel, closing the page.

Of course, he knew that in the unlikely event he ever *did* meet Sasha, he could always just confess the truth. She'd find out he wasn't twenty-five as soon as she saw him. If that wasn't a dealbreaker, would being white?

But Nathaniel also knew that he'd gotten this far with Sasha only by being someone else. Flirting *as Nathaniel*? Kissing *as Nathaniel*? Maybe even . . . *having sex*? It was so much more *doable* as David. After a lifetime of being doughy in every sense of that word, what would it feel like to be . . . a little less?

Nathaniel, in short, had no intention of going through with any of it and every intention of going through with all of it, which was why, the next day at work, he stuck the Post-it on which he'd written the details of his possible rendezvous with Sasha to the inside door of his locker—his version of a pinup, and a way to guarantee his aunt and uncle wouldn't find it—and, after morning meeting, repaired to the gift shop off the lobby where, just for fun and deadly serious, he bought a bottle of Hawaiian Tropic Dark Tanning Oil.

VIII.

Thus began the darkening of Nathaniel Rothstein.

To Uncle Bob's deep admiration and Aunt Marlene's muted horror, that Saturday Nathaniel went straight from the gym to a lawn chair in the Alexanders' front yard. There, he sunned shirtless, lifting his Umbros up and up his milky thighs, all 732 pages of *The Sword of Shannara* and a half-drunk can of Arizona Iced Tea at his side. ("I tip my hat to you, sir," Bob told him, chugging past with the mower.)

He woke the next morning pleasantly warm. In the bathroom, shower running, he stood before the mirror as he did the deed with Sasha, his chest and arms now slightly, agreeably blush. How many times had his mom told him "you could use a little color," not to waste the day inside? Why hadn't he listened? After he hung up, Nathaniel couldn't stop pushing his thumb into his sternum; each time, it left a white mark, a sign, he knew, that soon his strawberry skin would mellow and brown.

In the afternoon, he drove to a nearby shopping plaza to get Subway for lunch. Nathaniel usually took his Italian BMT back to the house but, pleased with his "little color," he decided to get some more and sat at one of the outside tables instead. This was how he noticed that directly across from the sandwich shop, in between a Souper Salad and a Smoothie King, sat DreamSkinz Tan & Spa.

A tanning salon. What were the chances? Would there be any harm in . . . checking it out?

Nathaniel had always associated tanning beds with the ultra-rich, unaware that in reality the chichi toasted themselves by home pools or in less conspicuous, and more discreetly named, parlors, no greater flare to warn away the 1% than an extraneous *z*. DreamSkinz was a land of restless suburbanites instead, a place for those who had white-flighted out of city centers and now, in a karmic twist, spent their days conspiring to darken. The average clientele: bored stay-at-homes, aged fitness instructors, the occasional status-conscious gay fabulist who yearned for, and oft achieved, the rusted skin of a genuine Vegas showman.

The owners had gone hard on the California vibes: a surfboard on one whitewashed wall, the scents of the lobby all Coppertone and coconut oil. On the glass shelves behind the reception desk: bottles of "dark tanning accelerator" and after-tan "browning lotion," "skin calming day cream" and teeth-whitening gel.

On the walk over, Nathaniel had concocted a rationale for being there (family vacation approaching, needed to work on his "base"). Unnecessary. Among the sun-hungry citizens of that place, the comers and goers were too preoccupied with achieving their own dream skinz to worry about anyone else's.

Why was Nathaniel Rothstein at DreamSkinz Tan & Spa? Who cared? Not the ladies browsing a rack of swimsuits. To those gingerbread women's icing-white eyes, the lightly tanned boy was translucent as Casper. Not the receptionist either, her bleached hair so overprocessed it had taken on the lifelessness of a merkin. She was reading a library copy of *Memoirs of a Geisha*, glanced up only briefly. "You eighteen?"

Nathaniel instinctively felt in the front pocket of his cargo shorts for his Velcro wallet. He'd only graduated from his learner's permit that spring, his driver's license so new it was still stiff and shiny. "Eighteen?" he said uncertainly.

"Rockin'," said the receptionist. She asked what length and level he wanted and, when Nathaniel took too long to answer, shut her book and decided for him. "Anything above a three, my dude, and you're gonna stick to the pan."

Inside the small tanning room, Nathaniel checked the door twice to make sure he'd locked it, left his clothing in a pile on the floor, and climbed into the bed. He'd been uneasy till then—was it weird he'd gotten totally naked?—but as he shut the canopy, he felt like an astronaut in a rocket ship, shivery with possibility as the engines rumbled before launch.

For ten minutes, he lay in the blue-lit solarium. It was otherworldly, the alien nature of the place giving Nathaniel license to explore himself in ways he never normally would in not-quite-private. He flopped his ball sack on his thigh, sniffed his pits. He removed the complimentary tanning goggles and put the left eye cup over his left nipple, couldn't say why, tried right on right, returned them to his head. From the safety of his spaceship he attempted, for the first time ever off the phone, to speak as David. "Well, hello there, young thing!" said Nathaniel, as deeply, as performatively, as the man who inspired him.

Nathaniel woke the next morning to find he'd burned his butt and inner thighs. There was an extraterrestrial thickness to the scalds, raw enough that even in his scrubs he waddled through the workday. "Why are you walking like you need to void your bowels?" David asked when they passed in the corridor. Nathaniel told him he was sore from the gym.

After work, he found a bottle of ancient aloe under Cousin Max's bathroom sink, lathered his irradiated areas like his mom had made him do to sunburns past.

Within a few days, the burns had healed. As he'd hoped, his strawberry skin started to become richer, deeper. Did he look *Black*? More like he was midway through a teen tour of Jerusalem. But white Jews come in only two colors—Tri-State or Tel Aviv—and, like his mother, who turned downright Sephardic in the sun, a few rays and Nathaniel began to move from the first to the second. Also like his mother, Nathaniel had to admit: he looked good.

He decided variation was key, committing to twice-weekly sessions at DreamSkinz, weekends in the front yard. Nathaniel's daily triage now involved applying sunblock and aloe to any burned regions, more tanning oil to the browning ones.

It was guesswork, nothing more. But like the actors of South Stars, who never whistled in the wings nor accepted flowers prior to a show, he stuck stiffly to these arbitrary customs. Nathaniel never deviated from the schedule, never missed a morning ablution, his holy water white and creamy, green and goopy, brown and slick, and in his discipline the boy conferred upon these made-up rules powers incommensurate with their powers.

And why wouldn't he? For as the outside Nathaniel started to turn, he began to feel a change within.

IX.

The first sign came at Terry Tucker's in mid-July, on the Thursday following his DreamSkinz scalding. For weeks, Nathaniel had futilely slapped at the speed bag, whacking it so hard it would swivel wildly, or else too gently to build a rhythm. That Thursday, forty-five seconds into the third round, he knocked the bag with his left fist just so and knew, somehow, to release his right as he brought his left back to guard his cheek, knew, in a way he hadn't before, how to rest his weight on his knees, how to make small circles with his fists, until *badada-badada-badada-badada*—

"There it is!" called David from one speed bag over. Nathaniel wasn't attacking it with the intensity of the regulars, let the bag rebound slowly, but still he was getting it: *Badada-badada*, "Keep it going," David called, *badada*, "one more minute," *badada-badada*, "twenty seconds now," *badada*, "that's what I'm talking about!" *Beep!*

The fight clock signaled the end of the round and Nathaniel, breathless, rested his hands on his knees. "See! This work pays off," said David, shaking the boy's shoulders in congratulation.

Two days later, on Saturday morning, Nathaniel found the pulse of the double-end bag for the first time, managed to pivot around the tether and keep punching, too. "You sure you're related to *Bob Alexander*?" said Jocelyn Carter, passing by. "Your uncle can't hit that thing for shit."

The next Tuesday, David excavated from underneath the ring a unicycle Terry kept there for core work. "All aboard," he said, helping Nathaniel up. David braced his palms against Nathaniel's flanks, the training wheels the boy needed to wobble about the gym.

He guided Nathaniel around the regulars working the bags—"Here comes trouble," etc.—past Old-Timers' Row, empty but for Carlos Ortega, lounging in a barber's chair. "This the fuckin' circus?" Carlos called.

"Since you're here it is," said Nathaniel, pedaling past. He realized what he was saying only as he was saying it, as astonished at having thought it, having let it out, as he was when he turned back to see Carlos raise an invisible beer mug. "Good one, bitch!"

Later, as David made his social rounds, Nathaniel worked the heavy bag. He still hadn't figured out how to pace himself, would go full bore, get winded, slow down. It was in one of these slow-down periods when Felix Barrowman stepped up to the bag next to his.

"You the disciple, right?" said Felix.

Nathaniel, starstruck, didn't know what to say.

"David's number two?" Felix offered his glove. "Barrowman."

Until now, Nathaniel had gone out of his way to avoid Felix, even more so after his electrifying presentation to the juvie kids. Working out no longer felt awkward in the presence of the just-for-fun crowd, but around a *true contender*? Nathaniel stared down at the older man's glove dumbly, then bumped it with his own. "Rothstein," he stammered.

"Minute left, Rothstein," said Felix, nodding toward the fight clock.

Nathaniel tried to keep it slow and steady this time, was careful to move with the bag like David had showed him. Felix let it rip, the thick chain anchoring bag to ceiling jangling loudly as he worked around it. *Pa! Pa-pa! Pa-pa-pa!*

"Don't bunch them shoulders, Rothstein," said Felix, without slowing down. "Open up now." Nathaniel relaxed his shoulders, spread his feet farther apart. "Yeah, Rothstein. Thatta boy. *Pa-pa!* Get it."

Get it, Felix said, and Nathaniel Rothstein complied.

It wasn't that he was showing meteoric improvement. He was at the exact level a pudgy kid who'd never taken athletics seriously should've been a month into working out. Nathaniel's footwork was basically nonexistent; David's calls for him to slip one way usually sent him the other. But by the third full week of July, Nathaniel had begun to feel what they all felt after long enough at the gym, the crazed charge that comes from unleashing a combination, from punching through to the end of the round.

What was it about the sweet science that bred in its practitioners such delusion? That turned each landed punch, no matter how soft or wild, into evidence that the puncher might one day rule the world?

Not near as dark as David, Nathaniel no longer had the temporary shine of the just-vacationed, either, didn't glow like his fourth-grade crush, Rachel Rosen-Levy, who'd famously returned from Club Med Punta Cana in January '92 near-phosphorescent, her loose curls pulled tight into cornrows. Did he *now* look Black? More russet, like a potato. He'd begun to shed pounds, too, and had to hold up his jeans with a braided belt he'd found in Max's closet.

Darker and darker, stronger and stronger, and as he transformed he got better and better: on the phone, in the ring, in his skin. Nathaniel knew the first wasn't leading to the second, yet he couldn't help feeling they were inextricably linked: the tanner he turned, the braver he felt, his browning skin the armor he needed to do battle with the world.

At DreamSkinz, Nathaniel upped his time and level. There were, he knew, inconsistencies in his skin tone, and he went about eliminating them with Ahab-like intensity. Most polychromed were Nathaniel's privates. After burning his butt the first time, he'd started wearing his leopard-print bikinis into the tanning bed, rendering that region lighter than everywhere else. His tush was still the pink-white it had always been, except out of the shower when it bordered on salmon. His balls didn't match the rest of him, but had they before?

Nathaniel's attempts at color correction were both wide-ranging and tempered by a fear of a nuclear-singed ween/ass. In the tanning bed, he tried flopping his package over his waistband to sun his front and save his back, tried going naked and wearing a sock like a condom to do the opposite. None of it seemed to have much effect.

His August 8 in-person date with Sasha ever closer, Nathaniel began to consider more drastic action. He wondered if the rays were stronger at Hippie Hollow, the rocky nude beach out on Lake Travis where Bob Alexander, to the good-natured revulsion of his wife and son, would occasionally swim.

And that wasn't even the wildest option Nathaniel contemplated. One afternoon, an even more off-the-wall possibility emerged from an even more unlikely place.

It happened when Nathaniel went to read to Gloria Abruzzi. The doctor answered the door wearing oven mitts. At first, Nathaniel figured she was just confused. But on her sofa, Dr. Abruzzi removed the mitts to reveal a horror: she'd woken to find her knotty fingers swollen to the point of near-explosion, the backs of her hands covered in raised red patches, themselves covered in dense, silvery scales. "Don't get old," she advised Nathaniel.

Dr. Abruzzi asked if he wouldn't mind fetching her pills from the kitchen counter, along with a glass of milk. "The treatment for this thing . . ." she called, as Nathaniel did as he was told. "*Byzantine* does not begin to describe it." In addition to the pills, she had to bathe her hands under a UV lamp. Her son, who lived close by, would be bringing one by that evening.

"What happened to you?" asked Nathaniel, setting the items down on the coffee table.

"Psoriasis," said Dr. Abruzzi. "An immune issue. Something. I don't know." She'd developed the condition in adulthood, in the past had only suffered mild flare-ups, nothing "a topical" wouldn't fix. This time, for the first time, they had to haul out "the big guns." Dr. Abruzzi asked Nathaniel to uncap the pill bottle. "It's not contagious, if you were wondering."

Psoriasis. Where had he heard that word before? Psoriasis . . . A UV lamp . . . Nathaniel looked down at the pill bottle. *Black Like Me*.

"Is it true these make you darker?" he blurted.

"Make *who* darker?" said Dr. Abruzzi.

"Like whoever takes them," said Nathaniel. If they were the ones that John Howard Griffin guy had used, they worked. From the picture on the book's cover, dude looked dark as Urkel.

"I don't understand what you're asking." Dr. Abruzzi repeated the question slowly: "*Is it true these make you darker?*" She squinted up at Nathaniel, bewildered. "They're for my hands."

Most of the time, Dr. Abruzzi came across solid as a bowling ball. It was only in these moments of confusion when she seemed small. This time, maybe because she was ailing, she even looked a little frightened. Nathaniel knew he'd erred. "Never mind, sorry," he said, shaking a single pill out of the bottle and placing it next to the milk. She hadn't asked him to do that, but he didn't see how she could manage on her own. "Just a dumb thing I read in school."

Dr. Abruzzi offered a close-lipped smile. "So," she said, moving on. "What children's book are you reading me today?"

Give the kid some credit: despite trying to turn himself Black in hopes of hooking up with a Russian phone sex operator, even Nathaniel Rothstein knew that stealing psoriasis medication from a nursing home patient whose hands were as bloated as the foam fingers at a basketball game was a bad idea. He never brought it up with Dr. Abruzzi again.

Still, if his initial intention had only been to give himself a bronzing, with each passing day he recommitted himself to the project, off-white Nathaniel succeeding in ways he never had in his original skin.

No longer did entering the staff locker room provoke near-paralysis, each swaying dong transfixing as a hypnotist's pocket watch. Now he entered those stuffy quarters like an almost normal person; he'd even begun to change into his scrubs out in the open, for all the world to see. In the cafeteria, when David ordered "Un double cheeseburger, mademoiselle," Nathaniel would follow up as his boss taught him, with an impish "Moi aussi."

"You two are dorks," Chef Alejandra told Nathaniel the first time he did this. "Texas is agreeing with you," she said another.

At the gym, wolf whistles and *looking good, mans* followed Nathaniel as he followed David from mat to bag to ring. "Rothstein," Terry Tucker had started grunting, approvingly, whenever Nathaniel passed. A fist bump here, an ass swat there. Twice when David was in the restroom, Terry had come over to offer pointers. The boy who had once stood out like a newly transplanted organ had, same as many a burgeoning regular before him, been absorbed into the body that was the boxing gym.

They accepted him because he kept coming back, day after day. Because he did the work. Because just for fun or deadly serious, there was no pretend training, no pretending in the ring.

But even if Nathaniel knew this, still it felt like they were responding to something more.

Now when he imagined thrusting into Sasha Semyonova, he envisioned not his body nor David's, but the body he described on the phone, a body he felt his own becoming, tight and tough and obsidian. The fat that masked Nathaniel's pecs and abs had begun to melt away. Standing naked before the mirror during his morning Sasha sessions, shower blasting, he'd catch glimpses of this new man through the steam. Flex here, suck in there, and he could just make him out: this other self inside himself, waiting to break free.

X.

He had his skeptics.

One evening, David running late, Nathaniel skipped rope in the gravel lot alongside a trio of Mexican guys about his age, including the stocky kid with the fat mole above his lip. "Hey, can I ask you something?" he said to Nathaniel at the break. The other two—more developed than the first, chests snug in their tank tops—looked on in anticipation.

The stocky kid asked him something in Spanish. The only word Nathaniel recognized for sure was *mexicano*. Was he asking if Nathaniel *was* Mexican? If he wanted to *be* Mexican?

"Sorry," said Nathaniel, realizing that his four years studying the language had not prepared him for this moment. "I don't—"

"*I said*," said the kid, and he repeated the question, this time enunciating every syllable.

Nathaniel looked to the others, their fists to their mouths like corks to bottles, stifling potential laughter.

"You should look up what that means." The others laughed for real now as the stocky kid turned back to his intended audience. "That kid's fucked up," he said, shaking his head.

Nathaniel knew enough about boys to know what had transpired, how one chunky kid had curried favor with a group by going after another. But if he was experienced enough in these painful dynamics to partially recognize the other boy's motivation, he didn't see all of it. He didn't see how his careful evasion of the other teenage regulars at Terry Tucker's, born of his own self-consciousness, made him seem stuck-up. He didn't see how even though the stocky kid—his name was Ernesto Barrientos—had been coming to the gym twice as long as Nathaniel, he didn't have his own minder paving his way. In Ernesto's three months there, David had never said anything to him at all.

So Nathaniel went inside and hung up his jump rope and prayed David would arrive soon, and when he did he stuck close to him as ever, and from then on took even greater care to avoid the stocky kid with the fat mole above his lip, and reminded himself it was the other boy's own insecurities that led him to make fun of Nathaniel, and on those occasions, later, when he did think about the incident, the shame he felt had nothing to do with the why of the other boy's taunting but only with the what.

A second doubter emerged in the latter half of July 1998, albeit a more reluctant one.

One Sunday, gym closed, Nathaniel asked to join his uncle at Barton Springs. Towels spread, Bob stripped down to his swim briefs, expecting Nathaniel to begin his reading, but when he looked over there was his nephew, removing his baggy cargo shorts to reveal baggy board shorts, stripping off his baggy T-shirt and lathering his piglet belly with tanning oil.

"What are you *doing*?" asked Bob.

"I dunno," mumbled Nathaniel. He made his way down the grassy hill to the eight-feet mark and jumped in.

Later, as they toweled off, a freckled, frizzy-haired girl ran down the hill toward the water, brushing Nathaniel's bare elbow. "Sorry!" she called back before leaping off the edge, shriek-laughing all the way into the pool.

"What say you, squire?" asked Bob.

Nathaniel shrugged. "Pretty hot," he said plainly. "Do you want to lay out for a bit?"

Pretty hot. Lay out for a bit. Was this the same kid he'd picked up from the airport less than two months before?

Truth was, Bob hadn't paid *that* much attention to Nathaniel since the boy arrived. He'd kept him sheltered, kept him fed, encouraged him with the boxing stuff. Their chemistry wasn't electric, nor did it need to be. Nathaniel was a visiting nephew, no more no less, and he received from his uncle the exact amount of consideration Bob felt such a person was due.

But now, sunning side by side with the boy, he saw the scope of his nephew's transformation. He was so much more confident, so much more relaxed. So much more . . . tan.

It pleased Bob to see Nathaniel coming into his own, to know he'd found a mentor in David. Pleased him that the kid might turn out to be less of a dud than it previously appeared.

Early the next morning, however, Bob Alexander experienced a pang of doubt after passing Nathaniel's closed bedroom door. He swore he heard the boy speaking to someone over the running shower, but when they met in the kitchen some minutes later, the younger told the older he must've misheard.

It was a small thing, yet it nagged at Bob—he was pretty darn sure he'd heard something—this tiny tear in the fabric of Nathaniel's tale of summer triumph leading Bob to stick his finger in there, rip some more. Was it kind of *weird* how much time he spent on the lawn? What sixteen-year-old was buying Hawaiian Tropic Tanning Oil? And why would he lie about talking on the phone?

Twenty-four hours later, Bob snuck past Nathaniel's room as he had the day before, heard the same muffled chatter. Heard it again two days later.

"I don't want to pick at the kid," Bob told David that Saturday, as they sat on the apron of the canvas, wrapping their hands. Through the open garage doors, they watched Nathaniel gamely attempt double-unders with his jump rope in the gravel lot. "I mean, what you're doing with him, it's unbelievable." Bob hesitated. "Do you think, though, that maybe he's . . . overdoing it with the sun?"

"Let him be," advised David. "When you jump," he called to the boy, "don't bring your heels to your behind." Then, to Bob: "I think Nathaniel is figuring out Nathaniel."

"Christ, you sound like Marlene," said Bob. "She says he's *finding himself*. I said, as what? Gunga Din?"

David couldn't deny that Nathaniel was darker. The kid was *everything*-er. Like the After photograph on the right side of a weight loss advertisement, he'd become slimmer and stronger, better coiffed and styled than Before.

"Do you know why people come to this place, Bob?" said David, lowering himself to the floor. "To *change*. So maybe we shouldn't fault the boy for changing."

Bob had to admit he had a point.

XI.

Here's what David didn't tell Bob Alexander: Nathaniel wasn't the only one transforming.

Until that summer, David's dirty tutoring had always provoked the occasional flash of self-loathing. He thought back to Nathaniel's first day, when David had become so pissed at himself for again engaging in his summer stupidity that he'd even tried to exorcise the apparition on the heavy bags at Terry Tucker's Boxing Gym.

Now, in the final days of his forty-seventh year, the final days of July 1998, things were different. At the gym, David's lessons were real. His stories were real. Whenever Ramona inquired about her husband's renewed passion for boxing, he'd tell her that it was a favor for Bob, nothing serious, *just for fun*. It went deeper than that, but it was also true: David was having a blast.

The future that summer felt full of promise. Movement at the gym led to other movement: in the kitchen, where, after workouts, he'd taken to concocting lavish meals of coquilles St.-Jacques and cassoulet; in the bedroom, where he and Ramona made love at rates unseen in years. Since June, David had dropped eleven pounds.

Sometimes, in bed, David reminisced with his wife over the same stories he'd shared with Nathaniel earlier in the day. *Remember that scuzzy Chinese restaurant we'd go to after fights? What do you think happened to One-Eyed Ralph?* He delighted in Ramona's sardonic take on those times, her theatrical groans. Those memories, once painful, had begun to remind David not of possibilities dashed but of the promise of possibility to begin with. He'd returned the photograph from his first fight, long stowed in the bottom of his dresser, to its rightful spot on top of it.

So *this* is why men have children, David sometimes mused, kneeling on Nathaniel's sneakers as the boy completed his sit-ups, holding the heavy bag as Nathaniel whaled away. He knew it was a silly cliché, but maybe not so silly because it was true. A second chance, a second act: to turn the boys they once were into the men they'd never managed to become.

How sweet it felt to have this smaller, pinker version of himself *jab cross!* when David told him to *One two!*, to call, *Keep it going, thirty seconds!* and know Nathaniel would: for thirty seconds, thirty minutes. Sometimes, it seemed to David, if he asked the boy to, Nathaniel might keep it going for life.

Until that summer, David had spent hours, days even, fantasizing his way out of his job and into something new. Lately, though, he'd started thinking that maybe his path wasn't *out* of Shoal Creek, that he didn't need an *instead of* but an *in addition to*. He had no delusions of training the next Felix Barrowman. But was it so crazy to think he might pick it up as a sideline? Train his own little crew?

Nathaniel had already mentioned it'd be cool to return next summer. He was hungry and malleable, strong and getting stronger. Why couldn't he run and lift on his own back in Massachusetts, return to train with David more seriously in June? Nathaniel would only be seventeen then; they could even try for one of the local tournaments if he got good enough. When Terry was seventeen, he didn't even know how to skip rope.

Terry's openness to the unlikeliest of boxers was why, David had always believed, the gym had succeeded in the first place. The man's life and business philosophies were pleasantly aligned. Terry knew people could change, could grow. He'd changed and grown himself. That spirit of possibility was what attracted more middle-aged women to Terry Tucker's than to the other local boxing gyms, more folks trying to lose weight. Inclusivity turned a profit.

A couple years before, when that *Statesman* piece on how everyone was welcome at Terry Tucker's came out, David had shown it to Ramona over breakfast, knowing the accompanying photo would get a rise out of his Terry-skeptical wife. Inside the ring, gymgoers of every size and color posed in fight position, Terry front and center, grinning. "The great egalitarian," Ramona had said, taking a loud slurp of coffee, her version of an eye roll.

"You know what that man is thinking?" said David. "He's thinking, if Terry Tucker of all people could make money boxing, literally *everyone else on this planet* has the potential to make Terry Tucker money boxing, too."

If Terry could fight, why *not* Nathaniel? If Terry could train, couldn't David Dalice?

Now, whenever David sensed Terry in their orbit, he found himself unable to resist the urge to put on a small show. In the ring, he shouted combinations louder than necessary, and, at round's end, would ignore the fight clock entirely, slamming his focus mitts into Nathaniel's incoming gloves harder and harder, as if to say, *Look here, Terry Tucker motherfucker, at what this student of mine can do*.

The student always executed, Nathaniel basking so fully in David's shadow it sometimes felt to David like he *was* his shadow.

On the last night of July, David asked Nathaniel if he wanted to feel what it would be like to spar. They ventured into the storage closet, moving damp cardboard boxes of gloves and unspooled hand wraps until they found the boy a worn body cup to step into, some beat-up headgear, chinstrap fraying, which David snapped into place. "And one more thing," he said, rummaging through his bag until he found an old mouth guard, which Nathaniel washed in a sad stream of warm water from the fountain, then shoved over his teeth.

The guard was way too big, Nathaniel's lips forced wide apart like a sock puppet. He gave David the thumbs-up, clenched his jaw tight to keep it in place, and followed the older man up the metal steps into the ring.

At Terry Tucker's Boxing Gym, David and Nathaniel worked until they were the only ones working, worked until they heard the rumble of the closing garage doors, Terry's sign to stragglers that it was time to go.

Could be . . . who knows . . . *what if*?

XII.

How close they came to avoiding it all.

On that last night of July, David still believed what he'd told Bob Alexander: the boy's evolving skin was of a piece with his evolving body. Thanks to David, Bob believed it, too.

If they'd kept on believing, it would've turned out differently for each of them in the summer of 1998. But though it seemed at this late date—Nathaniel's meetup with Sasha Semyonova only eight days away—as if no one in the boy's off-the-phone orbit knew what he was up to, that wasn't exactly true.

At the Shoal Creek Rehabilitation Center, a minor character in the life of Nathaniel Rothstein had begun to fixate on the weirdly tanning boy. Nathaniel had been a minor character in her life, too, at least until this nonsense with her hands. Since that cruel twist sidelined her, she'd had plenty of time to think, and she'd developed some theories about the once-pallid kid who read to her every afternoon.

Turned out, Dr. Gloria Abruzzi knew a little something about choosing to be one person, or another.

Memory Care

FOR THE FIRST SEVENTY-FOUR years, Gloria Abruzzi, daughter of Annunziata and Giampaolo, both of Pescara, daughter of Bensonhurst in the borough of Brooklyn, had been, it was widely agreed, a reluctant Italian. It wasn't that she tried to pass herself off as anything else. Gloria was olive-skinned and ample-bosomed, and in her prime sported a blast of salt-and-pepper hair that her eldest once likened to Madeline Kahn's two feet of frizz in *Young Frankenstein*. And though she'd married Marvin Robertson in 1950, and though at the Prewitt Psychiatric Center in Queens, where she served as chief psychologist from 1971 to 1980, she was known as Dr. Robertson, she was more than happy to unleash a little Abruzzian spavalderia when the situation required.

"I ain't talking to no tired ginzo whore!" an agitated resident roared at her one morning, in an incident emblematic of her tenure at Prewitt.

"Well, you're in luck, Mr. Matthews," said Gloria, "'cause I ain't tired."

No, she wasn't a closet Italian, the Gloria Abruzzi of 1922–96, but she never held that part of herself close, either. Not like her older sister, Sofia, who raised her own family in the same narrow 18th Avenue rowhouse they'd grown up in. Not like her younger brother, Anthony, who always said he'd die happy if he could spend three weeks in the old country, baking on the beach in Casalbordino, and, upon his retirement after fifteen years as FDNY battalion chief for the 42nd, Bay Ridge to Bensonhurt, promptly did.

No, Gloria didn't hold it close, *couldn't* hold it close, really, not if she wanted to Be Somebody, and oh did she, our Gloria, who even as a little girl was cursed with the knowledge that there was more to this life than the hundred yards between the pork store and Giantelli's Soda & Snack, that the Little Italy of Brooklyn was indeed little and this world was big big big.

Had she been a looker like her sister, Gloria might've aspired to the homemaking life that was expected of her. But from the start she knew she was plain, broad in the shoulders and heavy on bottom, near-sighted as soon as she was sighted: a pair of thick, round spectacles her binoculars to the world. Plain and peculiar, for Gloria hadn't gotten the memo that ungainly girls ought at least be quiet, too.

"I'm gonna be a doctor like Sigmund S. Freud," she announced to her family over dinner one Sunday soon after her eleventh birthday, having just completed a school report on the man. (Never one to take the easy way out: "It's 1933 and being an Italian in America isn't enough struggle for this one," carped her father in bed that evening. "No, our little Gloria needs to be an Austrian Jew!")

But the idea stuck—*Dr. Gloria Abruzzi*—for unlike her boy-obsessed sister, unlike the mawkish girls in her class, Gloria could see that the love story they all dreamed of starring in ended not with a kiss in the bedroom, as they imagined, but with a smack on the ass in the kitchen.

Yes, girl was looking to get out from the get-go, and get she did. In 1936, at fourteen, she applied and was accepted, on full scholarship, into the all-girls Danforth School on East 86th Street in Manhattan. She had to memorize her exact number of trolley stops without the aid of street signs: according to her mother, Gloria had enough going against her without wearing her glasses, of all things, outside the house.

An early lesson for this astigmatic ragazza: she wasn't the only one who had trouble seeing. Gloria should've been passable at piano, had previously shown an aptitude for math, but no one considered that the problem might be her eyes. Indeed, the word in the faculty lounge was that the Admissions Committee, whose members had long talked of funding a scholarship for the underserved, had chosen the wrong, er, guinea pig to start. Maybe she'd do better at her local school?

It was optics that nearly felled the girl, and optics that saved her. Gloria had no interest in her local school, and chucking the Italian was not the look to which the good liberals of Danforth aspired.

This, then, was how Gloria Abruzzi learned to be seen: by working her culo off. And if she refused to interrupt her studies for Sunday dinner, resulting in screaming matches between father and daughter that could be heard all the way down the avenue, and if her mother worried she'd end up a spinster and Sofia called her hoity-toity and little Anthony said it would be nice if she gave a you-know-what about her own flesh and blood, so be it. By the time, in 1949, she was applying for internships to complete her doctorate in psychology from Teachers College, Columbia University, Gloria Abruzzi, now sporting powder-blue "Leading Lady" browline frames, was plumb out of you-know-whats to give.

She met Marvin Robertson that same year through friends in her cohort. He was a mild-mannered resident in ophthalmology at Lenox Hill, a lank fellow whose wry blandness and moneyed nonchalance had rendered him an accidental feminist.

"For your information," Gloria told him, three dates in, "I'm not going to stop working on account of getting married."

"All right," said Marvin.

"And when we have children," said Gloria, "I'll continue to see patients."

"Seems prudent," said Marvin.

"And we don't overdo it with the religion," said Gloria. "The kids can just be *kids*."

"My mother will want them raised Episcopalian," said Marvin. He raised an eyebrow. "But she's getting up there, likes her gin . . ."

They married in 1950. For months prior, Gloria had tried and failed to secure an internship, the final requirement for her degree. No one, it seemed, was in a rush to return the calls of a lady-doctor-in-waiting called Abruzzi. As a Robertson, it proved less difficult. She began her internship in clinical psychology at Prewitt that September.

Within the year, she'd landed a permanent—though somehow always tenuous—position there. Within two, she'd had her first child, Richie, and, three years after that, a second, Benjamin. Finally, Dr. Gloria Robertson was living the life she'd dreamed.

Then again, Prewitt Psych wasn't exactly Mount Sinai. Understaffed, underpaid. Gloria's ascent to chief psychologist, in 1971 at the age of forty-nine, was made possible only due to the indiscretions of the previous chief and the chief before that, both of whom knocked up their secretaries. ("We assume in addition to discretion surrounding your predecessors' departures, we will not find in you a repeat offender," the unctuous board president had told her as she signed the necessary paperwork. "All lips are sealed," said Gloria.)

No, not Mount Sinai, but what a rush it was! To figure out what was going on in those unusual minds. To connect. "They all think I'm crazy," Bertha Anderson, a four-time returning champion who'd witnessed Gloria in her acid-tongued prime, once told her. "But Doc, I see behind those big ol' glasses"—by then oversized tortoiseshell Turas—"and I *know* I'm not as crazy as you are."

"Honey, you got my number," said Gloria. The women raised their hands above their heads and locked fingers. "How you been?" said Gloria.

"How *you* been?" said Bertha.

She saw her people, *saw* them, and they, in turn, saw her.

And if, when slapping together dinner after ten and a half hours in the psych ward, she forsook her mother's maccheroni alla chitarra for Hamburger Helper, and if, on Christmas Eve, she skipped midnight Mass and instead sat by the fire with some eggnog and called it a day, and if, when she and Marvin took the boys on vacation it was not to the Jersey Shore but to Cozumel aboard a *Royal Princess* cruise, it was not, she told herself, because she was hiding her heritage, but because with a life as full as Gloria's, choices had to be made.

Did she miss the traditional stuff? She didn't think so. At their house in verdant Riverdale, nods to Gloria's old life were buried like fossils beneath the Formica: Stella D'oro cookies dormant in the pantry, a dusty bottle of amaretto deep inside the bar. They hauled the kids to Gloria's childhood home on 18th Avenue for Labor Day and Thanksgiving, their boys both frightened and exhilarated by their scrappier, tawnier cousins, the adult men all too happy to give Marvin shit.

Gloria loved the rough-and-tumble ("So what Marv doesn't change his own oil? And I suppose when you need a cataract removed, you'll be doing it yourself?"), could give as well as she got. Still, she found her siblings' provincialism cloying, felt her hackles go up whenever that ear-piercing mamma from the Prince spaghetti commercials appeared on her sister's TV, as if every Italian woman were fated to spend her life screaming out the window for her kid to quit playing stickball and come inside for carbonara, which Sofia, most annoyingly, did in fact do.

"You should come more often," Sofia would always say at night's end.

"We will, we will," Gloria would respond, knowing they never would.

Her kids sensed it, too, the distance between their cousins' lives and their own, they knew, much greater than a handful of miles down the FDR. Like all young people, they were already miniature versions of their adult selves: Richie was built like Gloria, stout and bulldoggish, a suburban kid who seemed destined to wear his work collar off-white. Benjamin had inherited their father's long features, his dry wit.

"Am *I* Italian?" he asked at the age of eleven, as he completed a family tree for a school project.

"You're Benjamin Robertson," said Gloria, and, when that failed to appease him, "You're whoever the hell you want to be."

Benjamin wanted to be in advertising, which was how, by '79, he'd ended up in Austin, skinny and mustached, in the Graduate School of Business at UT. Richie left New York a year later, for Chicago, where he landed a job managing the Lou Malnati's in Elk Grove.

1980: that was the year Gloria was forced out at Prewitt, though she knew she had plenty of good work left in her. The board of directors was going in a "different direction." She was fifty-eight years old.

"If you're a pain-in-the-ass old man in charge, you're a *maverick*," Gloria told Marvin over the phone after hearing the news, one clip-on earring cupped in her shaking hand. "But if you're in charge as a pain-in-the-ass old lady . . ."

"What's the word for that?" asked Marvin.

"Exactly."

Unwilling to retire, Gloria began to see patients in a locale far less thrilling than Prewitt: her basement office. Now it was the bored women of Riverdale she counseled, that exhausting breed available in seemingly inexhaustible supply, the chance to lie upon the couch of, as one excitable homemaker put it, "a shrink for the criminally insane" the very antidote to the ennui that led them to her in the first place.

As these women unloaded, about opportunities missed and lives unlived, Gloria got the distinct sense she was freeing them of their languor by absorbing it as her own. While her clients "got out there," as Gloria advised, becoming aerobics instructors or hawking their middling arts-and-crafts projects to cutesy boutiques in White Plains, she remained in place, the big world she'd always hungered for starting, for the first time, to close in.

It was only a preview of things to come. One day in winter of 1993, when Gloria was seventy-one, she forgot to show up for a root canal, despite a reminder call not eighteen hours prior. On an icy Wednesday a year later, she face-planted on the pavement outside the Riverdale Cinema on her way, with Marvin, into a matinee screening of *The Pelican Brief*. Her gold-frame metal bifocals snapped right in two.

The decline of Gloria Robertson was immediate and never-ending, as abrupt as it was ghoulishly gradual. The fall was from a transient ischemic attack, her physician explained, a ministroke, and probably not her first, either. Gloria's risk of developing dementia was high, but the process could be slow-moving. She might lose her mind for years and years, all the while knowing she was losing it.

Gloria was able to maintain a semblance of normalcy thanks to Marvin, then retired. With his encouragement, she kept working: a few longtime clients, two afternoons a week. Marvin insisted Gloria stay active, accompanying her on walks in the early evenings. Never a cook, he procured from Key Food watermelons carved into shark heads, their mouths stuffed with fruit salad, to make sure she was getting her nutrients.

For a time, they plodded on, until one morning in late 1995, when Gloria woke to find Marvin dead beside her. She combed his hair and straightened the collar on his pajama top before calling an ambulance, held it together until that night, when, sitting with a glass of port on the couch in the living room, she began to cry, for her husband and for herself, because she'd fought so hard to become Dr. Gloria Robertson, and that person, she knew, had died right along with him.

Richie and his family flew in from Chicago, where he now owned three Quiznos locations; Benjamin came from Austin with his wife and two kids. Gloria put on her game face, which now included, as a replacement for her taped-up bifocals, king-size honey-gold plastic frames, the lenses so thick they made her look Bambi-eyed.

And after the funeral, after the masses descended on the house for the ritualized emptying of the widow's bar and the wolfing of the miniature delicatessen sandwiches, tongues swallowing catered tongue, heads bowed and cheeks bulging with deviled eggs and lemon bars lest anyone have to figure out what to say to one another, after the hoi polloi bundled into their coats and the grandkids were tucked in and the daughters-in-law had retired to their husbands' boyhood beds, Gloria sat with her two sons at the same kitchen table they'd eaten at as children, for the conversation she knew was coming.

"The thing is, Ma . . ." started Richie, rubbing over his heart. He'd grown heavy in middle age, and the emotional stuff always gave him reflux. He looked to his brother.

"Look, Mom, some night the phone's gonna ring," said Benjamin, taking his mother's hand, "and something's happened, and we're both gonna be thousands of miles away."

"It's terrible," said Gloria solemnly. "Awful. But I have a solution."

"You do?" said the Brothers Robertson.

She leaned in close to her children. "*Don't answer the phone*."

A nursing home was out of the question, Gloria declared. She'd seen enough dementia patients to know how it would end for her, but she wasn't there yet; after getting pushed out of one locked facility prematurely, she wasn't about to get pushed into another before she was ready.

"What about an apartment of your own?" ventured Richie. "Maybe somewhere near one of us?" tried Benjamin. The boys had come with brochures. "They call it *semi-independent living*," said Richie, pointing to a glossy photograph of a not-especially-elderly woman on a walking path, mid-stride.

Semi-independent, Gloria knew, until she broke a hip or lost her mind, for all of these "assisted living" centers were part of larger facilities with no exit signs. A resident "upgrade" in that topsy-turvy world meant not nicer accommodations but more oversight, Gloria's penultimate resting spot destined to be a fusty room in what one of the catalogues labeled its "memory care village": a whole little community of the demented.

"*Make every day a fresh start*," Gloria read aloud. "Oh, that's *good*," she said, amused by the grim comedy of the slogan. "That is *gooooood*." She pushed away the stack of materials. "This isn't going to end well, is it?"

In the spring of 1996, forty-five years after receiving her doctorate, twenty-five years after becoming chief psychologist at Prewitt Psychiatric Center, four months after the death of her husband, Gloria Robertson, seventy-four, moved into a one-bedroom apartment in the Assisted Living wing of the Shoal Creek Rehabilitation Center in Austin, Texas, first floor, well aware that as her situation deteriorated they'd move her up a floor to Continuing Care, up a floor to the locked Special Care unit, up and up, until she was high enough that the only direction for her to go was down down down.

Gloria had spent a lifetime navigating institutions, and she arrived at this new one with the wry knowing of a person fluent in their maddening language. Despite the marketing team's endless crowing about Shoal Creek's "amenities," Gloria understood she was entering a minimum-security prison. Her children's repeated reminders that she wasn't "stuck there" may have been true in the literal sense—Benjamin *was* only ten minutes away, she *could* always call a taxi—but they weren't true in spirit, since Gloria had nowhere to go and no one to see and would die in this place, on one floor or another.

These were the sort of ugly truths the institutional tongue always obscured, and Gloria wanted the varied professionals who trod Shoal Creek's long halls to know she saw through the linguistic mist, hopeful they might recognize a fellow traveler in her magnified eyes.

It was not to be. What $225 a day in "tuition" bought Dr. Gloria Robertson was what it bought all the residents, regardless of professional history: a few choice pieces of furniture from the old house giving this new space the vague look of home but none of its feel, a singsong greeting from her captors as they passed. "Good morning, Mrs. R!" Always in the brisk walk-and-talk style she had seen countless higher-ups employ at Prewitt: big smile, then head down and a few murmured words to themselves, a way of ensuring no further conversation.

Who the hell is Mrs. *R?* she wanted to scream.

And then there were the residents. What a peculiar breed, those Texans, so insular and proud. "Nothing in there you can't get in the *Statesman*," clucked a speed-walking old biddy, wind pants whooshing past, as Gloria read the *Times* from the armchair outside her apartment. One neighbor, Hank Foster, brought over a box of Entenmann's to "welcome her to the neighborhood," but had to excuse himself ten minutes in so as not to miss the start of Rush Limbaugh ("Major Dittohead here!" he proclaimed, cookie crumbs flying). Another, Helen Bowers, wouldn't shut up about her "land" in West Texas. "If I have to hear one more time about all the fun this lady's having on her *fourteen acres . . .*" griped Gloria on her nightly call with Richie. "That hump of hers gets any higher she's gonna be yelling 'Sanctuary!' from a bell tower. What, she's roping cattle out there?"

Gloria had always been proud of her ability to make room for herself in unlikely spaces. Now, at Shoal Creek, she wondered if she'd finally found her social Kryptonite.

How could she ever make a home in *Texas*?

And this is where the story of Dr. Gloria Robertson takes an unexpected turn, for when, a few weeks after arriving in that infernal state, she met her son Benjamin at CHEW, the Assisted Living wing's "restaurant-style" dining room, she was surprised to find that after she'd asked about Beth and the kids, after she'd breathed some of that customary fire ("Is it called CHEW as a reminder?"), Gloria Robertson let loose with an observation she'd resolved not to observe aloud, for she didn't quite know *why* she'd been feeling this way, and feeling something without knowing why one felt it, while trying to prove one's suitability for *semi-independent* living, seemed a good way to get kicked upstairs:

"The problem with this place . . ." said Gloria, trying to sound casual as she picked at her salad. "The problem with this place is it's not all that welcoming to *our kind*."

Benjamin took a nervous gulp of iced tea. "Our kind?" he said, aware that a vintage Gloria unloading was in the works.

Gloria checked behind her to make sure no one was listening in. "Look around, sonny boy," she whispered. "Not exactly teeming with Riccis, is it? You think these people are named Esposito? Romano? *Bianchi?*"

Benjamin Robertson looked at the table next to theirs, where two ladies were finishing off lunch, then to the table behind, where three more were just sitting down. Five puffy-haired women, puffs high but thin. Who could say if they were Everetts or Espositos? Brookses or Bianchis? They looked just like his mother. They looked, well, old.

"Where are you going with this, Mom?" Benjamin asked wearily.

For seventy-four years, Gloria Robertson had forced her way into the world on the brute strength of her intellect. But now, at this place, among the Williamses and Andersons and Joneses of Shoal Creek Rehabilitation, she felt strangely unmoored. Even at that still-early stage in her unspooling she couldn't parse it, but an earlier incarnation of herself would've explained it to herself this way: that stripped of her profession, stripped of her husband, stripped ever so slowly of her mind, Gloria Robertson needed something to anchor herself to this mortal plane, something to remind the people of Shoal Creek, to remind Gloria, of who *she* was. And if she couldn't find that anchor, couldn't tie its chains tight around her waist and listen to the scrape of the thing as it dragged behind her, she was sure whatever was left of her, the *actual* her, would just up and float away.

"I'd like to go back to Abruzzi," she told Benjamin. "*Dr. Gloria Abruzzi.*" She knew it sounded crazy, but as soon as the words were out, she knew they were the right ones.

Thus began, seventy-four years after Giampaolo and Annunziata Abruzzi of Pescara welcomed a baby girl to an 18th Avenue rowhouse in Bensonhurst, in Brooklyn, the re-Italianification of Gloria Robertson.

Gloria threw herself into the process. For years, every Monday night, Gloria had phoned her sister, now seventy-seven and at a nursing facility in Dyker Heights, but whereas before these conversations were pleasant but brief, now she took to grilling Sofia about their mother's old recipes, recording them in a composition notebook she'd bought for this purpose.

In public, she brandished her new (old) identity with the all-in fervor common to the newly out. Feeling hemmed in by the distinctly not-ethnic decorations festooned on the doors of her neighbors—folksy *Welcome Home* signs and patriotic garlands—Gloria ordered, from a shop in Toms River that Sofia recommended, an "Italian flag wreath" of green, white, and red silk peonies.

To the dismay of her children, who'd taken over her bills when she moved, the wreath arrived alongside the shop's 150-page catalogue. By Memorial Day, Gloria had acquired a new doormat, *Benvenuti!* splashed across the coir, and a three-foot-tall plastic Santa, which she'd planned to keep in the coat closet until Christmas but loved so much she put right outside her door. For reasons neither of Gloria's kids could discern, St. Nick had apparently taken up a side gig as a waiter and wore a green, white, and red apron, offering a tray of plastic delicacies—spaghetti and meatballs, tiramisu—to all who passed.

And passing was all Gloria wanted her neighbors to do. Dr. Robertson had never had many close friends and saw no reason Dr. Abruzzi needed them, either. "Your father was my friend," she'd tell her boys. But they were on her about it, desperate, she thought, for evidence that they hadn't kenneled their own mother like a dog.

"It's not like there's a shortage of social events," Richie told her one evening, an understatement given the administration's fanatical devotion to holidays. Major, minor, made-up: no anniversary was too obscure to be commemorated at Shoal Creek, allegedly national celebrations of cookie appreciation and fibromyalgia awareness on the calendar same as Valentine's and Easter. It was a way to give cohesion to the residents' days (the company line), or at least, thought Gloria, to keep the bulletin boards fresh.

"These people, they're not like me," Gloria griped to Richie. "They're very . . . you know . . . *white*." A few conversations like this and Richie had stopped pushing back with what he thought was obvious. "Just be yourself," he suggested. "You've never had a problem with that."

Indeed. When, at an ice cream social in honor of National Hot Fudge Sundae Day, a well-meaning tablemate asked where she was from, Gloria declared her "people" from "Pescara."

"And that is— " said the woman, mid-polite-spoonful.

"North of Sambuceto," said Gloria, irritated. Then: "Abruzzo region." Finally—what the hell was wrong these people?—"*Italy*."

Through the summer of 1996, Gloria added to her catalogue-inspired menagerie of tchotchkes, the outside embellishments prompting complaints from her neighbors, a fussy collection of former gated-community doyennes and HOA scolds. Richie decreased her credit limit in a mostly unsuccessful bid to rein her in from afar. "You may be an Abruzzi, Ma," he told her, "but you spend like a friggin' Robertson." Her eyesight was iffier than ever, and she'd begun wearing tinted lenses in her honey-gold frames.

Most worrisome, Gloria's short-term memory was now declining in earnest. "You know what's nonsense?" she told Benjamin over lunch at CHEW. "*Memory like a sieve*."

It was an inapt metaphor, Gloria explained, since a sieve held on to what was solid and drained away the excess, whereas Gloria could remember with precision the most irrelevant details of other people's lives—a favorite television program of the gift shop cashier's, something funny a server had said weeks before—without being able to recall if she'd spoken to them earlier in the day.

This was Gloria at her best, when she could turn her clinical skills on herself, her moments of lucidity so dazzling they made Gloria at her worst even more confounding. She became angry so easily now, raging at what other people forgot rather than acknowledging what she couldn't remember. "I don't answer to that!" she'd snap at staffers or other residents who hadn't retained, or ever known about, her departure from Robertson-dom.

Gloria battled bouts of paranoia, convinced that the staff was conspiring to snatch away her apartment on the first floor. *Anti-Italianism* was invoked often, an ironic twist as it was her hot-tempered father who'd acted, well into *his* seventies, as if Sacco and Vanzetti had been executed just the day before, and Gloria who was forever explaining to him that times had changed. Had his fear and fury been in her all along?

At least the far past she remembered. Whenever someone referred to a more recent incident she couldn't recall, Gloria refused to admit it, sure her *semi-independence* was on the line. She'd respond instead with a tight-lipped smile.

But Gloria's semi-independence *was* on the line, her fear of losing it only expediting the process. The final straw came when she set the smoke alarm off in her kitchen during a botched attempt at pizza pugliese. Within the day, Shoal Creek's executive director called for a meeting with the Robertson sons—Richie on the phone, Benjamin in person—to gauge whether Assisted Living was still the "appropriate" floor for Gloria, who wasn't invited.

The executive director, Zelda Phelps-Heifetz, was a malignantly cheerful fifty-something whose spiky hair and jutting chin suggested a caricature come to life. Her insistence on referring to Gloria as Mom ("When Mom is happy, kids are happy, *we're* happy") was but one of many qualities that had bred in all Robertsons and Abruzzis a deep mistrust of the woman since move-in day. The curled sideburns. The penchant for long scarves. Her transparent obsession with avoiding litigation.

"Assisted Living is a *community*," she said, once Richie had beeped in. "And it's *essential* that all of our residents feel *part* of that *community*." Zelda was well-versed in the euphemistic language of "extended care" common to all the Grim Reaper's support staff, but her message was clear: no one was paying for a "luxury apartment" and an air of independence to live next door to an extra from *Titicut Follies*. Loopy Town was upstairs. Gloria was free to go by Abruzzi, Robertson, or Thomas Jefferson if she wanted, but temper tantrums and fire scares meant one thing: *time to ascend*. "Let's get Mom away from kitchens and revolving doors." Continuing Care, on the second floor, was the place for Gloria.

The Robertson brothers had agreed coming in that they were willing to go into light battle to keep their mother where she was, the prospect of moving into a gussied-up hospital room enough, they were sure, to kill her.

"Listen," said Richie, "these issues she's having, aren't they par for the course?"

"Absolutely," said Zelda. "As is recognizing when a situation requires an adjustment."

"She burned some pizza," said Benjamin.

"It's more than the pizza, Mr. Robertson."

"But isn't it your job— " started Richie.

"To *assess* what is best for our residents."

"There's a quality-of-life issue— " said Benjamin.

"The quality of life in Continuing Care is just as— "

"*We're paying you two hundred and twenty-five dollars a day*!" roared Richie suddenly, his voice topping out the normally clear long-distance connection. It was the sort of honest eruption one didn't like to hear from other adults. Zelda and Benjamin looked to their laps. "Sorry," said Richie. "I, uh . . . I didn't mean to be that loud."

Zelda sighed, her veneer of customer servitude dissolving into the normal, tired look of a lady who'd had this conversation many times before. "I get it, guys, I do. This is not fun." She opened her desk drawer. "Can we compromise?" If the Robertsons would sign a waiver acknowledging that she had recommended otherwise, Zelda was willing to let Mom stay put for six weeks, after which they'd re-assess.

"By the way," she said, as Benjamin initialed each paragraph, "has your mother met our Director of Hospitality yet? He runs the activities for our residents, has a real way with . . ."

"Problem parents?" said Benjamin, still initialing.

Zelda Phelps-Heifetz said she'd send him by.

This was how it happened that on a bright morning in September 1996, Gloria Abruzzi answered the doorbell at Apartment 103 in the Assisted Living wing of the Shoal Creek Rehabilitation Center to find David Dalice, Director of Hospitality, a bouquet of zinnias in his outstretched hand.

Gloria had seen him around, of course, a bulky Black man in scrubs oft engaged in playful banter with the more outgoing residents. From afar he'd seemed like every other saccharine soul who worked at Shoal Creek. Worse, since her neighbors seemed to get a genuine kick out of him. "What can I do for you?" Gloria asked, standing in the doorway.

"I have wanted to meet the arsonist of Shoal Creek Rehabilitation for some time."

"A wiseass," said Gloria. "Unexpected."

Coffee was brewed. A box of store-bought biscotti opened. And as they chatted at the kitchen counter, Gloria sensed she'd finally found her fellow traveler.

"I am told you are a doctor for the highly disturbed," said David.

"I'm sorry," said Gloria, "but I do require a referral."

"Madam, citizens the state over can vouch for my insanity."

Gloria *ooo*-ed in approval. "Say, do I detect a slight accent?"

David told her he'd come to the Texas capital from the Haitian one as a young man. "Over twenty-five years ago now."

Gloria leaned in. "It's such a relief to meet someone else who isn't *from here*."

Later, as she washed the dishes after he'd gone, Gloria felt a bit of her old self returning.

Madam, he'd called her, *Yes, half-and-half, ah, thank you, madam, merci beaucoup*, and though she would've found this tic irritating in others, she felt in his delivery a flicker of something else, a wit, a bite, subversion masked as sycophancy.

Back at Prewitt, Gloria had learned that she didn't just have to be better than her colleagues but bigger, too, her outsized brassiness protection against men who'd otherwise think her weak. She sensed in David something similar, his fulsomeness the armor he needed to survive in this lily-white land.

They arranged a standing coffee date for Fridays at her place, where the healthy and addled parts of Gloria's brain melded to produce questions inappropriate and true. She wanted to know what it was like to be Black at Shoal Creek, Black in the world. "*What's it like for you* to be married to a white woman?" "*How is it* being the only Haitian here?"

Gloria's sense that David's experience was her experience—"Italy and Haiti, we know a little something about being on the outside"—would've rankled some. But when David started at Shoal Creek there were still residents whose great-grandfathers had fought for the Confederacy. He'd take clumsy connection over that.

His answers straddled the border between jokey and real, candor always tempered with maudlin optimism, Gloria's most dangerous questions answered with questions of his own. There were always going to be naysayers when it came to interracial marriage. "But since 1971? Oh! We've come a long way, haven't we? It's the nineties, madam!" Being the only one could be difficult, of course, but everyone has difficulties, don't they? "One just keeps going. Like you."

With David's support, Gloria led a one-hour Italian cooking class for a dozen fellow residents (at his suggestion they made bruschetta: "Your track record with heat leaves something to be desired"). He helped her enroll in an Italian for Beginners course at the nearby YMCA.

By then, the six-week waiver had been extended to twelve weeks, then eighteen. Now that Gloria had a person to vent to, her public rages subsided. When she complained that Shoal Creek was unwelcoming to her "kind," David didn't urge her to get over it as her children did. The truth, David knew, was that Gloria's neighbors were, like their hall decorations, conspicuously Anglo.

It had always been this way. The aging abuelos of the city's sizable Mexican community largely lived with or near their own adult children, while members of Austin's small-but-mighty Jewry were more likely to send their bubbes to Meadowbridge (aka the Hebrew Hilton), the kosher dining plan so good that more than one geriatric goy had sacrificed shellfish for the privilege. To the Wonder Bread eaters at the Shoal Creek of the mid-nineties—many of whom were entering this world just as Sacco and Vanzetti *were* being frog-marched out of it—an Italian *was* a little exotic. "But there is nothing to worry about," David assured her. "A little exotic goes over well in this place. And you're the right kind of exotic, too."

She greeted this statement with her tight-lipped smile, which David knew signaled she didn't understand. What he meant, but didn't say, was that by the time today's residents were coming of age, violent displays of Italophobia had gone the way of the icebox. The current Creekers had been in their primes at the height of the civil rights era; some were on the wrong side of the "race issue," even more on no side: a side itself. A proud Italian offered them some satisfying spice without the guilt or shame they might've felt had Gloria been any darker.

A few days after the cooking class, Helen Bowers, she of the fourteen acres, rang Gloria to see if she'd join her for lunch at the Olive Garden. They cabbed over together. "I know it's not your kind of Italian, *real* Italian," said Helen, "but honestly? That lasagna?" A stage whisper: "*Heaven*."

Later, when Richie called to see how it had gone, Gloria's review was, by her standards, a rave. "Would I die for this woman? I would not. Would I do lunch again? I'd consider. Did you know the salad is unlimited?"

A year passed.

When she'd first arrived at Shoal Creek Rehab, it had felt to Gloria as if she were nearing the end of the final chapter, a few pages left of semi-independent life. Turned out, it was only the end of Gloria Robertson.

The occasional lunch with a neighbor, pleasant greetings in the hall. Gloria's Italianness made her legible to the people of Shoal Creek, kept her legible to herself. Four million from her parents' generation had passed through Ellis Island a century before, from Abruzzo and Apulia, Basilicata and Sicily. They made this hostile country their home, found a way, as Gloria had done in her old life, to make it work.

Amidst all the forgetting, Gloria's rebirth made her remember: there was strength in being on the outside. Outsiders were survivors. Outsiders knew how to adapt. Take a stumble? Find a walker. Lose your tinted glasses? Start wearing them with neon green Chums (a gift from the grandkids). While neighbors ascended, she remained. Like any good second-generation Italian American, Gloria stayed long enough so that eventually others became the unwelcome newcomers.

The connections she forged with her fellow residents were not deep. Gloria made no dear friends, found no second Marvin. It was enough. She wouldn't die for these people, didn't need to. They seemed to have that covered.

And when she lost the thread or lost her temper or, in Shoal Creek–ese, "got herself a little turned around," with David in her corner she was somehow always able to keep turning, turning until she found herself going again in the proper direction.

She knew she'd never have made it without him.

David felt something, too, a kinship that transcended friend-for-hire. His own mother had died of pancreatic cancer at a hospice place near her home in Miami a half-decade before, and it was a comfort to have someone of her generation asking after him. Gloria Abruzzi knew more of his Shoal Creek story than anyone else in the building. She was the closest to family any of the residents had ever become.

It was for this reason, in the fall of 1997, that David confided to Gloria that he had been thinking about going back to school, becoming a therapist himself. In the decades since he'd dropped out, David had steadily climbed the ranks at Shoal Creek, becoming, in his current role, as much a counselor to the residents as the social workers on the payroll were. A PhD seemed a little ambitious for a forty-seven-year-old still many credits shy of a college diploma, but a master's in social work? It felt . . . doable. Possible.

"Do you think it's a silly idea?" he asked, surprised that, as he said it, his face went hot. He was embarrassed, he realized, at how much he wanted her to tell him that it wasn't silly at all.

"I can't think of anyone better," said Gloria. "I mean that truly." She vowed to write him a letter of recommendation, help him study for his licensing exam when the time came. But the next Friday, when he told her their talk had inspired him to take the first step forward—he'd signed up for spring classes at Austin Community College—he could see from her tight smile that she had no idea to what he was referring. David never mentioned it again.

The rash came without warning in July 1998, Gloria's hands fine one morning and the next covered in lesions, red and thick and scaly.

She'd been diagnosed with plaque psoriasis in her fifties and had suffered the occasional mild flare-up. The itch and inflammation were a nuisance, the treatment never more than a prescription cream. This was a different beast. It was a strange part of getting old: how midlife aggravations could metastasize into humiliations with age.

Till her skin betrayed her, Gloria hadn't given much thought to the poor schmo who'd been reading to her in the afternoons that summer. She understood he was a gift, of sorts, a wink, from David, even if he was an undeniable putz, even if she got the sense he viewed her as a nonperson, which was certainly how she viewed him. Sometimes, Gloria needed a little reminder why he was even there.

But then the boy had gone and asked about her pills. The kid's name, the books he'd read her: by the time of Gloria's outbreak, all those details had leaked right through the sieve. What remained, like the gift shop clerk's favorite television show and the server's goofy joke, was that peculiar question—*Is it true these make you darker*?—and the reality that every time the kid returned, he was, in fact, more dark.

In the days ahead, Gloria Abruzzi began to consider the *why* behind the ever-toasting child. Having never paid attention to a word he was reading before, Gloria now pretended to, inspecting him for shifts in color, the smell of tanning lotion in the air. She asked what she thought were leading questions—"Sunny out today?" or "I used to love to sit by the swimming pool. Do you?"—to which he responded with his usual *Kind of*s and *Not really*s. What was his motivation? She couldn't say.

Gloria's treatment called for her to shine a UV lamp on her hands four times a week and, two hours before each session, to take a capsule of methoxsalen with a glass of milk. Even with her kids keeping track as best they could, it was hard to remember when to do what. She didn't feel comfortable leaving the apartment in her state, took meals at home. Her hands were always so itchy.

A week went by, a week and a half. July became August. On good days, she chatted on the phone, had Benjamin and the grandkids over for a visit. On bad ones, she sat on her sofa in the dark and worried about what would happen if she messed up on her treatment; she knew if she didn't heal on the first floor, they'd move her to the second. When it all became too much, Gloria thought about the boy. Why fixate on her skin when she could fixate on his?

Her ideas were inchoate. Strange images consumed her. There he was, in a colorful woven cape, leading sheep across the Andes. There he was, almost busting out of an intricately embroidered skin-tight suit, the guitarrón player in a mariachi band. Once, she saw the boy hunched over a breakfast table in striped boxer shorts and a ribbed undershirt, yelling at the newspaper. *Her father*. "What is he *up to*?"

She hadn't meant to say it aloud. This was on Wednesday, August 5. It had been a bad one, so far, at least until David arrived to check in, a near-daily occurrence since she'd taken ill.

It was the day before David's forty-eighth birthday, and his spirits were high. He went to the kitchen to make coffee, Gloria's mind drifted and . . .

"What is who up to?" said David, setting a cup and saucer on the coffee table before her.

"Oh, no one, no one," said Gloria. But now the damage was done. And David seemed curious. Would it be so bad if she did a little fishing? "It's just, he used to be so *white*. Your friend."

"My friend?" said David.

"The reader," said Gloria.

"Ah, that one." David took a seat in the armchair. "Maybe Nathaniel just wants to look a little less pasty."

"Italians and Haitians: we're blessed with good skin, aren't we?" said Gloria.

"So, Dr. Abruzzi," said David, changing the subject. He could indulge the Italian-Haitian business only in small doses. "How are we feeling today?"

"You know, *maybe* . . ." said Gloria. She couldn't stop herself. "Maybe that's why he wanted to know about my pills."

"Your pills? For your hands?"

"Oh, haven't you heard?" said Gloria wryly. "*They make you darker*."

David didn't follow. "They make *who* darker?"

"Whoever takes them," said Gloria, parroting Nathaniel.

Not two weeks before, Bob Alexander had also mentioned Nathaniel's darkening skin to David. He hadn't thought much of it at the time. But now Gloria, too? "Tell me this, madam," said David. "Why do you think my friend would be interested in your pills?"

Until then, it hadn't made sense to the old woman, either. With David there, it clicked. She'd been in this place as her old-new self and as her new-old one, too. Which did she prefer?

Dr. Gloria Abruzzi gave him a look: *Isn't it obvious?* Then, in a knowing whisper: "I think he wants to look a little more like us."

Like Us

WHAT IN THE WORLD? thought David as he continued his rounds.

Even Dr. Abruzzi's kookier claims—her accusations of anti-Italianism, for one—had always been rooted in something, bits of actual fruit floating in the gooey marmalade of her mind. Had Nathaniel *actually* pestered her about those pills? Could they possibly do what she thought they did?

David assured himself it was nonsense, went on with his day. That evening, however, while Ramona took a bath, he found himself opening the French doors to his wife's paper-strewn office, putting on a pair of her cheaters, and, using only the computer monitor for light, dialing up AOL. He hunted and pecked at the keyboard: *psoriasis medication*.

Had David spent six minutes browsing instead of seven, that would've been the end of it. But he was new to surfing the web, new to the sensation of clicking onward for no other reason than that he could, past Pfizer and Blue Cross and Healthscape.com, from the third page of search results to the fourth, which was what led him to the same John Howard Griffin fan site that Nathaniel had found a month before, that same squint-to-read-it story in bright yellow Comic Sans about a white man who took some pills—Gloria's pills—and turned himself Black.

Can you imagine, thought David, a white boy voluntarily Blackening, in *this* place? Oh yes, this must be Nathaniel's plan! Surely, he, too, wanted to experience what it was like to see white women clutch their purses tighter whenever they passed him by, clutch tighter and then relax, their faces flush from the shame of tightening in the first place. Did the boy feel he was not being pulled over with enough frequency?

Yet that night, as he tried to fall asleep, David couldn't help but consider his pupil's evolution in the two months since they'd first met. Nathaniel's mustache had started to fill in, parted in the center, like David's. Just the day before, they'd ordered matching brisket plates and Chef Alejandra had responded, "Like father, like son." David had previous underlings who'd adopted his scent, picked up a couple of his favored phrases. He'd known for weeks that this was something deeper. Could it be deeper than he'd imagined?

Was there a chance Nathaniel was trying to . . . become David? Or if not him then . . . *Black*?

Nathaniel's time in Austin was fading fast. In the days since they'd donned protective gear and stepped into the ring, David had mapped a training plan for Nathaniel to follow back home. Core and cardio and diet were the fulcra. Sit-ups and jump rope, proteins and planks.

David didn't write any of it down. Nor had he broached with Nathaniel the logistical questions they'd need to consider for the boy to come back to Austin. Could he stay with Bob again? Would he want to return to Shoal Creek? David didn't know for certain that Nathaniel was committed to returning at all.

He'd resisted sharing his ideas for next summer when they were still having fun in this one. The rush came from the plotting. No easier way to wreck a good plan than by saying it aloud.

In bed that night, David told himself that the prospect of Nathaniel trying to become him was weird and ridiculous, a silly distraction from the tasks at hand. But David told himself a lot of things. The next day he'd be forty-eight, and he sometimes still lived his life as if it weren't his life, as if real life were David the Lawyer, David the Therapist, hell, David the Boxer, and this was just rehearsal.

Yes, weird and ridiculous was how David pretended to feel because how he actually felt—disconcerted, a little bit flattered?—was too weird and ridiculous to admit.

He did think he ought to remind Nathaniel that he shouldn't be asking residents about their meds, no matter the reason, and he resolved to do so the next day, Thursday. He might've, too, except that in the bright light of morning, even that felt embarrassing to follow up on.

Anyway, it was his birthday, which meant coffee with Ramona and a shower of coos and crafts from the still responsive of Shoal Creek. In Apartment 103, Dr. Abruzzi had arranged for her son to drop off a box from Reale's to celebrate. "Ten a.m. and cannoli this fresh?" she told David between bites. "It's gonna be a good year for you." If she was still thinking about the vial of pills on the coffee table between them, she didn't let on.

By the time David arrived at the gym, he'd almost forgotten about Dr. Abruzzi's wild musings entirely. And that was even before, as he and Nathaniel wrapped their hands, the boy announced he'd gotten David something for his birthday.

"Not a present, exactly, but, well, I'll just give it to you." From his gym bag, Nathaniel presented David with a folded sheet of paper.

It was a printout of the short article that Nathaniel had found via Ask Jeeves the month before. *Newcomer Rasta Dalice gives hometown hero Bandit Bengochea a run for his money!*

"You found *this* on your computer?" said David.

David hadn't seen the article since it had been lost in the move those many years before, disappeared with his Haitian passport and the letter from his mom. But he didn't need to read those twelve lines from the Alvarado *Graphic* to remember the time in his brief fight career when he got close to being more than one of Lem Pugh's tomato cans, more than a guy who would lose so others could win.

"What you got there, old man?" called Felix Barrowman from the heavy bags. Soon a small crowd gathered around boy and boss, first

Terry and Felix and then a few of the other fighters, too. David couldn't help but be amazed: to learn Nathaniel had spent time searching him, to know that somewhere on that amorphous thing called the World Wide Web, which David had always sensed was for and about other, bigger lives, somewhere on there he existed, too.

"You remember our ring walk?" David asked Terry. Whenever RastaMasta entered an arena, his corner did a little jig. "We'd go two steps forward, take one hop back, and *clap*!"—David clapped—"all the way down the aisle!"

"I have a vague memory," said Terry, who'd served as permanent caboose in this train of merry men. He didn't seem overly amused.

"*That* was your ring walk?" said Felix. "How many hours it take you to get to the ring?"

"Are you kidding?" said David. "This was a crowd-pleaser, man! We didn't need all your loud music. We had the moves!"

This made Felix laugh. "Hey, Tuck," he said to Terry, "if this Poland thing works out"—there was talk of a fight in Warsaw—"you think this is how I should come out?" Off Felix went, snaking around the heavy bags: two steps forward, one hop back, *clap!*

"That's right. And *clap*!" called David, delighted.

Later, as David and Nathaniel sat on the apron of the canvas, sucking at their water bottles between rounds, Terry called them into his office, told them to bring the article printout.

Terry nodded toward the collage of clippings that covered the wall behind his desk, stories about Golden Gloves winners and Friday Night Fights champs and Felix Barrowman, too. "Forty-eight, huh?" said Terry, folding away the blank part of the paper and thumbtacking the remains over someone else's glory. "We've come a ways."

And if, as David's loss was added to Terry's wall of wins, David was chagrined—if he wanted to point out that Terry wouldn't have a career if David hadn't trained with him in the first place—he didn't act it, because the truth was it felt good to receive this overdue acknowledgment, the acknowledgment, to David, overshadowing the overdueness, even though he didn't want it to.

"A good gift," he told Nathaniel, poking him in his belly. "A good gift."

The boy beamed.

Oh, Nathaniel.

If only the gods of pits and pubes and come-filled Kleenex had cut the kid some slack, Nathaniel and David would've returned to their workout then and, two days later—Saturday, August 8—the boy would've gone to Sasha Semyonova's apartment or wimped out, left Austin chastened for attempting his weirdo racial transformation, or, depending on the reality of Sasha, left Austin finally, finally unchaste. If Terry hadn't said, "One more thing," perhaps this peculiar episode from that peculiar teenager's life would've ended once Nathaniel's return flight touched down at Logan, and he would've gone on to graduate high school and college, meet Mrs. Rothstein, make little Rothsteins, and leave this world with the same name he came in with.

But now Terry was saying that the kid had been looking good lately, "got some fortitude, Rothstein," and if he wanted, no pressure or anything, but Saturday morning—Saturday, August 8—there'd be a couple high school kids sparring for the first time and maybe he'd like to cycle in.

"If I get some time tomorrow, maybe we can work on cleaning up that footwork," said Terry. "Got a few other ideas for you, too. That is, if it's OK with your manager here." And then he winked, not at David but at the boy.

David knew that Terry's invitation to Nathaniel was his way of saying, *I see you, kid, keep at it.* But David was also the world's leading scholar of his own counterfactual history, of what might've been and never would be, and he could see how this was going to go. For the first time since he'd started working out with Nathaniel, he felt that old urge resurfacing. *Real power was making them live vicariously through him.*

"You think I'm ready?" Nathaniel asked David.

It was not David's country and not David's people, it was not David's gym, which was why he said of course Nathaniel was ready, and that he'd be there cheering him on.

One of David's former minions had been pyro-curious, his thumb forever striking the spark wheel of a cheap lighter. The kid liked to see how close, and for how long, he could float his palm above the nozzle without getting burned. David's bawdy storytelling had always been a little like that. He'd never set his own life on fire, had only flirted with the flame.

Standing before his old disciple and his new one, David Dalice experienced that familiar desire to toy with truly exploding his existence. Like the gay kid who scrawls *faggot* across his dorm room door and reports it as a hate crime, he knew that sometimes the easiest way to avoid getting burned by others was to light the match yourself.

The passport appeared two hours later.

David and Ramona had gone for a late birthday celebration at Guero's, and after, bloated on queso and margaritas, they browsed the funky shops along South Congress: Allens Boots, where David usually insisted on trying on a Stetson and a bolo tie; Lucy in Disguise, where they'd rented matching Sonny and Cher jumpsuits the Halloween before.

They were walking the long, creaky aisles of a rambling antique shop when Ramona found the passport. She'd been waiting for the right time to ask if David would like to invite his "new friend" over for supper before summer's end, knew she had to be spontaneous lest he think she'd given it any thought. Her husband had been careful to downplay his commitment to the gym, his friendship with the boy. Not a thing, never a thing. *Not every thing must be a Thing*. But Ramona could see it: from the casually insistent way he'd talked about his new trainee—"no harm letting him have some fun in the ring"—to the hours he put in.

She found her chance in that cavernous shop, where it was perfectly acceptable to converse with your partner while staring at a dusty shelf full of leprous dolls instead of at each other.

"No, no, there is no need for that," David assured her. "You know, Terry offered to help him a bit this week, too. It's not just a me thing."

That's when Ramona spotted it, on an end table covered with vintage travel documents: a REPUBLIQUE D'HAITI PASSEPORT, the country's coat of arms embossed in silver, a dead ringer for David's long-vanished passport.

The passport was fraying at the edges, one of its two staples missing. "You don't think . . ." said Ramona. In the upper left corner, a round orange price sticker: $1.25.

It seemed unlikely, thought David, picking it up off the table. How would it have ended up *here*? And yet it had been lost in Austin . . .

"Ah, no," said David, forcing a chuckle. He turned the passport so Ramona could see the front page. The date of issue was 1988, well after David's arrival in Texas. Despite the guy in the photograph having David's same complexion and being in his late teens, he otherwise looked nothing like David had at that age. This kid had high cheekbones, springy hair.

"Hubba hubba," said Ramona, starting toward the door, ready to split a cone at Amy's Ice Cream across the street. "That would've been *too weird* if it was yours." But David remained in place, staring at the kid in the photograph.

Where *was* his passport? he wondered. Was there some other thrift shop, in some other city, where his twenty-year-old self now inexplicably lay, a buck and a quarter for a tatty three-decade-old booklet with only one stamp? What had become of the young man in this passport, the student visa pasted onto its second page long ago expired? And in whose pocket would this document end up? A collector? Some dumb kid with an especially stupid plan for a fake ID?

David imagined the others in the shop—at the moment, all white—flipping through the book's now-soft pages: offering respectful nods or uttering that vague *huh* he'd heard on outings to the Blanton Museum with Ramona. It was the *huh* people made while pretending to read the wall captions, the *huh* meant to signal, *Despite my profound disinterest, I am indeed alive!*

Would these people even think to consider where this man had come from, to what he aspired, what he'd achieved? That behind the laminate lay a life?

"I'm thinking Mexican vanilla," Ramona called back to David. "Don't tell me you're not in the mood!"

"Coming, coming," David said, mustering his usual good cheer. It came to him so naturally after all these years. Masking pain behind that easy façade. As natural as waking up in the morning, as easy as slipping a stranger's passport into his pocket and heading out into the night.

The day before he was to spar for the first time, the day before he was to meet Sasha Semyonova, Nathaniel Rothstein drove to Shoal Creek Rehab and met David Dalice for morning meeting in the staff locker room.

David laid out Nathaniel's tasks for the day and, after the maintenance men had snapped on their tool belts and the nurses had smeared their pits with Old Spice, a final, feeble counter to the smells awaiting them, David, alone with Nathaniel for the first time that morning, told his charge that there was something they had to do to prepare for sparring tomorrow and, electric razor in hand, instructed him to take his shirt off and approach the sink.

Nathaniel did as he was told, tentatively hanging his scrub top over the closest bathroom stall, unsure of what the older man had in mind. Nathaniel's chest was cinnamon, shoulders freckly.

"A real fighter must look like a fighter," said David. He flipped on the razor and, after getting the OK from Nathaniel, began to strip the boy of his high and heavy puff of hair.

He worked in silence but for the buzz of the razor, Nathaniel and David each absorbed by the image reflected at them, a Black man and that Black man now beige and fun-sized, the boy's coarse brown fluff landing in chunks on the floor.

After, they moisturized their elbows and faces, squirted their necks with Acqua di Gio, and then David told Nathaniel that he'd brought him a small gift for his Terry Tucker's debut.

"In honor of where you started and where you're going," David said, and from his locker took the passport he'd stolen the night before.

Nathaniel opened the booklet. "It's . . . awesome," he said, flipping through the wilted pages. "Who is this?" he asked, studying the photograph inside the front cover.

David explained the passport's provenance. "Seeing it on that table last night, it almost felt like fate," he said. "I'm not very emotional, you know, but I suppose it's my way of saying we come from the same stock, eh? I've trained you as a fighter. As a svelte young Casanova, too! And should you want to train more, I'll be ready to help. That is my word as your brother." He put his hand out to Nathaniel. "My brother. Frè mwen."

"My brother," repeated Nathaniel, taking David's hand in his own. "Frè mwen."

All day, as he played Chinese checkers with Mr. Foster, as he got the VCR set up in the common room for the afternoon showing of *E.T.*, Nathaniel felt for the passport in the pocket of his scrubs to make sure it was still there. He found himself inspecting the photograph in off moments, even once, alone in the yoga studio, comparing it to his driver's license. In a few years, his license, brand-new, would expire, but it felt as if the dull-eyed boy in its photograph had already expired, the current Nathaniel closer to the handsome, confident young man pictured in the passport. Cross-legged on the floor with the documents in his lap, Nathaniel imagined his tomorrow in the ring, in the bedroom, imagined a life, his life, so much bigger than the one, until that fateful summer, he'd feared he was fated to live.

At 2:50 p.m., Nathaniel changed in the quiet of the staff locker room, transferring the passport to the front pocket of his jeans, which also held his car keys. He moved quickly, as he always did, necessary if he wanted to squeeze a Sasha session in before the gym.

He was about to close the locker when he remembered the Post-it, which he'd affixed to the inside of the door the month before. If he was really to meet Sasha tomorrow, he'd need her address. It was only when he went to grab it that he noticed there was something on the upper shelf of the locker, something that hadn't been there that morning.

No way, thought Nathaniel. *Who could've done this? Could've known?*

We've all had the urge, haven't we? To float our palms too close, too long? To see what will happen if we actually do it. To find a way to say the things we'll never say.

Some of us have affairs or tell stories of affairs that never happened. Some of us drink too much or take up shoplifting in middle age. We've heard the stories. Middle-class folk swiping stuff they don't want or need. A scarf, cheap jewelry. A passport off the table in an antique shop.

A vial of pills.

In the staff locker room at Shoal Creek Rehabilitation, Nathaniel heard a toilet flush, a single shower spray to life. He glanced back to make sure no one was watching, then took his second gift.

PART TWO

1-900 Texas

BELINDA ST. JAMES, NOT her real name—Playboy Playmate of the Month (April 1978), dancer at EXPOSE! (1979–1980), stylist at Sexy Cuts (on and off, 1982–91), SportsClips (1993–96), and the hip new Fresh on South Congress (three fraught days, March 1997)—knew how to make a little money on the side.

For years, she'd made ends meet cutting hair after hours in her home, #2E at the Shady Creek Condominiums on South 1st Street in Austin. Belinda had convinced her plumber neighbor to covertly install a salon basin in her living room ("We traded parts for labor," she liked to say), and offered her patrons peppermint Starlights, which she kept in a ceramic seashell on her cutting table and received in pilfered half-pound boxes from a ponytailed cashier at Jason's Deli in exchange for a ten-dollar touch-up every six weeks.

She also worked Monday through Thursday evenings as a "concierge" at the Residence Inn on West 6th Street, serving all-you-can-eat quesadillas out of hot trays in the "VIP Lounge," then cleaning the place up afterward, and every Saturday afternoon at the back of Aisle 9 in Twin Liquors as "brand ambassador" for a ghastly tequila called Colima Blue. ("They ought to call me an off-brand ambassador" was her go-to line.)

Belinda had red, wavy hair and freckles and a small gap between her two front teeth. Motherhood had rounded her out some, but she'd mostly kept her figure, and if she carried a little more in her belly than she'd have liked, well, she still had her three Bs—booty, bust, and brains—and knew when and how to employ each of them, always with one objective in mind: to maintain the sovereign state of Belinda St. James.

Yes, over forty-one years, Belinda had learned a little sumthin sumthin about how to stay solvent in this big, nasty world. And though she was not living the life she'd imagined for herself in the days and months after she'd bared her body for 18 percent of all American college males two decades prior, she made her own money and owned her own home and was beholden to no man. ("Not even you," she'd remind The Sixteen-Year-Old.)

For Belinda St. James, that independence was threatened at 2:25 p.m. on the first day of June 1998, when she returned home from an afternoon of errands to find a note taped to her door: "Janine – Come over as soon as you get this – Dot (1E)."

Trouble. It was always trouble when someone used Belinda's real name. It was the name she saw only on overdue bills, junk mail, and, of course, her downstairs neighbor's pale pink notepaper. Dot Meese, sixty-seven, lived directly below Belinda. Dot was Shady Creek's one-woman neighborhood watch, known for documenting, on her Nikon Tele Touch 300, all manner of infraction—vehicles parked in fire lanes, pets she suspected were over the twenty-pound limit—and mailing her findings to the property management company.

Though Dot knew about her upstairs neighbor's illegal activities, she knew, too, that Belinda was doing her best, raising a troubled soul to boot. So Dot pretended not to notice when the judges and lobbyists who Belinda had poached from her previous employers parked their pickups in the guest spots, nor when they returned fifteen minutes later, necks shaved and talcumed, Belinda's flirty style evident in the sprightly way they hoisted themselves into their trucks. Dot Meese may have liked a good rule, but she was a Christian first. So long as it didn't affect her well-being, she wasn't going to stand in the way of a woman feeding her family.

Christian, widow, mother, grandmother. Also, a thirteen-year cocker rescue foster-volunteer ("If they've got another few years of life they'll go to a family," she'd once told Belinda with a laugh/shrug. "If they're bleeding out the eyes they come to me"). A dedicated thrifter, Dot had given Belinda, over the years, both the fold-out couch on which The Sixteen-Year-Old slept and the two cast-iron patio chairs on Belinda's front balcony.

"Motherfuckit," Belinda declared, tearing the note off her door. The Shady Creek Condominiums faced onto the parking lot like at a drive-up motel, and now Belinda St. James made her way down the same exterior staircase she'd come up, because if she knew one thing about Dot Meese's notes it was that, like tumors, it was best to determine quickly if they were malignant or benign.

Belinda rang the doorbell. This triggered the familiar caterwauls of Dot's latest batch of dying cockers, the familiar unlatching of the brass chain door guard, the familiar sight of Dot Meese—liver-spotted, with a swish of white hair that The Sixteen-Year-Old oft noted was reminiscent of Ursula in *The Little Mermaid*—hunched down and holding those bloody-eyed gremlins at bay.

"Janine," said Dot, looking up from her hunch. "I don't mean to be a"—and here she mouthed *pain in the ass*—"but would you come look at this with me?"

Dot's apartment was covered in a thick maroon carpet that Belinda swore was damp, though she'd never dared set foot in the place barefoot. She'd recently read a book on the art of minimalism, Dot had, and cleared out all but the essentials. Dot led Belinda into the living room, empty except for a floral-print couch in front of a television and a black coffee table on which lay a thick tome called *Understanding the End Times*, a bookmark slipped in about page 3.

"You spartan as a monk," said Belinda. Dot wasn't paying attention. She was looking up. There, in the plaster ceiling, directly above where Dot sat each evening to watch the local news, was an ominous brown water stain, a water stain so severe that the plaster had begun to puff out along the perimeter—a stain in the precise shape of the bottom of Belinda's salon basin.

"Oh my word, is it just me or is that little spot on your ceiling in the exact outline of Jesus Christ?" tried Belinda. Dot crossed her arms.

It'd cost hundreds to pull the plaster out of the ceiling, assuming black mold wasn't rotting up there, which it probably was, not to mention the lost revenue of having to cancel all her clients until God-knows-when, figuring out what was wrong with the basin. "Mother-*fuckit*," she repeated, and started back up the stairs.

When Belinda St. James returned to #2E, she found The Sixteen-Year-Old on the front balcony, sitting cross-legged on one of the cast-iron chairs, listening to Belinda's beat-up Discman. He was a long, lank thing, six foot and not done growing, with blond hair that fell just past his shoulders. Belinda bent down and gently lifted one of the earphones. "Your hair's getting long."

The kid stared at her: *What you want?*

"I need the place for an hour," she said.

The Sixteen-Year-Old put the earphone back in place and didn't say a word.

Belinda worked the phone sex hotline whenever they needed a little extra something, didn't mind it much, neither. The pay was insulting but not piss-poor, and she could work from home: just gave the dispatcher her code and calls came straight to her landline.

Belinda was an old pro, which meant she could scrub dishes or fold laundry or, if there was no housework or she wasn't in the mood to do it, sit in her salon chair and watch *Another World*, sometimes not even that softly, all the while tonguing and licking and clenching, some fat trucker's dirt-caked finger three inches up her poon. She would've been fine using her own voice—sex was sex was sex—but the proprietor of this operation, Mr. Jim Kamden of Spur, Texas, had been a Slavic studies major back at Texas Tech, said he was "committed to keeping this thing Eastern European." As a result, Belinda spoke in a vague Soviet accent, asking her callers if they "like horny Uzbek girl" or instructing them to get down between her "thick Ukrainian thighs."

Who called the 900 number? Doctors and butchers. Teachers and electricians. Businessmen and the unemployed. Always whispering like their wives were in the next room, which half the time Belinda assumed they were. Guys who liked to spank or get spanked, piss or get pissed on. Incest, bondage, some good old-fashioned boinking. Didn't matter if you were a pervy piggy pounding your Pomeranian or a syrupy suitor whispering sweet nothings to your phone whore with a heart of gold, by call's end the tighty-whities were going in the hamper.

"Happy penises are all alike," Mr. Jim Kamden had told Belinda years before, when she'd answered his ad in the back of Austin's alternative weekly, looking for voice actresses "in the mold of Raisa Gorbachev." She could hear him snapping chewing gum, the creak of his chair as he threw his cowboy boots on his desk. "And unhappy penises? All alike, too."

Two dollars and ninety-nine cents a minute, and twenty-seven cents went to her. Belinda's aliases were Natalia, Natasha, Sasha, or Sabrina, and if the men noticed that these ladies all sounded more or less the same, or if they noticed that sometimes they sounded altogether different (Mr. Jim Kamden, who took in the remaining $2.72 per minute, had Natalias, Natashas, Sashas, and Sabrinas from Amarillo to the border), they never said anything to Belinda, probably because if you're laying out $62.79 for twenty-one minutes of aural oral, you don't want to spend too much time litigating who's who.

Twenty-seven cents a minute, $16.20 an hour, eleven hours and she could pay her utilities and the monthly HOA, and so, on that first day of June 1998, after Dot Meese showed Belinda the stain on her ceiling, Belinda locked her door and called the dispatcher, and, after the dispatcher put her on hold, paced her small living room, then approached the front window, blinds drawn, and lifted a single faux wood slat to make sure The Sixteen-Year-Old was still wearing those headphones. If she had to have fake sex in a fake accent to keep a real roof over their heads, Belinda didn't need her one and only child hearing her as she did it.

Her one and only. She'd taken to calling him The Sixteen-Year-Old because he was a pain in her ass, and, also, because he wouldn't answer to his own name and she wasn't about to call her own flesh and blood X. That's how he'd started signing his schoolwork, what his co-workers and even his supervisor at the Whataburger across the street called him, which was how she found out about X in the first place.

Three months prior, that March, The Sixteen-Year-Old had come down with the flu over spring break and, in typical Sixteen-Year-Old fashion, forgot to call in to work about it. "X not coming in today?" asked the supervisor, Kelvin Williams, over the phone.

"And who the hell is X?" said Belinda.

"When I grew up there was a toothless illiterate in town called Egbert Bridle who looked as if he'd been the product of a one-night stand between his mama and his peepaw on the *maternal* end," Belinda told The Sixteen-Year-Old later that night. The boy lay on the fold-out, swaddled in blankets. "And when the postman came around and Egbert Bridle had to sign for a package, you know how he signed it? *X.*"

No child of hers was gonna be no Egbert Bridle–style no-name. C.R.M. were the initials her boy would one day monogram onto his silk pajamas if she had anything to say about it. *Charles Rex Markham.* She'd named him like a king, for this world was his to inherit.

"You can be anything you want to be, my little man," she used to whisper to him as a child. Sometimes she'd still tell him that, even if she knew it meant he'd get surly, look away.

Belinda inspected him through the window, watching as he stared out onto the parking lot from his perch on the front balcony. He wore a black tank top, black jeans even though it was pushing 90 degrees. "What I'd give to be that skinny," Belinda said softly, though she knew her boy hated it, hated how if he puffed out his chest in front of the mirror, every rib of his rib cage was visible.

If she was square with herself, Belinda knew it wasn't the new name that bothered her so much as the destruction of the old one, and all that went with it. The week before, Belinda had gotten off early from the Residence Inn and walked in on Charles Rex in the bathroom by accident. She'd shut the door right away, but she knew what she'd seen: her only child naked, his penis and testicles tucked between his thighs, her Colour Riche by L'Oreal in fuchsia applied too thin across his lips.

It wasn't exactly a shock. The boy had been feminine from the beginning, in spirit and body, too, with a nose that extended slightly at the tip, face fragile as a porcelain doll's. At five, he'd fallen in love with Belinda's lime-green mohair sweater, and when Belinda told him that he couldn't wear it outside the house—it's a *girl* sweater, she explained, and it was down to his knees anyway!—he'd cried so hard she'd had to go to Fabric Warehouse to buy him a swatch of the stuff, told him to carry it in the pocket of his little blue jeans and rub at it if ever he needed comfort.

She'd noticed the way he scrutinized the girls in the movies they'd watched and rewatched together a thousand times, as if, in Baby from *Dirty Dancing* or Alex from *Flashdance*, he might find a model for himself. She'd seen how he'd adopted some of Belinda's own affectations, how when he got sassy his voice went smooth and sultry as a shoulder shimmy. The year before, he'd claimed his backpack hurt his neck and had subbed it out for an old ESPRIT beach bag which he'd begun to carry like a purse. Hell, last Halloween the boy announced he was going out dressed as a goth and Belinda had taught him the correct way to apply eyeliner herself.

"There's your inside self and your outside self," she'd told him then, as they both penciled over their lids. "But if you gonna bring that inside self outside . . ." Belinda whistled. "You gonna need to learn to fuck some folks up."

"Oh, Mama," Charles Rex had said. "You know I never fucked anyone up in my life."

"You fucked me up," Belinda said, reviewing the job she'd done. "Gonna end up dead in the asylum on account of you."

So the bathroom penis incident wasn't a shock, exactly, but it shook her nonetheless. Later, she'd realized it wasn't the lipstick or even the boy hiding his parts that so rattled her, but his pubic hair, the first blond wisps of it, a reminder that if he was gonna grow out of this thing, it would've happened already. The prepubescent, Belinda knew, were kinky as all get-out—fellating their thumbs and fingering their noses and joggling their tiny joysticks for all the world to see—but most of the time they sucked and picked and jiggled that gunk right out their systems before the change came. Once the hair grew under a boy's pits and over his manhood? It seemed to Belinda that was a barrier, forever trapping any mess that remained inside.

Belinda didn't say anything the night she caught him in the bathroom, but the next morning, she made sure to be up before he went to school. She found him in the kitchen on his way out the door, ESPRIT bag already slung across his shoulder, Eggo in hand.

"You wanna talk about it?" she said.

"Talk about what?" grouched The Sixteen-Year-Old. He made like he was going to brush past her.

Belinda put her arm across the doorway. "Listen, now, everybody's got their *thang*, okay?"

"Mama—" he said, head bowed so as not to make eye contact.

"And maybe this is yours. But this a man's world, sweet stuff, and you got the Golden Ticket between those legs." A lock of hair, still wet from the shower, had fallen over her son's face, and Belinda gently tucked it behind his ear, lifted his chin to make him look at her. "So you gonna hold on to that."

It wasn't like she was one of those Christian psychos, Belinda told herself now, still spying through the window as she waited for the hotline dispatcher. She'd known that her child would grow up to love men before her child knew it. Knew her state and her country and her countrymen, too, knew them so intimately that even back when Charles Rex was a toddler wrapped up in Belinda's feather boas, playing with the microphone on her home karaoke machine, even back when something was killing homosexuals and no one knew what it was, even then Belinda told herself to be thankful, that birthing a thousand gay boys was preferable to birthing even a single boy-loving girl, because science and medicine were ever-evolving but from the beginning of time to right this second, men—all men—had always been exactly the same: on top.

She'd grown up in West Texas, endowed with sparkle and skepticism and, though they wouldn't bloom until her late teens, two breasts so perfectly round that more than one man would compare them to the map they'd seen in their grade-school geography primers of the western and eastern hemispheres side by side. Belinda knew those dated primers well. As a little girl she'd pored over them, dreamed of going to darkest Africa to hunt lions, do wild tribal dances, and escape quicksand. In junior high, she read in an old issue of *Life* about bush pilots in Kenya, including one, a glamorous British woman with—this she couldn't get over—her same last name, who, in between affairs with dukes and magnates, enjoyed flying low over antelopes and Thomson's gazelles as they tore across the savannah. Birthed to some other family, in some other town, in some other time, that might've been Belinda, but she was born Janine Markham in Sweetwater, up in Nolan County, 1957, and *Baby doll*, her mama always told her, *you too pretty for nonsense.*

From an early age, she learned to keep her interior life interior. Her curiosity about the world was too much for her parents, who'd survived the Depression and the Dust Bowl and World War II, which was her mama's murky explanation for why, in *her* house, under *her* roof, "funny business is not welcome." It didn't matter if Janine asked whether, if she put a stick of dynamite in a hot dog bun and gave it to their mean old neighbor, Mrs. Baker, to eat for lunch, it would be considered murder in the first or second degree, or why they were only friends with other white people: the responses were always the same. "Sweet girl like you don't need to worry about all that," her father would say without looking up from his newspaper, followed by her mother with that ever-present adage, which Janine sometimes imagined her squawking out like a parrot:

Too pretty for nonsense! Too pretty for nonsense! Cacaw!

No, in the Markham home, good girls spoke only when spoken to, so she learned to ask those questions and dream those dreams in her mind alone, to bury one Janine deep inside another. To the people of Sweetwater, she was just your average girl: not brash nor bashful, shy nor chatty, shrewd nor stupid. Not anything, really. She was *pleasant*, which, according to her mama, was what the men of this world most desired.

They lived in a brick ranch house on three acres along Highway 70, no neighbors in sight. Janine's father was a plant engineer for United States Gypsum, her mama kept the house in order. Good folk, those Markhams: churchgoing but not fanatical, responsible but never stingy. They gave their three daughters three hot meals a day, a turkey with all the trimmings on Thanksgiving and Christmas, a penny for each lost tooth: luxuries they'd only dreamed about as too-skinny kids who'd watched their own parents turn hunched and brittle tilling the dry land of the Dirty Thirties.

No man-made cataclysm swirled over Janine Markham's youth. The Sweetwater of the 1960s was on the up and up: new gypsum and cement plants, a burgeoning business district over six blocks of downtown. And then there was the Rattlesnake Round-up, the largest of its kind in the whole United States, according to the Nolan County Chamber of Commerce. The impetus for this event was the area's rattlesnake infestation: townsfolk hunted and captured them all through the year and, in March, gathered in the rodeo arena, where they sold snake meat and rattlesnake wallets and boots, and the girls of the town competed for Miss Sweetwater, donning ball gowns and tiaras and, for the talent competition, putting plastic ponchos over their evening wear and skinning snakes dangling from meat hooks.

"A little slice of Heaven," Janine's mama used to say from her rocking chair on the porch, looking out onto that nothing highway that led to nothing in particular. Sometimes, Janine imagined she was an alien who'd been assigned the Markhams, for all the other women in her family seemed not just accepting of their roles but downright tickled by them: her mama delighted to cook and clean all day ("This pecan pie's gonna send your father into cardiac arrest!"), her sisters, eight and ten years her senior, thrilled to be wives and mothers before Janine had finished fourth grade.

Good folk, nice folk, but Janine didn't desire nice but more, wanted to see what lay beyond Highway 70. In those early years, she sated her appetite exploring the foreign terrain of her own developing body. At age nine, tucked beneath the same quilt under which her mama'd slept and *her* mama'd slept and her mama'd slept before that, Janine Markham touched herself for the first time and suspected then that she'd found something no one else knew about, because it was hard to imagine anyone else in that town feeling such untamed pleasure.

Janine went to Sweetwater Junior High School, Sweetwater High, earning marks same as boys who would go on to work for First Texas Bank or in office jobs at National Gypsum. Still, it was not her B's and (mostly) C's that inspired admiring whispers from classmates and teachers alike, but those marvelously spherical 36Ds, which had tumbled forth in full by the fall of her junior year.

And if she burned to get out of there, if she thought the boys were plain as milk and the girls a nasty bunch of bitches, if she didn't want to be a homemaker like her mama, if waitressing or teaching or even nursing didn't make her blood run hot, she was fourth generation in that place and didn't have a model for what else to do, for how else to be. And so she made out in the back of the bland boys' cars and smoked cigs in the bedrooms of the bitches and kept her comments mostly to herself. Janine planned to enroll in the beauty school in Wichita Falls after senior year, would've too, if, at her mama's insistence, she hadn't entered Miss Sweetwater in March '74 at the age of seventeen, hadn't smiled wide and pushed her chest out like she'd seen the other girls do. If she hadn't taken the crown.

It wasn't the winning that got her out of Dodge but what happened after. They'd gone to celebrate where all the seventeen-year-olds celebrated anything in Sweetwater back then, in some pasture, and there, around a bonfire, everyone crowded around her, the frenzied adulation of her admirers and the palpable envy of her nemeses disproportionate, she knew, to her own bleh accomplishment.

"This might be the biggest day of your *life*," squealed her best friend, Lucy, and a shiver ran down Janine Markham's spine. Oh, hell no, she thought, and knew then that it was time to get moving.

Wit and brains and boobies: it didn't take Janine long to figure out which two of those four would be paying for her ticket. She'd heard about a talent agent in Abilene, forty miles east, cut school the Monday following to meet him. He was thirty, if that, not bad-looking either: sandy-haired and coppery, with a handlebar mustache and a long, lean figure. Cute enough that Janine told herself he was safe, even if he did work out of a construction trailer on a country road miles out of town, even if, after she climbed up into his bare-bones office, he got up from his desk and, as she settled into a folding chair, locked the door behind her.

The talent agent's name was Warren Earl: "like the judge but backwards," he'd told her, proudly hoisting up his jeans by the belt loops. Not bad-looking and a sweet talker, too. We'll start modest, he declared, told Janine they'd get her posing for some of them department store catalogues ("You know Lichtenstein's, out in Corpus? What if I told you I *knew* Lichtenstein?"). And with that smile? "Girl, before too long we'll be out in Cali-forn-i-ay, shooting commercials for the idiot box." At meeting's end, they agreed to reconvene the next day at the Diamond K Indoor Rodeo Arena, a few more miles down the road, to shoot her comp card: the sample shots Warren Earl would send out to his connections far and wide. He had a contract with the owner to use the arena during off-hours, he said. They'd have the whole place to themselves.

Warren Earl told Janine to dress casual and she did, showing up at nine the next morning in her favorite rose-pink knit sweater, pair of jeans. "Hoo dog," said Warren Earl when he saw her in the parking lot. Once inside, he announced that Janine was too fine to be some Gee,

Your Hair Smells Terrific Jergens-brand shampoo girl. Girl like her, there was *real* money to be made, if she was willing to show a little skin.

"Why don't you take that shirt off," he said gently, sitting wide-legged in the front row of the metal bleachers as Janine stood in the dirt before him. "Brassiere too, now."

Janine hesitated but did as she was told, and as her bra fell to the ground, Warren Earl placed a hand over the crotch of his Wranglers, whistled. "Girl, you got titties like the world!" he told her. "And the world can be yours if you learn how to use 'em."

He said if she was willing to take it all off, he could send her comp card straight to Dallas, to Tony LaBianca of *Flesh* magazine, so long as she could offer twenty dollars upfront to cover printing and developing. "Once that ol' wop sees what I seen, girl, you'll get a return on that investment thirtyfold, *forty*fold, guaranteed."

A no-name country girl in the centerfold of a national magazine? It wasn't what Janine Markham had signed up for, but she'd be lying if she said the idea didn't turn her on: her sex, herself, not buried below her mama's quilt or shielded from her suitors under clasps and snaps and buttons or obscured beneath a plastic poncho and a pageant gown, but out in the open, for all the world to see. Turned her on and frightened her, too, and because her greatest fear was that she'd end up where she started, and because she was seventeen years old and didn't yet have the poise or the presence of mind to say, "Hold on a second, let me think this through," soon she was naked, straddling the top of a steel bucking chute, doing her best to spin a lasso.

At first, she told herself she liked it. Sure, she had to clench tight to stop her privates from scraping against the top of the rusted gate, the metal against her thighs cold as a doctor's speculum. Yeah, Warren Earl was too close, for though he'd started on a tripod a few yards away he'd since moved in, working his lens only inches from her nipples, from the crack of her ass, for what he described as "some intimates." Still, she was doing it, doing it well, too, if the fevered way Warren Earl discharged his commands was any judge: "Swing that rope, girl, aw yeah, you got it cowgirl, yeah.

"Now drop that rope and get down here," said Warren Earl, offering a callus-free hand as she dismounted. He told her to get on all fours in front of the gate.

"In the dirt?" Janine asked.

Warren Earl grinned, and she did as she was told. "Oh yeah, arch that back, girl, spread those legs, girl, aw yeah . . ."

Yes, Janine Markham told herself she liked it, told herself that each click of that camera represented a mile she would travel, so that soon she'd be out of Sweetwater, out of Texas, out of the country even, on a jumbo jet to Gay Paree.

Truth was, she *did* like it. Janine had lost her virginity five months before, to one of the bland boys, her senior-year steady, Carl. Sex with Carl was neither awful nor pleasurable. Mostly, it was short-lived, since "sex," in Carl's mind—and, to that point, Janine's—ended the moment Carl orgasmed. Still, Janine let him climb on top of her most nights, if for no other reason than she'd realized a climaxing Carl was his most interesting self, his otherwise blank face gone tense and desperate. The sweat Janine wiped off after was always his sweat, never hers.

This was different. Watching Warren Earl's eyes go bovine as she posed, as if, despite his greater height and strength, she were the one in control. Letting air into places she'd never let it. There was power there. Power in the promise of making her own money off her own body, taking that money and that body wherever she pleased.

Course, feeling powerful and wielding power were not the same thing. But Janine didn't figure that out until after she'd straddled the chute and swung the rope and got on all fours and arched her back and spread her legs. Didn't figure that out until Warren Earl set the camera down beside her and took a single step back.

"Can I get up now?" she said.

"We almost there, girl," said Warren Earl. And then her talent agent of seventeen hours and seventeen minutes unbuckled his belt, pushed his blue jeans down to his ankles, and, his crotch inches from the top of her head, took his penis in his hand.

"We gonna make some money together, girl." He spoke plainly

and without malice, spoke as if she weren't on all fours in the dirt. "See, I can see the future. I'm a seer, see. An *orkle*. Knew you wanted this, didn't I?" He shook it at her. "I could see that."

She told herself he wasn't forcing her. Wasn't touching her. Told herself it would be a funny story to tell at some later date. He didn't, as far as Janine could tell, want her to take it in her mouth, didn't want her to do anything except stay docile, like she did for Carl. Warren Earl, she saw, was aiming for her face.

Her shot, Janine Markham now understood, was inextricably linked with his, and she resolved to let him shoot it. Would've too, except for this: desperate to get it over with, she tried to think of something else, found herself imagining those transfixing images she'd conjured in her youth, Janine as adventuress-socialite, clinking champagne glasses in exotic embassies, Janine flying low across the plains, tried so hard to concentrate on them that she didn't realize she'd begun to tremble.

"Aw, darlin', don't clam up on me," said Warren Earl. "C'mon, girl. *You too pretty for nonsense*."

Like a sleepwalker who'd blundered into a river, Janine Markham now shot awake, the briny water flooding her nostrils courtesy of her mama's insufferable refrain. She stared up at Warren Earl: five fingers wrapped around his shaft, five fingers now cupping his ball sack, not a single finger pushing down to release the shutter.

No Paris, no jumbo jet, no out of the country. Sweetwater, Texas, for life.

"C'mon, boy, you got this," said Warren Earl, desperate not to soften despite his subject's recalcitrance.

Janine knew from her own boyfriend what spilt seed heralded: not one thing. Nothing ever happened after a man's orgasm. The end of "sex," the end of the conversation. There was only one shot to be shot that day at the Diamond K Indoor Rodeo Arena and it was not Janine's. If she wanted more, no one was going to give it to her. She'd have to take it for herself.

"Yeah, you got this," he repeated. He closed his eyes and tried to come.

Thus, the man was wholly unprepared when Janine, alert, alive, snatched the camera next to Warren Earl and started to scramble toward the exit.

"What the—?"

Warren Earl went to grab her, except he forgot about the jeans around his ankles, began to tumble toward her. Halfway to the ground, he got hold of Janine's foot and took her down with him. She smacked her heel into his face hard as she could, kept moving.

It gave her enough time to grab her tangle of clothes by the bleachers and bust naked out the employee entrance into the empty parking lot, sun stinging her eyes. She fumbled to find the keys to her mama's white Buick LeSabre in her blue jeans, was quivering so bad she had to use one hand to steady the other so she could open the car door.

Janine chucked the camera and clothing onto the passenger side as a hollering Warren Earl, pants unzipped, stumbled out of the employee entrance. By the time he was banging on her window, Janine had turned key in ignition. She slammed bare foot to pedal and tore out of the lot.

Down that country road she flew. Girl hauled ass, ten miles in ten minutes, muttering that hateful phrase under her breath—*too pretty for nonsense*—as she pressed harder and harder on the gas. It was only once she was outside the city limits that she'd calmed enough to pull over into the empty dirt lot of a small church, the building's white paint peeling. Janine sat silent for a moment, determined not to cry, then checked the rearview mirror to make sure no one was behind her and gingerly opened the car door.

The ground was cool and rough on the bottom of her feet, a few kernels of flesh dangling off her skinned knee from when Warren Earl had taken her down. Janine, nude and trembling and clutching her mama's car keys like a tiny pistol, tiptoed a few feet out toward the road to make extra sure no one was coming, turned back to the car to get dressed.

It was then that Janine noticed the church reader board, announcing, in faded Gothic lettering, that she was on the grounds of the Church of God of Prophecy and, underneath, in the block letters common to most church marquees:

REMEMBER TO WHOM YOU BELONG!

Janine read this message, read it again, looked to the sky. And though she'd been holding back tears since escaping Warren Earl, and though she'd expected that now, alone, she'd let them flow, reading that sign just about did her in, and instead of crying, Janine Markham unleased a deep and guttural scream. She took a breath and, unfulfilled, went at it another round, crazed as the Pentecostals who gave themselves over to the language of the spirit in that very place each Sunday. After, Janine inhaled deeply, wiped her mouth with the back of her hand, dressed in the church parking lot, and drove on home. Like the girls who'd come before her, she never considered reporting Warren Earl to the authorities.

Unlike those other girls, however, Janine Markham had Warren Earl's camera, had his film, and had, she felt, in her screaming, allowed that long-buried version of herself, her inside self, to crawl up out of its grave in the bottom of her belly and grab for her heart.

The next day, just before 6 p.m., this new Janine, the old Janine, drove toward the few blocks of squat, pale yellow brick buildings that constituted downtown Sweetwater, smoked a cigarette on the cement steps of the hardware store, and surveyed the goings-on inside Felson's Camera across the street.

The proprietor of the shop, Mr. Fred Felson, collected cameras from all eras and had arranged them on tripods in the window display. Through this window, Janine could see the old man, a small fellow in suspenders, counting bills on the counter next to the register. After a minute, a teenage boy she didn't recognize emerged from the back room, walked to the front of the shop, and flipped the sign in the glass door from open to closed.

Janine took a long drag on her cigarette. *You can get a return on that investment thirtyfold, fortyfold*, Warren Earl had told her. Even if everything else he'd said had been a lie, when, right after school, Janine called directory assistance, Dallas, please, connected to *Flesh* magazine, and asked who was in charge of picking centerfolds, the man who answered said, "Tony LaBianca, who wants to know?" And if Warren Earl had been right about that . . . $20 times forty was $800. Janine flicked the cigarette onto the street.

Janine had again worn her rose-pink knit sweater, this time without a bra. She'd heard stories from her mama about Fred Felson. He'd opened the shop in '49: "*family money*," Janine's mama always noted, as if it were a secret only she knew. For most of his career, Mr. Felson had taken the annual portraits of every student, K–12, under a contract with the school district.

That job had gone elsewhere a few years before. To that point, he'd kept his own artistry separate from the business. A documentarian of the American West, his photographs had shown in Dallas, Phoenix, Santa Fe, his neighbors in Sweetwater never knowing. Everything changed in 1970, when Fred Felson, then sixty-five, had his first-ever gallery opening in New York City; it garnered enough attention that word got back to his hometown. Turned out, for years, the man had secretly been making formal portraits of civil rights activists who passed through Texas. SNCC organizers and Freedom Riders, even (Janine's mama couldn't bring herself to say the words above a whisper) *Black Panthers*. More appalling still: each of his subjects had posed sitting on a stool in front of an arctic-blue cloth backdrop, the same stool and same backdrop Sweetwater's youth had posed with for the previous two decades.

The Markhams, of course, got their film processed at the Rexall Drugs two blocks over. According to Janine's mama, it had nothing to do with "all that": "*As you know*, I have no problem with *anyone* doing *anything*," she'd once told Janine. "But he develops those photographs *in store*! As if I wanted that little man knowing all our business."

At 6:05, the old man exited the shop. It was Fred Felson for whom Janine had planned to lift her sweater in exchange for developing (and keeping quiet about) her naughty photos. Sweater would be her initial offer. She'd lose her jeans and panties if she had to, scraped knee be damned, was willing to pay up to double the regular cost for the processing (Janine was still flush off the forty dollars she'd earned as Miss Sweetwater, minus the twenty that had already gone to Warren Earl).

Now, watching Mr. Felson hobble down the sidewalk, she had her doubts. He was frailer than she'd remembered. But maybe there was a tidier solution to her problem. She hadn't anticipated the shop assistant. Why seduce an old man if there was a teenage boy available?

Twenty minutes later, the boy still hadn't emerged from the shop. Janine crossed the street, peered through the glass door. Felson's Camera appeared empty. She walked down the adjacent alleyway to see if he might've left out the back: no exit. Only when she returned to the storefront did she find him, locking up after himself.

"Hey, I've been looking for you."

"Sorry, we're closed for the night," said the boy, his back to her.

"You've been closed for a half hour. What all were you doing in there?"

The boy turned to face her. He was almost a man, but not yet: his neck, sloped as a brontosaurus's, hadn't yet figured out how to support his head, and the pimples from above his lip to under his chin formed a Van Dyke of acne. Faded green cords, a well-worn striped T-shirt. Tousled red hair, darker than hers, that swooped forward and fell past his ears, like a Pilgrim.

"You new around here?" said Janine.

"No," he said, shifting uneasily. "Lived here my whole life. You're Janine Markham, right?"

"How you know that?"

"I'm a sophomore. Over at the high school? James Wilmer? Probably seen you every day, last two years at least."

"I don't think I've ever seen you."

"Yeah, well," said James. "You're not the only one." He was careful to look past her, as if he were searching for someone over her shoulder. "Anyhow, like I said, Mr. Felson's gone . . ."

"I wasn't looking for Mr. Felson, James. I was looking for you."

James didn't follow. "Thought you said you didn't know me."

Janine smiled. "Why you locking up so late anyway?"

"Working on my own stuff. Mr. Felson lets me, after close."

"You any good?"

"I dunno," said James. He looked down at his Pumas. "Know some things."

"Bet you do," said Janine. She brought her lips close to his ear. "So listen, James. I need a favor."

She told him about everything that had happened with Warren Earl, told him she had to get out of town pronto and this was the only way, listed the parts of herself she'd show him and the amount she'd pay him if he helped. At this last part, Janine took from her jeans the film she'd stolen and transferred it to his corduroys, kept her fingers in his pocket.

She felt, as she did this, the same strange power she'd felt posing on all fours in the rodeo arena. In offering her body she was defending her body. In surrendering control, in playacting surrender, she was taking it: a queer kind of freedom.

"I don't—" said James.

"It's okay," said Janine, burrowing her hand deeper into his pocket.

"I mean, I can't— I'm not—"

"You can, James," she whispered.

Janine rubbed her pocketed hand against his crotch.

The boy jerked away. "Can you get off me? What the hell—?"

Janine pulled her fingers out of his pocket with some difficulty, drew her hand back as if bitten. "I'm sorry, I—"

When he finally looked at her, she saw the boy's eyes had filled with tears.

This was what Janine Markham learned from James Wilmer: how to open a film canister and cut off the end of the film, how to load the developing tank, how to dry the negatives (on a clothesline along the back wall of the darkroom). How to wait.

James maneuvered around the darkroom with only the red glow of the safety light as guide, operated with a confidence Janine hadn't expected. He handled the film like she'd sometimes seen women handle their children, with a rough assuredness that didn't comport with Janine's sense of their fragility. "Developer, stop bath, hypo," he told her, pointing to plastic jugs of unlabeled chemicals on the back counter. "Got that?" It was as if James, who Janine had never noticed in the hallways of Sweetwater High School, could only be seen in the dark.

After they'd processed the negatives, Janine monologued about the likelihood of Warren Earl coming for his camera ("I'd like to be gone before he tries it") while James sat on a stool in front of the enlarger on the back counter, working on his own pictures.

"You've seen the negatives," said Janine. "You think I got what it takes?"

"You're Miss Sweetwater, so probably, right?"

"But do *you* think I'm sexy?"

"Yeah," he said, "course," without looking up. "We probably got another hour before this all dries, if you wanna take a smoke break."

Alone in the alleyway, Janine wondered why the boy was so reticent, if it was born of embarrassment or he was just awkward. Later, she'd realize he was probably homosexual. Far as she knew, she'd never met one before, found the idea of a man wanting another man's ding-a-ling nasty and a little intriguing. (In the Markham house, boys had *ding-a-lings* and girls had *unmentionables*, a fact that, many years later, she liked to remind The Sixteen-Year-Old of: "Now, which sounds more fun to you?")

Back inside, Janine learned from James how to use the enlarger, learned the giddy-sick feeling that came every time they placed the photo paper in the developer, waiting for another Janine Markham to appear from the shallow depths of the chemical bath. She learned that she was fine using her looks and her voice to get what she wanted, but that it'd ruin her if she was ever forced to use her touch, James's wet eyes when she'd felt his crotch reminding her a little too much of her own the day before.

Never once did Janine ask, nor did James offer, any explanation as to why, after she'd done it, he'd wiped those wet eyes on the shoulder of his T-shirt, unlocked the door to Felson's Camera, and said, "C'mon, then."

The closest to an answer, she thought, came from James's own black-and-white photographs, headshot-sized prints hanging from the clothesline, which she studied as James cleaned up.

They were close-ups of body parts in action: an extended index finger, which she realized was attached to Drunk Sam, always in excited conversation from his park bench on Main Street; the strained neck of Rev. Daniels mid-sermon.

There was a striving to James's subjects. He favored striding legs, outstretched arms, bulging eyes. It was as if the parts James photographed were trying to escape the confines of the bodies that contained them, trying to escape the confines of the photo paper, the confines of that town.

"You itching to get out of this hellhole too, huh?" Janine asked, staring up at eight knuckles, the connected fists wrapped tight around a Brookshire's shopping cart handle.

He joined her before the clothesline, half covered in her images, half covered in his. "I sure hope so," he said softly.

"We gonna do it, James Wilmer," said Janine. She gave him a playful elbow. "This whole world's gonna be yours and mine."

She left with eighteen five-by-sevens, plus the negatives. In forty minutes with Warren Earl that was all he'd taken: eighteen shots of Janine humping and riding and arching, though for all Warren Earl's faults, Janine had to admit, he had some talent as an amateur pornographer. She deemed ten of the shots worthy, and within twenty-four hours had sent them to Mr. Tony LaBianca, c/o *Flesh*, with a note outlining her terms:

If you'd like to use call Janine at the number below and say you're Henry, friend from biology. $100 each.

Five days after that, Henry from biology did call, and as Janine's mama fried steak in the kitchen, her daughter, bedroom door locked, sat cross-legged, fully underneath her quilt of sin, a patchwork ghost, and negotiated her first contract.

"Bad news, sweetheart," Tony LaBianca informed her. "You're out of your mind."

According to Tony, "A hundred per" would be reasonable if Janine was Lauren Hutton offering exclusive rights to her "slit": "and not the one between her teeth, you read?" Fifteen dollars for the bundle was more than fair—generous given that half the shots, Warren Earl's "intimates," were unusable ("who did the lighting for this glorious epic of the Old West? Ray Charles?"). If she wanted, he'd also put her in touch with an actual photographer in Austin. "Someone who'll do more than takes close-ups of your culo, bellisimo as it is, capeesh?"

"Don't you know anyone in Dallas?" Janine asked.

"Not anyone you can afford," said Tony. "Say, how'd you hear about me, anyway?"

Janine hesitated a split second, told him.

"*Warren Earl*, huh? Who's his brother? Frankfurter Felix? Never heard of him."

Anger and profound relief flushed Janine's cheeks. She would eventually do some asking around and find out that Warren Earl's real profession was preying on West Texas girls who didn't know better. He had a thing for cowgirls, and since the girlie mags of the day hadn't caught up to his particular tastes—busty gals in buckskin suits, nude women bound in piggin' string—he'd taken to creating his own.

He'd shoot his roll and shoot his load, most of the time never to be seen again. That was Warren Earl's racket, with an assist from the manager of Diamond K Indoor Rodeo Arena, round-faced and mutton-chopped as a nineteenth-century industrialist, who, for a five-dollar cut and a duplicate of the negatives, was happy to leave the employee entrance unlocked "on accident": "weekdays only and out by noon please and thank."

"And one more thing," said Tony LaBianca. "No one wants to

beat off to a cowgirl named Janine. It's a little too . . . real. I'm thinking Denise. Delilah. *Belinda*."

"Belinda Markham?" said Janine. She liked the first name well enough, didn't think it sounded right with her boring old family name. She thought back over the last few days. The boy at the camera shop, James Wilmer, sure had helped her. An angel that one turned out to be. A saint.

"What you think about Belinda St. James?"

A certified check for fifteen dollars arrived a week later, only a five-dollar loss on her initial investment. Combined with her leftover earnings from Miss Sweetwater, the sum was enough for a bus ticket to Austin, a few nights in a motel to start out. Just for the summer, she'd assured her mama, and if this whole modeling thing didn't work out (what exactly she'd be modeling went left unmentioned), she'd go on to beauty school in the fall as planned.

So off she went, and eight years passed. Belinda St. James waitressed at Hoffbrau Steaks and Threadgill's, served beer and enchiladas from the snack bar at the Dart Bowl. Austin wasn't Gay Paree, or Hollywood, or even Dallas, but she could live cheap and easy, and if, on her one half-day off a week, she wanted to sit with a Lone Star and a 99 cent Hobo Plate at Hector's Taco Flats and flirt with college boys, or get sweaty grooving to redneck rock at the 'Dillo with cowboys and hippies alike (different costumes, same joint passed between them), in Austin that wasn't called nonsense. It was called Tuesday. And always, when she could find the work, she'd model: with her clothes on for a little money (for a local jeweler in the *Statesman* and a hosiery company that failed to pay), and with them off for a little more.

A Texas-sized irony: thanks to Warren Earl's predilections, she developed a reputation from the start for her Wild West tableaus. The girl who wanted nothing more than to get out of Sweetwater became a perpetual cowgirl, a regional attraction occasionally—very occasionally—featured in national skin mags: $50 to pose for *Flesh* again in January 1975 ("You win Most Improved," declared Tony

LaBianca); $400 to ride a mechanical bull in *Gent* nine months later; a whopping $5,000 for *Playboy* two years after, which provided her the starter money to take out a mortgage for #2E in the Shady Creek Condominiums a decade after that. The photograph was set in a hunting lodge. Belinda posed on a cowhide rug in white cowboy boots and an open mink stole.

And though she was industrious, she never made enough to settle on a coast, where the real money was made. And though she was pretty, she was never considered beautiful: too short for high fashion, too round for TV. And though she was independent, in that world, at that time, she too often had to rely on talent scouts and managers and photographers, all men, who took too big a cut for too little work, who were handsy, or worse. (Poor Warren Earl: he *should've* been an agent, Belinda often mused, for it wasn't atypical for those debauched souls to come up from behind and press their distended dongles into the repulsed rumps of their clientele, and off their women they made more than twenty bucks.)

In short, Belinda St. James did what she had to do to live something closer to the life she'd always wanted (not the life she did want, but closer, and closer was better than farther away). And when, in 1981, she made good on her promise to her mama, now two years deceased, and enrolled in beauty school, earning a license from Austin College of Cosmetology, Belinda did it not to have a secondary income to support a husband, or as something fun on the side, but so that she could keep living that closer-to-the-life life she'd been living.

She became pregnant soon after, the father an on-again off-again who, upon learning his girlfriend was expecting, went off, again, never to return. Belinda St. James had never been religious, but when she decided to keep her child, she prayed to God above and to Jesus Christ and to her obstetrician to give her a boy, because she knew firsthand what it took to survive as a woman in this world, had done it once, and felt no need to relive the experience.

She'd have a boy, Belinda told herself, and if he was brainy, he would use his brains, and if he was strong, he would use his body, and whatever life he wanted to make for himself he would make, with her help, and it would be his choice.

And now, some sixteen years after she'd given birth, on this first day of June 1998, Belinda waited for the dispatcher to send the first caller to her portable phone, and assured herself, as she stood on the oak laminate she'd paid to have installed, peeking out the blinds she'd bought, at the child she'd created, that she wasn't some Christian psycho. No, she just wanted her boy—her one and only boy—to take this world for everything it had to offer.

You can be anything you wanna be, thought Belinda, watching her son, *but don't be that. God, don't you make him that.*

Suddenly, the dispatcher returned to the line. "I'm ready to send the first one your way," he said. The dispatcher's voice was young and chipper and Belinda pictured a Boy Scout operating an old-timey switchboard. She knew the aw-shucks thing worked on some of the younger girls, how a little cloying flattery could convince them to take on slower shifts or fill in for someone who was out. Belinda let the slat of the blinds fall.

"So whaddya say, Ms. St. James?" said the dispatcher. "You good to go?"

"You just leave it to beaver now," said Belinda, settling into her salon chair. She cleared her throat. Her accent was awful, she knew, her only basis for the character Bond villains and Natasha from *Rocky and Bullwinkle*. The day's events had left her feeling old and fat and tired, and she swiveled around in the chair so she wouldn't have to look at herself in the mirror above her cutting table. But she pushed off with too much force and the chair came to a squeaking stop 360 degrees from where it had started. Belinda was once again face-to-face with Belinda. *Mother*fuckit, she thought, and then the first call came through.

ONE

Three months before his mama returned to the phone sex hotline, X told Margaret Clanahan that he was a fag for Jesse Filkins.

That was the word he'd used as they lay on the green shag carpet in Margaret's bedroom, heads propped up on her Pillow People, passing a box of Snackwell's Devil's Food Cookie Cakes between them.

It was the first night of spring break 1998, and X and Margaret were playing one of their favorite games, where one would name a teacher and the other would have to imitate what they imagined that teacher's farts sounded like first thing in the morning. X had given Margaret a gimme, pig-nosed Mrs. Margolin, their tenth-grade history instructor, who always drank an entire Big Gulp during their B-block class. Her morning wind could be simulated, in Margaret's rendering, by puffing up one's cheeks, making a small O with the lips, and slowly exhaling, and that's what Margaret was doing when X blurted it:

"I'm a fag for Jesse Filkins."

"Oh my god," said Margaret. "*X!*"

They'd been best friends since the first day of freshman year, X and Margaret, when they met on the track in P.E. Coach Beaupre, stout as a measuring cup, had announced they'd be "trying their groins" at the hurdles, had split the class into two groups behind parallel starting lines, so that each student would race another.

"Is this, like, a *joke*?" a befuddled Margaret, last in the first line, had asked X, last in the second. Plump and freckled, Margaret Clanahan wore a long black T-shirt and black-and-white striped leggings, which X would later learn she referred to her as her Wicked Witch of the Easts. "I mean, *hurdles*? Isn't this a little—"

"Ambitious?" said X. He was still going by Charles Rex then, his shoulder-length hair and six long feet belying his quiet nature. "I don't think I can do this," he'd said, watching as the most athletic kids, who'd happily taken the lead, glided over the hurdles.

"I definitely can't," said Margaret. "Should we just say screw it and run full blast?"

When it was their turn, Coach Beaupre blew his whistle and they did as Margaret suggested. All it took was one glance passed between them, X running high on his toes, Margaret already wheezing, for the giggles to set in, so that by the time they'd reached the first hurdle they'd descended into full-blown hands-on-knees weep-laughter. "OK, folks, let's try to hold it together," said Coach Beaupre, instructing them to get back to the end of the line.

They'd been best friends ever since, and though X had never, until now, officially declared his preference for boys, their conversations tended to focus on those strange and sweaty creatures, and in particular on Margaret Clanahan's deep-seated fear that she'd leave high school having never dated one, then get a brain tumor and die.

"Margaret Clanahan: perennial singleton," she'd lamented on one of their first after-school "dates," over double scoops of Mexican vanilla on a bench outside Amy's Ice Cream. "I mean, it's not like I'm asking for *Hugh Grant*. It could be, like, Rudy, right?"

The Sean Astin movie about the squirt of a Notre Dame football player who walked onto the team and, after years of tireless effort, finally got to play in the last minute of the last game of his senior year, was an obsession of Margaret Clanahan's.

Margaret licked a dribble from the base of her cone. "He's just so *widdle*," she'd cooed. "You have to admit: Rudy'd be nice . . ."

"Rudy'd be nice," repeated X, in a way that left open whether he was saying it'd be nice for him or for her.

No, he'd never outed himself as a boy-lover to Margaret (and she'd never pressed), until the first night of spring break in this, their sophomore year, when X announced he was a fag for Jesse.

Margaret Clanahan would, in the years that followed, go on to become a vocal coach in Houston, marry an electrician, and have children of her own. But in March 1998 she was still a husky musical theater girl, forever relegated to sidekick status or comic relief. Just the month before, she'd prayed the cast list for *Little Shop*, about a man-eating plant, would reveal she'd play Audrey, the female lead, only to find she'd been assigned the voice of the sociopathic Venus flytrap.

Never an Audrey, always an Audrey II was our Margaret, and, like many a husky musical theater girl of that time, she was a little bit in love with her not-so-hetero-seeming best friend, which was why she'd never broached the subject of X's sexuality herself. Still, deep down Margaret had always known X was probably a fag for someone, and seeing as how, while she was stuck in play rehearsal after school, X had been hanging out with Jesse Filkins, she'd sort of assumed it was him. And because Margaret Clanahan was not only a little bit in love with X but also loved X, she snuggled up to him and put her head on his chest and told him that as soon as he came out to the world and she lost thirty pounds (2003, she predicted), they'd hit the clubs in New York City and go man-hunting together.

"So you do anything with him yet?" Margaret asked.

"He started talking about us going somewhere. Like, overnight. But . . ." X hesitated.

"You not ready?" said Margaret.

"I don't know," said X, staring up at the stippled ceiling. "I mean I want to be. I just . . . he's a little strange, right? Like, those pants?"

"Those fucking *pants*," said Margaret.

They sat in silence for a moment, stoned on Snackwell's, and then X made a brief sputtering sound with his lips, the noise they'd agreed on for Coach Beaupre, whose first-light toots, they'd decided, were short and hot, and on the fart-to-poop continuum smelled closer to the latter.

TWO

Those fucking *pants*.

That's how X had first noticed Jesse, how everyone at Travis High first noticed him when he'd transferred over midway through the year: those ultra-wide-legged JNCO jeans, so comically capacious that X had trouble even fathoming their manufacture. Who was in the market for pants like these? Even among the fledgling skaters and tyro Juggalos who favored that baggy look, Jesse's dark blue JNCOs seemed excessive.

They'd met at the start of spring term in Mrs. Eisenhower's Russian I class. X had signed up to fulfill his foreign-language requirement and also, given his mama's occasional side hustle, to poke at the outermost Matryoshka doll from which he'd emerged. ("I'm just glad you're being practical," was all Belinda told him when he showed her the textbook, adhering to one of her favorite maxims: "Don't get to be an old fish if you always takin' the bait.")

Mrs. Eisenhower, angular and curly-haired, spoke the way all foreign-language teachers do: talking with her hands, overenunciating to the point it appeared at any moment her jaw might dance right off her face. For reasons that made little sense to X, the only kids who took Russian at Travis *were* the few Russians, mostly big boys with names like Vitaly and Ivan who wore gold chains and slicked their hair forward. Vitaly and Ivan and X and Jesse Filkins, who entered the first day in those giant-legged pants and a long-sleeve Korn T-shirt, and sat in the back row, two desks over from X, no one between them.

There were only ten students in the class. That first day, they learned the Russian alphabet off a worksheet: the eight Russians ably repeating back to Mrs. Eisenhower their *ya*'s and *yo*'s and *zhe*'s, X self-consciously mouthing these new sounds, eyes fixed on his paper. Not Jesse Filkins. As soon as he got that handout, he flipped it over to its blank side, buried his head in his elbow, and began to draw, scribbling insistently, pressing his stubby pencil hard into the page.

X tried to ignore Jesse, was careful not to stare. He hadn't found school to be an abject horror, even if he'd been pegged a sissy since elementary, even if, on occasion, he was called a faggot or a cocksucker. It hadn't been *fun*, exactly, but X had kept his head down, tried his best to make himself invisible and mostly succeeded, too. When you're an X, you got enough going against you without getting lobbed in with the angry weirdo in the denim pantaloons.

Unfortunately for X, his ability to survive high school had not been factored into his new Russian teacher's lesson plans. Midway through the period, Mrs. Eisenhower announced they'd be breaking into pairs to practice their *pree-vyets* and *kak de-las*, their hellos and how-are-yous. She made the couplings herself, pointing to each student as if it were their own names they might not understand—"Ivan ee Vitaly, Irina ee Elenka"—before coming to the non-Russians in the back.

Earlier in the class, X and Jesse had been asked to choose Russian names. X, not knowing any, had stared blankly at Mrs. Eisenhower until she'd started listing them. She'd paced in front of the whiteboard, offering a theatrical shrug after each option, the shrugs getting grander as she went down the list: "Vsevolod? Vyacheslav? Afanasy? *Bogdan*?"

"Bogdan," repeated X, having decided at the start of this charade he'd have the best chance pronouncing correctly the last one she said.

Mrs. Eisenhower waited for Jesse to choose.

"Vsevolod," he said dully, without looking up from his drawing.

Now Bogdan ee Vsevolod were supposed to practice greeting each other, and, since Vsevolod didn't appear to be relocating—indeed was drawing still, elbow blocking his work—Bogdan moved over one chair-desk, then, once seated, dragged his new chair-desk so one corner of the desk touched one corner of his partner's.

On the surface, they could've been half brothers: dark- and shaggy-haired Jesse and flaxen X, both tall and thin, two crooked string beans off the same rancid vine. But whereas X had almost no muscle, hated the thought of his arms turning sinewy, everything about Jesse was strained and tight: a grubby hemp choker taut below his bulging

Adam's apple, Korn tee failing to hide broadening shoulders, even his drawing style tense and uncompromising.

X felt intrusive watching as Jesse created on the page, but soon Mrs. Eisenhower was coming their way, and he knew they couldn't just sit in silence. "Pree-vyet," he tried, hoping Jesse might relent. Jesse didn't give an inch, didn't even acknowledge X until Mrs. Eisenhower was upon them.

"Kak de-la, *Bogdan*?" he said then, drawing still. He spoke with the same blah intonation as before, until he got to the name, which he spat out bitterly.

X wondered when Mrs. Eisenhower would tell the boy to "get with the program," as his other teachers would all do. She said nothing, just waited for X to respond, and so he said, "Horosho, ah oo teb-ya?" with little trace of a Russian accent, and Mrs. Eisenhower offered an approving, "Mm-*hmm*, Bogdan!" at a pitch bordering on falsetto, and told them to switch roles, gone before Vsevolod had a chance to *pree-vyet* Bogdan, which, with the instructor out of the picture, Vsevolod didn't bother to do.

It occurred to X that maybe Jesse Filkins made Mrs. Eisenhower uncomfortable, that she wanted to avoid whatever scene she thought that boy capable of making. And yet, at the end of class, X had watched Jesse fling his seemingly empty backpack across his shoulder with one hand while hitching up those enormous pants with the other. X, despite himself, had smiled at the absurdity of this maneuver, and Jesse, noticing X's smile, had, despite himself, smiled too, though only for a second. "See ya, *X*," he said.

X felt his face go hot. When he'd adopted the moniker at the start of the school year, he hadn't intended to make it permanent. He'd just wanted to try something other than his horrible given name, yet here we were.

X. X Markham. X Markham the spot. Oh, X. What on earth.

The ridiculousness of it all had come into stark relief in October, when every sophomore at Travis High School took the PSAT and the boy, who'd never determined if X was his first, middle, or last name, bubbled in the Xs next to all three. "Fuck a duck," he said under his breath after he'd done it, staring at the "legal name" the Educational Testing Service would match with his scores: XXX. He'd erased the Xs, then bubbled in the seventeen letters of Charles Rex Markham.

No, he didn't plan to be no *X* for his entire life. Frankly, he'd have been an ex-X months ago, if everyone hadn't adapted to it so quickly. It was weird: poor Katie Barnett had tried for their entire eighth-grade year to get everyone to call her Katherine to no avail, but as soon as Charles Rex said he'd be going by X, X he was. Kelvin Williams at the Whataburger even had a new name tag made up for him:

X

PROUDLY SERVING *YOU* SINCE 1997

"You think I can pull it off?" he'd asked Kelvin at the time.

"X suits you," Kelvin had assured him. Kelvin was thirty-nine and had been proudly serving YOU since '91. He liked that Charles Rex didn't bitch like the other high school kids he employed part-time, figured a boy like that had a long row to hoe without him serving as another weed. "X is mysterious. All-encompassing. X could mean anything! Could mean *everything*!"

"Could mean nothing," Charles Rex had said, and Kelvin had to admit he had a point.

So he was X now, whether he wanted to be or not, X in name and everything else, since the more he thought about it, the less sense it all made.

What was X's gender? X.

X's sexuality? X.

Could X be a woman? On the for side: he felt, in his bones, more woman than man, always had, when he imagined what his adult self might look like, it was not an aged version of the person he saw in the mirror but a woman, that just as a boy knew he was a boy and a girl a girl, so, too, did X know he was closer to the second than the first.

On the against, to use the terminology he'd gleaned in high school

English: a single main argument and two supporting. In the school library, X had found only one book that mentioned *gender identity disorder*, a 1981 tome called the *Kever-Barr Manual of Mental Dysfunction*, and there it had stated plainly that sufferers of this "condition" often regarded their genitalia as an affront. "It is not atypical for a boy with gender identity disorder to report hating his penis."

But X *didn't* hate his penis, regarded it more as an object of fascination, that curious trespasser dangling between his legs. And then there was this: when he awoke in the mornings, it was that troublesome organ which had produced the evidence of his dreams the night before, and when he thought about what he'd like to do to certain boys at school, what he might let them do to him, it was X's penis that responded, and when he responded to its responsiveness, it felt so good.

Later, it would all become clearer, this knowledge that X's outsides didn't fully match X's ins, that the testosterone produced inside that body was a colonizing force, planting hair where it didn't belong, spreading scent where none should've existed, and that, like Gandhi battling the British, to find independence, Charles Rex Markham, X Markham, ex–Charles Rex Markham, would need to drive the invaders from their host.

But this was 1998 in Austin, Texas, *zir* and *they* and *hir* and *them* not yet part of the conversation, or at least not any conversation X was hearing. Only in activist circles were the varied members of what would later be labeled "the queer community" even joined in acronym, and like that breed of poor white whose only real sense of worth comes from not being Black, so, too, did reviled *L* and dying *G* and is-there-really-such-a-thing-as *B* keep their distance, taking solace in the fact that at least they weren't that lowest caste, *T*.

As for anything beyond the *binary*, well, X had never heard the word.

In short, there was no language for X to use to understand himself (or, more precisely, X-self), which was why, in hindsight, he'd thought to give up on language altogether.

See ya, X.

That first week, they fell into a familiar routine. Jesse Filkins would re-appropriate Mrs. Eisenhower's daily worksheets for his artistic pursuits, speaking to X only in those moments when Bogdan and Vsevolod were in the spotlight, Bogdan always taking the lead, Vsevolod chiming in with a well-timed, if dispassionate, *Kak vas zavoot*?

Travis High School was a bustling, bawdy little city, and X had seen his share of kids mouth off to teachers, the occasional fistfight in the halls. Never had he met a boy like Jesse, though, who wielded his sullen weirdness with such effectiveness it seemed to have bought him the one commodity X most desired: a little bit of room.

On the first Friday of the spring semester, X worked up the nerve to ask Jesse what he was drawing. Jesse didn't acknowledge the question in class, but after, as X walked to woodshop, the other boy called for him to wait up, handed him that day's worksheet, folded over, then turned and walked the other way.

X Markham had, by his sixteenth year, reconciled himself to the fact that dating and sex would not be part of his agenda anytime soon, might never be part of it, that he'd die a "spinster," to borrow a word from Margaret Clanahan's dictionary.

What X dared fantasize about (and even this seemed far-fetched) was a kiss, one kiss, and it was his unkissedness that kept him up at night, the certainty that he'd be one of those outcasts who entered adulthood with virgin lips. Entering adulthood an actual virgin seemed, to X, a given.

When, then, on the just-buffed road to Industrial Arts, he opened the worksheet Jesse had given him to find, drawn across the width of the page, a rock-hard dick, X did the only thing he could do. He folded it back up quick as he could, folded it again and again like origami and stuffed it into the back pocket of his Levi's, and spent the rest of the day thinking about that hand-drawn penis, and wondering if that penis was the penis attached to you-know-who.

A bored kid doodling a D? X had been in high school long enough to know that dick scribblers came a dime a dozen in these parts. But this penis, that penis—*his* penis?—was no doodle. It was a veiny behemoth, realistic in its rendering (shading was involved), almost manga-like in its vigor: head bulbous as Toad's from Super Mario Bros., shaft tumid to the point of almost-detonation, nuts so full and symmetrical they could've understudied as the plump buns of a naked woman in a Victorian painting. He'd included dark pubic hair around the base of the shaft, signed it J.FILK in neat block letters at the bottom right.

That afternoon, as X walked home along Oltorf, a Ford Taurus station wagon pulled up beside him, Black Sabbath blasting out the driver's side window, the right side of the bumper smashed in. Jesse Filkins didn't say anything, just reached over from his seat and opened the passenger-side door.

This was before developers had taken over the stretch of South Austin between Travis High School and the Shady Creek Condominiums, where X and his mama lived. These were in the days when the trailer parks on those roads still housed big Mexican families and white retirees who'd spend their afternoons sipping Lone Stars from webbed lawn chairs, not campers retrofitted to serve lobster rolls and shawarma. Oltorf was a semi-scuzzy strip of money-loan stores and fast-food restaurants. Some days, X would pass an old man who rode around on an adult-sized tricycle, selling Good Humor bars from a freezer in the front. The man wore black shorts and bifocals and kids swarmed around him whenever he sounded his bell. X had stopped him only once, on an unusually hot day the school year before. The man kept his eyes on X as the boy pulled a dollar from his canvas bag, seemed to be inspecting his long hair, his fragile features. "Well, if you ain't the prettiest little girl I ever did see," the old man said as they traded cash for ice cream. The man adjusted himself on the bicycle. "Bet on this hot day you got one stinky little pussy." Since then, whenever he saw the tricycle swerving toward him, X would walk blocks in the wrong direction to avoid it.

Now, confronted with an open door into Jesse Filkins's Ford Taurus, X threw his bag onto the floor of the passenger seat and clambered in after it, without considering whether or not he wanted a ride from this person in the first place.

"*Time again to save us from the jackals of the street!*" wailed Ozzy Osborne as Jesse bopped his head to the music. "No AC," Jesse yelled, nodding to the window crank on X's side as X fastened his seat belt.

"Oh, I'm fine," said X. Jesse ignored him, reached across X to roll the crank down halfway. X put the canvas bag over his crotch.

"So you live close by?" X asked.

Jesse didn't answer, only kept bopping. Each time X told him to go left or right, Jesse said nothing. He followed the directions all the way to Shady Creek.

"All right, then," said X, getting out of the Taurus, "thanks for the ride." Outside the car, he watched Jesse lean over to crank the passenger-side window back up. "Thanks again," he called as Jesse drove away.

Well, that was peculiar, thought X. He tried to put it out of his mind, the cartoon willy and its flesh-and-blood inspiration. Was this how boys *flirted*? Did it *work*?

All weekend, as he handed off bags of Thick & Heartys to the hungry drivers of South Austin from the drive-thru window at the Whataburger, X found himself fingering the back pocket of his Levi's, making sure that maybe-Jesse's boner was still there.

The following Monday, when Jesse entered Russian I, he sat next to X instead of one seat over. After Mrs. Eisenhower announced it was time for "oral exercises" (a phrase, X noticed, which always provoked in the boy a slight snigger), Jesse pulled from his backpack a composition notebook, tossed it onto X's desk. "My *oeuvre*," Jesse deadpanned.

"Wow," said X, flipping through. X meant it, too. It was a downright Lolly-palooza in there. Sharpie dicks, colored-pencil dicks, dicks of all sizes but of only one shape: *that* dick, across a hundred wide-ruled pages. "So this is, like, your thing?"

It was Jesse's thing, all right. Dicks in his notebooks, dicks in his textbooks. Take a seat in any stall in a Travis High School boys' room between 1998 and the renovation eight years later and find yourself eyes-to-eye with a Filkins original on the inside door. "Tried tits once but they didn't come out," he confessed. "Guess it helps I've been looking at wang my whole life, right?" He curled his lip ever so slightly: a wink disguised as a smile.

That afternoon, Jesse drove X home again, remembered how to get there without X showing him the way. The next, he told X he was in the mood to drive for a bit, so off they went, too fast down the interstate, the rush-hour traffic not yet begun.

On the open road, Jesse Filkins began to open up. He spoke with the same hostile precision with which he drew. The problem with the metalheads at Travis, Jesse explained, was that they were dilettantes, one and all, had a basic understanding of "nu metal," sure, but no appreciation for their influences. In Houston, San Antonio, there was more of a "scene, y'know? Jam sessions and shit." As for the general Travis population, he reserved his most heated ire for the jocks: "These corn-fed *assholes* think *I'm* a faggot? I'd like to see just one of them last ten seconds in a Wall of Death."

Wall of Death? Jam sessions? Had Jesse Filkins lived in Houston? San Antonio? Jesse Filkins didn't say. There was a lot he didn't say: why, if Korn was "nu metal" and he was more into "old" (olde?), did he wear a Korn shirt so often? Why, if he didn't like *faggots*, was he driving around with what the citizenry of Travis High School had long ago deemed one? Also, re: faggotry: how many avowed not-cocksuckers drew penises all day?

X had never had a boy show interest in him in this way, in any way, really. So, in the spring of 1998, an unlikely friendship was born. Every morning, in Russian I, X and Jesse would ask each other where the restroom was or take turns ordering knishes as Bogdan and Vsevelod, and every afternoon, they'd get in Jesse's Ford Taurus and drive.

If X didn't have work, they'd go all the way up to Cedar Park and back, or down to McKinney Falls, near empty on weekday afternoons, where they'd lie out on a mass of limestone overlooking the squat and tepid waterfall, and talk. Well, Jesse talking, X punctuating these lectures with "I never thought of that" or "What was that lyric again?"

And though X didn't care for Korn or Limp Bizkit, found even the allegedly "more accessible" melodies of Pantera and Jane's Addiction to be virtually unlistenable, though Jesse's intensity scared him a bit, still he liked when their arms grazed as they walked down the halls, feeling Jesse's jeans against his own on the warm limestone, this other body at his side.

Also: for all his excesses, Jesse Filkins did have the ability, on occasion, to see the unadulterated absurdity that was Jesse Filkins. The titan trousers! The profusion of pricks!

Sometimes, as they watched the clouds drift above McKinney Falls, Jesse would go off on the nastiest of diatribes only, after, to sputter his lips and let his head flop to one side, shake like he was having a seizure. Then he'd stop suddenly, sit up like a zombie coming back to life. "*Fuck, man*," he'd say. "Glad I got that out of my system."

He could be playful, too. Once, while Jesse was driving, X worked up the courage to ask what, pray tell, a Wall of Death was anyway. Jesse explained it was when people at a metal concert split into two columns and charged at each other full bore.

"Hope you got better pants for it than those," said X, in a tone he'd learned from his mama. X hadn't meant to say it aloud, was sure he'd gone too far.

But Jesse just curled his lip. "Fuck you," he teased.

"Fuck me, huh?" said X, stunned he'd let himself talk like that.

"Yeah," said Jesse, his eyes glazing over in a way X would later understand was Man for *Doinker rising*. "Fuck you."

Was Jesse Filkins into boys or girls? He used the word *faggot* with the regularity of a conjunction, had more than once referenced Elenka Voskresensky from Russian I as "pussy" he'd like to "slam." He was preoccupied with *real men*: those corn-fed assholes didn't fit the bill, creatine supplements shriveling their ball sacks. "A real man knows you don't plow a girl with your *biceps*." X had noticed that after Jesse made these declarations he'd always pause, as if to give X the opportunity to engage. X never took him up on it. Jesse always moved on.

As for what X was, it seemed as if Jesse Filkins knew, knew without having the words for knowing, and when they were alone, they began to shed their identities as Vsevelod and Bogdan, as Jesse and X, and fall into the roles of Man and Woman.

Each afternoon, X walked out to the student lot to find Jesse already waiting in his Ford Taurus. And each time he got in, it felt to X as if he were meeting someone he hadn't seen just three periods earlier, as if he himself were someone he hadn't *been* three periods earlier, as if a whole new day started each time X shut the passenger door.

"Hey girl," Jesse took to greeting him. The first time he said it, X rolled his eyes and Jesse snorted, but they both liked it, could both tell the other did, too. Jesse said it again the next afternoon, and the afternoon after that, until the phrase was bereft of its leeriness, until the only normal response to "Hey girl" was "Hey you," always said as X fastened his seat belt. "Tell me about your day."

Jesse bitched, and X comforted. Jesse bemoaned the plight of Jesse and it was X's job to confirm it was, indeed, a plight.

The boy, X knew, lived in Travis Heights. X had never set foot inside any of the houses on those lush streets. He'd driven the neighborhood with his mama, who admired its little Austin quirks: front gardens blooming with sunflowers, even the most modest porches bedecked with elaborate gingerbread trims.

X had always theorized that the bedraggled inhabitants of his own condo complex had moved there either to start their lives or to die. There were no teenagers except for him, only adults, young and old. As far as he could tell, the only way out of the place was via ambulance: either as the result of a complicated pregnancy—nothing signaled to a Shady Creek woman that it was time to move like birthing a child, the For Sale sign never far behind the placenta—or else underneath a sheet on a stretcher.

Travis Heights was different. There, some families even had entire pools to themselves, a far cry from the small one at Shady Creek, from which X had once spied, early one morning, their neighbor Dot Meese using a long net to fish out a dead possum. The long-haired guys and tramp-stamped girls who monopolized that pool could spend hours behind its corroded aluminum gate, their drunken revelry invariably descending into a sloppy summit on their hatred for the smaller, shittier Texas towns they hailed from: fuck Waco, man, fuck Texarkana, we in the ATX now, *livin' the life*!

In Travis Heights, they really were living it. Jesse's parents were attorneys, had enough money, apparently, to send him to St. Stephen's, though not so much to stop him from getting kicked out mid-year. It hadn't been one big, bad thing that led to Jesse's banishment, just not showing up or showing up without having done his work, social surliness and that troublesome fondness for peen-art. "I'm apparently in need of an *attitude adjustment*," Jesse had scornfully reported to X, due to what Jesse's mother had diagnosed as "abstract unpleasantness."

Yes, Jesse complained and X did a lot of *I know what you mean–ing*, and because it was Jesse who had the car, it was he who always drove, and because it was Jesse who had the money, it was he who always paid for the migas plates at Magnolia and the burgers at Fran's. And they liked this arrangement, Jesse playing the man and X the woman, both of them too young and scared and horny to consider if these were the types of men and women they wanted to be.

They were drifting into something, they both knew. Sometimes, at school, Jesse would surprise X from behind and whisper nasty questions in his ear. He'd ask them dead serious—*You ever licked a hairy asshole? You ever gagged on hard cock?*—and X would turn and slap him lightly on the elbow, say, "You perv," and Jesse would say, "You like it. I know you do."

The boys in X's life had always treated him *as* a boy, and if they called him faggot or sissy, it was because they'd decided he wasn't boy *enough*. But Jesse treated X as he'd sometimes seen those boys treat girls, as if he were a teacher and X the pupil, endearing but a little dumb. And though X didn't always like it, he did like it, too, for if being a girl in this world meant being debased, well, maybe part of him wanted to be debased, too.

On the first day of spring break, Jesse invited X over while his parents were at work. They'd rented a Martin Lawrence movie from Vulcan Video, and when Jesse turned on the combo TV/VCR in his bedroom, a paused image appeared of a curvy blond girl face-forward, naked on her knees, five undressed men semicircled behind her, only their lower halves visible: one's erect penis on her head, another's in her mouth, the others in the grip of their owners.

"Oh, shit," said Jesse, "didn't mean for you to see that." X was lying atop Jesse's made bed, and Jesse chucked the porno onto the edge of the mattress so that the video's label was faceup—*Blow Bang Vol. 2*—popped the other movie into the VCR.

"No worries," said X, crossing his legs.

Jesse flopped onto the other side of the bed, a denim backrest pillow between them. "Dudes have their needs, right?"

They watched the whole movie apart, Jesse's bare right foot occasionally drifting over to X's socked left one, Jesse's T-shirt riding up so X could see the elastic of his flannel boxers above the waist of his JNCO jeans.

After it was finished, Jesse rolled toward him, and though X's mind told his body not to get ahead of itself, his goose-pimpled neck told his brain that Jesse was leaning in for a kiss.

"Do you ever just want to, like, get out of here?" asked Jesse instead, propping his head up on his elbow.

X pushed himself up so he was parallel with the boy. "Like move to Hawaii or something?"

"Like just get away for a night, blow off steam."

X asked what Jesse had in mind.

"Like, what if we just said fuck it all? No parents, no bullshit, just like, *lived*, like actual adults." Jesse glanced toward his shut bedroom door. "You know that Days Inn up north off 35? By that all-night café or whatever?"

X was never up north on 35, had no idea about any Days Inn or an all-night café. "Yeah, I know it."

According to Jesse, you could stay there even if you didn't have ID to prove you were eighteen, only $19.99 a night. "We could rent some shit on pay-per-view, smoke some weed, just, like, see what happens."

They could see what happens. It sounded so simple. A rom-com, a joint, maybe some light anal? But X didn't really want to go to some fleabag motel to get naked with Jesse Filkins, would've preferred to stay right there on his bed, feet flirting. Besides, didn't people, like, decide if they were *dating* first? Make out a little?

The year before, puberty had sprung up on X like a bad cold. Beneath the loose, striped T-shirts he wore to school, X kept expanding in ways that felt mutant, as if he were having an allergic reaction to his own body. Reddish-blond wisps had sprouted above his crotch and underneath his armpits. He'd wondered about shaving everything, or some things. His pits, his pubes. Would Jesse *want* hair there? Did X?

"Yeah, maybe," said X vaguely. "I'll think about it."

In this, X was true to his word. The rest of the afternoon, it was all he could think about. The pros (sex! normalcy!), the cons (did he even *like* Jesse?), those stomach-churning what-abouts (condoms? AIDS? what exactly was the deal with *lube*?).

This was how it happened that, four hours later, resting his head on a Pillow Person atop Margaret Clanahan's green shag carpet, X, unable to keep it in any longer, interrupted the teacher fart game to tell his best friend that he was a fag for Jesse Filkins, which felt like not the whole truth but closer to the truth than he'd ever given her.

And because Margaret Clanahan loved her friend, she told X he had plenty of time to decide on the Days Inn, no need to rush, and that she'd support him no matter what.

Until he'd done it, X hadn't realized how much he'd wanted to tell Margaret what had been going on with Jesse. Hadn't realized how much he'd wanted Margaret to react as she did. So great was his relief that when X got home, he went immediately to sleep, and woke late the next morning cold and shivery, his body's defenses, on high alert for so long, breached the moment they were given a reprieve.

The flu lasted the rest of spring break. X forgot to call in to work about it—this was how his mama learned about his new name—but didn't forget to call Jesse. They spoke daily during their week apart, and when school resumed so did their flirtation. (Ever-faithful Margaret Clanahan now raised her chin in mock salute whenever she passed the two of them gangling down the hall, but otherwise gave them space.)

At first it seemed that X's less-than-enthralled reaction to the Days Inn proposal hadn't had any effect on Jesse. But as the weeks passed, Jesse began to allude to their getaway with greater frequency, becoming increasingly irritable in the face of X's indecision.

"I'm just so sick of this fucking *routine*," Jesse announced during one of his McKinney Falls tirades. He paced shirtless on that strange lunar landscape as X, shirted as ever, sat cross-legged, looking at Jesse instead of at the Texas history book open in his lap.

"School. Sleep. *Jacking off*," griped Jesse. "Don't you want something new?"

X had hoped Jesse might forget the motel thing and kiss him in the Taurus like a normal person. If he wanted to make out so bad, why couldn't they just do it in his bedroom while his parents were at work? But sussing this out would've required a level of candor X didn't feel capable of, and he instead found himself offering up ever more jokey excuses each time the subject arose. "If you're gonna spend nineteen ninety-nine on me, why don't we just do the snow crabs at Red Lobster?"

The final blow-up came the last day of April. "If you don't like me, you can just say it," Jesse snapped as he drove X home from school.

"It's not that, Jesse—I just—I mean—"

Jesse cut him off. "It was just an idea, OK? Yes or No. And you went with No. Nyet. *X*. Big surprise, right?"

No matter how X responded he knew it would enrage Jesse

further, so he said nothing, eyes fixed on his own reflection in the passenger-side window.

"Talk to me when you're ready, OK?" said Jesse finally. "Till then quit wasting my time."

And that, it seemed, was that. When X dialed Jesse's cell phone later that night, it rang once and clicked over to voicemail. X didn't leave a message and Jesse never called back.

In just a few months, X marveled, he'd managed the impossible: to conquer every stage in the entire life cycle of a high school relationship—from early flirts to sour end—without ever once getting kissed.

Even more X-like: within a few hours of the break, he found himself longing for Jesse, unable to get the kid off his mind. Was it possible he now *loved* a boy who only a day before he wasn't sure he *liked*?

"Fuck him," said Margaret Clanahan at lunch the next day, as X eyed his sorta-ex, sitting alone on the far side of the cafeteria.

"If only, right?" was all X could manage.

Russian I became intolerable. Jesse had moved himself up two rows, and at partner drills now paired off with Elenka Voskresensky while Bogdan got stuck with fat Ivan. The day they learned animal noises was a special horror: Jesse cracking Elenka up with his cock's crows—*koo-rah-re-koo*—while Ivan stared blankly at X, who let out a listless *eeyah-eeyah*, which was how, according to the worksheet, one brayed like a Russian ass.

Four days passed. A week. Now X found himself waking at odd hours and slipping out to the balcony to ruminate from his cast-iron chair above the dead parking lot. He'd lost Jesse because he was scared to "see what happens" at the Days Inn, was scared that an encounter like that would force X to make decisions he wasn't ready to make.

But what if this was his only chance?

He was sixteen years old, for Chrissake. Wasn't it about time that he figured out if he was man or not-man? Faggot or not-faggot? It wasn't possible to be not-man *and* faggot, was it? And what do you call your ex-boyfriend if he wasn't your boyfriend to begin with?

THREE

In the end, X never would've gone if not for Belinda.

At least that's how he would rationalize it, for in the wake of his not-a-breakup his mama had somehow become even more intolerable than before.

They'd long been overly tangled in each other's business, the condo not big enough for the both of them now that X was grown. He was too old to be sleeping on the fold-out in the living room, to have only the bottom two shelves of the dresser in his mama's bedroom for himself. Worse, in X's view, Belinda had loaded down the place with cheap furniture and gaudy embellishments, showy garbage she claimed gave #2E its "dazzle."

This was his number one objection to his mama, that she thought appearances were the end-all be-all, believed that if you looked a thing convincingly enough you were in fact that thing. "These boys coming in for their cuts are gonna think they're at a genuine Paris salon!" she'd enthuse before investing in one of her signature decorative touches. Her most recent purchase had been a "sitting bench" for waiting customers right by the door; it was upholstered in "parchment ivory" and "exclusive to HomeGoods," or so said the saleswoman. After X had pointed out that *all* benches were for sitting, his mama had begun grandly referring to it as the "Diane Miller Home Collection settee."

And though the white leather fold-out on which he slept was fake, the material so thin that on hot nights he sometimes thought the sofa's skin might peel off and stick to his own, and though, during the school year, he had to do his homework on Belinda's cutting table (forever trying to find his reflection in her glass jar of blue Barbicide disinfectant rather than finish his algebra), and though he didn't feel there was room enough in that place to move, to think, to take a goddamn breath, well, "truth is in the eye of the beholder," insisted his mama, though nothing in X's sixteen years on this planet had indicated this was true.

She wasn't a liar exactly, Belinda, but she fudged the facts to make them work in her favor. "Linda Lies," X called them. Whenever he heard one, he'd clear his throat, then raise his left hand, tap thumb to index finger twice—L L—an indication he knew she was full of it and wanted her to know he knew it, too.

"Linda Lies": always small, and usually about him. Stupid stuff, mostly to her customers. An 84 percent on a biology test inflated, in Belinda's telling, to an 89. X being named employee of the month at the Whataburger when it was for the week.

"Oh, you," she'd say, whenever X tapped his fingers at her in the double L.

"What's that *mean*, anyway?" he'd asked her once. "*Oh, you*?"

"You know what it means," she'd said, in a tone that suggested she didn't know, either.

And then there were Belinda's deeper lies, lies for which the double L never felt like adequate retribution. Lies like the one she told Judge Ulbrecht nine days after X and Jesse had stopped speaking, the one that drove X to "see what happens" at the Days Inn.

This was midmorning on a Saturday in early May. The judge had been going to Belinda for his haircuts since X was little, and between the man's preference for coming straight from the gym (in disturbingly thin sweatpants) and his god-awful breath ("He does like his whitefish," Belinda admitted), X made it a habit to already be in his mama's bedroom watching television when he arrived.

X was halfway through a *Road Rules* when he heard his mama, whose voice, till then, had been muffled by the shut door and television, speaking at a volume intended for X to hear: "Girls love that boy, but no, he ain't brought anyone home yet to meet his mama since you asked." Then, even louder: "Waiting for that special someone, ain't that right, C.R.M.?"

The rest of the day, while Belinda offered tequila samples at Twin Liquors, X stewed in silence, and at dinner that night he left untouched the frozen meatballs he usually loved, which Belinda always put individual toothpicks in.

"What's got your goat?" she asked.

What's got my fuckin' goat? he wanted to say. She *knew* X wasn't interested in girls. Didn't know about Jesse specifically, but she knew. Why else would she sometimes whistle when she got to one of those Calvin Klein men's underwear advertisements in her *People* magazine, hold the page open for him to have a look? "Now, *there's* a man," she'd say from her end of the sofa, ogling Marky Mark grabbing his stuff over his underpants. X had never admitted to liking boys exactly, but when she showed him those photographs, maybe he'd blush or say, "Oh, Mama," but he always looked and she knew he looked, too.

Ain't brought any girls home to meet his mama, my ass, thought X at dinner, tapping both feet hard against the laminate floor, trying and failing, as usual, to find the words to articulate his anger.

How could he explain it to her when he couldn't explain it to himself? How could he say that he'd been *seeing someone*, kind of, but didn't know if the someone he was seeing really saw him?

X couldn't tell his mama all that was going on, so instead he opted for what he hoped might be the next most satisfying thing: "Oh, fuck you."

Belinda just sat there for a minute, so unperturbed it made him want to scream. "Well, then," she said, holding up a toothpick-speared meatball for inspection. "Fuck you, too." She plopped the meatball into her mouth.

X couldn't storm out, couldn't get at his mama nearly as good as she could get at him. In that moment, the vastness of the questions before him was too overwhelming, and so X did the only thing that he thought might offer answers: he grabbed the portable phone from its charger on the cutting table, shut himself inside the bathroom, and called Jesse's cell phone.

Jesse answered on the fifth ring. "*What?*" The barely bottled wrath was such that X half-expected Jesse's spittle to fly through the receiver.

"What you up to?" asked X, trying to sound casual.

"Nothing."

"Same."

And though X may not have known, as he'd dialed Jesse's number, if he could muster the courage to go through with it, all it took to push him to it were six words hollered from the living room:

"What you doin' in there, hun?" called his mama.

"So you wanna try that getaway thing or not?" said X.

FOUR

They blasted down I-35, windows open and Anthrax blaring, all the while X experiencing that strange sensation endemic to adolescence, that feeling of not believing something was happening even as it was happening, not believing it was happening until after it was done.

Past Cesar Chavez, past downtown. At MLK, Jesse's hand drifted over to X's thigh, covered in a pair of baggy sweats. X had been so desperate to escape his mama he hadn't even packed a bag, just told Belinda he was spending the night with Margaret and hauled ass out of there in an undershirt and his fuzzy house slippers, waited for Jesse on the curb outside Shady Creek.

Jesse wore a striped button-down, his enormous JNCO jeans traded out—to X's astonishment—for a pair of rumpled khakis. He'd spiffed up the Taurus, too, candy wrappers and empty bags of Fritos no longer stuffed low into the cup holders. All that remained was a black overnight bag, which sat in the back like a small passenger.

"Sorry I didn't get all dressed up," said X, poking at the yellow Christmas tree air freshener Jesse had hung from the rearview mirror. "We goin' to the courthouse or something?"

"*Fuck you*," said Jesse, grinning his grin. (This was all they could think to say half the time, Jesse to X and X back to Jesse, X to his mama, those two neat syllables protean as *shalom*.)

"Yeah, yeah," said X. "Fuck me. Fuck you."

He quieted after that, fearful if he spoke too much the spell would be broken, that what had seemed like it couldn't be happening would be revealed to not, in fact, be happening, the dream of Jesse's lips on his lips only that.

But it was happening, happening fast. There was Jesse, pulling into a well-lit lot off the frontage road, the upper deck of the highway shooting through the sky *Jetsons*-style behind them. There was Jesse, opening the back, and, overnight bag now slung over his shoulder, hustling past the DAYS INN pylon sign glowing so bright X could hear its fluorescent innards buzzing. There was Jesse, moving between the two squat glazed pots that stood to either side of the entrance like the guards at Buckingham Palace, those strapping men replaced, in true Austin style, with agave. And there was X, doing the thing X always did, and following.

A few days after X had started using the ESPRIT beach bag instead of a backpack, a story had appeared in the *Statesman* about a "transvestite" who was beaten half to death for "manipulating" a construction worker into unzipping his pants behind a roadhouse outside San Antonio. It was a one-day story from another city; X would never have heard about it if, that night, when he'd gone to the kitchen for a Pepsi, he hadn't found himself staring at the article posted to the fridge. In its center: a photograph of the victim, Rosario Vega, her face so swollen it looked like a pair of lips had grown around each of her eyes, her chin stained with blood.

"What the hell is this?" X had asked.

"That's the real world is all," said Belinda from the couch in the living room. According to her, the life of a transvestite was one of poverty and violence. This was why Rosario had gotten beat, why she was working as a "woman of the night" in the first place.

"What's a *woman of the night*?" said X.

"It's a ho with a thesaurus," said Belinda, impatient to change the subject. "Just thought you should see it."

X had crumpled up the article, thrown it into the trash. Brushed it off as typical Mama.

The story had stuck with X as all his mama's stories did, like a grass burr on a pant leg, easy to forget until he scraped against it the wrong way. Following Jesse toward the motel lobby, X sensed that maybe he'd been reluctant to go with him because doing so would prove his mama's prophecy correct, that while the regular couples of Travis High went bowling or out to eat, the Xs convened only in shadows: behind roadhouses, inside sleazy motels.

But the Days Inn was not the ramshackle motor lodge way down South Congress that X, who'd never stayed in a motel, imagined when he imagined them. This was not that place, where his mama claimed sad tweaker prostitutes gave blow jobs for twenty-five cents a head. This was another place, a place he'd seen on VHS and on TV. This was the place where a normal, well-liked suburban high school boy—a boy raised in a stately red-brick house, a boy from a John Hughes movie—might take his normal, well-liked suburban high school girl, for the night that would change their lives forever.

X had imagined all sorts of scenarios like these, imagined himself as Baby from *Dirty Dancing* and Andie from *Pretty in Pink* and all the rest. But he hadn't really, hadn't dared imagine he'd *really* be the one, shuffling toward a motel lobby in his wooly house slippers with his boyfriend at the Tom-Cruise-in-his-undies, everyone's-forgotten-Molly-Ringwald's-birthday, so-normal-it-never-occurred-to-him-it-could-happen-to-him age of sixteen.

X knew then that Jesse had been right, that no parents, no bullshit, just *living*, was exactly what they needed. X knew then that he'd give himself to Jesse Filkins that night, wanted to, too, because if a sixteen-year-old X could be the one to walk into that motel lobby to lose his virginity in the year of our Lord 1998, then anything was possible. As the automatic doors to the Days Inn Austin/University/Downtown opened, X felt like they were opening just for him.

They didn't dare touch, or speak, as they approached the front desk. Still, they could feel it now, how close they were. X walked with his hands stuffed into the pockets of his sweats, noticed Jesse had angled his duffel so that it covered his fly.

The front desk clerk was paunchy, his oval glasses flecked with dandruff. When he said it would be $39.99 cash or card and he'd need to see some ID, X steeled himself for it all to fall apart, for Jesse to say "C'mon, X" and storm out, steeled himself for the grim car ride home, Jesse on a tear about how to do anything in this world you needed to be eighteen goddamn years of age . . .

Instead, Jesse pulled from his duct-tape wallet, connected to his khakis via chunky chain, a shiny MasterCard and what even X could tell was some not-remotely-Jesse-looking redhead's probably fake ID. The clerk glanced at the license, then at Jesse, back at the card. "Y'all sure you're eighteen, right?" he said. "Yeah," said Jesse, and the man swiped and slid what needed swiping, sliding, returned the license and the MasterCard to the boy with two magnetic keys.

"How'd you do that?" whispered X, as they quick-walked to the elevators.

"You think some faggot *receptionist* cares if it's a fake?" said Jesse, as if it were the job title that was the slur. He pressed the UP button and the elevator door opened right away. "Guess I have the magic touch."

"Money talks and bullshit walks," said X, trying out a Belinda favorite.

Even inside the elevator, keys in hand, X couldn't shake that *this isn't really happening* sensation. Course, if it wasn't *really* happening, maybe X wasn't *really* doing whatever he did.

It was this sense—that in this place X wasn't X, exactly, that in this place, the rules and the body that had forever constrained him were more pliable than they'd seemed—which allowed him to talk fresh like his mama, to poke Jesse in the soft part between his hip and ribs, another Belinda move.

"You saying I'm bullshit?" said Jesse.

"Maybe," said X.

"Bitch," teased Jesse, poking X in the spot X had poked him.

"Am I?"

"Are you?"

X shrugged and, as the elevator opened onto the second floor, grinned the grin that Jesse was always grinning, the slight-curved lip, those mischief eyes, and said, "We'll see."

Years later, the ex-X Markham would be waiting for a friend at Oilcan Harry's, the gay club on 4th Street, when a paunchy man in oval glasses—glasses flecked with dandruff—would approach the bar and order a G&T. It was only then this former X would understand how Jesse had gotten away with it in '98, how they'd lucked into an unassuming fairy god-daddy, averse to standing in the way of a happy ending. X should've picked up on it at the time, since the man hadn't bothered asking the one question that every front desk clerk always asks, had recognized what X and Jesse would want to see after they inserted the key and flung open the door and switched on the lights, knew only a king would do for those two queens.

"Wow," said X. He'd never slept in a bed that big.

"Fuck yes," said Jesse, dropping his duffel. He did a trust fall onto the bulky floral comforter. "*This* is the life."

The boy turned onto his side so that he faced X, still lingering by the door. "Look, I know I can be a giant pain in the ass or whatever," said Jesse, in a tone X didn't recognize: bashful and sweet. "It's cool, y'know? That you'd do this for me."

Jesse sat up. "I got you something. Nothing, like, *amazing*, and you can return it if you don't like it." He pointed to the small black duffel. "I still have the receipt."

X sat on the edge of the bed next to Jesse, put the bag in his lap, and unzipped it. He sorted through the boy's belongings with the care of an archaeologist mid-excavation: a pair of Jesse's flannel boxer shorts, a toothpaste-smudged toiletry kit, five four-pack strips of Trojan condoms.

"Under all that," said Jesse softly. At the bottom of the bag were Jesse's giant JNCO jeans, and beneath them, draped under his Korn shirt, as if its contents were fragile, a wide, shallow gift box.

X knew what it was right away, would've recognized those red-and-pink stripes anywhere, for though his mama was all about T.J.'s or

JCPenney when it came to the day to day, if she ever had a date night, out came what she called her "thank-you-for-dinner skivvies."

X ran his hands across the embossed Victoria's Secret logo. Jesse had taped a small envelope to the front of the box. Inside was one of those thank-you notes they sold in sets of sixteen at Target, *Thank You* written in red cursive across the front. Jesse had neatly crossed out the words with a thin black Sharpie. On the card's interior he'd written:

TO: X
FROM: JESSE

"I didn't really know what to say," said Jesse.

X didn't know what to say, either. He'd always sensed that Jesse saw him as, if not an out-and-out woman, then at least a known X. Still, it hadn't occurred to him that they'd be moving from unknown to female, from X to XX, so quickly.

Holding the box, X finally understood why Jesse had been so committed to coming here, saw what Jesse had seen all along: that maybe if they escaped their houses they could escape themselves, too. Maybe here, at the Days Inn off I-35, X could be the X he sometimes imagined he was, X in a bra and panties, X nuzzled up to his man, and Jesse, who X was pretty sure was a virgin, too, could be the sort of Jesse who made love not to his faggot boyfriend but to his girlfriend, who wasn't just in the business of losing virginity but of taking it, too.

"You want to see how it all fits?" Jesse asked. He nodded toward the bathroom door. "Or I can go in there and you can change out here, or whatever."

X told him no, a girl needs her mirror. "Gotta see if I'm fairest of them all."

Inside the shut bathroom, X laid the box on the sink counter and, hands quivering, opened it to see what he was dealing with.

He hoped Jesse might've opted for something X could pull off despite not having an inch of tit: maybe black briefs and a black camisole like his mama wore when she was "slumming it," which, in X's opinion, was when she was at her most beautiful.

Jesse had been more ambitious. In the box, under the pink tissue paper, X found a satin bra and matching high-leg bikini panties, both a glossy crimson.

X took off his tank top and slid the thin straps of the bra over his shoulders.

"How'd you know my size?" he called, door still shut, hoping Jesse wouldn't grow impatient.

"Just told the lady my girl was flat as me."

"Well, ain't you a knight-in-shining," said X, arms knotted behind his back. How did anyone have the dexterity to clasp these things? Every time he thought he might've done it, he'd let go, only to feel the air on his back and know he hadn't.

"You OK in there?"

"Oh yeah," said X, trying not to panic. X took the bra off, laid it across the sink. *What's the trick with you?* He took a deep breath, the kind you took only when telling yourself to take a deep breath. X went to try again, an idea taking hold. He put it on backwards this time, without the straps. He clasped it easily, then shimmied the bra around his chest so it was right side forward, slipped the straps back on.

X slid off his wooly slippers, then his sweats and underpants, and stepped into the panties. They rose just over the top of his pubic hair, narrowed into a small triangle at the crotch, a triangle not built for what X carried. He pushed his penis between his legs, knowing he'd have to waddle out if he wanted to maintain some semblance of the illusion.

"You good?" Jesse called from the bedroom.

"Just give me a second," said X uncertainly.

X popped a rubber band off his wrist, put his hair into a ponytail, then, unsatisfied, pulled the rubber band off, letting his hair fall to his shoulders. There was the X X wanted to be and the X X was, and he knew if he spent too much time in that bathroom all he'd see was the latter. Look too long, too close, and he was just X, minus the Y-front tighty-whities that he'd girdled his junk behind for sixteen years prior. But go fast, look and look away, and X could see it . . .

Was it possible to go into a motel bathroom as one thing and come out another?

FIVE

"What you think?" asked X from the bathroom doorway. He'd meant to say it seductively, knew as soon as it was out that he'd sounded too . . . hopeful?

"Wow," said Jesse. The boy had stripped to his underwear and socks and now sat up in the bed, pillows propped behind him. Jesse scratched at his sternum with one hand, the other flirting with his boxers, a couple fingers just under the waistband.

"Good wow? Bad wow?"

"*Wow* wow."

X shifted his weight from one leg to the other. "*Wow* wow," he repeated. "That's nice to hear."

"You're nice to hear," said Jesse. "This bed is comfortable as fuck, by the way."

X had to walk with an almost comic deliberation to keep everything where he wanted it. Jesse didn't seem to notice. "Come join me."

X sat on the bed with his back to Jesse, trying his best to keep his bulging panties out of Jesse's sight. He pulled his legs up and lay on his side, ass in Jesse's direction. Jesse understood and rolled that way, taking X in his arms. X could feel the poke of Jesse's boner.

"You're everything I've ever wanted," Jesse whispered into X's hair. "I'm so fucking lucky."

"*You're* lucky?"

He kissed X in the crook of his neck, a hard and toothy kiss that made X cup his own crotch with both hands.

"Yeah, girl," said Jesse. He slid his hands over X's bra, kept them there. "You like that?"

"Yeah," X admitted. "Will you kiss me?"

"Yeah, you like that," said Jesse. "You like being my girl."

"Keep going," X whispered, rolling his head to one side to give Jesse more neck to nibble. "Kiss me."

"You wanna kiss?" said Jesse between bites.

"Yeah," said X. "Kiss me. Please."

Jesse let go of X, turned onto his back, raised his knees and pulled off his boxer shorts, tossed them to the carpet. X rolled to face the boy and found him prone, his dick forming a near-right angle with his flat belly.

And there it was. X surveyed the specimen, comparing it to the illustrated version he'd seen hundreds of times before. Was it *that* penis, thick as a thermos? Until now, the only penis X had inspected for any length of time was his own. Jesse's was circumcised and stuffed into a fatter package: a wrestler, perhaps, whereas X's might've opted to join the track team, try its luck throwing a small javelin. Otherwise they were . . . not dissimilar?

It was a penis: sturdy, swollen, of this world. What a tremendous relief.

"So there it is," said X.

Jesse raised his chin to inspect it himself, lay back. "It what you were expecting?" he asked. It was the same trying-to-sound-sexy tone X had employed earlier. It made him sound needier than he'd intended. Only made X want him more.

"I wasn't expecting anything," said X, and then, realizing that didn't sound right: "It's perfect."

Jesse's pubic hair was thicker than X's, his scrotum lolling peaceably against one thigh. The boy pushed the penis toward his belly, then used a couple fingers from each hand to make it stand perfectly straight so X could get an unobstructed view.

How comfortable Jesse was, handling himself. He had an ease with the thing that X had never felt with his, and as X moved closer to the boy, he noticed Jesse's eyes were not on X but on that other object of his affection. Jesse was transfixed: a snake charmer charmed by his own snake.

X had never witnessed this before, the way a man loses himself in these moments, turns dumb and malleable. It was ridiculous and unexpected and the hottest thing he'd ever seen, and now he straddled the boy, grinded into him, panties on bare crotch, this not-quite-X feeling the same assertive looseness he'd felt on the elevator ride up, as if maybe it was not the boy but the X with the power.

"You want to kiss it?" asked Jesse.

"I want to kiss you," said X, and bent forward to do it.

Just as X made his move, Jesse turned his head, and so X kissed him on the neck, as Jesse had done to him, licking along his jugular, then gnawing into the flesh under the boy's jaw, Jesse grunting and writhing beneath him.

"Kiss me," said X.

"Yeah, girl, yeah," said Jesse. He put his hands on X's shoulders and pushed lightly, directing X to lick lower down, and because X wanted to please him, and because it seemed like Jesse needed it, *needed it*, X complied, licking his neck and across his sternum and around the few hairs that had begun sprouting from his nipples.

It was wild, to taste Jesse in this way, salt and sweat and Irish Spring, and now they were in a frenzy, Jesse talking low and dirty, X licking harder.

Lower X went, around Jesse's belly button and down his burgeoning happy trail, across the border of flesh and pubic hair.

"Kiss it," moaned Jesse. With one hand he angled his penis so it touched the soft part beneath X's chin. It was warmer than X expected, already wet. X's own penis required constant upkeep and, to his never-ending horror, would give off a sour scent if left unwashed, which, like the other smells that came from X's body, felt more unnatural to X than the boy parts themselves. Jesse's had the same Irish Spring odor as the rest of him, just the slightest hint of something curdled underneath. "*Please.*"

This was not where X Markham had long dreamed of landing that first kiss. Still, it seemed appropriate, X had to admit. Jesse wasn't sketching lips all the livelong, after all. Yeah, it seemed appropriate, and to that point everything *had* felt good, and so when Jesse said please, X consented, and at Jesse's suggestion repositioned himself so that he was on all fours, his pantied backside in Jesse's face ("I wanna see my girl's ass"), and down X went.

A word to the wise for those who have never sucked knob. Smoking pipe is like smoking pot: you probably won't get high the first time. Sure, there are the prodigies, the Little Men Tate of pharyngeal flexibility; the rest of us need our education. No sooner did X go down, only the tip at first, then X came up, a little queasy, not that it was gross exactly, just new.

"Oh yeah," said Jesse, who, when X turned back, had his nose buried in his own armpit. He didn't seem to notice X's tentativeness. Didn't seemed to notice anything at all.

X sensed that this was a test of some kind, not a test from Jesse but a personal test, and that were X to fail it, it would have meaning beyond "On this one day in 1998, I did not successfully make this one guy come in exactly the way he had in mind." This wasn't just X's first time, but maybe his only time, his only chance. So down he went again.

This time he went a bit lower, told himself to breathe through his nose, to count *one* when he lowered his head, *two* when he raised it. *Down on one up on two*, and when Jesse pushed his hips up, the boy's signal he wanted X to take more of him, X kept counting, hopeful that as long as he accounted for each bob, he'd get through.

It was a workmanlike performance, a true blow *job*. Up and down X went, faster and faster, like a plunger. Not sensuous, this inaugural beej. A dozen sucks in, X lost focus, didn't pull his lips hard enough against his teeth, could feel his incisor catch on Jesse's shaft. If the boy felt it, he didn't show it or didn't care, grinded harder, forcing himself closer to the back of X's throat.

Jesse called X *girl* as he went at it—*fuck yeah girl do it yeah*—spat it like a curse word. He slapped X's ass hard. And X, who'd been having fun until the blow job, suddenly wasn't.

It felt embarrassing, and boring, too, X on all fours, erection fading, bra askew. Nightmare scenarios began playing out in X's mind: a thrust-induced throw-up, a runaway fart. *Fuck yeah girl suck it girl yeah.*

Onetwo girl yeah onetwo: Jesse was going too hard now, too fast, jamming himself deeper. X could feel the saliva building. It was make a change or dry heave time, find a way back into it or call it quits, and so from his position on all fours, X did the only thing he could think to, and as he worked Jesse's dick with his mouth he shoved a hand down his panties and retreated into his own mind.

No bad blow jobs in X's dream state. In his fantasy, he was straddling Jesse, riding Jesse, Jesse holding X's hips, rubbing his breasts, Jesse inside of him, biddable and at his mercy.

Jesse thrust and X imagined, and it worked. They began to find a rhythm they'd lacked before. When X imagined Jesse the way he wanted him, he wasn't imagining all the things that could go wrong when he had him this way that he didn't.

Jesse's penis was sloppy with spit, saliva dripped down X's chin. "I'm coming," Jesse groaned, "fuck, I'm coming," and X, who didn't want to ruin those pristine satin panties, who needed, right then, not to be constrained, pulled balls and penis over waistband, and they shot as one.

X wiped his mouth with his index finger and lay back, propping himself up on his elbows, head to toe with Jesse. They'd done it. They'd done it! And even if X had gagged a little, didn't get all of it, still they'd done it and in the end it had felt, well . . . *kind of good*?

Earlier, face-to-face with the bathroom mirror, X had seen it, when he'd looked and looked away, and seconds ago, lost in his own imagination, he'd seen it again, too: an image of X that wasn't X, the not-X that X knew X-self—knew *her*self?—to be.

Maybe there was a way to live normal, to live happy, more normal and happy than X had ever conceived. Maybe there was a version of this person inside him who wasn't Charles Rex or X either, and maybe now X could make that person real.

Sure, Jesse had been a little rough, a little selfish. He was a guy. A man. How many times had X's mama told him that that's just who men *were*? But Jesse hadn't *hurt* him, and X, in turn, hadn't disgraced himself. Just a happy, normal couple getting off together, barf- and fart-free.

X wanted to shower, snuggle. Maybe get some dinner from the vending machine, watch a shitty movie on the free HBO.

But when he looked at Jesse he could tell something had changed. Jesse wasn't looking back at him, was staring at his own belly instead, at the goopy pile X had left there. "What the fuck, X?" he said softly. He ran a few fingers hard over his stomach, inspected them, then wiped the mess on the comforter. "What the *fuck*."

"You didn't like it?" asked X.

Jesse looked up at X, winced and turned away. "Jesus. Put that away."

X didn't follow. "What are you—?"

"Could you not hear me?" said Jesse, louder now. "*Put it away*." He grabbed a pillow and covered his own crotch with it, rose to collect his clothing off the floor. "I mean, just *look* at yourself, X. Look at yourself."

X did as Jesse instructed and realized then that in his post-blow rapture he hadn't covered himself back up with the panties. His junk drooped over the top of them.

"Oh," said X quietly. "I—"

"So you're just going to, like, leave it there?" Jesse hissed, struggling into his boxers.

"No," said X, tucking himself back in as best he could. "It's . . . I . . . Why are you angry?"

It made no sense. It wasn't as if Jesse thought X had been born a woman, parts-wise, or that X had ever pretended he'd been.

"Why am I angry? *Why am I angry?*" Jesse snapped, as if saying it twice might bring him closer to an answer. "For you to fucking . . . This wasn't the . . . You were supposed to be . . . to be . . ."

"I was supposed to be *what*?" said X.

"I didn't pay for this room, for this night, to fuck some *faggot*."

"I'm not a—I—what did you think—?"

"Fuck," said Jesse, fumbling with the buttons on his shirt. "*FUCK*."

X got out of the bed, covered himself with a pillow of his own. If he could just get close to Jesse, make him remember who he was dealing with, maybe he'd get a hold of himself. "Just calm down, OK? It's just me, remember? X?"

"Calm down? Calm down?" Jesse got right up in X's face. "You fucking calm down, all right? *X?*" He was crying now. "You fucking calm down."

"I don't understand your problem."

Jesse grabbed the pillow from X, slammed it with both hands hard onto the ground. "That's my problem," he said, pointing at X's crotch. "OK? That's my fucking problem."

Jesse's fists were clenched. X knew the boy was going to hit him, figured it was better to take a punch to the face than to expose his bulge again, provoke Jesse further. X covered himself with both hands, brought his arms close together.

But Jesse didn't hit him, offered instead that one thing more male than violence: silence.

X had always told himself not to be stupid. Even when something seemed like it was going well, *don't be stupid, X, remember who and what you are*. But on that night, in that room, he'd allowed himself to believe that the ending to his story might be different. Maybe he'd always believed it, because even if X wasn't a boy he'd been raised one. "You can be anything you want to be, my little man," his mama always told him. And it was this—not the bewildering change in Jesse Filkins, not even the threat of violence, but being so freakin' *stupid* as to let himself believe—it was this that brought him to tears.

"It's OK," X tried again. "I can do better. We can figure it out." Why was he pleading? "I thought we were having fun. Jesse, I, please, just sit down and we can, please—"

But Jesse wasn't hearing him. Jesse was in Jesse World, bracing himself against the wall, forcing his feet into his sneakers without untying them. Jesse was in Jesse World: on a tear about what was he thinking, "What the *fuck* was I thinking?" Jesse was in Jesse World, his one palatable option, because the only other place for Jesse to be was in the actual place where he was.

And then he was gone. Up and left, taking the small duffel with him. Out the door, and down the hall and into the elevator, and by the time X had thrown on his sweats over the panties and switched the bra for his undershirt and slid on his wooly slippers and hurried down to the parking lot, the Ford Taurus had disappeared.

SIX

Three weeks later, Sasha Semyonova was born.

Like Eve or Aphrodite, she sprang to life fully grown. Sasha wasn't the result of sperm joining egg, didn't enter this world through the birth canal (a terrifying thought: doc, nurse, expectant dad all huddled close as, from between the legs of a screaming mother pops an adult woman's head). Rather, she came by way of portable phone, delivered by two best friends in the throes of adolescence. Two best friends: each with an ear to the receiver, their foreheads fused like conjoined twins, one's imagination mixing with the other's.

This was the first day of X's summer vacation, the first day of June 1998. Take in the pre-Sasha scene: X marooned on the front balcony, stuck outside #2E. "I need the place for an hour," his mama had told him an hour before. The impetus for Belinda's return to the 900 hotline: a leak in her salon basin, which the downstairs neighbor apprised her of earlier in the day.

Next to X: Margaret Clanahan. She'd shown up unannounced,

as was her way, midway through X's exile. X hoped Margaret would want to go somewhere, seeing as she had a car; as soon as he told her why they were locked outside, she'd insisted they stay put.

"She's doing it *now*?" Margaret kept saying. "Like *right now*?"

Even after Belinda emerged from #2E looking distinctly unsexy in her Residence Inn polo, announced she was off to her next job, and started down the exterior stairs, Margaret—too tongue-tied to offer more than a meek wave goodbye—still wasn't over it.

"A phone sex operator for a mother!" she said, watching from the balcony as Belinda drove her red Camry out of the lot. "What I'd give!"

According to Margaret, her own mother—"Old Lorraine"—was a total prude. "The other day, I asked her what a dildo was and do you know what she said?" Margaret looked a little possessed. "*Nothing!* She refused to answer. I don't think she knew!"

"You asked your *mother* that?" said X, Margaret devolving into ghoulish laughter. X excused himself to pee, leaving the door to #2E open so they could keep chatting.

"If you hear a scream," called Margaret, "it means Jesse showed up and I kicked him in the *nut bag*."

This was how they'd talked about Jesse Filkins in the three weeks since Margaret picked X up from the Days Inn. As soon as he'd gotten into her car, X had started crying, the inward, face-scrunched kind that even best friends tried not to do in front of each other. It was only when Margaret went off about doing damage to Jesse's *nards* that he started to smile, and because X didn't know how to tell Margaret what had happened and Margaret didn't know how to ask, they instead listed all the different words for balls and scrotum they could think of and what Margaret would do if she got her hands/knees/elbows on Jesse's, until their faces contorted into the inconsolable visages of sobbing widows and they screamed out gonads, testes, acorns, *plum*, this last one so hilarious Margaret almost had to pull over.

"I think Jesse's, like, *following me* sometimes," X had confided to Margaret in the cafeteria a week later.

"What do you mean *following you*?" asked Margaret.

"Like in Russian he won't say hi or anything, won't even look at me, but then I'll see him staring at me from the parking lot."

"Like the school lot?"

"Like *my* lot. Like I'll go out on the balcony and he'll just sort of be . . . *waiting*."

It happened twice in the days after the Days Inn: X went outside to leave for his shift at the Whataburger only to find Jesse in his Ford Taurus, parked in one of the spots below #2E. Both times, Jesse drove away as soon as X spotted him.

"That is fucked," said Margaret. "Like *fucked* fucked. Like, *what the fuck*?"

At Margaret's urging, X confronted Jesse in the hallway after Russian, asked why he'd been hanging around Shady Creek. "There's obviously some stuff that's been left unsaid."

"What are you even talking about?" was all Jesse could manage, screwing his face into a bitter swirl. He hitched up his pants and stormed off. "Hey, Elenka, wait up."

Even after, Jesse kept coming, not every day but some days, and now, on this, the first day of June 1998, Margaret Clanahan played lookout on the balcony, so bent on coming up with a new word for balls that at first she didn't register the phone ringing inside or X calling for her to get it, at first didn't quite register who she was speaking with—

When, thirty seconds later, X came out of the bathroom, he found Margaret running in circles inside #2E, the portable phone in one hand, both arms wigwagging violently above her head, like a member of the studio audience who'd just heard her name called on *The Price Is Right*.

Margaret managed to get out that it was *the dispatcher* from *the place*. She brought the phone back to her ear. "Still on hold!"

"The place?" said X.

"Mother Russia!" she bellowed. Then, in a tone one might use to announce their engagement: "They're short-staffed!" That's why the dispatcher had called back. "*Did Belinda want to hop on for another couple hours?*"

"Did you say she wasn't home?" said X.

"I said yes!"

"What?"

"I *know*!"

"Why?"

"I don't know! He thought I was your mom and . . . I panicked!"

"Well, hang up," said X.

"I know, but . . ." Pleading. "Aren't you *curious*?"

"No," said X. "*Hang up* . . ."

"What if we did just one?"

"I'm serious, Margaret."

But now Margaret Clanahan was saying, "Oh god, it clicked. The phone *clicked*. Does that mean someone's—?" And then the girl's eyes went so wide that X had no choice but to bring his ear to the receiver, too.

"Hey there," came a voice from the other end of the line. He had the punch-drunk cadence of a dusty old cowboy. "This Sasha?"

SEVEN

Hang up, thought Margaret. *Hang up*, thought X. The friends regarded the receiver, then each other: *What should we do?*

X had learned the truth about the 900 number when he was thirteen. By then he'd tired of being told he needed to read on the balcony at odd hours while Belinda made her "work calls" ("you *cut hair*," he'd begun to retort). Twice he'd overheard, after he was supposed to be asleep, his mama making sounds he'd never heard her make. "You're doing something bad on the phone, aren't you?" he'd asked one morning on the drive to school.

She told him some men needed company and that she provided it. "In a sex way?" X had asked, and she'd said yes, in a sex way, and now that they'd talked about it, they could stop talking about it.

In the years since, he'd picked up on the Russian thing, but had little idea what happened on the hotline. Before Jesse, X had little idea about most sex stuff, really.

Truth was, despite her job and her history, Belinda St. James was her own kind of prude. She spoke of the birds and the bees only in euphemism, updating the ding-a-lings of her youth to peckers and peters and Golden Tickets. The act itself was *doing the horizontal tango* or *a little bow chicka wow wow*. After making an especially oblique reference, Belinda would follow up with a suggestive *If you know what I mean*. X never did.

The few times she'd tried to "get real" with him, Belinda had stuffed her advice with so many code words that it became almost Yoda-like in its circuitousness. "Lambskin, latex, ultra-thin," she told him once, "but you cover up Miss Tink with something cause that's one fairy that don't want no clap."

Belinda's sex talk came doused in hot sauce or extra-salted. Why couldn't she ever tell it to X plain?

But now here it was, plain as day. A man on the phone. A man wanting sex. In the abstract, X knew going through with it was a bad idea. Confronted with an actual voice—an actual man—he remembered the change that had come over Jesse, how the boy, in bed, had become an animal version of himself.

So X did what all teenagers do when their minds are telling them, to use a phrase from the era, *Don't go there*. He went there, stayed there. *This Sasha?* the man had asked.

"Uh, yeah," X started, then corrected himself: "This Sasha, yes," he said, doing his best approximation of Mrs. Eisenhower's Russian-inflected English.

Margaret dry-heaved a giggle, slapped a hand theatrically over her mouth to stifle it.

"Sure is nice to hear your voice again," said the man, unfazed. "You remember me? Eddie? Out in Buda?"

"Out in Buda?" said X. He looked to Margaret: *Am I doing this right?*

Margaret spun one hand in rapid-fire circles: *Keep going!*

"Yes," said X. "I remember."

"That's nice to hear. I've been thinking about you."

"About me?" said X. He couldn't find any words Eddie hadn't used first.

"Don't just repeat him," whispered Margaret.

"Sure have," said Eddie. "About how young and beautiful you are."

"Yes," said X. A stilted pause. "I am."

"That's right, Sasha, you are."

"I am?"

"You are."

X looked to Margaret.

"Maybe *do* repeat?" she said.

X did as Margaret advised. Eddie from out in Buda said what he desired—"You're a schoolgirl, right, Miss Sasha?"—and X said it back, his accent oscillating between movie Russian and Irish brogue.

They held it together, X and Margaret, the situation too real, too dangerous, for the seizing-on-the-ground fall-aparts that accompanied crank calls to Mrs. Margolin's house or Mr. Gatti's Pizza. This was a quieter rush, their giddiness contained, apparent in the heat in their cheeks, in the strands of Margaret's frizzy hair that had begun to stick to her face, in the glances passed between them.

"Hey, Miss Sasha," said Eddie, "you mind if I take my pants off as we talk?"

"No mind."

X heard rustling, then the relieved sigh of a belt unbuckled, a fly unzipped. "That's better," said Eddie.

X knew from the man's tone that their flirtation was now over, that the change that had taken over Jesse three weeks before had come for Eddie out in Buda, too.

"What does it sound like when I'm inside you?" asked Eddie.

The only sex sounds X knew to draw from were the pretend ones he'd overheard his mama making on this same phone all those years ago, and he tried to go for those. What came out was pained and pornish, too much moan for where they were in the process. X went up a note at the end, making it sexier than he'd intended.

Too much, too sexy, at least for Margaret Clanahan. She separated herself from X's forehead and began walking fast in small circles, *ohmigodohmigod*, shaking her hands as if they'd fallen asleep. It was *funny*: this was what Margaret meant to convey. This was funny, right?

X sensed he should end it there, and might've too, if Eddie hadn't said, "That's good, Sasha," if X hadn't responded, "That good, yes," and moaned again, and on it went, until X heard a gasp, a shudder, and again that *click*. Eddie from out in Buda: come and gone in eighty-two seconds.

X stared at the phone. Had he actually done it? Had it actually . . . *worked*?

"Oh my god," said Margaret. "*Oh my god*." She was wet-eyed, vermilion. "You just made that guy *splooge*."

"We should hang up," said X, not hanging up.

"Like, he *creamed his pants* because of you."

"Let's pretend it never happened."

"I didn't think it would be so . . . *sexual*," said Margaret.

Another *click*.

"Umm . . ." said X. "I think a new one is—Margaret, do you want to—?" He motioned for her to take the phone.

"Nah," said Margaret, plunking down into the salon chair. "I think I'm better behind the scenes, y'know?" She told him he should try again. "You're, like, *really* good."

Hang up, thought X. He brought the receiver back to his ear.

And so the men talked, and X repeated. A few called just before climax, the mere fact of a person on the other end of the line enough to push them over the finish. Mostly, in those opening moments, theirs were the same voices that crackled through the drive-thru speaker at the Whataburger, the same ones X heard flirting with his mama while she cut hair. They were the voices of men, regular men. It was the knowledge of what those men would soon become that kept him on the line.

And though X may have lacked his mama's wit, he made up for it with that willingness to repeat back, verbatim, whatever the man had just said, a trick so obvious it seemed like it would never work, but always did.

His only true improvisation came when a guy with a thing for sex between sisters asked for Sasha's family name. X signaled for Margaret to grab his Russian textbook, still on the cutting table from studying for finals the week before. He scanned the cover for the editor's surname.

"Semyonova," said X.

At first Margaret played along, offering double thumbs-ups when X repeated back an especially lascivious command. Ten minutes in, she announced she had to get going, wasn't feeling well. Maybe it wasn't so funny, after all, hearing the person you kinda maybe sorta loved moaning lustily at weird old strangers. "I think I'm lactose intolerant," said Margaret. They hadn't had any dairy.

"Don't go," said X. She waved him off and he didn't hang up the phone.

X told himself he'd make it up to Margaret later, regaling her with stories of how Dustin seemed "Dueling Banjos"–level country and that Norman Ogden III—this was how he introduced himself—breathed so heavy he must've weighed 500 pounds.

It was all a joke, he'd tell her. Gross and ridiculous. It wasn't as if X was *turned on* by them. God no. But what Margaret could sense and what X would never admit was that the process itself, that *did* turn X on, and as Eddie slapped Sasha's bottom and Dustin worked his tongue between her thighs and as Norman Ogden III held her head to his crotch, it was not those actions that compelled X to keep going but the men's desperation, their desperation a confirmation that how Jesse had needed X, others could need X, too, a confirmation that Jesse's hunger was every man's hunger, and X could be the one to placate it.

What's more, as X repeated back to these men their dirtiest desires, not one of them seemed to think Sasha was anyone other than who she said she was. Did they believe she was *Russian*? Impossible. Still, to them X *was* Sasha, and while he prepared himself for a caller to state the obvious—there was no way he was a grown woman of any nationality—no one ever did.

As the fear of being outed dimmed in X's mind, he found himself leaning forward in the salon chair, elbows braced against knees, and speaking in a way only three weeks before he'd never thought capable of speaking.

"How all you say boobies in Russian?" Dustin asked.

"How you say boobies in Lakeway?" sassed X.

"Aw yea, girl, keep talkin' like *that*."

In this way, X Markham learned to speak this strange new tongue.

"Who this?"

Twelve minutes.

"Of course I call you Papa, Papa. And what does Papa call me?"

Seventeen.

"I *slut*, I *bitch*. Whatever you like. Or call by my given name—"

And on it went—

"*I Sasha Semyonova! I anything you want me to be!*"

EIGHT

The last call came at 4:09 p.m.

"Hello?" said X. No response. "Hello?" X tried again. "Is no one there?"

"Heh." A voice. Breathy, husky. A familiar grunt of a greeting. X had heard sounds like this in the halls at school. Heh, sup, goin' on: said with the lifelessness of the just-out-of-the-tub. The half-formed *hey* of a teenage boy.

"Heh," said the caller, and then, as if X needed further confirmation that he was speaking to an agemate, the caller added, in that same, soft grumble, "Uh, which one's this?"

"This Sasha," said X. An awkward silence.

Every previous caller had taken the lead, X a competent enough follower. But confronted with this shyer breed, X had no idea what to say. He spun in the salon chair, willing the caller to fill the quiet. When the boy said nothing, X asked him what he wanted.

The boy's breathing intensified. He began to snivel like a dying animal. X didn't like the ones who called just before blast-off. A passing thought: *if you make the guy hard, it's phone sex. If he* <u>*starts*</u> *hard, it's listening to a stranger jerk off.*

Another: *if high school kids called the hotline, did that mean they did it with—*

X stood, suddenly claustrophobic. He took the portable out onto the front balcony, asked again what it was the boy wanted to do.

The caller gabbled on, making sad sex noises without actual words. If only X had parroted the boy like he'd done the others, matching those wounded whimpers with whimpers of his own, he could've ended that clumsy caller's afternoon hots and his own foray into phone sex, too, killed two birds with two drained stones.

But X was no longer paying attention to the boy, for there, in the spot Belinda usually parked her Camry, was Jesse Filkins's Ford Taurus.

Why was Jesse doing this? What did he *want*?

Had X only felt anger, or fear, he would've gone back inside. But as he held the phone to his ear and stared down at the Taurus, X felt what he always felt when he caught Jesse out there. He knew he was supposed to hate the kid ("You're being, like, *literally stalked*," was Margaret's not-altogether-unhappy take). But the only thing he hated more than Jesse lurking outside #2E was when he looked down into the parking lot and saw Jesse wasn't there.

Did he *love* Jesse? After everything Jesse had done? And if he did love him, or even *liked* him, wouldn't it be better to just go down there and say it?

So consumed was he with the drama below, it didn't occur to X that his own intensifying urge to talk to Jesse had anything to do with that timorous caller's groans. Yet as the boy moaned and tried to speak—making it as far as *I want*, *I need*, what was *wanted*, *needed* left unsaid—it was as if, in the caller's inability to get out what needed getting, X heard something a little too familiar, each *uh* and *um* compelling him toward action.

X looked down at the Taurus, the glare from the windshield obscuring Jesse's face. X raised a hand: *hey*.

In the past, Jesse had driven away as soon as X stepped onto the balcony. Now Jesse lingered, X certain his wave was enough to start the thaw. Soon the blow-up that needed to happen would happen, whatever needed to be said said, and Jesse would smirk and X, embarrassed, would roll his eyes, and maybe they'd start the cycle again. Flirt and fuck and feud and yearn: a true high school relationship.

X touched his thumb to the on/off button on the portable. If he'd pressed it, that nickering boy on the other end of the line would've heard the dead air of disconnection, and when he tried the 900 number again would've been directed to a different Natalia, Natasha, Sasha, or Sabrina.

But just as X was about to hang up—sure Jesse would get out of the car and ascend the steps—the Taurus began to reverse out of Belinda's spot.

Wait . . . seriously? Had X somehow managed to allow himself to be abandoned by Jesse Filkins *again*? How pathetic could X be? He watched the Taurus disappear from the lot.

On the phone, the boy bleated.

Why were guys always like this, so incapable of communicating like everyone else? X returned inside, shut the door. And why couldn't he just get over Jesse? Just . . . *man up*?

That was the obvious moral to the tale of the Days Inn, wasn't it? Man up, nut up, grow a pair. But in the last three weeks, X had gone in the opposite direction, experimenting in ways he never had before. He'd taken to posing in front of the bathroom mirror, piling his hair high on his head and holding it that way, messing around with Belinda's makeup. The week before, she'd even caught him, though he'd be lying if he said he didn't hear her coming.

What was he *doing*?

Of all the places X could've been born, of all the times he could've been born, he'd been birthed in the most powerful country in the world at the height of its power. Born with a dick in the United States of America, 1982. My God.

What incredible, unlikely fortune!

How many times had Belinda told him that men had the power in this world, that she'd had to work twice as hard for half as much? X had never met his grandparents, but he understood enough from his own mama to know that the parameters on what that child from Sweetwater was supposed to imagine herself becoming were set as soon as she emerged from *her* mama. *It's a girl!*

Three jobs, four jobs. Forty, fifty, sixty hours a week. If she had to show titty, she showed titty. Had to talk dirty, so be it. And what did it get her? A five-hundred-square-foot condo in a sweltering parking lot? A four-drawer dresser she had to share with her own kid?

X couldn't put it into words yet, but he was old enough to understand that you only live once, that entire generations of entire demographics had missed out, lost out, born too soon or in the wrong body or in the wrong country or in the wrong skin.

He couldn't put it into words, but sixteen years on this planet as an X was enough for X to know that these accidents of birth dictated the contours of our entire lives, that in this world, he versus she wasn't just semantics or biology, plugs versus jacks, but how far you could go and how big you could dream.

To give up his birthright? For what? To feel *relieved* when the guy he blew didn't turn around and hit him? To stand on a balcony like some misguided Juliet, still pining for the Romeo who'd abandoned him at a Days Inn?

X knew in the taxonomy of high school how each of them would be classified if what happened at the motel ever got out: Jesse a *dick* and X a *pussy*. Men fought and women didn't. Men didn't tell their enemies to *talk to the hand*, as the girl combatants on *Ricki Lake* did; they clenched their fingers tight into fists.

What was the incentive to be a woman in this world if you could be a man?

In the mirror above his mama's cutting table, X looked and looked away. X looked and kept looking. X saw what he always saw, knew what he'd always known. If you are a thing, you are that thing, and X was it, was that.

And because of what he saw in the mirror and because of what he heard on the phone, and because X loved Jesse and hated Jesse, and felt those same ways about his mama and about himself, when the boy let loose with a high-pitched moan, X countered with a mean-spirited imitation, loud and girly.

"Do you not hear me first time? I say *what you want*?" demanded Sasha. She asked again, and again, the boy's refusal to answer only provoking her further.

Sasha said he was like all the others, too weak and soft to get his girl off. She ordered him to say something. Anything.

More groaning.

"Pa-tet-ic," she snarled.

X wanted to crawl out of his mind and body, let the wild force that escaped his flesh hunt Jesse down like the creature that busted out of the guy's stomach in *Alien*, let his inside self out.

"Do you know how lucky you are to have someone like me?" said Sasha.

"I—" the boy managed.

"But you do *nothing* with it."

"Um—"

"Oh, you think you're such *big* man?"

"I want—"

"Such *strong* man?"

"I want—"

"I ask you one last time," growled Sasha. "*What you want?*"

A spitting sound, a low moan. "I want you," said the boy. His voice was different, deeper than before. "I fucking want you."

"That's it. Say it." *Say it*, Sasha commanded.

Now the caller spoke as if it were *he* who'd escaped *himself*, he who was the alien, busted through the belly of a boy. It wasn't like when the change had come for the others, transforming them into raw but recognizable renderings of themselves. This was a wolf-bit man on a full-moon night, Jekyll hardened into Hyde.

He spoke in an accent X hadn't caught at first, sounding a little like the Jamaican bobsledders from *Cool Runnings*, forever on TBS. In that rich and peculiar voice, he described how he would use his body—his *Black* body, he kept noting—to please her.

Every other guy had used this moment to tell Sasha where he'd put it, each's big reveal the same reveal, give or take a couple inches. This boy's fantasies were closer to X's: tongue on tongue, bodies tangled. He nuzzled Sasha's neck and kissed her breasts and licked across her teeth and lips.

X felt the same sensation he'd felt at the Days Inn before it all went wrong, X transcending himself, becoming himself. He was suddenly, wildly hard.

X put the phone on the cutting table and stripped frantically, pulling off and pulling down, a fisherman desperate to hold on to a catch. He stumbled into the salon chair. "You want me so bad," said Sasha, "how you take me?"

The boy wasn't funny or loose, like Dustin of Lakeway. He didn't have Norman Ogden III's weird imagination, or the easy manner of Eddie from out in Buda.

But he spoke with a rigid precision X recognized from Jesse. He ached in a way the others didn't, ached in a way X did, the line between wanting and needing, coming and crying, love and lust and fury, as blurry as the line between late girl and early woman, between the end of boyhood and the beginning of man.

He spoke with such conviction that X began to see, in his mama's cutting table mirror, the person he imagined the boy seeing. He spoke with such conviction that Sasha began to do the things the boy asked her to, began to tell the boy the things Sasha wanted him to do to her.

Thus, on the first of June 1998, Sasha Semyonova made love to that strange boy over her landline. At times, Jesse Filkins encroached on X's imaginings. He wasn't whole Jesse, had been deconstructed as all objects of fantasy are, a slideshow of Jesseian parts: flat ass, floppy hair, pulsing Adam's apple.

But as they kept at it, those pieces of Jesse began to fade away, until just before climax, when he disappeared entirely. In those last, glorious seconds, X fixated neither on his ex nor his current, his past nor present self. He was focused on Sasha, on pleasing Sasha, on being Sasha, until the deed was done, the phone clicked off, and X was X once more.

NINE

He hadn't planned to call the boy back.

Yet as X scrubbed in the shower after hanging up, he couldn't stop thinking about how good it had felt. Like, *really good*. So much better than with Jesse, those two like puzzle pieces that looked as if they'd fit together, but didn't, no matter how hard either of them pressed.

To experiment as Sasha without any of the complications of actually *being* Sasha . . .

Why *couldn't* it be a thing, or at least a *sometime* thing? All this time, X had thought he wanted a boyfriend. Maybe, he realized, all he needed was a boy.

"Wait . . . you called him *back*?" Margaret Clanahan asked the next day. They were cruising around in her Dodge Neon as X explained how it all went down. He could tell she was trying to decide how to feel about it. "Do I need to do a DTMTTSLS?" she asked.

"Please don't," said X, exhausted from the goings-on of the previous day and not sure he was ready for one of Margaret's classic Don't Take Me to the Second Location Screams.

The intricacies of procuring the boy's phone number revolved around three characters that loomed large in the lives of X and Margaret Clanahan: *69, which allowed a person to dial back the number of their last incoming call. Margaret considered herself an expert in the dark arts of the vertical service code, could've told X for sure what would happen when he tried it, that *69 would direct him back not to the boy but to the dispatcher.

When the dispatcher answered, X knew he should hang up. "There's this feeling I've been getting lately . . ." he told Margaret in the car. "It's like what I'm doing, I'm not *actually* doing. Because *I* would never do it, but then the person that isn't me *does* do it, and . . . it's the best feeling in the world. So when he said hello, I just *went for it*."

X tried to think what his mama would say to the dispatcher, told him that the last caller had been an old friend, believe it or not, they'd gotten disconnected on accident, and seeing as she—"Belinda"—was already doing the dispatcher a favor, maybe he could give her the guy's number, just this once, "a little *tit for tat*."

"All you had to do was say *tit*?" said Margaret.

"It's not exactly Fort Knox."

That night, X waited for Belinda to go to sleep, his urge to channel his brassy Sasha self mixing with a vengeful horniness. Once his mama's lights were out, X burrowed deep under the covers and phoned the boy and, when no one answered, waited a few hours and tried again, his quilted lair heavy with the stench of impending fluid.

X tried one last time the next morning, before Belinda had woken. This time the boy answered, proved as game as Sasha to re-engage. X planned to call him again at 4:09, same as the first day, an ideal time since X's mama was usually away then at one job or another.

"What's he like?" asked Margaret.

"*Real* self-confident. Knows *exactly* what he wants," said X. "Oh, and get this: he's *Jamaican*. Accent and everything."

Margaret sighed longingly. "Black guys are *so* hot."

X asked Margaret if they could stop at Walgreens; he needed to buy a calling card so Belinda wouldn't see the charges.

"So you two are . . . a couple?" said Margaret.

"Not a couple." The boy didn't even know X's name, only Sasha's. "It's, like, *just* for sex. Is that . . . gross?"

"*Gross?* Why would it be *gross*?" said Margaret, so emphatically that X knew she was a little grossed out. Margaret could tell X could tell, regrouped: "Honestly? I'm in awe. This is the most *adult* thing either of us has ever done."

The rules were simple, established in that first call: Sasha would ply and play until her phone-mate's *uh*s and *um*s stiffened into words, until that strange, shy boy—his name was David, X would learn—ceded power from his outside self to his inner one.

Their initial liaisons were efficient as Navy showers, from on to off in under two minutes. Once one had announced a physical attribute about the other it became canon: a surefire way to drive David wild, Sasha learned, was to reference the long legs he'd invented, and nothing electrified Sasha like when David spoke of the shoulders she'd broadened, the torso her mind had made tight. Like master improv comics, they *yes and*–ed each other to completion.

When David told Sasha he was twenty-five, then, she accepted it, said she was twenty-five, too. X had more fun inhabiting a grown-up anyway, far from the scent and sweat of high school. Even more titillating, David claimed he, like Sasha, lived in Austin, an assertion X sort of doubted (what area code was 617?), but that lent new heat to the proceedings.

In the beginning, it was simple enough for X to contain her. Sasha would evacuate the moment they'd finished, the only physical remains of her wiped up with a Kleenex or flushed down the toilet. But after a few weeks of slipping Sasha on and off as easily as Sasha might a fur coat, X found that, like the odor from Belinda's haircare products, his alter ego had begun to linger.

It started one afternoon when Sasha invited David to play the question game after sex. Favorite movies, favorite food. This became a regular thing. Sasha always did most of the talking, David painfully shy post-hookup. She offered tidbits from the drive-thru, complained about her "slobs of sisters." He managed to convey that he worked at a nursing home, was pursuing his true passion—boxing—on the side.

These little chats failed to satiate either's growing appetite for the other. Sasha and David added early-morning and late-night sessions to their routine: before Belinda had risen or after she'd gone to sleep. X would do it in the bathroom, water running at full blast to mask the noise. He was pretty sure David sometimes did this too.

"Who was your last guy?" David asked one night after they'd finished, Sasha splayed out on the floor next to the tub. She told David about Jesse: "Some asshole." Sasha explained how after they broke up, he'd hung around her parking lot like a creep. "He only stop when you appear." This was, strangely, true. X hadn't seen Jesse once since David entered the scene.

"Would he hurt you?" asked David.

"I hope not," said Sasha. "Would you protect?"

"Course," said the boy. "I'd never let anyone hurt you."

Soon, Sasha was surfacing off the phone, too.

During the day, when X wasn't working and needed to be out of the house, he roamed the land with Margaret Clanahan. If what happened on the hotline had created a minor gap in their friendship, Sasha proved a capable filler: a constant conversation piece, their mutual imaginary friend. Now they spent their free hours driving to thrift shops by UT and cutesy clothing stores up north. There, they'd suck down Frappuccinos and outfit Sasha in their minds.

They wrote her biography anew each day, depending on where they landed. At a bohemian-themed boutique on the Drag, Sasha became a patchouli-ponged fortune teller who lived deep in the Hill Country and dressed like a gypsy: jangly bracelets and hammock-like shawls she'd crocheted herself. In a funky vintage place off Airport, they found her a high-waisted peplum swimsuit in a gaudy floral pattern. Once-wild Sasha had settled down in the 'burbs, spent her afternoons eyeing the pool boy from her kitchen window. Her hairy-backed husband had left her sexually unsatisfied: he was too busy breaking bones for the Russian mob.

And if none of these Sashas matched X's conception of grown-up X—if he couldn't imagine his future self reading tarot in Wimberley or keeping house in Round Rock—still it felt good to try on these varied personas, to transform into someone so sturdily defined.

X had never wanted to be his mama, but hers was a language he knew how to speak, Belinda's shakes and shimmies like markers on a map, leading him closer to his next port of call. Sasha was Belinda supercharged, her traits the same as the bangles and ear cuffs X and Margaret would play with at Claire's. To be tried on, tossed back, occasionally kept and incorporated.

"Do you ever feel like a man?" X asked Margaret one morning. He was still high off Sasha's fumes, hadn't meant to be so blunt. This was in the Dillard's at the Barton Creek Mall, where they were costuming Sasha for what they called Dallas Date Night.

"God no," said Margaret, sorting through a rack of low-cut dresses. "Can you imagine *me* with a dick? It'd be stumpy. And *clammy*. Oh my g—" She caught herself, realizing her friend's question might've had more weight to it than her response. "I mean . . ." She spoke gingerly. "Do you ever feel like Sasha? Like, *really* feel like her?"

X didn't answer, and they continued to sort in silence.

"*Booyah!*" said Margaret suddenly, pulling a slinky red number off the rack and holding it up to X. "This is *so* Sasha," she said, which X assumed was Margaret's way of changing the subject.

That afternoon, though, as they lay in her bed watching *Rudy*, Margaret Clanahan announced her nails looked like shit and got up to get a bottle of Wet n Wild from her desk drawer. "Your nails always look like shit," called X.

"Let's do yours instead, then," said Margaret, making no effort to conceal that this had been her plan all along. "Gimme," she said, sidling up to him on the bed.

"Margaret," protested X.

"*Gimme*," said Margaret, grabbing for his hand.

The color was a shimmery sapphire, Denim Chrome. X would've preferred something less in-your-face. Still, after they'd finished and returned to the movie, X couldn't stop extending his fingers to marvel at them. "What you think?" he asked Margaret.

"You look like one bad bitch," she said softly.

TEN

David confessed he wasn't from Jamaica just after Fourth of July weekend.

Since X had inquired about—and David had confirmed—his Jamaicanness during their second encounter, X hadn't given it much thought. David's accent, like Sasha's, was inconstant, his unaroused voice the grumble of every boy. As for the country David apparently *was* from, X didn't know one thing.

"Where's Haiti?" X asked his mama the morning after David's confession. They were in the frozen desserts aisle at H-E-B, Belinda squinting at the dietary facts on the back of a tub of Blue Bell, pretending to calculate if she could get away with it.

"What you need to know about *Haiti*?" she asked, chucking the Blue Bell into the cart.

"There's a new guy. At work," said X carefully. "He's from there."

"Haiti, huh?" She continued down the aisle. "He handling *food product*? I hope he's wearing gloves. That place is—"

"You been?" asked X, following behind.

"To *Haiti*?" said Belinda. "Heeeell to the no." She pronounced *hell* like *hail*. According to Belinda, Haiti was the worst country in the world. Hail on Earth. Stick children so hungry they'd gone potbellied. The scourge of AIDS. "I'd say I was from anywhere before I said Haiti. *Anywhere*."

No wonder David had claimed he was from Jamaica. Sasha didn't bring it up again.

If they avoided discussing David's origins, the same couldn't be said of his race. Nothing turned David on like referencing his body parts, his *Black* body parts, and the wild arousal this provoked in him turned X on, too. Sasha would repeat back whatever he'd said—turning his *I*'s into *you*'s, saying *Black* where he'd said *Black*—and each time she did the boy would groan in pleasure, and so she'd do it again.

X didn't *think* this was racist. Sasha was following David's lead, after all. And even if it wasn't David's skin that got X going—and even if it felt a little weird to be pretending that it was—wasn't the attractiveness of Black men just conventional wisdom?

Black guys are so *hot*, Margaret had said when X first described David. X's mama sometimes talked this way about Black guys, too. Smokin' hot. Fine as hell. More than once, Belinda had told X she even felt God had *intended her* as Black, "given my resilience in the face of adversity."

The ways of Black folk was a subject on which Belinda considered herself something of an expert. "The Afro-American culture is rich rich rich," she liked to say, usually when *Sanford and Son* came on Nick at Nite. Her best friend at the strip club had been a Black girl named Candy—"biggest areolas you ever did see"—and Belinda had been with a Black man for a brief spell in the eighties, a mechanic named LeFrank Bufkin, whose name she now invoked only during times of nationwide racial crisis.

"I don't want to say LeFrank would've done anything like *that*," she declared during the O.J. trial, "but after what we've put them through, *historically*, there is some untapped anger that needs to be explored." (X's mama saved her real venom for Nicole Brown. "Football player-cum-actor going with *that* two-bit piece? Guess Orenthal James just never met me!")

As for Black people coming around the house for haircuts, well, *prejudice* wasn't the reason none ever did, Belinda had assured X the few times the subject came up, though broadly speaking she did feel that letting Black folk into #2E might put her at risk for anonymous HOA complaints from certain downstairs neighbors. "The real problem is I just don't know what to do with that *ethnic hair*," said Belinda. Different textures, different products. "I just tell 'em, uh-uh, honey, that hair's too gorgeous for the likes of me."

X had always sensed there was a fontanelle-like softness at the center of this argument, as if, were he to poke at it too hard, his finger might just bust right through. "So you'd be fine with me dating one, right?" he'd asked her once, as she sat on the couch, gawking at a shirtless Tyson Beckford in her *People*.

"Boy, don't start with me," she'd told him, not even looking up from the magazine. "You got enough problems as it is."

The only Black person X knew well in his own life was his manager at the Whataburger, Kelvin Williams, who'd always looked out for him. The few times X had allowed himself to consider how Kelvin would feel if he ever learned the way Sasha talked, well, it made X try hard not to think about it.

But the truth was not thinking about Kelvin was easy. Not thinking about *anyone* else was easy in the summer of 1998, the summer X left X behind.

ELEVEN

The announcement came without warning.

Belinda's longtime haircutting client Judge Ulbrecht and his wife, "the Judgess," were off to the coast for a night in four weeks' time, had asked her to stay over and watch their cats. She'd agreed, which meant X would be responsible for #2E while she was away. Belinda said it so casually—her exiting the condo, X entering, "Oh, by the way . . ."—that the shock of it didn't hit him until after she'd shut the door. His mama hated cats.

That wasn't the only weird part. It was early July: Why was she telling him so far in advance? Also: couldn't cats be left for a day or two? Whatever his mama was up to, X doubted it involved any of the nouns she'd used in explaining her impending absence. Were it any other summer, X would've followed up with the obvious: *Is he cute?* In this summer of David, he didn't question this incredible, improbable turn: the promise of a mamaless night.

Belinda told X; Sasha told David. *But then the person that isn't me* does *do it, and . . . it's the best feeling in the world.*

X didn't know if they'd go through with it, only knew that after Sasha gave David the date and time (August 8, 9 p.m.) and address (X's *actual* address!), they had the wildest session of their lives, the kind of sex that, upon completion, doesn't curtail horniness but leads to more of it. X had less than a month to prepare.

That night at Margaret Clanahan's, the friends dug deep in Margaret's crusty Ziploc bag of pancake makeup and expired lipstick, which, before then, came out only when she was about to go onstage.

A smear of lip gloss, maybe something subtle around the eyes: this was the future X who X imagined. But understatement would've raised the stakes too high for those two, made it all too real. Instead, he sat on the closed toilet in Margaret's bathroom and let her transform him into the suburban mob wife they'd imagined in the gaudy floral swimsuit.

They approached this act as if it were a summer diversion, *just for fun*, for reasons psychological and practical. Margaret rarely wore makeup herself, was more face painter than cosmetician. "I'm *so bad* at this," she declared midway through.

"No, you're not," said X, trying to hold still. "Anyway, who cares?"

Who cares? *Who cares?* Not them, they told themselves, even if Margaret's hands trembled as she finished with the brow brush, her eyes wet in the same way they'd been during the phone sex: *This is funny, please pretend with me that I am finding this funny*. Not them, even if, after Margaret finished, X held the hand mirror so tight his nails dug into his palm as he examined every painted inch.

Good Lord. Margaret *was* bad. She'd slathered on the cherry red lipstick, raised his eyebrows high as a cat from *Cats*.

Still, they kept at it: the next day and the day after, these experiments becoming part of their routine. And if each understood this process was important to the other, Margaret intuited X's motivation better than X intuited Margaret's: that this was her chance to get this right, that she *had* to get this right, because her inability to make X up correctly was a reflection, in her view, not of X's imperfect womanhood but of her own.

Together in those dog days of summer 1998, X and Margaret Clanahan figured out how to wave their mascara wands and work Margaret's mother's terrifying eyelash curler. X showed Margaret how to do eyeliner as Belinda had showed him the Halloween before, and together they experimented with concealer, both spellbound as their freckles (hers) and zits (his) disappeared. Margaret took to concealing one side of her face, leaving the other unadorned, like Two-Face in *Batman Forever*. "Best Actress," she'd say, turning toward the mirror so only her unfreckled side reflected back. She'd turn her head the other way, only freckles showing. "Best Supporting."

Always, they had to make clear they were just messing around before getting real. But after the giggles and the two-facing, get real they did, Margaret working on X and X on Margaret and, as the days progressed, both standing in front of the sink top, working on themselves side by side.

They'd paint their lips or lashes and talk about sex stuff, not in the way they used to, speculating about Mrs. Margolin's o-face or debating *taint* versus *chode*. This was the kind of sex talk that couldn't have happened if they weren't doing an activity also, something to occupy their eyes and hands.

What did it feel like, to grow breasts? To have cramps? To bleed?

How big were penises, *really*? Were they ever *too* big? Like didn't-fit big?

How bad would it hurt, exactly, the first time?

TWELVE

And slowly Jesse faded.

He'd still come up on occasion. Sometimes, driving around town, Margaret would ask X how Jesse's *thing* compared to various candies. Was it wider than an Airhead? Longer than a Twix? "*Jesse*," she'd always scoff when they were finished talking about him. She'd say his name like others might say *Jesus* after hearing some vile story on the news.

Jesse. It was weird how much real estate he'd taken up in X's life until the start of summer break. X still hadn't seen the Ford Taurus since then; now he'd often go whole days without wondering about the kid's whereabouts.

Even so, he sometimes *did* wonder: Where had Jesse gone?

Later, there will be more people in X's life like Jesse, as there are in all our lives. Exes, former colleagues, friends we've lost touch with or fallen out with or drifted from. At sixteen it was still a novelty. Jesse Filkins: *a person from my past*.

It felt nice to have a past. A past implied intrigue. A past suggested *a story to tell*. A past meant the present was different.

But what X had not yet learned in the weeks leading up to his fateful date with David was that even when change is fast it's slow. Breakups don't stick and must be repeated; fallings-out are interrupted by halting attempts to fall back in. Feelings linger, exes linger. Even the gone are still with us, passing down features to faces, gifting their progeny with wealth or poverty, cherished heirlooms and genetic conditions, mostly-bad ideas.

Leave a romance, leave your country, leave your body, leave this world: the consequences of your foibles and your furies and your passions remain.

X will not be X forever. But the next iteration will inherit the hope and the heartbreak and the history of this one. The memories of this one. Of David, of Jesse. Of that summer of becoming.

Nothing's ever as dead as it seems.

Jesse

BELINDA CAUGHT JESSE THE second week in July.

She'd known something had been going on in that parking lot. Twice in May she'd walked in on The Sixteen-Year-Old peering out the blinds like he was waiting for someone. Both times she'd asked what he was doing. "What are *you* doing?" he'd countered.

Then, coming home from late-night karaoke on a Wednesday at the end of June, Belinda had found a Ford Taurus in her parking spot. Inside was a shaggy-haired kid staring up at #2E. He drove away when she signaled the space was hers, and Belinda wouldn't have thought much of it except it happened the next Wednesday, too.

Even then, she might've let it go if it weren't for everything else going on with Charles Rex. The naked lipstick incident, the "fuck you" meatball dinner. How he'd started waking and showering at the ass-crack of dawn before Belinda's alarm even went off, was always angling to go to bed early.

The final straw came one evening in early July. Belinda got off her shift at the Residence Inn to find her boy had cleaned #2E bottom to top, cooked mac and cheese for dinner. "What I do to deserve all this?" said Belinda, collapsing onto the couch as Charles Rex finished up in the kitchen.

He was chattering away about how a guy's car had broke down in the drive-thru lane at work. It wasn't until he set the food in front of Belinda that she noticed his fingers, inexpertly painted a shimmery blue.

Belinda waited for her son to wave them in her face, say, "What you think?" in that tone he used when he wanted to get a rise of her.

"Gummed up the whole line for an hour," he said instead, grabbing his own bowl and joining her on the couch. "So," he said, digging into the macaroni. "How was your day?"

"Mm-hmm," said Belinda. "Mm-hmm."

"You OK?"

"Oh, I'm fine. Had a good day, good day . . ." Belinda finished her meal without saying another word.

Belinda didn't have much to say the rest of the week either. She was saving up for the Wednesday following, when, again returning from late-night karaoke, she left her car in guest parking near the front entrance, walked up to the Ford Taurus idling in her own spot, knocked on the passenger-side window, and, before the driver had time to respond, let herself in through the unlocked door.

"And who the fuck are you?" she said, plopping down next to him.

"Jesse," said Jesse, eyes fixed on the windshield, and Belinda said, "Jesse, are you the reason my child is workin' me to my last nerve?" and Jesse said, "I don't know," and Belinda said, "You wouldn't, would you?" and then explained she had a "hypothesis" about the happenings of the last few months. "You want to hear it?"

Jesse said nothing. Belinda said nothing. "Whatever," said Jesse, eyes still averted, and Belinda knew then that her hypothesis was correct.

"I've seen you here on *multiple occasions*, seen my son hoping to see *you*." This got Belinda thinking that perhaps the boys had been "an item," and their breakup was the reason Charles Rex was "acting out" in ways she didn't much care for. "So maybe instead of sitting in this Mom-mobile like a little b, you could right this train before I throw myself in front of it."

Belinda told Jesse she was going out of town for one night only: August 8. (Upon learning Belinda couldn't cut hair for the foreseeable future on account of her leaking salon sink, Judge Ulbrecht's wife had called and offered her $75 to cat-sit on that date. At first Belinda had turned Dolores Ulbrecht down—it was charity, basically—but in light of recent events, she'd reconsidered.)

The plan, Belinda explained, was simple. If Jesse wanted a second chance with her son, he was to follow her instructions closely. First, he needed to quit lurking around the parking lot like a sex pervert. Second, a wash and cut over at SportsClips would do him good. On the "night of," he was to pick up some tulips at H-E-B ("you can save roses for when you also buyin' rubbers, which will *not* be that evening, am I getting through?") and get his skinny ass up those steps to apologize, preferably in something other than the pioneer woman's skirt he was currently wearing. ("I know you think you look tough, honey, but what you really look like is Dr. Quinn, Medicine Woman.")

She closed with a requisite *If you hurt my child again I'll scalp away that and cut off those* and out she went and out Jesse drove and out Jesse was, just like that.

How had she figured all that out, Jesse wondered in bed that night.

He'd gone to Shady Creek that first time with the intention of apologizing, but facing X meant facing Jesse, so he'd sat there like an idiot instead, imagining himself climbing the steps two at a time, tapping lightly at the door, admitting he knew he'd acted badly but maybe, I dunno, we could start again?

Jesse liked that image of himself, which was why he kept coming back, each time telling himself this was the time, each time wimping out. The worst had been when X had waved at him from the balcony. Jesse knew that was his chance, knew he'd blown it, and from then on had only indulged in his stupid fantasy from behind the wheel of his car when he knew X wouldn't be looking for him: at night.

He spent his daylight hours in his room, trawling internet chat rooms for cybersex with other guys. He'd type one-handed, his pants so stupendous that unbuttoned and shoved down they still almost came up to his knees. His dad liked to say that Jesse's JNCOs were a sign of how "out there" he could be. Really they'd been the boy's attempt to mask his true "out there" nature, to wrap himself in a recognizable high school form. Jesse wanted to be normal, always had, and if he couldn't resist his urges to log on, then at least he'd figure out what constituted normal in those rooms, be that.

Online, he'd abandon his JNCOs for other costumes: the soccer shorts of a dude in the locker room, the scrubs of a doctor who required his patients to strip down. He'd try on the guises of soldier and student, frat bro and leather boy, all of whom, inexplicably, sounded the same once they got going, the same as everyone else in those rooms. Ensconced in that land of faceless guys, where professed Division I athletes from towns without colleges wrote, without irony, that they were interested only in "real men," Jesse could hunt for hours. But he never felt like he was with the right person, in the right room. X was the closest Jesse had come to what he wanted, and he'd lost him.

But what *was* X? What was Jesse?

That had been the best part about what they had going in the spring: they didn't talk about what they were, they just *were*. With X's mom, it had felt a little like that again. "Y'all were an item," Belinda had told him. As if it were the most natural thing in the world.

Jesse always assumed he'd keep his sexuality a secret. Belinda had, without knowing she was doing it, suggested a different path forward. It was only a nudge, but only a nudge was needed, and in the weeks between Jesse's encounter with Belinda and "the night of," he embarked on a reinvention as audacious as X's into Sasha.

Jesse got a haircut as Belinda suggested, ditched his pants for a pair of Abercrombie cargo shorts his own mother had bought him the summer before.

In the afternoons, he started to visit the places he'd gone with X. McKinney Falls, desolate during the school year, was a scene in the summer, and he took to hiking away from the crowded water, wandering the dirt path to the campgrounds, Discman in his cargo pocket, headphones on.

Cedar elms and Mexican plum trees separated the campsites. Walking past them, Jesse felt as if he were changing the channel every few yards, every site its own universe, intricate as the inside of a snow globe. He liked how the inhabitants of each world seemed oblivious to the existence of neighboring planets, the tanned and Teva'd girls relaxing in their fold-out chairs unaware of the struggling couple next door, a mess of poles and pegs and groundsheet, too caught up in their mutual resentment to pay any mind to the Mexican family one site over, picnic table piled high with foil pans of meat and beans, with frosted cake and bags of Ruffles.

What would it be like if Jesse and X laid claim to their own plot, too? Jesse would assemble the tent and, after, sun still out, they'd climb in and lie atop their sleeping bags, staring at the trees through the polyester filter. At sunset, they'd sit in matching camping chairs, palm in sweaty palm.

When Jesse shunted aside all his unanswered questions about who they were, he could see it. See them. And if the problem with this sort of imagining was that it was never as easy as actually *doing*, without the imagining who would think to try?

In that summer of 1998, shorn of shag and shorn of JNCOs, Jesse Filkins became a lighter version of himself. Each day he was powered forward by the promise he'd made to Belinda, and by his vision of that promise fulfilled. He'd stay away from the Shady Creek Condominiums until the night of August 8, and there and then he'd make it right.

August 8, 1998

MARGARET CLANAHAN ARRIVED AT 6:21 p.m.

They peered into the oval-shaped makeup mirror that sat atop Belinda's vanity, X's face magnified by five. X, seated with a towel wrapped under his armpits, did his makeup as Margaret stood behind, hands on knees like an umpire. "You look *so good*," said Margaret once he'd finished. "It's perfect."

"Margaret," X said. "This isn't, like, the end of our friendship."

"I know that. Of course I know that! I'm fine. I'm *thrilled* for you. I just—"

X knew what was coming next. He saw it in her putting-on-a-strong-face, as if she were preparing to send X off to war. The *are you ready* and *is it safe*, the *I don't want to see you hurt*.

"I'm gonna get dressed," said X. He went to the bathroom, shut the door almost all the way: enough to let Margaret know he was annoyed but not so annoyed he wanted to stop talking.

It hadn't seemed like a dumb idea when X proposed it a month before. Everything had felt so natural that summer. Experimenting with David, with Margaret. With each passing day, X felt his limbs getting looser, felt himself shedding more of his X-ness, coming closer to the underneath.

At first, X doubted it would actually happen. But the possibility had set both X and David off, turned them both on. *See you soon*, they'd tell each other before hanging up. Repeated and repeated, until a wish began to sound like a promise.

X would've preferred to stay in sweatpants and an undershirt, to keep it low-key in the way he had in those early days with Jesse. Still, he understood the rules he'd established with David, knew what was expected of him, had seen, with Jesse, what happened when one met those expectations, and what happened when one didn't.

And so, back into the bra and panties Jesse had given him three months prior, into the slinky red Dallas Date Night dress, a gift from Margaret. "You shouldn't have bought this," called X. "It's too much."

"We could go and return it," tried Margaret.

Through the door, X assured Margaret he'd thought this through. David knew. Knew *something*. That Sasha wasn't Russian, maybe that she wasn't *she* in the way X had presented her. Even if he didn't know, and even if it seemed like he wouldn't be happy when he found out, Sasha would Sasha her way out of it. She'd get him naked while she stayed clothed and wrap her hand tight around him like a fist, or she'd use her lips, extrication begetting extrication.

"That doesn't sound like you," said Margaret.

X couldn't explain it. "It's different when I'm her."

Back in his mama's bedroom, X let Margaret attend to him. She adjusted the straps on the dress, tousled his hair. *Beautiful*, she kept saying under her breath, like a ballet instructor offering praise without wanting to disrupt her students' flow.

X didn't feel beautiful. He knew his shoulders were too broad. Kept tugging at the hemline of the dress, wishing it ended closer to the knee. "Why did I tell him I was a 36D?"

"So he'll be here at nine, right?" said Margaret, even though X had already told her that. "Promise me, no matter what happens, you'll call."

"If we get to the point of *doing it* doing it, is that like a *here* thing"—in his mama's room—"or do you think I ought to make up the fold-out with new sheets?"

"*Promise* me."

"Oh, Margaret, you know I will."

"And if he seems sketchy *at all*, you remember our code for *I'm in trouble*—"

"'*Just calling to see if you remembered the Depends for Old Lorraine*.'"

"God, you're gorgeous," said Margaret. She gave his shoulders a final squeeze. "Personally, if it was between having sex on my parents' bed or literally offing myself?" Margaret Clanahan put an invisible knife to her neck and slowly slit her throat.

It was only after his best friend left that X could admit to himself maybe this wasn't the best idea.

He'd invited David over in the moment, but as the actual moment approached, the evening had taken on a significance way beyond what he'd intended when Sasha told David *the shadow of the blue moon now shines upon us*.

X had always assumed his outside self *was* his self, his inside self the fantasy. But what if the way he held his head low as he skulked the hallways, how he always looked past drivers when he asked if they wanted extra ketchup, what if *that* was the act?

What if X on the phone, daring and sexy and droll, was the true X, or more true than the timid soul from Travis High School, the milksop at the Whataburger?

He thought of Rosario Vega, the woman whose beaten face his mama had put on the fridge the year before. He thought of Jesse screaming at the Days Inn.

Of course X knew it might not be safe, knew that every terrible outcome in this world was a possibility. The problem wasn't that everything that was bad *could happen*, but that the badness wasn't guaranteed. The worst was possible, not preordained, and if something was possible it meant the opposite of that thing was possible, too.

X knew it would be better to know, knew he *had* to know, if there was a place in this world for an X that wasn't abandoned in a motel room or on the ground in an alley, a place in this world for an X to flirt with strangers, to make bad choices. To be sixteen.

Either there was or there wasn't, X was sure. You could be inside *or* outside, man *or* woman. Not everything had to be so *complicated*. Some stuff was just black and white.

Come sundown, it would be deciding time.

Till then, all X could do was wait.

CLOWN

NOW HERE'S AN OMINOUS sign: man goes to hunker down on his preferred snoozin' bench little past two in the a.m., half a bottle of rotgut keeping his insides snug, and before the first cock a-doodles, he wakes to a boy peering over him like the pale rider himself. Shoulda known then and there to say no siree, but I was taught it best to be an all-loving God in business as in life. I have paid and paid again for my munificence.

This was at my international headquarters, abandoned but for a couple mutts curled up beside the gazebo, flies tanning theyselves in the lamplight. Back in 2001, when that boy found me, I was crossing into Hidalgo County three, maybe four times a week. Locals called me El Payaso, and anyone who was seeking me out in that moonlit plaza in Reynosa was looking for one thing.

"Texas, Our Texas! All hail the mighty state," I burbled, still prone. Boy couldn't have been more than fourteen years, but even in my bleary-eyed delirium 'twas apparent he was playacting the tough: sweat-hood up, chin jutting. "What you want, son?" I asked. That boy just stared me down from two paces back, like he was trying to determine if I was real or apparition.

In fairness, I should confess that whilst south of the border, my habit was to stay clowned up. Not my normal going-out look, but circus cosmetics are a little more science than art, and I like to take my time with the outlines: nice big ovals round the brows and under the eyes, little horns curling off the ends of my spout. “Don’t tell me you never seen a man in a romper before,” I said, sitting myself up.

Boy started to speak, hesitated. He was a small fellow, fists burrowed in the kangaroo pouch of his pullover. “You a coyote?” An amateur ruffian, this one, never sure if he was ending his words in a period or question mark.

“Kai-oh-tee? I look like a coyote?” I rubbed at my polka-dotted paunch, bit of the dyspepsia kicking in. “Use them peepers, son. No coyotes in the circus.”

“You’ll take me across?” he asked, accent thick as a water moccasin.

“Across?” I rose and began to circle him, nice and slow, my shoes squeaking against the cobblestones of the plaza. No fun sleeping in your rainbow laces, but forty-five years old, five foot eight, one sixty: you try stuffing your bunions each morning into red-and-blue sixteen-inchers with bulbous toes. “You DEA?”

He stared blankly.

“INS?”

Boy craned his neck to keep me in sight.

“DPS? FBI? CIA?”

He scrunched his face, confused. “I’m no one.”

“We all someone, I’m afraid.”

Whilst I scoured my deep pockets for some dip, that boy explained he’d been trying to get Texwards but didn’t have the money. Said he’d spent the last summer in Austin, needed to get back before the next one. Said he had three hundred dollars U.S. and word was The Clown would go for that.

“That’s what the competition saying these days, huh?” I leaned in to inspect him. “How old you anyway?”

“Sixteen.”

“Liar,” I scoffed. “You ain’t close to sixteen. Fourteen, maybe. How stupid I look?” Spit some chaw on the cobblestones. “How you learn English?”

Boy shrugged. “Just learnt it.”

"Liar," I said louder, coming in closer, our snouts almost touching, foam to flesh. He was a bumpy-skinned creature, little wisps of hair above his upper lip. "You don't just learn nothing. Someone teaches. What's your name, boy?"

He looked to those mutts like they might give him the right answer. "Juan," he tried.

"Bullshit your name Juan. That's a lie. You a liar. And how you get that money, assuming you actually got it?"

"It's my money."

"Liar!" I shouted and slapped my knee and grinned a grin beneath my painted one. Boy didn't flinch. "That's good, son. We can make that work. Now," I said, pointing to his jeans pocket, "let's see the skrilla."

He took out three crumpled C-notes, returned 'em where they came from.

"Funny little co-inky-dink," I said, ambling back to my snoozin' bench. "My brother's up in Austin. Love of my life, my brother. Best man I know."

Boy nodded, but I 'spect he didn't understand. "You take me across, I gotta wear the paint?"

"Shit, son, won't be any worse than the skin you got. We got a deal?"

Boy gave me one of those tough-guy nods, so slight it almost weren't no nod at all, then moseyed off into the darkness real slow, like he had a fifty-pound weight between his legs. Adolescence a fun time, ain't it?

"Clown car moves out ten tomorrow," I called after him. "All three hundred *before* I paint you up. And wash up beforehand, kapeesh? With a mug like yours, I'm gonna need to be Pablo fuckin' Picasso to do this right."

Lucky Larry's Clown Spectacular: *Affordable birthday parties in English and Spanish from Texas to Tamaulipas!*

The idea was simple, see: No papers but wanna ditch that peso-an-hour at *El Rey de Hamburguesa* to flip pink sludge in service to the American King? Smile wide and jump on in to Lucky Larry's 1984 wood-paneled Plymouth Voyager of fantasy and fun.

None of this lips-so-chapped-you-don't-got-'em-anymore dying-across-the-desert kai-oh-tee nonsense with me. No, Lucky Larry Hooley provides you with proper documentation and a seat belt all your own, only fifty dollars extra for air-conditioning from pick-up to drop-off, and I'll throw in half a can of Fanta to be shared with your neighbor and a Slim Jim for good measure.

See, border crossing ain't so complex long as you follow one simple rule: get that pigmentation out of your system, sister. BP sees so much as a hint of tanning oil darkening your sideboob and they're on you like a roof rat to dog food. Pelt like marshmallow is to what we aspire. And you know the *blanco*-est species on God's green don'tcha?

Step right up for the Greatest Show On Earth!

I mean, who's to say that bright white little lady in the tricolor wig *ain't* Sally M. Wilson of Alpine, T-X?

You, Agent Miller? Go ahead, wake her up.

You can see those papers are valid . . . Brown eyes, four-foot-eleven . . .

. . . well, no sir, we didn't wash it off 'fore we left. That takes the magic out of it for the little ones, and besides, this is the professional stuff, heavy duty, and you know the water down there . . .

Yes, Lucky Larry's Clown Spectacular. Beaucoup bucks and a near-perfect batting average! The secret ingredient: my clowns *clowned*. Never know when a patrolman with a hornet in his helmet gonna want you to pull a quarter out from behind his ear or blow and twist the condom in his back pocket into a short dog. We'd practice entire afternoons, not rolling out till my zanies could handspring or headstand sure as any merry-andrew worthy of the name.

'Course, by the time I met that boy in spring oh-one, whole country was tensing up. And after the September of that fateful year, border patrol took it to a new level and I had to close up shop altogether.

These days I'm back on the coast, cornering Galveston's door-to-door cutlery market. But nothing's brought me closer to success than the Clown Spectacular.

See, I was the big shit in Reynosa's nappy before those narco thugs started angling to shut the big top down. In fact, just the day before I met that boy, I had an ugly encounter in that same plaza with the gilt-fanged representative of an organization that shall not be named. Sat right down beside me and, without even turning his neck, murmured that next time he saw a patron of mine clowned up, he'd chop that jester's head square off with a machete, as a message to anyone else thinking 'bout joining my circus.

A lesser man might've hightailed it home then and there, but I wasn't just providing for myself, see, for a portion of my profits were intended for my beleaguered twin brother—the one and only Ed Hooley—without whom I could not comfortably walk this earth.

That's the only reason I said yes to that boy. A few final pennies to drop into the collection jar, even if it meant dealing with a child drenched in the stank of pubescence!

Yes, I owed it to my duplicate to earn for him what little I could. Pure of heart and troubled of mind, my brother. A hearer of sounds and seer of sights hidden from the rest of us. Would care for him myself, but a medical professional is not what the Lord made me. And Mama always said it ain't about being together makes a family, it's about looking out for each other from wherever we are.

She's the one who taught us how to survive in this cruel world. Best rodeo clown ever come out of Galveston was Claudette Hooley. Woman could juggle five torches whilst Irish dancing atop a star-spangled barrel: hell, even the bulls couldn't look away. On the circuit she was known as Johnny Fingers. Maybe some of those boys suspected Señor Fingers had a secret, but Mama, she was flat and wiry, knew how to tamp those native orange curls down under her bald cap, and she brought in enough scratch for the overlords no one bothered fussing in the first place.

Well, almost no one.

Once, at five years, I barged in on her pissing and, acting the wise-ass, asked if she was man or woman. She didn't even get up off the commode, just signaled me close and slapped me hard from her throne. "You got more or less than me down there?" she snarled, pointing at my crotch. When I whimpered "more" she said, "Yessir, and let that be a lesson. Don't you ever take less when more is an option."

Ed and me, we grew up on the circuit with her, which is how we mastered all manner of the performing arts: cloud-walking and unicycle, prat-falling and basic pickpocketry. Seven days a week before sunup, Johnny Fingers could be found in the main arena, barking instructions as we rehearsed our two-man somersaults, smacking at our stilts till we could umbrella-step from twelve foot high. Mama always told us when you're poor, versatility's a necessity. Ain't no point in stealing a coconut unless you planning to drink the milk, eat the meat, *and* halve the shell for a young girl's brassiere.

Another Fingersism: know your strengths, which was why she taught me to throw a punch and Ed to evade one. Cowboys on the circuit called me Offense and him Defense, and more than one puffed-up 4-H-er lost his balance swinging at Ed only to make contact with my fist as he fell.

Even back then, Ed was different: a twitch in his eye where a twinkle should've been, a most sensitive soul, unlike his brother. Ed was a daydreamer and a dawdler, with a taste for the simple things, like a moist Ho Ho on a cool autumn day. While I could leave no tent unscoured, was always checking out the pre-menstrual set at the broiler competition, he was content to watch steer roping for hours, and in Room 212 at the Beachcomber, where we stayed during the off-season, Ed could entertain himself with little more than a Warner Brothers coloring book.

'Twas only his sweet tooth that could lead my brother astray, resulting in our one persistent collaboration: the Hooley Switcheroo. On a weekday afternoon when ticket sales were slow, we'd repair to the nearest village green to scout out the local confectionery. Ed would loiter outside while I strutted in, stockpiling as many Walnettos and

Flipsticks as my denims would allow. Then I'd dash out like a common thief, Ed lollygagging behind. Every time those bumpkin storekeepers would nab him, thinking they'd nabbed me, and every time they'd end up apologizing to my empty-pocketed doppelganger.

Later, Ed would scarf down his Abba Zabbas, clean out a Pixy Stick or two, but once the feasting subsided, he'd confess a guilty conscience. "Quit your brittle-brattle. We ever get caught, I'll take the rap," I always assured him, but he'd calm only after we'd swung by the main arena to offer a sacrifice to our Almighty. "That's a nice haul, boys," Mama would say, popping Razzles three a time. "A nice haul."

'Course, if any of those candy hawkers paid a lick of attention, they mighta noticed the difference between Ed and me carved right into our scruffs: a numeral 1 on my neck and a 2 on Ed's, supplied by Mama's cold steel bowie at the age of two and one quarter. She'd carved a crooked zero into the top of her own sternum afterward. Always said this was what linked us, for without her one and two, she was nothing.

Miss Johnny Fingers. Our mama was a good woman but cursed with the aching knowledge that she was destined for something greater than what she was born into. Promised one day she was gonna open up a three-ring all her own and would bring us in to run it with her. Had the faculty and the flair, she said. Just needed the bacon. Two children in tow, well, once she'd taught us to survive, that was an expense she could no longer bear. Her parting words to me the final night she tucked us in: "You a man and you American. No excuses not to prosper."

And thus, at the age of ten years, when my brother and I awoke at the Beachcomber to find ourselves alone but for the talents our mama had bestowed upon us, I knew then that Ed was my responsibility.

Which brings me back to that boy . . .

We met at this itty-bitty dive bar mornin' after he found me in the plaza. Place didn't exactly scream happy hour, especially at ten a.m. on a Wednesday. Three grizzled old dogs in Texas tuxedos half-slept at the bar, enough dust on the counter I could've signed my name with my ring finger. A single string of white Christmas lights hung along the wall, only one bulb still flickering. Found the boy in the way-back, at the only table in the place, a Coke-stained plywood number next to a jukebox with its glass smashed.

He kept up the silent macho act from clown white to setting powder, legs spread, arms crossed, a master of the sulky shrug, the international sign of the puerile. Was especially surly after handing over the dinero, and who can blame him? Fourteen on your own at a dive in the red-light? I'd feign courage, too, lest I reveal myself the mark.

Tough guy or no, once I had the moolah secured under my corkscrew peruke, I insisted we imbibe, as I've found it best if everyone's a smidge loosey-goosey before the big show. Boy examined the inside of that first bottle like there might be a soupçon of cyanide in there, but once we got going . . .

"Let's have some real talk, grumpkin," I said, my paintbrush slathered in ruby. We was halfway to Bozo and two brews in. "Lot of tittle-tattle about Lucky Larry among my rivals. He not a *professional* because he ain't *affiliated* and this prevarication and that, so I know why you suspicious. But truth is, here we are and *soon*"—I pointed skywards, indicating north—"there you'll be. And hell," I added, passing him my compact mirror, "this *artistry*." Couldn't see a speck of burnt umber on him: high-arched ebony eyebrows and a devilish incarnadine grin. "So what gives, huh? Running from the cartel? Po-lee-see-uh? A&B? B&E? DUI? D&D?"

Boy brought the mirror real close to his face. "I'm going for my girlfriend."

"Your girlfriend?"

"Izzy," said the boy.

"You kill her or somethin'?"

From the same pocket he'd taken the greenbacks, he pulled out one of those wallet-sized photographs. She was a strumpet of some possibility, I admit: wavy hair past her shoulders, just the teensiest hint of a smile, like she thought the whole arrangement a bit silly but knew she looked fine. "How old this one?"

"Quince."

"Sweet fifteen! Man after my own heart. Austin gal?"

Boy gave his tough-guy nod, finished his drink.

"Dos más!" I called to the barkeep, a grim-faced man with jowls like the dewlap of a heifer. From my doctor's case, I procured my best persimmon hairpiece. "One hundred percent yak hair. Retails for *two fifty*." I stood up and moved around him barber-style, ready to disguise that buzz-cut pate. "So let's hear it."

Every summer, or so the boy claimed, he'd leave his grandpappy in Tampico for Austin, where he stayed with his auntie in a mobile park. Last summer, that girl moves into the double-wide next door. Three months, boy says, this duo gallivanted about town, she teaching him Americanese and, if I had to guess, the intricacies of touch. Summer ends, boy goes back to his grandpappy, and for seven months Romeo and Hoo-lee-etta exchange mail. Then old abuelo drops the bomb that our protagonist won't be returning to Tejas this summer forthcoming, and boy takes matters into his own hands. The dénouement to this tale o' woe: "I'm gonna marry her someday. I'm gonna make her my wife."

"*Tampico?*" I said, returning to my seat. "You telling me you voyaged three hundred miles north on your lonesome, stole a purseful of shekels from someone who's undoubtedly gonna want 'em back, and now you trampling across international borders with *me* all so you can visit your three-months girlfriend?"

"I told you," boy said softly. "It's my money."

"Fuck, son." Downed another brew. "You *are* fourteen." One of the drunks had roused from his siesta and was gaping at us. I winked to confirm for him he wasn't suffering a hallucination, watched as he twisted himself back toward the bar.

"Thing is," boy said, slurring a little. "I got a plan. I'm a boxer. Good, too." Soft-jabbed the air. Said he was gonna train in Austin, get himself a belt, settle down . . .

I told that boy I didn't see how he was affording a gym subscription on his limited budget, and you know what he tells me? Says last summer he worked out of this establishment called Tucker's Boxing

Gym where the proprietor would train certain individuals in exchange for them cleaning the mirrors or wrapping folks' hands. Said one time he lost his house key when his auntie was out of town and Tucker even let him sleep in a room at the back. "Gonna make me a champion someday."

"That so?" I said. "Sounds like quite a place. Have to check it out sometime. And what name should I be looking for on that marquee outside the Astrodome? Juan, right?"

Boy clinked his empty against mine. "Alexis," he said. "Cepeda."

"Alexis Cepeda, huh? You was my kid, Alexis Cepeda, we'd have a real sit-down to discuss your situational awareness." I reached into my jumper pocket, took out the driver's license. "But you're not my kid and you're not Alexis Cepeda." I tossed him the license.

"*Nathaniel Rothstein*," I said. "Born in Newton, Mass. October 27, 1981. Moved to Texas for his education: currently a student at Lucky Larry's Clown Academy and a fine addition to the Dallas Jewry."

"Where you get this?" asked Cepeda, examining the license. "And what's a Jewry?"

I explained I'd come into this fine example of fresh American identification a few summers back, in '98—the where and how was not his concern—and lucky for him it was a license perfect for a male clownling. "Haven't had occasion to use it yet. You get to break it in."

Cepeda pocketed the license, tried his new name on his tongue: "*Nathaniel Rothstein*."

"That's you." I saluted. "Shalom, cabrón. Say, how you feel about heights?"

Back room of a boxing gym: I'd be lyin' if I said the idea didn't stick in my cerebrum as a possibility for Mr. Ed Hooley. Would be another few years after that boy told me about Tucker's 'fore I'd have occasion to bring my brother there, but sounded like a place my simple twin might be at ease, for he knew a little something about the sweet science.

It was in Sinton where we perfected the act, at a rowdy roadhouse called Monk's Saloon. This was back in '66, just before our eleventh birthday. Ed and me, we'd been traversing the coast for weeks, using the gifts Mama gave us to put meals in our bellies: thimblerig outside North Beach in Corpus, coin smack and other small cons in Aransas Pass, all manner of misdemeanor in Texas City.

That night in Sinton, it was cold and we were hungry, so I told Ed to wait out in the parking lot and snuck inside, hoping to find me a yokel of the inebriated variety whose money clip might somehow end up in my breeches. "You be careful," Ed chirped, left eye twitching, as it did when he was nervous. I left him with his crayon book, Indian-style against the bloated bumper of a Chevy pickup.

Inside 'twas a regular charivari: dance floor crowded with two-steppers, drunkards packed tight against a long bartop, the sickly sweet smell of cigarette smoke and whiskey breath, hot piss and peanuts. All would've gone smoothly if I'd found a mark right off the bat, but I had to feel the place out some, and Ed got scared outside, came in to find me.

Later, Ed would tell me that man's wallet was practically falling out his back pocket. "I had to try," he would declare, but Ed was too slow, and no sooner had he 'tempted to make our money for the night than I heard my brother yelp and turned to see him by the bar, in the grips of an overalled brute to this day I swear was not fully human.

A crowd had formed around them by the time I made it over from the dance floor. "You let go of him," I called, and before that man knew what was happening I'd climbed up on a bar stool and leapt toward him, left-hooking him in the ear. He dropped Ed and we ran as the crowd cheered, which made me think there was money to be had from this particular attraction.

We developed something of a reputation after that. Folks called us The Fighting Hooleys, This One and That One, Kind of Good and Mostly Evil. We worked every ramshackle beer joint, dingy gin mill, stinky taproom, and sticky public house from Brownsville to Beaumont, Brazoria County in between. Late in the evening, usually when the mean blood alcohol level was approaching the mean IQ, I'd climb atop the counter and announce we had a presentation the likes of which none of those people had ever seen. Then I'd give Ed a helping hand up and we'd spar a round or two, all choreographed, me jabbing and Ed ducking past smoking ashtrays, around half-drunk bottles, every good ol' boy and their good ol' gals tossing coins our way in appreciation.

'Course, all this was just a warm-up, for next Ed would clear his tiny throat and declare that his brother Larry was the toughest 'leven-year-old this side of the Rio Grande, and any man who thought he could withstand the child's punch ought line up and try his luck.

Here's a secret: any grown man drunk enough to think this a good idea is drunk enough to get punched out by an eleven-year-old. They'd come for me, smirking and snarling, "Gimme all you got boy," and I'd throw my cross with my full strength straight at their jaws. Some would bust out laughing, caught off guard by my velocity, others would tend to their wounds with cold bottles, but they'd return again and again, thirsty for flesh against their numbness, punched and punched again until the lot of 'em passed out, heads against bartops or stomachs down on tacky floors.

Ed would pluck their wallets from the sleeping ones as I distracted the others—strutting around the counter, charming the womenfolk as I do—and then we'd scram, off to the next hamlet before those saps knew what hit 'em.

Oh, what a glorious time! Tenting on the beach, cabbage in our pockets, every supper a smorgasbord of Heinz Baked Beans and fresh-stole Lemonheads . . .

We coulda gone that way forever, Ed and I, if not for the changing body times. Hit us both at the dawn of our twelfth year: deepening our voices, stretching our appendages, stealing our act. Boy hits a man, it's entertainment. Man hits a man, well, that's just a fight.

For me, maturation meant fresh wonders daily: new associates who understood wampum and women; the pulsing finish to a marked-down tryst with a competent fellatrix, her teeth lost to the scourge of amphetamines (God be praised!); my body suddenly as greedy as my ever-needy heart.

But the change changed Ed in ways unanticipated and malign. That eye started twitching as never before, and though one would never describe my brother as clack or magpie, his word-faucet slowed from tepid trickle to irregular drip. He turned somber and suspicious, and on occasion I would find him walking the coastline, murmuring to souls unseen.

In our trade, shyness and capriciousness led only to lost lucre, and a pauperized Larry Hooley would do good to no one, my beloved twin most specially of all.

And so, early one June morning, on a quiet patch of beach near Baytown, I taught Ed Hooley how to throw a punch. "Don't need to know," he kept muttering until I shoved him to the sand, and, once he rose, shoved him again. He swung a wild and most ineffective blow in my direction, and using this maneuver as our rough draft, we set about revision, Ed smacking at my tummy and thumping at my gourd, each smash ever so sharper, little bit more precise.

We went about this work in silence but for the low growl that emanated from somewhere deep inside my brother each time he came for me. After an hour, I could announce any limb or organ and Ed could make contact there. At the ninety-minute mark he broke my nose.

"Sorry, Larry," he mumbled, his first words since I'd thrust him to the ground, for Ed was not accustomed to violence inflicted on him by his other half.

"Again," I said, and though Ed wavered, he knew I would not budge until he followed my command, and threw again, a power right, and again, and again, the thin stream dripping from my beak-holes strengthening into an epic gush, until my chin and chest were covered in the sanguine meat juice of a broken Hooley.

Seeing what he'd done to me, Ed began to cry. I'm not too much the man to admit I cried, too. Cried for my mama. Cried for my brother. Cried for what I knew I had to do.

"Pull yourself together now," I said, as much to myself as to Ed. I tried to remember what my mama always taught us: *It ain't about being together makes a family.* "Say, here's an idea," I told him then, wiping my nose with the back of my sleeve. "In honor of your newfound talents, how's about a Hooley Switcheroo?"

We set out on foot toward Sadie's Candy Haven downtown, the gleaming jars of jellybeans and jawbreakers no doubt etched into Ed's mind. So transfixed was he by this prospect that my brother did not think to wash the dried blood from his fists, nor did he notice, a mile before we arrived, when I dropped a single Big Hunk chocolate bar into the back pocket of his dungarees.

And when he was apprehended, I did not turn back, for though I wanted Ed at my side, wanted it with all my soul, I knew he'd be better off if I watched over him from afar. I did not turn back till I was all the way to the city of La Porte, eleven miles south, observing the seagulls as they made their rounds above Galveston Bay.

It was there I vowed that, best I could, I would keep eyes on Ed from a distance, and every nickel I netted, every penny I pilfered, would one day go to ensuring my dear brother never went wanting for nothing again . . .

Now here's some hard truth: Every now and again turns out that blue-tongued skink they sellin' at the exotic pet shop ain't nothing more than a common lizard force-sucked a grape lolly.

Yes, for all that bluster, the newly minted "Rothstein" née Alexis Cepeda proved himself to be a downright *feeler* once perfused with ale. It was plans, plans, plans after brewski numero seis. He was gonna move that girl to a McMansion in the suburbs where they could re-watch his pugilistic triumphs on a big-screen teevee. Six kids, seven kids, maybe I'll call 'em all Alexis he said, just like George Foreman. "An Alexis Cepeda Grill," he said, and laughed his sloppy laugh.

"A *Nathaniel Rothstein* Grill," I corrected. "No pork patties need apply."

Boy didn't follow. He was pickled, plastered, hammered, tight. And, sorry for me, turned out that a besotted Cepeda-turned-Rothstein lost the ability to ever once shut the fuck up.

After I got him wigged and rompered, we went out to the alley behind the bar, where I'd left the clown car, to find a talent for the child. I opened up the back of the van as he leaned against its side yammering, no foreseeable terminus to his boozy harangue. Trunk was teeming with all manner of whangdoodle: metal horns and giant toothbrushes, putty eggs hidden in the ductile be-hinds of rubber chickens.

"In Texas," he declared, "everyone's gonna know my name."

"You the big man, huh?" I said, sorting through a Piggly Wiggly bag of squirt flowers. I stepped over to face him. "Tell me now, honest. Where'd you get that money?"

Boy stifled a burp. "Washing dishes," he said, at a steakhouse off the interstate last summer. Three hundred dollars all he had to his name. "Worth it," he mumbled, "'cause I'll see Izzy, you'll see your brother, everyone'll be happy." He put his paw on my shoulder like we was old pals. "Has it been long? Since you seen him?"

That's when I noticed it: a sign from the heavens. The paint wasn't settling on him like it should. It was clumpy round the forehead, too thick atop the ears. He'd been picking at his chin and one of those pimples had popped, a squirt of dark blood now dry on his otherwise-Elmer's-like exterior. That boy looked like a clown, all right, but not the kind we were going for.

"What you just say?"

"Just asked if it had been a long time," he said. "Since you'd seen him."

"What business that of yours?"

"Not my business. I was just—"

"I'll see him this time. Taking you. That's when I'll see him."

"That's all I was asking."

"Been providing for my brother my whole life. What kind of person would I be otherwise?"

Boy shrugged.

"Will I see my brother? Yessir, what in the hell kind of person would I be?"

"Not much of one, I guess." He laughed then, a short little smirk of a laugh, a laugh I didn't much care for. "I gotta piss."

What was so funny, I wondered, about a lifetime spent raising funds for my beloved twin? Did he think he would've acted different had he to care for a troubled child *as* a child? Did he think his situation—trying to prance cross countries for some three-months girlfriend—was akin to mine?

Boy piddled his fiddle, and when he turned 'round he found me leaning against the clown car, holding an old pair of six-foot cloud-walkers upright betwixt my legs.

"You want me to wear those?" he asked uncertainly.

"You talking the big man, figured you might like the height." Told him to hoist himself up onto the hood of the van. "Aluminum adjustables, son. Step on in."

"Maybe I can do something else?" he suggested as I buckled him into the stilts, leaning them at a diagonal against the ground.

I told him to use the vehicle for leverage, gave him a helping shove. Boy almost half-mooned right into the ground, would've too if I didn't grab those long legs to keep him from toppling. "Careful now," I said, releasing the stilts so the boy could stand on his own.

"I don't think I can walk," he called, still wobbly. Boy was too high to brace himself against the van.

"Sure you can," I said. I went and slammed the trunk shut, returned to face the boy. "Try taking a step now."

Boy started to lift his leg, shuddered. He yelped and regained balance.

Who'd he think I was, anyway? Offering three hundred for a job worth thousands. Some mark he could con into smuggling on the cheap? "C'mon now: Take a step."

"I can't."

He wasn't even in his right head if you thought about it. Hundreds of miles, life savings, all for some girl he hardly knew.

Above, the boy stood paralyzed.

"I thought you was the big man. What kind of big man can't walk the sky?"

"Just get me down," he said. "For real, just get me down."

And to question my loyalty to my own flesh and blood? He acted as if it was always so easy, running toward the ones we love.

It was then I knew that enduring hours more under the forever-raised eyebrows of the child-clown I could not abide. If he was above it all, he could stay above it all. I'd gotten what I came for.

"You want down?" I called. "You so wise and good, boy, I'm sure you'll find a way." I got my car keys from my romper, headed toward the driver's side.

He tried to move again and faltered, arms windmilling to keep himself afloat. "Where you going? You can't leave me here," he yelled, voice cracking.

What all was he complaining about, anyway? I'd painted him white as boiled chicken, given him the only thing he truly needed to cross the border: a valid license. All he had to do was flash it at the border officer, say he was *Nathaniel Rothstein* if asked, and the Land of the Free would be his to roam under whatever name he pleased.

"You got my money!" he cried. "My money!"

That boy called and called but El Payaso was no longer listening. In the van, I ditched the wig, uncrumpled the cash, and drove off. Sometimes, the only choice you got is to leave.

PART THREE

Leonard District

DAY 1

It's the first call of her first night as a police officer, and Miriam Lopez doesn't know if Corporal Bennington is messing with her. There have been multiple reports of lewd conduct at this construction site—a "one-man show," according to Bennington—and now, perp long fled, the corporal is suggesting Miriam "put herself to use": "Why don't you see if he's left behind any *DNA evidence*?"

Until recently, 603 South 1st Street was the site of the Shady Creek Condominiums. It was a shabby, forty-unit complex, a raggedy remnant from an earlier Austin. Now, in August 2008, this splintery section of city is being sanded down. Shady Creek has been demolished. A new complex—the Residences—is on its way: digging for the underground parking garage here is about to begin. Portable light towers illuminate the site like a movie set. A bulldozer, Port-a-Potties. Security fencing on all sides.

Across the street is a Whataburger, and it was customers waiting in line for the drive-thru who called in the incident: a man behind the fence, jeans around ankles. A large polyethylene banner advertising the development company runs the length of the fence on the side facing the restaurant. The banner covers only the upper half of the fence, which meant the customers could see only the perp's lower half. The Dick Without a Face, the other officers are calling him.

Reports of a live one first came in at 9:14 p.m. Four officers responded, driving their vehicles right into the site, parking in a semi-neat row, each at a slight angle facing the fence. Miriam still had paperwork to fill out back at the station, has only just arrived at 9:52. But now the action is over and, as Bennington issues his maybe-serious order to Miriam, the others start to get moving.

They'd all met her at that night's staff meeting, and they offer warm farewells—*You need anything tonight, you let us know*—their banter fading as they head back to their cars.

—*You think you could shoot your load once you heard sirens? That'd be it for me.*

—*Is it c-o-m-e or c-u-m? Like, technically?*

For eleven weeks of field training, Miriam has heard this sort of chatter, would like to master it herself. She knows it's a way to deal with the shit they see every night, knows it's how guys—and it's almost all guys on the overnight shift in Leonard District—show affection. Her attempts always fall flat. She's never considered herself a funny person.

Miriam wants to ask Bennington if he's giving her a hard time. Instead, she begins to pace the fence line, inspecting the ground as instructed. What if she *does* find some? Hard to imagine they'll send a vial off to the forensics lab. Lewd conduct is frowned upon, sure, but not exactly a high priority in what her field training officer would've referred to as the *Getting to the Bottom of It Department*.

A few yards away, Bennington chats with the manager from the Whataburger, a heavyset Black man. He'd walked over when he saw the first police lights flashing, said he'd witnessed the whole thing. "You think you could ID any part of the guy?" says Bennington.

"Like his you-know-what?" says the manager. "I'm not sure I could pick it out of a lineup, if that's what you're asking."

Bennington sends him back across the street, approaches Miriam. The corporal's in his early fifties: up there for a cop. Acne scars, deep blue eyes. The buzzed bald head of a man who still gets haircuts despite having no hair. "So, Lopez," he says, "any evidence of this nocturnal emission?"

"No come stains here," says Miriam. She's going for levity, trying to talk how the others talk, but as soon as she says it, she knows she's erred.

Bennington winces. "I know it's your first night, Lopez, but let's be a little more precise with the vocabulary, shall we?"

"Sorry," says Miriam. Why was she trying to be clever? "I, uh, I can't find any ejaculate, sir."

Bennington glances to the heavens: *Am I talking to an idiot?* "That's not what I meant, Lopez. What I meant is: you're not looking for a come *stain*. You're looking for *come*."

Miriam is relieved to return to her cruiser, her roving refuge for the next nine hours.

She fastens her seat belt, turns on the car. "Remember: you can always quit," her dad told her when she'd headed out for the night. He is a mild man in build and temperament, an electrician who spends his free hours fiddling with model airplanes in the garage like a father from some earlier time. "Thanks for the support," Miriam said.

She is twenty-two, a ghastly age, and has spent her life on the fringes of friend groups. Her people have always been her parents: he a Texican, second generation in Austin, she an Anglo, also two generations here. They had her in their late thirties, too old and old-fashioned to pursue the surest route to hooking an introverted kid up with a social circle: befriending parents of similarly aged children, tossing their offspring into the mixer.

Miriam was never hated, never miserable. Just an awkward interloper in the lives of schoolmates who, years later, will flip through yearbooks, or scroll MySpace, see her face, and have the vaguest recollection. *Oh yeah. Her.*

It was track that gave her a place. A team. Since high school, she's run the 1500 meters: fast enough for a full scholarship to Southwestern (though not so fast to launch a career beyond it). On the track she found a grit she can access only when she is silent and moving and deep inside herself. She's always wished life were more like sports. A single set of rules for everyone to follow. An assigned group: *no matter who you are, Miriam Lopez, your people are here.*

She's found it a little at the boxing gym, where she works out most mornings. For Miriam, it's a place of quiet camaraderie, alliances built on chin nods and staying out of each other's way.

Miriam had hoped policing might give her something similar. Eight months at the academy and eleven weeks of field training and she's learned she is uniquely ill-suited for her chosen line of work. This is not a physical job. On patrol, it's about performing control. Perform control and people submit. Perform control and you're in control, a lot of the time. The gun doesn't hurt, but what does a gun do if no one thinks you'll pull the trigger?

What confers authority on the police is the way they speak, the way they are. A vibe: *You really want to go there with me? Really?* People are fine going there with Miriam Lopez.

Manic tweakers, mangy hair like cult leaders; olden hookers with curled upper lips. They'll back-talk the others, but never like they'll back-talk her. With her they'll keep going. Shriek in her face, spittle flying. *Dumb bitch. Fuckin' pig.*

Every night of field training it was some variation, and every night it was her field training officer who'd swoop in to her defense. Her FTO had a nice gut and a back brace and no problem getting up in anyone's face. "Call *me* a dumb bitch," he'd say, and that would be the end of the conversation.

"Dogs smell fear," he'd.told her once. "So I was you, I'd run out to the perfume shop and pick myself up a nice big bottle of *I Don't Give a Shit.*"

Miriam Lopez is not that person. She knows it, knows everyone else knows it: her superiors, her cohort. Random strangers on the street.

Yesterday—Tuesday—her last in field training, she'd run into that old man from the gym, Bob Alexander, at APD headquarters. The one with the missing nephew, ten years gone. Even Bob could see it. *You're a cop?* he'd said.

Still, Miriam isn't a quitter. She has promised herself she'll give it a year. A year on patrol in Leonard District. A year in this new world to figure out how to be.

DAY 11

The city is split into nine districts—each given first names, like hurricanes—and this sideways sliver south of downtown now belongs to Miriam Lopez. *Leonard District.*

It's foreign territory: her field training was on the east side; she grew up north. But Miriam has never felt like any part of Austin was especially hers, and there is something appealing about the idea that over time she will come to know this turf more intimately than the people who inhabit it.

Leonard District is a microcosm of its city, of its country, which is to say less a melting pot than a TV dinner, its components varied and apart. It's the Craftsman bungalows of aging environmentalists—hale white women in sun hats and their elven husbands, ponytails wilting—and the modest ranch houses of the secretaries and bus drivers who have long made the city run. It's bingo parlors that still have smoking sections, and bougie wine bars where appetizers masquerade as *small plates*. It's a seven-mile stretch of I-35, beneath whose exit ramps and overpasses reside the scraggly denizens of an Austin under Austin, a subterranean second city.

On patrol in Leonard District, Miriam Lopez is learning that her job is not to stop crimes. Crimes happen, then she appears. She arrives after the drugs have been ingested, the shots have been fired, the semen shot. In these first days of her career, she is often backup, or crowd control, or swapping in for someone else: the third, fourth, seventh officer on the scene.

Tonight, she arrives after a smash-and-grab in the parking lot of a 24 Hour Fitness, after a three-car accident on 71 near Montopolis. Miriam dons a reflector vest and lays flares amid the shattered glass, uses a light-up safety baton to keep the rubberneckers moving. She is never exactly sure where to park, where to stand. The other officers move like synchronized swimmers, Miriam a beat behind.

At 4:45 a.m., she pulls up to a run-down home set back from the road on an otherwise tidy street in Galindo. An ambulance and two cruisers are already there, lights flashing, plus an unmarked SUV. Miriam can smell it before she even opens the car door, like someone's holding her head down in a bucket of hot sewage. She starts to gag, swallows it.

Miriam passes through the chain-link gate, across the overgrown lawn, to the porch, a wide hole in its lattice skirting, as if an animal had once been trapped inside, busted through. An officer is bracing himself against the paint-peeled railing. Jug ears, freckles. Another rookie.

"You OK, Ross?" Miriam asks.

"Just needed a minute," he says, wipes his mouth with the back of his hand. The homeowner's daughter lives in Tulsa, Ross explains, had requested a belated welfare check on her dad a few hours before.

"How belated was she?" says Miriam.

"*Belated*." It's the medical examiner, now coming through the propped-open front door. She's a plump woman in her fifties: the face of a chronically unimpressed person framed inside a disposable Tyvek suit. Following her: two EMTs, wheeling a gurney. The body bag strapped to it seems weirdly small, like a child's.

The deceased has been gone so long the corpse had started to melt into the floor, the medical examiner explains. "I'd guess Mr. Samuelson expired in . . . mid-June?" It's now the end of August. She shakes her head, walks down the porch steps. "Happy Father's Day, right?"

DAY 55

The boxer is alone in a booth at the back, finishing off a burger and a beer, when he spots Miriam at the hostess stand, waves her over.

"Really?" he says, eyes widening. "*Really* really?"

"Really what?" says Miriam, perplexed.

"You're a *cop*?" he says. "*Oh, man!*" He shakes his head theatrically. "All this time, I had no idea. Good thing I never told you about all my illegal activities."

He is wearing a flat-brimmed Spurs cap, a red Nike tank top. Thick black eyebrows. A goofy, knowing grin: an inside joke in the body of a twenty-one-year-old.

"What did you think I was?" says Miriam.

"Physical therapist, maybe?"

"Your name's Alexis, right?"

Alexis Cepeda contorts his face: *Are you kidding me right now?* "How long have you been coming to the gym? Months, right? I see you *every morning*. We say hi *every* morning. I'm like, *Hey, Lopez!* And you say hi back. Every time!"

"Yeah, but we don't *talk* talk."

"Yeah, because you're doing your thing. It's a *gym*. But I *know* you." He squints up at her. "You gonna keep standing over me like a *cop*, or you gonna sit?"

Alexis Cepeda has huge reactions to Miriam. He howls with laughter. He buries his face in his hands. He isn't making fun of her, exactly, but he isn't not making fun. He is fake appalled at everything she tells him, or semi-fake appalled, or appalled. Miriam isn't sure.

Alexis can't believe she doesn't speak Spanish. Alexis can't believe she's a cop. Alexis can't believe she's a cop who is sitting across from him at "Mags" at 1:18 in the morning. "Mags" is Magnolia Cafe: a kitschy twenty-four-hour diner on South Congress, its vinyl booths half-filled with college kids, tatted hipsters post-gaming over pancakes.

“Do people call it *Mags*?” says Miriam.

“Never called it that before now,” Alexis confesses. He cocks one of his movie star brows: a question. “I always thought cops ate in *groups*.”

That’s how it was during field training, her FTO forever pushing tables together like a disheveled maître d’ or scootching over to make room for one more guy at Denny’s. So far in Leonard District, the few times she’s stopped for a proper meal she’s eaten alone.

“So why are you here so late?” asks Miriam.

Two days before, Alexis made his pro debut, first fight on the lower card at the Heart O’ Texas in Waco. Won in two rounds. A knockout. He mugs for Miriam: “Not a scratch on me.”

Ever since, he’s been too hyped up to sleep. It’s this or McDonald’s, and if Terry Tucker ever heard he’d been at the Golden Arches? “I don’t even want to think about it.”

“How’s he feel about beer?” asks Miriam.

“Probably not great,” says Alexis. “But I’m getting over a breakup, so . . .” He lifts the bottle. “I deserve one, right?”

“Yeah, totally,” says Miriam with more conviction than is warranted. She does this sometimes, presses the pencil too hard on the page. “Anyway, the *groups* thing. I think it’ll be like that eventually, y’know? Eating together. I just need to get my bearings. Maybe prove myself a little?”

“For sure,” says Alexis. “I know how it is.”

“Do you?”

“Yeah. Of course.” He says it so casually, more casually than maybe anything Miriam Lopez has said in her entire life.

It isn’t fair, is it, how easy it is for some people just to *be*?

They sit in silence for a moment, Miriam staring into her coffee, until the boxer raises a finger: an idea. “If I was you, you know what I’d do?” He leans across the table. “*Solve a cold case.* Biggest one I could find. Like a serial killer. I’d crack that shit *wide* open!”

DAY 63

Miriam Lopez is developing a reputation as conversational deadweight. She can never find ways to insert herself into the patter, can't do like the other officers and ride its rhythms like a wave. She is at her most self-conscious during those frequent and interminable waiting periods: in the parking lots of rickety apartment complexes, safety lights flickering; exposed in service lanes, passing cars not slowing all that much.

At the scenes of hit-and-runs, of aggravated assaults, the officers of Leonard District stand on the civilian side of the police tape to make sure passersby live up to their name. They wait with suspects as higher-ups bicker over jurisdiction. They wait for some reason no one has bothered to explain.

Jokes are cracked, shit shot. Miriam is always on the cusp of entering the fray, but the jibe or the aside or the good-natured insult reveals itself to her only after everyone else has moved on. She is listening—listening more intently than anyone else there—but she contributes nothing, doesn't even laugh when someone says something funny for fear of calling attention to herself, not realizing, exactly, that the not-talking, the not-laughing, is what's calling attention in the first place. Miriam Lopez remains silent, and it is this silence that irks the others.

A man has beat up his girlfriend, a man has raped his daughter, a man has strangled his wife, and these officers are here in the after: not preventing, not investigating, simply minding the world's shittiest store. Keep talking and you're not thinking. Talking is *something*, something other than standing around after the bad thing has happened, the bad thing that can never be undone.

12:02 a.m.: a stick-up at the Valero on I-35 at Oltorf has been reported and a small cadre of officers descend on the scene.

Inside, the mood is festive. The cashier, a lanky Indian kid living under a cloud of frizzy hair, had pissed his jeans, a normal reaction, but someone has scrounged up a pair of APD athletic shorts. Now he's returning to himself, gaining confidence each time he retells the story, until the fuzzy details from the scariest incident of his life—a hunting knife, a soiled army jacket—harden into the facts of the case. The owner has just arrived. He's a garrulous Persian versed in the art of Central Texas diplomacy: "Complimentary ICEEs," he announces, "for my friends in blue." Inside, there is a sense of Things Happening. One officer gathers witness statements, another takes photographs. In the back, a detective watches surveillance footage. Momentum!

Outside, by the pumps, Miriam and two other junior officers have been charged with keeping the scene clear. They stare out at the highway like stoned teenagers.

On Miriam's mind: the wrong turn she made responding to a suspicious person in Travis Heights. Corporal Bennington told her if she'd taken any longer to get there, he might've had to "I don't know . . . *call the police*."

On the men's minds: roadhead.

—*I'm telling you, Ross: three percent of all traffic fatalities. What a way to go.*

—*I don't know, Aguilar, might not be that bad.*

—*Not bad if it's <u>your</u> knob, dude! But you really want to die for another man's blowie?*

Miriam wonders if it's ever a woman on the receiving end, if that's included in the three percent. This is, in fact, the precise observation that would most endear her to the other officers in this moment, would inspire a lengthy back-and-forth on the subject of death-by-eating-pussy, would culminate, after Miriam goes on her way, in one man remarking to the other, "Lopez is weird as shit but I like her."

But Miriam is a slightly strange person who has never learned to hug that part of herself, whose mild attempts to embrace her essential Miriamness ("No come stains here!") always seem to get her into trouble, and so she says, "Anyone need anything inside?" and one says, *Nope*, and the other says, *I'm good*, and Miriam says nothing, but also then doesn't go inside: the weirdest possible move.

Now the bad thing. Silence. Miriam has asked if anyone needs anything, and no one needs anything and no one is needed. A souring of the mood.

And then: a reprieve. The detective emerges from the Valero. A woman. A woman detective. Forties, small and sturdy. "Robbery, man," she says to the trio. "Got more sleep when I was in Missing Persons, I'll tell you that." The other officers chuckle. "Y'all have a good night."

Miriam has not, until this moment, taken seriously Alexis Cepeda's unserious advice from the previous week, but also: she could really use a win. *Cold case. Missing Persons.* She remembers what Bob Alexander, the First Thinger from the gym, said of his vanished nephew. *You ever hear anything about his case, maybe you'll let me know.*

Miriam trots after the detective. She is still not used to moving with all this extra heft: the twenty-pound duty belt, her department-approved black Reeboks, chunky as orthopedic shoes. "Excuse me," she says, catching up to the detective. "Sorry to bother you, I just . . . I was wondering: Do you happen to remember a kid named *Nathaniel Rothstein*? Disappeared like ten years ago?"

The detective tells her there are four hundred cold cases in the city. "You have any information about him, Officer—" She peers at Miriam's bronze name badge. "M. Lopez?"

Miriam says she doesn't.

"Good talk," says the detective.

DAY 77

Where Miriam has excelled is in learning the formal language of police.

Police never use the words civilians use for a thing if there are special police words they can use instead. Women are females; children juveniles. Words have different meanings on the job. SANE is Sexual Assault Nurse Examiner. HEAT is Help Eliminate Auto Theft. In the academy, they'd studied a seventeen-page packet of "useful" acronyms, many of which seemed irrelevant to the task at hand. The IRA is the Irish Republican Army. AKC? American Kennel Club. Miriam knows them all.

It's a language distinct from how any normal person speaks, but it's a language Miriam can learn, and she gloms on to it.

"A *female*?" says Alexis Cepeda, performatively aghast. They are back at Mags at 1:25 a.m., and Miriam's telling him about a woman who barfed all over herself during a DUI stop. "Who says *female*? You sound like the kids in juvie."

Alexis has never been arrested as an adult, but in high school he was twice sent to Gardner-Betts—juvenile detention—both times for weed, a couple days each.

"Seems kinda harsh," says Miriam.

Alexis says kids were locked up for stuff like that all the time. Drugs, truancy. "Except the white kids." The white kids were scary. For a white kid to end up in juvie? "You had to do the most fucked-up shit imaginable. This one dude was in there for *raping a horse*."

"That was probably a rumor," says Miriam.

"I doubt it," says Alexis, shaking his head. "Kid ate apples all the time. You know who loves apples?"

This is their third meetup in as many weeks. Some nights, Miriam can't even take a pee break, is catching up on paperwork so late into the morning she misses the gym. Others, she might have a whole hour to herself. The habits of hooligans and of busybodies are no different from the habits of anyone else in Austin. Low-key on Sundays; disinclined to venture out in the rain. On those nights, Miriam calls Alexis Cepeda. He's never not answered on the first ring.

At the gym, little has changed between them, except that Alexis now addresses Miriam as "Officer Lopez," salutes after he says it. He does his thing, she does hers. *It's a gym*. They save their *talk* talk for when it's dark.

"I'm not up to any *funny business*," he told her when he gave her his digits at the gym. Mags is only a five-minute drive from Alexis's "pad," so it's an easy spot to meet. "Just, like, you know, if you ever want someone to eat with," he'd said. "Until you break your big case."

Miriam takes a final bite of omelet. "About the apples thing," she says, getting up to leave, "would that mean he *raped* a horse or thought he *was* a horse?"

Alexis slaps both palms on the table. "And *that's* why you're the cop!"

DAY 95

Halloween passes, the presidential election passes.

The officers on the overnight in Leonard District live in upside-down world. Their sunrise is sunset; the worst day of your life is any old day in theirs. They note the markers that signify the passage of time mostly after those markers have been defiled, after the time has passed. A smashed jack-o'-lantern; campaign signs tagged or in tatters.

Miriam was aware of the election like she's aware of hold music on the phone: a persistent tinkle in the background. She's heard grumblings from the others. Aguilar is sure Obama's from Kenya; Bennington thinks he's soft. In the waking world, investment banks are collapsing; there is talk of a second Great Depression. In upside-down world, it's just another Saturday. Every day in Leonard District is a global financial meltdown for someone.

DAY 101

Miriam is in the staff lot of the Leonard District substation, about to go home for the day, when Corporal Bennington approaches. "I don't know what you're up to, Lopez," he says, "but someone way above your pay grade stopped by last night on unrelated business. Left you a gift."

He hands her a manila envelope, stuffed full. It's addressed in Sharpie: M. LOPEZ.

Inside her Corolla, Miriam opens the envelope. It's the entire file on Nathaniel Rothstein, maybe 150 pages. Miriam has planned to go to the gym, now has second thoughts. *If I was you, you know what I'd do? I'd crack that shit wide open.*

At home, she spreads the documents across her bedroom floor. The first page: a missing persons report from two days after the boy disappeared. The last page: the note Bob Alexander found on his windshield ten years later, the one he'd shown Miriam outside APD headquarters. It's blank but for Nathaniel's birthdate, written in the unsteady scrawl of a child. On the pages in between: leads that didn't pan out, transcripts of interviews from witnesses and onetime suspects, a bad Xerox of a photograph of a Velcro wallet.

It doesn't take long to understand the basics. Nathaniel Rothstein was going through it. Sixteen: ugh. Miserable at home, violent at school. Then: Austin. He finds the gym, makes friends. From an interview with Bob Alexander: "Back east, it's gloomy! My nephew loved the sun." From an interview with Nathaniel's supervisor at the nursing home where he'd volunteered: "That boy was having the time of his life."

Even in her short time with the department, Miriam has learned that the most obvious answer is usually the answer. Suburban white kids aren't kidnapped for no ransom or murdered for no reason. The end of summer meant the end of Nathaniel's new life, a return to his old. Before that could happen: sayonara.

Nathaniel Rothstein ran, and either he wanted to stay missing or whatever bad thing happened to him happened at some later date, probably far from this city. There is little Officer Miriam Lopez, 101 days on patrol in Leonard District, can do about it. Nathaniel vanished before Facebook, or YouTube. Before Google, even. Disappear before the start of the twenty-first century and it was possible to disappear for good.

Still. It's fun to think about. Cracking a case, making a name. Miriam returns the pages to their proper order, piles them neatly on her small desk. She imagines creating a crime board on the pale yellow wall of her childhood bedroom: string connecting pieces of evidence like on TV.

Miriam knows it's a silly daydream, a way to make her life seem like something other than what it is: standing and waiting, sitting and writing, confronting a man at his angriest or his saddest or when he's most out of his mind and pretending—*trying* to pretend—not to be afraid.

Being a cop is just being a hundred other professions, armed. A hundred other professions Miriam is also unqualified for. A secretary with a gun. A social worker with a gun. An actor with a gun, performing for an audience of the hysterical and the deranged.

Miriam finds her father in his garage workshop. He looks up from his latest model airplane, waits for her to speak. Francisco Lopez never asks about her nights unprompted; Miriam rarely prompts. There is enough crazy out there, no need to invite it in here.

"Hey, Pop," she says. "Weird question but: Do you have any thumbtacks?"

DAY 118

The boxing gym is five miles north, in a different district—Edgar—with its own set of known miscreants and socially toxic personalities, none of whom Miriam is familiar with, thank god.

Since she started at the gym during field training, she has kept a low profile. Miriam has an idea of the comers and goers but says little. It is only now, in her after-midnight meet-ups with Alexis at Mags, that she begins to put names to faces.

The built Black guy in the shiny red shorts? "Fe-lix Bar-row-man," says Alexis, emphasizing each syllable as if he's teaching Miriam a foreign language. According to Alexis, back in the late '90s Felix was a legit contender. Fought on ESPN, *Boxing After Dark*. "Got knocked out at this big fight in Poland," says Alexis, transitioning to ghost story mode. "Never the same again." He makes the hand gesture for alcoholic: glug glug glug.

"Really?" says Miriam. "He's so *built*."

"You know it's possible to drink and still be *very* sexy." Alexis Cepeda raises his beer bottle. "Look at me."

DAY 124

It is scary. This is the thing that no one told Miriam Lopez, that no one seems to admit. This job is fucking terrifying.

Miriam alone in Leonard District's farthest reaches: a forlorn patch of frontage road out by the airport. The area around Austin-Bergstrom is for driving *past*. The airport itself is the clue: it's for coming or going, not staying. Only for the most unfortunate is this the end of the road.

The owners of the decrepit attempts at commerce here don't even have the juice to name their establishments. The pawn shop is called Pawn Store, the strip club Men's Club. The only foot traffic after dark: scattered vagrants, the occasional prostitute.

It's 3:08 a.m., no other cars in sight, when Miriam sees the man in the middle of the road. He's a white guy in his forties or fifties or sixties. The hermit's beard, the dirty face: who knows? He wears no discernable expression, which, standing in the middle of the road at 3:08 a.m., is an expression in itself. He's dressed like a teenager: loose cargo pants, a baggy thermal. Miriam stops her cruiser a couple yards from him, flashes her lights. The man doesn't move. It's as if he's been waiting for her.

The man begins to walk toward the cruiser. Slowly, deliberately. *Fuck*. Getting out of the vehicle seems like the right thing to do, the *brave* thing to do. What if he needs help? What if he's a danger to himself, or others?

Miriam wants to call for backup but can't. She'd never hear the end of it. The man hasn't done anything. She thinks, *You are armed.* She thinks, *The doors are locked, the windows up.* Miriam remembers something her field training officer once told her: *some rules supersede other rules*. The number one rule: *stay alive.*

When the man reaches the driver's side window, he stops. Miriam looks at him; he stares at the road ahead. Then he slaps his open palm against the window.

He does it with enough force that Miriam gasps at the sound. He holds it there. Two seconds, three seconds, four . . .

Miriam stares at the lifelines on the man's palm, at his extended fingers. She has forgotten how to move, how to breathe.

At five seconds the man releases his palm from the window. Then he keeps walking. Past the cruiser, into the night. Miriam turns to watch him. The man does not turn back.

On nights like these, Miriam Lopez knows she'll skip the gym come morning. On nights like these, she'll spend her final waking hours at the small desk in her bedroom: researching, taking notes, adding scraps of evidence to her pale yellow wall.

She has written the names of the key players on neon index cards and tacked them up there. Nathaniel Rothstein (Victim). Bob Alexander (Uncle). David Dalice (Boss). Also: a list of important dates; the Xerox of the note Bob showed her months before.

Miriam has made little progress. The "leads" of the previous ten years have led nowhere. There is zero evidence of foul play. Her tools are the tools of a layperson. Google, her imagination. Miriam is undeterred.

At Southwestern, a couple guys in her freshman dorm were serious gamers. It always seemed so dorky, but it's started to make sense to Miriam since joining the department. Immersing yourself in another world, another role. Forgetting.

She knows her FTO would've confronted the man out by the airport, taken him in. *Threatening a cop?* Corporal Bennington or any of the other officers would've, too, and, if they'd thrown him in the back of their vehicle with a little too much force, if they'd torn his shirt or his legs got twisted, well, guess he'll know for next time.

Miriam did not take the man in. Miriam did not report the incident. Miriam kept driving.

You seem like a normal person, Bob Alexander had told her months before. If that were the case, Miriam would've kept on driving all the way back to the substation, handed in her badge, her gun. One hundred and twenty-four days in Leonard District: no one could say she hadn't tried.

But there is the person Miriam is and the person Miriam wants to be, the person she thinks she *can* be, maybe, if she can figure out the route. She has always been so *contained*. What would it feel like to throw her weight around like the others do? To say, *Sir, I need you to step <u>back</u>*, and watch the man comply.

And make the man comply.

Would it feel like running?

DAY 139

"You know the guy who stays in the room at the back, right?" says Alexis.

Ed Hooley's been living at the gym for three and a half years. Since August, he and Alexis have developed a ritual of sorts: before the boxer spars or fights, he taps Ed in the gut. "He's my good luck charm," says Alexis. "With Hooley in my corner, I can't go wrong."

Miriam knows Ed, all right. He has a twitchy left eye, is always staring at her as she works the speed bag. Hair combed forward in the universal style of the not-all-there. And that unsettling marking on his neck: a jagged *2* carved right into him.

"Wait, you brought *him* to your *fight*?" Miriam asks, genuinely baffled.

Once, when Miriam was still in field training, she'd run into Ed in the wild. This was at an all-ages amateur competition at the Pan Am Rec Center; Terry had a couple kids fighting and knew it was Miriam's territory, invited her to stop by before her shift.

Miriam had never been to a community boxing match. The event had an eventless quality: gymnasium lights on, rafters packed but only the relevant parents, girlfriends, paying attention to what was happening in the ring. Around it, fighters warmed up on whatever lacquered floor space they could find: the teenagers and twenty-somethings throwing at air, or at their trainers' mitts, the under-12s attacking the bare palms of their fathers.

Miriam stuck by the popcorn vendor close to the exit, relieved, for once, to be in uniform, to not have to explain who she was or why she was there or who she was with. She watched a couple fights, figured she'd done her duty and could head to the substation. Then Ed Hooley appeared.

"Hey there, Miriam Lopez," he drawled. "Hey, Ed," she said, and they'd stood like that, up against the wall: Miriam pretending to watch the fight, pretending to ignore Ed's tremendous BO; Ed not even trying to pretend he wasn't watching Miriam.

So distracted was she by Ed's peculiar presence that she didn't even notice the photographer coming toward them, realized what was happening only when she heard, "OK, you two, *Statesman* here, get together . . . ," the interlocutor a narrow body clad in black with a camera for a head.

Just before the photographer pressed the shutter release, Ed rested his head on Miriam's shoulder, obscuring the number carved into his neck. Miriam forced a smile and—why was she always making the most awkward choice?—pressed her cheek into his greasy, combed-forward hair. She didn't know why she did this, didn't *want* to do it. Ed's hair smelled like nicotine. "Adorable," said the photographer.

A few days later, she noticed Terry had taped a short *Statesman* write-up about the event to his office wall; Miriam was not exactly shocked to learn they'd chosen a different photograph to run with it.

How was Ed Hooley, of all people, Alexis's good luck charm?

At Mags, Alexis admits he used to get a bad vibe off Ed, too. "But it was just first impressions. Ever since we started working together, I've been *good like gold*."

Alexis has been coming to Austin every summer since he was a kid and moved here permanently in eighth grade. His English is solid, but he sometimes mixes up prepositions, adds an *s* where one doesn't belong ("You know what I could use about now? *Spaghettis!*"). Miriam's never sure if he's misspeaking or just being a goof.

"I don't know if I'd say you tapping his stomach is really *working together*," says Miriam. "Like, is there more to the story?"

For the first time in Miriam's presence, Alexis doesn't look like he's kidding even a little. "Why would you say, *Is there more to the story?*" He sounds genuinely concerned. "Does it seem like there's more?"

Did she say the wrong thing? "Sorry, I—because, um—the story makes no sense?"

"Yeah," says Alexis, "because *luck* makes no sense! That's why it's *luck*." He's back to his jokester self, feigning indignation. "Y'know, Officer Lopez, not everything is a mystery to be solved."

"I guess," says Miriam. "Ed just kinda gives me the willies."

"*The willies?*" says Alexis, laughing. "What's *the willies*?"

DAY 151

Miriam can't understand why Alexis is friends with Carlos Ortega. "He's such a douche," she says, signaling for the check. "*And* he's old."

"Forty-two ain't young," Alexis agrees.

Carlos wears jean shorts and white athletic socks with work boots, untucked polos, and a ribbed beanie. He likes to lurk around the heavy bags, lying in wait for earnest newcomers so he can tell them they're wasting their money. Carlos retired from boxing some years ago. Miriam's heard him claim to be in the flooring business, but he frequently arrives while she's still working out in the morning. He never seems to have anywhere else to be.

Miriam was shadowboxing in front of the mirrored wall in the weight room the first time Carlos addressed her directly. "You for real, girl?" he rasped, squinting at her reflection. He pointed at her mirrored chest. "Burn that shit up! You hear me?" When she didn't respond, he shook his head, disgusted, skulked away.

It was only after the round ended that Miriam figured out what Carlos was talking about: her black Austin Police Department T-shirt. It was the first and last time she wore it to the gym, but now, whenever Carlos sees her, he uses those words in truculent greeting—"Burn that shit up!"—before turning to whomever happens to be in spitting distance and offering another favored exhortation: "*Never* trust a cop!"

To Alexis, everything Carlos does is hilarious. "Can you believe that fool?" he says now. "*What* an idiot!"

Miriam says she has a serious question about Carlos Ortega. "You think he wears the same shorts every day or does he have, like, ten pairs and they all look alike?"

"I don't go around smelling people's shorts, Officer Lopez. Is that a cop thing?"

"I'm just saying!" says Miriam.

Alexis looks around the room as if Carlos might be eavesdropping. "Same every day," he whispers. "*Definitely*. Carlos is nasty."

DAY 159

Bob Alexander is Bob Alexander.

"Did you know his nephew disappeared?" Miriam asks.

Alexis had no idea.

DAY 167

The most intriguing document from the Rothstein file is a retired detective's typewritten notes from an interview with one Emmett Wombley.

Miriam tacks the notes to her wall, along with the mug shot of Wombley, included in the file. He is a spindly old Austinite, a skinny Santa in an Aloha shirt. Wombley's rap sheet is like Wombley: long and marginal. Disorderly conduct. Public intoxication. A scroungy Parrothead from the seediest edges of Margaritaville.

The weekend of Nathaniel's disappearance, the Travis County Sheriff's Office received numerous reports of petty theft at Hippie Hollow, a "clothing-optional" swimming hole on the outskirts of town. The following Wednesday at 6:57 a.m., a deputy sheriff making his regular rounds came upon a startling sight. In the middle of Hippie Hollow's expansive and otherwise-vacant parking lot: a man spread like a snow angel. At his side: a tote bag from a local grocery, Wheatsville Co-op.

Wombley was dead drunk, not dead dead. The deputy revived him, then arrested him. Inside the tote was a weekend's worth of goods reported stolen. One monogrammed money clip, moneyless. One fanny pack, ransacked of cash. Not reported missing, but also in the bag: a Velcro wallet, empty but for an appointment reminder card from Newton Centre Orthodontics. Next to PATIENT NAME, in teacher-clean cursive: NATHANIEL R.

According to the notes, the cashier at a nearby liquor store identified Wombley as a regular. On the Saturday before his arrest—August 8, 1998—Wombley had spent around one hundred dollars on beer and vodka. The cash reported stolen from Hippie Hollow added up to seventy dollars; Wombley confessed he'd made the other thirty selling a driver's license he'd taken off the Velcro wallet.

The buyer of Nathaniel Rothstein's license was the associate of an associate, a "first-class mouth" from the coast whom Wombley had heard was always on the lookout for "fresh ID." What did the man use them for? "No idea," said Wombley. What did he look like? "I'm a drunk, detective. You think I remember? He looked like every other fuckin' clown."

In the end, Emmett Wombley—like the others questioned over Nathaniel's disappearance—was cleared.

Still, the whole thing strikes Miriam as odd. What was a sixteen-year-old kid doing at a *nude beach*? She wonders if Bob knows about that part. And if Nathaniel's license is out there somewhere, why hasn't it ever turned up?

DAY 174

At Terry Tucker's Boxing Gym, Miriam and Alexis flirt in the way of many nascent boxing gym couples of yore. They begin to work out together.

For someone as inexperienced as Miriam, it is the runway that she needs. She has never had a boyfriend, never had sex. There are no obvious reasons for these things, no unaddressed trauma or horror from her past. She didn't date in high school or college and then it felt too late. *A twenty-two-year-old who has never been kissed?*

Of course, they've been flirting for months. He is cute, maybe more than cute, his loose tank tops showing off not the cartoon delts of a bodybuilder but the subtler musculature of a man who needs strength *and* speed. Five foot seven and he could probably beat the crap out of every cop Miriam knows. She is two inches taller, and though she, too, boasts the unfussy physique of a practicing athlete, still it is inconceivable to her that Alexis, so open and easy, would be interested in the forever unsprung jack-in-the-box that is Miriam. He seems to move so lightly through the world, no footsteps in the snow. Miriam has always left deep tracks in her plodding wake.

And though she feels so loose around Alexis, so much looser than she is *out there*, she's convinced herself it's the unreality of their situation that allows her to be like this. Alexis isn't part of her real world, her real life. He is a break from those things, a break from Leonard District.

DAY 186

It happens in broad daylight, on the way home from her workout.

Miriam stops at Central Market for a coffee. In the parking lot, a man bear-hugs her from behind, slaps a palm over her mouth. "Gimme all your fuckin' money," he whispers.

Until now, crimes happened and *then* Miriam Lopez appeared. She has exactly as much a chance of being in the wrong place at the wrong time as the rest of us, except our wrong place is her right place. Or, at least, it's supposed to be. This is the moment she's trained for: a crime in progress, a crime she can stop.

The man releases her suddenly, collapses into a fit of exaggerated guffaws. "You shoulda seen your fuckin' face!" He's slight and stooped, a single swoosh of salt-and-pepper hair escaping his beanie. "Saw you driving in and I thought, I can get her *good*," says Carlos Ortega, delighted.

Miriam struggles to catch her breath. "Yeah," she says. "You did."

Carlos raises both hands in peace signs high above his head, a deranged Nixon. "Burn that shit up!" he says, then turns around and starts big-footing back to wherever he came from.

Inside Central Market, Miriam is too shaken to stand in line for coffee. She paces the grocery aisles, pretending to look for something, pretending she isn't hiding out in there, hoping Carlos won't still be lurking in the lot when she returns.

She tells herself this isn't like the incident by the airport. This time, she would've done something if it hadn't all happened so fast. Elbowed him in the stomach or swept her foot behind his leg. Except doesn't it always happen so fast? Isn't that, like, the most basic fact of violent crime? Miriam didn't even tell him to fuck off afterward. She walked away, let him walk away.

How is it that every day she confronts weird, broken people behaving badly, and every day Miriam Lopez is the one who ends up feeling like she did something wrong?

The police can't run a background check on just anyone. They need cause, and Miriam knows she doesn't have it. From her bedroom, she searches the Department of Public Safety Crime Records Division website. His most recent arrest was three years ago, in '06. Google turns up a last known address. *Of course*, thinks Miriam. *Leonard District*.

Still in her gym clothes, Miriam drives her Corolla south. The apartment complex is like everything built in Austin in the seventies: the slacker vibes of the era extending to architecture, construction. Tenuous wooden posts supporting crooked balconies, the buildings identifiable only via the pale remains of the big plastic letters once affixed to their sides. All the trappings of a skeevy beach motel except the beach.

The parking lot carries the vaguely hoppy scent of undergraduates; a small Catholic college is only a couple blocks away. At #21J, the blinds are drawn, no welcome mat. To one side of the door: a large soil-filled ceramic pot, cigarette butts where there should be flowers. Miriam rings the bell, knocks.

It feels weirdly freeing to be doing this out of uniform, stripped of her duty belt, her gun and holster. Dress like a cop and you'll feel like a cop, Miriam had once hoped. What Miriam has learned over six months in Leonard District is that if you dress like a cop without acting the cop, without *being* the cop, you just feel like a civilian dressed like a cop. She may not be able to Tase anyone, or beat them with a baton, or pepper-spray them in the eyes, but she doubts she'd do any of those things anyway. At least in gym clothes she can run.

The man who answers wears cycling shorts, a baggy tank top. He is sixty, seventy. Hard green eyes. Thinning gray hair that has no business anywhere near his gaunt shoulders. The loose skin of a drinker. He is the man from the mug shot, ten years aged.

"Emmett Wombley?" says Miriam.

It is a cold, gray day but Emmett Wombley does not invite Miriam in. Instead, he steps out to the balcony, braces himself against the slivery railing, and peers out: a dying king surveying his dying kingdom. "I don't like cops," he says, though all Miriam has given him is her first name.

Whatever she thinks he did, Emmett Wombley says, he didn't do. He hasn't been arrested in three years because he hasn't had a drink in three years. "Funny how that works, isn't it?"

Miriam stutters out why she's there: 1998. Hippie Hollow. Nathaniel Rothstein. It is a pained, laborious explanation. "You might have been the last person to see him," she finally manages.

"Are you suggesting I was messing around with a *naked teenage boy*? I'm a drunk, Officer, not a pervert."

"I—no—I'm—" Why can she never say the right thing? "I'm not suggesting anything."

Emmett Wombley doesn't remember the license or to whom he sold it. Maybe if he saw a picture of the guy, but he doubts it. "A thing about drunks is we're not known for our photographic memories." The Wombley story is not an inspirational one, he says. He was a bad husband, a bad father. He is not a good person but is less bad sober. "I've contributed nothing and I ask for nothing, except to be left alone." He turns to Miriam. "Aren't you going to ask how I knew you were a cop?"

Miriam doesn't want to know. "How?" she says weakly.

"Cops are like drunks," says Emmett Wombley. "Scared, little people who need a badge or a bottle to make some sense of ourselves in this big, scary world. We're *cowards*. The good ones, they just know how to hide it. And you and I . . ." A sour sneer. "*We're not the good ones*."

Miriam wants to ask Emmett Wombley what it is about her that makes this so obvious to him. To everyone. Instead, she takes out a scrap of notepaper on which she's had the foresight to write her name, her cell number. "If anything jogs your memory, I hope to hear from you."

Emmett Wombley takes the paper and goes back inside. His parting words as the door closes behind him: "You won't."

DAY 199

On her days off, Miriam runs with Alexis Cepeda.

She learns that she can talk to him side by side in a way she's never able to face-to-face. They run on the residential streets behind the gym, on the crushed granite trails around Town Lake. They run and talk, and because, until last summer, Alexis had been with the same girl since he was thirteen, it's new to them both: this Tell All portion of courtship, taking turns as confessor and priest.

It's on a run that Alexis asks Miriam if she feels more Mexican or white. "White, I guess," she tells him, but mostly she feels Lopez, her insular, eccentric family an ethnicity unto itself. Her parents found something in each other that they lacked before, and once they had it, whatever it was, they didn't need anything from anyone else. Holidays are just the three of them. Travel is rare and mostly in-state. She's never been to Mexico, never had ceviche, Alexis's tía Lola's specialty. "Is that your favorite food?" she asks.

"Hell no," says Alexis. "Pluckers ten-piece, baby. *Baker's Gold*."

It's on a run that Alexis admits that his "pad" is the back room of Lola's in the Live Oak Estates, a mobile home park off Oltorf. It hadn't occurred to Miriam that Alexis has a job outside of boxing, and back at Mags he'd never volunteered this information, but of course he does, as a busser at a Brazilian steakhouse. "Place is *mad* sketchy, but the money is OK."

"So that's why you're always up in the middle of the night," says Miriam. "You're just getting off your shift."

"I didn't lie," says Alexis. "I *deleted*." Hauling dishes may be what he does some nights, but boxing is who he is. "That's all that matters, right?"

In late February, Miriam and Alexis run alongside the water, both dressed like scuba divers: long-sleeved compression shirts and running tights, Alexis's accentuated with a pair of neon green shorts. "For *modesty*," he says in faux solemnity.

Alexis is cheerful enough the first half mile, but as they progress, an unfamiliar heaviness sets in. He is now 3–0, with three KOs. Terry has arranged these initial encounters using his contacts across the state, but it's time for Alexis to sign with a manager, a promoter.

"That's good, isn't it?" says Miriam.

"Would be, if I didn't have to deal with *The Law*," Alexis says, like he's in a Western.

Alexis isn't in the country legally. He has a truck but no license; a bank account but no social security number. He can commit to fights only within driving distance: he can't get on a plane. He could fight as a Mexican national, but this would involve living in Mexico. His gym is here, his people here. The grandfather who raised him in Tampico for much of his childhood is dead. "Missed the funeral, but—" He glances at Miriam, turns back. "I think he'd understand."

The rules make little sense to Miriam. For years, the steakhouse paid Alexis in cash; a barback told him he'd make a little more if he used a fake social to get "on the books," so as of last fall he's official. Since then, his situation is what it's always been, except now he pays taxes.

"Should you be telling me all this?" says Miriam.

"You gonna call ICE, *cop*?"

Miriam asks Alexis what he's going to do.

Bob Alexander taught at UT for forty years, and he has a friend who runs the immigration clinic at the law school. Alexis is meeting with her next week. "I'm just hoping we can figure something out."

What he knows for sure is that if he wants a fighting chance, he can't mess up in any way, like he did a couple months back. At Christmas, Alexis was pulled over for speeding, then cited for driving without a license.

"You never told me that," says Miriam. "What happened?"

"What do you mean, *what happened*?" says Alexis, trying to laugh. "I paid the ticket."

The ordeal Miriam Lopez has survived over twenty-two years is being a human on this planet. Alexis, Miriam sees now, has survived actual *Things*. She wants to confess to him something as significant as he's confessed to her, but the truth is that the worst things that have ever happened to Miriam seem so ridiculously small compared to what Alexis is going through. *I've never fit in, never had sex*. Boo-hoo.

It sucks sometimes, but Miriam is self-aware enough and content, enough, to know the truth: her things are not Things.

Miriam knows there is only one confession worth confessing now, because it's the only one she doesn't want to confess. They run in silence, heels hitting granite in unison, until she can't not say it any longer: "I think I'm a terrible cop."

DAY 211

He offers his first lesson as they skip rope in the weight room at Terry Tucker's Boxing Gym. They each try to outdo the other: if one jumps heel to toe, the other side-sways; if one goes criss-cross, the other does it in reverse. "You don't even *like* cops," says Miriam, jumping on one foot.

"*You* don't even like cops," says Alexis, kicking his legs out like a Russian dancer.

Alexis may not like cops, but he has endless ideas for Miriam about how to become a better one. He loves *CSI: Miami* and *Training Day* and *Rush Hour 2*. He's seen every episode of *Lockup*, the prison docuseries on MSNBC, and has perfected imitations of his favorite characters, including a fast-talking Crip at San Quentin ("I don't think you should do that one in public," Miriam has suggested) and a sadistic Mexican Mafioso serving life in Pelican Bay ("Alexis Cepeda está loco, ese! Alexis Cepeda gonna fuck you up!").

According to Alexis, cops don't look *at* you, they look *through* you.

According to Alexis, cops' two favorite phrases are *Shut the fuck up* and *Step the fuck back*. "So if you ever don't know what to say, just pick one."

According to Alexis, nabbing a criminal, stopping a crime, is like knocking an opponent out in the ring. "To have that much power? Even for a couple seconds? I'm telling you, Officer Lopez: it feels *scary* good."

DAY 228

Alexis teaches Miriam *Boxer Face*.

They're midway through a set of bicep curls, watching each other in the mirrored wall. "*This*," says Alexis, face relaxed, "is Normal Alexis. And *this*—" Alexis clenches his teeth, juts out his chin. "Is *Boxer Alexis*." Alexis claims he does Boxer Face fifty times in the mirror before bed each night.

"No, you don't," says Miriam. She tries to focus on her own arms, slender and lightly sculpted, and not his. She has never seen a person so secretly strong, his working body a different body from his unflexed self.

"You don't know me!" says Alexis. He switches to lateral raises. "For real, you think I go into the ring looking all scared?"

"I don't think you're knocking everyone out because you make some face," says Miriam.

"That's true," says Alexis, checking himself out in the mirror. "I'm knocking everyone out cause they're horrible at boxing." This is something Miriam has only learned recently: up-and-comers always fight duds to start. There's an entire industry of these people, apparently. Tomato cans.

She remembers something Corporal Bennington told her after some low-grade fuck-up the week before: *Your peers should be thankful, Lopez. You make these knuckleheads look like geniuses*. "Must be nice to be you and not them," says Miriam.

"For now," says Alexis, going to rack his weights. "But that's why I practice! 'Cause one day, soon, I'm gonna be in a *fight* fight, and I *will* be scared, and no one will know it." He returns to Miriam, still lifting. "And you know why, Officer Lopez? 'Cause I'll have made that face so many times, *it'll be my face*."

DAY 260

They do not kiss, do not have sex. This is the thing: it is nice to have a friend. Two hundred and sixty days in Leonard District, and Miriam Lopez *needs* a friend.

Now she and Alexis eat together, run together, tell each other their secrets. In the weight room at the gym, Miriam braces her palms on Alexis's boxing shoes as he completes his crunches and learns the point on his inner thigh past which his dense, curly leg hair fades into sparser terrain. They sit upright, toes touching, and toss a medicine ball at full force into each other's guts, never acknowledging that the grunts they emit when they work out by themselves and the grunts they are emitting now, together, are not the same grunts.

And sometimes, after work, Miriam crawls into bed and imagines her and Alexis doing the things they never do.

Miriam has never known herself in this way. As an athlete, her singular focus was her body. Disciplining her body. She was so careful about what she ate, so obsessive about training. She didn't get her period once during her senior year. Now her body no longer belongs to a team, to a sport. Her period is back. She is at the start of her twenty-third year and it is almost as if, after eight years on the track, she is only now allowing herself to experience the full sticky breadth of adolescence.

In late April, Miriam makes herself orgasm for the first time. She wants to scream out, wants to call his name, but in her childhood bedroom, in her childhood bed, she inhales deeply to stifle the sound.

Miriam is relieved she never told Bob Alexander she'd been poking around his nephew's case. It has been weeks since she even thought about the documents posted to her pale yellow wall. Miriam has reappropriated the creative energy she spent on one boy for another. Masturbation, it turns out, is a better stress reliever than investigating a decade-old missing persons case. Alexis Cepeda is her new Nathaniel Rothstein.

DAY 281

At Mags, Alexis tells Miriam the story of how he came to Texas.

After he finishes, they sit in silence, staring into their mugs. "OK," says Miriam finally. "Now tell me the real story."

"I'm telling you: dude was a *clown*. Makeup, wig, *everything*," says Alexis. "*Lucky Larry*," he adds, as if that makes the story more plausible. "El Payaso."

"So let me make sure I got this," says Miriam. She retells Alexis the story he just told: "This clown *dresses you* as a clown, then he gives you another kid's driver's license, then he abandons you *on stilts*, so you walk to the border crossing *by yourself*..."

Alexis makes a buzzing noise: the wrong answer on a game show. "First I had to get *off the stilts*. Remember, I broke my toe coming down?"

"So you walk to the border with your broken toe, *still dressed as a clown*, and at the inspection booth you show the license to get across?"

"I know what you're thinking," says Alexis. "But—" He raises a finger: *Now I got you*. "*You didn't need a passport back then.*"

"Are you *ever* serious?"

"I'm *always* serious," he says in his regular tone: serious and not. Alexis claims he still carries the license for good luck. He goes for his wallet.

On the radio: a hit-and-run on the 2200 block of South Lamar.

Miriam throws a couple bucks on the table for the coffee. "Next time, payaso."

The next morning, Miriam skips the gym, climbs into bed with her laptop. She Googles various combinations of "border" and "smuggler" and "Lucky Larry" and "clown" and comes up with nothing. She does find a story about nineteen immigrants who were abandoned in a tractor-trailer and suffocated to death in South Texas, another about a fourteen-year-old boy who was raped by a man claiming to be a coyote, then left for dead in the Sonoran Desert.

She decides she won't ask Alexis about crossing the border again.

DAY 306

A 10-39 to the Umlauf Sculpture Garden. *Use lights and siren.*

The Umlauf is an unexpected oasis off Barton Springs Road, its eccentric bronze statues—squat animals and strangely slender religious figures—scattered across six wooded acres.

Miriam arrives at 12:03 a.m. At the pavilion near the entrance, a wedding is being disassembled. Cater-waiters stack folding chairs, buffet trays. The vibe is Austin dropout culture, professionalized: shirtsleeves concealing inked sleeves; thin dreads atop a tanned blond head, the coils tied back in a sprightly burst.

Miriam's forays into the upper echelons of Leonard District have mostly involved property crime, or "persons of suspicion." "Gunshots" that turned out to be fireworks, which the homeowners would also like investigated. This is different.

In the garden proper, Miriam finds officers spread among the statuary, interviewing the remaining members of the wedding. The revelers speak in low voices and try not to seem as drunk as they are: the bony bride, a thirtysomething white woman in a billowing ball gown that screams *My turn now*; the bearish groom and two rosy groomsmen, all with ties around their heads like prep school pirates.

Miriam approaches Brendan Ross, her fellow rookie, the one she smelled her first corpse with all those months before. He's talking to a stately, gooselike woman in wide-legged linen pants and a flowing tunic: a Roman senator by way of Eileen Fisher.

"Mother of the groom," Ross tells Miriam, by way of introduction. "Mrs. Simpson here is an art history professor at—"

"Dr. Simpson and University of Pittsburgh," she says amiably. "As I was explaining to *Officer* Ross, this piece is less a representation of the *person* than the *time* in which it was made." She gestures toward the statue in front of them: a waifish naked woman, contrapposto on long legs. Her hair is parted in the center, one hand behind her back. It's Eve, Dr. Simpson explains.

"Like *Adam and*," says Ross.

"Except it's *not* Eve," says Dr. Simpson. "It's *1970s Eve*. Look at her. This woman isn't *biblical*. She could be in the Partridge Family."

Ross asks Dr. Simpson if she's sure she'll be OK.

"I'll manage," she says unconvincingly. "I *am* an art history professor. Nothing I haven't seen before, right?"

Ross thanks her for her time, catches Miriam up to speed. The wedding ended at 11:30 and most of the guests departed. The groom couldn't find his mother—the professor—so he and a couple members of the wedding party went looking for her. She'd come into the garden for a final wander, and it was here that she saw the man: his face hidden behind Eve's face, his front against Eve's back, jeans around his ankles.

"Stroking it," says Ross. "*Right between Eve's legs*."

The wedding party departs, the other officers depart, leaving Ross and Miriam to give the grounds a final look. "You know, I saw something just like this a few months back," Ross tells her. A late-night masturbator outside the post office at Congress and 71: on his knees behind a mailbox, only his member and his pumping fist visible to passing drivers.

Miriam says the same thing happened at the construction site across from the Whataburger on South 1st last August.

"Serial jerker, huh?" says Ross.

Miriam shines a light on Eve's backside. "Oh, damn." Cradled in the statue's hidden hand: the forbidden fruit. An apple. A viscous substance drips across it like a toga. She calls Ross over. "I don't think that's bird shit, is it?"

"Nope," says Ross. "Not bird shit."

Miriam remembers the corporal's instructions from her first night on the job. "You think we should, like, save a sample?"

Ross gives her a look. "A *sample*? You're on one tonight, Lopez."

She says it without thinking, says it like Alexis suggested: "Shut the fuck up."

Ross peers at her: *Did you just say what I think you said?* He chuckles. "You're weird as shit but I like you, Lopez. You think we'll catch this freak?"

Miriam returns to the substation at 7:17 a.m. In the break room, Corporal Bennington is pouring himself a coffee. "Hey, Corporal, guess who's back?" says Miriam, chummier than she's ever allowed herself to be with him before. "The Dick Without a Face."

Bennington has been with APD since 1989; he's been a cop since '86, the year Miriam was born. "The Dick Without a Face," repeats Bennington. He furrows his brow. "Who the fuck is that?"

DAY 323

School's out, shirts off. Summer in Leonard District: a broiling frenzy. "Can't spell *temperature* without *temper*," Corporal Bennington says of the season. Also: "*Dead things smell worse.*"

The most recent police academy class is ending their field training, and a new batch of rookies has begun to trickle in, as Miriam did the previous summer. Once backup to the backup, she is now often just backup.

Miriam arrives after the drag racers cross the finish line, the coke is flushed, the bicycle stolen. After an unknown person takes a shit in Little Stacy Pool (well after, unfortunately for everyone involved).

At the end of June, Alexis wins his fourth fight, returns from Fort Worth with a busted lip, a decent shiner, another KO. A few mornings later, he meets Miriam in one of the small parking lots off the

Hike-and-Bike Trail at Town Lake. She's traded out her normal racer-back tank for a black sports bra, wonders if he'll notice.

"Ouch," she says, inspecting his bruised left eye.

"Don't hurt too bad," says Alexis coolly.

"Really?" says Miriam.

"It's, like, my *eye bone*, dude! It kills!" He sneaks a glance at Miriam's bare stomach. "See I'm not the only one with a new look."

Miriam scrunches her face. "Too much skin?"

Alexis pulls off his T-shirt, tucks it into the waistband of his shorts. His chest is hairier than Miriam expected. He looks like a boardwalk caricature: a boy's head on the body of a man. "Too much skin?" he says, setting off.

DAY 333

Alexis's immigration attorney has a plan to allow him to keep training in Austin: a skilled worker visa. It's a long shot: he'll need to apply for a waiver first, since he's been in the country illegally, and he doesn't have one of the jobs that most often make for a successful application, like scientist or engineer. "But I am skilled," he tells Miriam at Mags. "Guess I better keep winning."

"And staying out of trouble," says Miriam.

DAY 342

At Terry Tucker's Boxing Gym: a wild development. Carlos Ortega is being sent away.

"To prison?" asks Miriam from the bench press, Alexis spotting her.

"To *Africa*!" says Alexis, an upside-down head.

"Where in Africa?" says Miriam, bringing the barbell down to her chest.

"I don't know," says Alexis. "*Africa!*" It's a long story, he tells her, but Felix Barrowman—glug glug glug—has agreed to fight an exhibition match "over there" at summer's end. Carlos will serve as his cut man. Felix is broke, and Carlos is the only one weird enough to do it for free. "How crazy is that?"

Miriam raises the barbell. "Isn't being a cut man, like, an *actual skill*?"

DAY 348

No single moment leads to this moment. They weren't ready, now they are. Alexis has the place to himself for a few days; they both have the night off.

He'd called that afternoon, inviting her over under the pretense of watching a movie.

"Is that really why you're inviting me over?" asked Miriam.

"No ma'am," he said.

She's always assumed she'd keep her virginity a secret, even as she loses it. But now the moment is here, she is naked in Alexis Cepeda's bedroom, in Alexis Cepeda's bed, and all she can think is *What if I bleed*?

The bedroom is Alexis distilled: adult and child, kidding and serious. He is fastidious: twin bed perfectly made (until they unmake it); his small, doorless closet organized by item, then color. On the walls, neat as paintings in a gallery, he's thumbtacked full-size movie posters. *2 Fast 2 Furious*. *Live Free or Die Hard*.

On the dresser across from his bed, Alexis has a modest flatscreen that he keeps on at all hours. The sound offers a semblance of privacy in this home that isn't his home; *SportsCenter* highlights and the *dun-dun* between scenes on *Law & Order: SVU* his version of white noise.

Alexis is above her, putting the condom on, when she says it. "I've never done this before." He eases himself on top of her until they are face-to-face, parts aligned. Alexis is dense and warm: a weighted blanket that doesn't quite reach her toes. He tells her that he's only had sex with two women in his whole life: his ex-girlfriend and, after they broke up, a one-night stand. "And that time," he offers plainly, "I almost couldn't come."

Before now, Miriam believed that she lacked the technical know-how to be intimate, that when the time came, she wouldn't know what to do. But when he kisses her, she kisses back. She lifts her hips ever so slightly. "I don't think that will happen this time," she says.

It is not earth-shattering. Miriam does not transcend herself and rise above her writhing body to watch, does not make wild noises, does not come. It is polite sex: not sex, even, so much as a quiet conversation about what hurts less, what feels right, Alexis adjusting, adjusting, until amid all that movement he loses the ability for quiet conversation and buries his face in her neck.

After, he wants to go down on her, wants to "finish my job," but she says, "It's finish *the* job," and he says, "I know it's finish *the* job," and they're back to their old jokey ways. Alexis has kept the television on at low volume: his prison reality show, *Lockup*, is in the middle of a marathon on MSNBC. He takes the clicker from his bedside table, presses INFO. "Now you'll always know," he tells her.

"Know what?" says Miriam.

"Know that the first time we had sex it was to—" He slowly reads aloud from the program information displayed at the bottom of the screen. "Season Two, Episode Four. Inside Holman Correctional Facility."

They watch TV, flirt, make out. Alexis gets up to pee and Miriam doesn't hear him return, but when she looks in the doorway there he is: arms hugging himself like white kids do when they're pretending to be rappers. He's scrunched his face into a swirl of befuddlement and irritation. Miriam doesn't know where it's come from, but he's wearing a ribbed beanie.

"What are you *doing*?" asks Miriam.

"Who am I?" he asks, his voice the scratchy rasp of Carlos Ortega.

"Alexis, that's so gross," says Miriam, wince-laughing. "I don't want to think about that guy naked."

Alexis comes back to bed, beanie still on. He's a little bit hard. "Who's Alexis?" he says.

The weirdest part is that it doesn't feel weird. Miriam has spent these past months learning her body could do things that she'd never allowed it to do. Training it to do those things. Now, here, finally, she's putting that training to use. The result: it feels right. *She* feels right. She feels right with him.

At some point, *Lockup* transitions over to the news. One story has dominated the headlines for days, the sort of racial dust-up whose grabby particulars are easier to fixate on than the underlying causes: perfect for TV. Miriam has followed it like she follows all stories: via the side comments of her fellow officers, from glances at chyrons on blaring televisions inside the homes of hoarders or the deceased.

A white police officer responding to a 911 call arrests a Black man for breaking into a home in Cambridge, Massachusetts. The problem: the man is a celebrated Harvard professor, the home his home. Then, at a press conference, President Obama says the police behaved "stupidly." In Leonard District, the president's comment has agitated those officers who become easily agitated by this president. Now, in an effort at modeling reconciliation, Obama has invited both the professor and the cop for a beer at the White House—an event to which Corporal Bennington claims he would refuse the invitation.

Miriam thinks it's obvious that arresting a man for breaking into his own home is, at the very least, in the general direction of stupid. She does not care about this story, is not focused on the television. She thinks Alexis is asleep, turns on her side. He big spoons over. "Yo, Officer Lopez," he grumbles, as Carlos Ortega. "You wanna go one more round?"

"*Nooooo*," she says, groaning into the pillow. "That voice is scary."

Alexis straddles her. "What voice?" he says in the voice. She laughs as he kisses her neck. "Never trust a cop!"

DAY 349

The messages start coming at 8:25 a.m. A long-lost track pal: "Looking good, girl!" Officer Ross: "That ur boyfriend?" Miriam's still in bed; Alexis is in the shower. She texts Ross back: "???"

Before Miriam gets a response, Corporal Bennington calls. "Have you picked up the paper this morning?" Miriam is twenty-three years old; the year is 2009. "The paper?" she asks.

Three hours later, Miriam's at APD headquarters as instructed, in the small, unadorned office of Public Information Officer Gary D'Angelo. PIO D'Angelo is in his thirties, tall and long-limbed, with a prominent Adam's apple and a dark mustache and the glint of a formerly gawky person who has found his spot, relaxed into himself.

On the desk between them: the morning's *Statesman*. Across the front page: a color photograph taken under the bright lights of the Pan Am Rec Center gymnasium many months before. His head on her shoulder, her cheek in his hair. *Edward Hooley, 52, shares a moment with Officer Miriam Lopez of the Austin Police Department.*

D'Angelo explains that in light of the professor-and-police kerfuffle dominating national news, the *Statesman* is running a series on community relations with the department. Today's story is on cops and the mentally ill. Ed and Miriam aren't mentioned in the article; why should they be? "The photo says it all," says D'Angelo. He takes a slow sip from an APD mug. "*There is no bad press* doesn't apply to the police. So this, it's nice to see."

Miriam cannot believe they've published this photograph. She was not comfortable in that bizarre position. Even now, she thinks her grin looks strained and tight. Ed is Ed-like: hair combed forward; eyes gently closed and smile soft, like a sleeping puppy. The department has already posted the photograph to its Facebook page. Miriam doesn't have Facebook, but she knows she's meant to be impressed when D'Angelo says, "Over *twenty-four hundred* likes."

D'Angelo has pulled Miriam's file. Fewer than a quarter of APD officers identify as Hispanic or Latino. Women? Under 10 percent. "People trust people who look like they do," says D'Angelo. "And you look like a whole lot of people."

The Public Information Office is always on the hunt for bright young officers to serve as spokespeople for the department. If Miriam keeps her head down, keeps up the good work, he'd love to see her application in a year or two. "Just remember, we're the face of the department. The best of the best." A droll warning: "So keep it clean, Lopez. Don't go destroying any evidence on us, all right?"

Miriam brings Alexis a copy of the paper, excuses herself to the bathroom, and when she returns, finds him in bed, pretending to jerk off to it. At the substation, the front page is everywhere: on printer paper in the staff mailboxes, blown up on posterboard in the break room. During their staff meeting, Corporal Bennington presents Miriam with a toy Academy Award.

When, eighteen minutes later, on patrol in Leonard District, an unknown number appears on her cell, Miriam assumes it's another well-wisher. "Lopez here," she answers jauntily.

"You're truly awful at your job, aren't you?"

Miriam hasn't thought about him in months, but she can picture the caller right away. The hard green eyes. The sour sneer. "Mr. Wombley?" she says.

She'd asked him to call if anything "jogged his memory." Now something has. "That inane picture in the paper." The man he sold Nathaniel Rothstein's license to: "Galveston scumbag, pardon the repetition," says Emmett Wombley. "Guy claimed he was a professional party clown, but from what I remember he was just a *clown* clown."

"Like he dressed like a clown?" asks Miriam, confused.

"No, he wasn't dressed like a clown," says Emmett Wombley. "Is English not your first language? He *was* a clown. An asshole."

"What does that have to do with the photo in the paper?" says Miriam.

"*That's him*, Sherlock," says Emmett Wombley. "The man you're with is that fuckin' bozo. I only dealt with him that one time, forgot him best I could, but then I saw that picture and the stench came rushing back. Bigger juicehead than I was. General Grant's piss probably smelled less boozy."

Emmett Wombley says he's 99 percent sure that's the guy Miriam's looking for. The only discrepancy is the name. He wasn't going by *Edward* then. "Called himself Lucky Harry or Larry or something. If he wasn't resting on your shoulder like that, I'd know it was him for sure. Had a real gnarly carving in his neck. A number *one*."

Emmett Wombley is still talking but Miriam is no longer listening. *Lucky Larry*. Where has she heard that name before? And why would a person look just like Ed Hooley but have a different number carved into his neck? It makes no sense. How can a one become two?

DAY 350

Crimes happen, and ten years later Miriam Lopez appears.

A lesson from three hundred and fifty days in Leonard District: if it's too much of a coincidence, it might not be a coincidence at all. Turns out the guy who's always mysteriously wide awake when you call at 1 a.m. gets off work at 12:30. Jeans around ankles at a construction site, behind a mailbox, in a sculpture garden, isn't a sign of an epidemic of public masturbators, but of one handsy, headless man. Two names, two personalities, two numbers, one face? Maybe Ed Hooley has an alter ego. More likely, he has a twin.

7:34 a.m.: Miriam Lopez, still in uniform, reviews the dusty evidence on her pale yellow wall. In August 1998, a "clown" on the lookout for "fresh ID" bought Nathaniel's stolen license off Emmett Wombley. According to Wombley, the clown's name was Lucky Larry.

Alexis has also told Miriam about a clown with this name: a literal clown—a clown in wig and full makeup—he'd hired to take him stateside, where Alexis had already begun training at a boxing gym in Austin. Some years later, a homeless man named Ed Hooley arrived at this same gym, desperate for a place to stay. Had Ed heard about the gym from his twin brother, who'd heard about it from Alexis?

And if the Lucky Larry who bought the license of a teenage boy off Emmett Wombley in Austin is the same Lucky Larry who gave the license of a teenage boy *to* a teenage boy named Alexis Cepeda, it's likely that the license Alexis used to cross the border, the "good luck license" he's carrying around right now . . .

You ever hear anything about his case, maybe you'll let me know.

How is this possible? *Could* it be possible? Once, Miriam would've never even considered it. Too connected. Too bizarre. But if she's learned anything over three hundred and fifty days on patrol it's that too *anything* doesn't exist. In college, Miriam had an English professor who liked to say *you can't create a world you can't imagine.* A year in Leonard District has taught her that most people can't imagine the world we've already got.

Miriam checks the time. 7:39. His aunt should be at work by now. Miriam texts Alexis: "Gonna skip gym today." She texts again: "Get back into bed."

It is a privilege to decide.

To run or not run. To stop or not stop. To let him go or pull your weapon. It's a privilege because it means you're in the moment, in the now.

For a year, Miriam Lopez has tried to talk, think, act like a cop. No matter what she did, she could never locate those facets of herself that she needed on patrol. The decisive self who never flinched at the starter pistol or glanced back to see who was gaining on her. The resolute self who moved only in one direction: straight ahead.

Now she has a reason to act. A person to act *for*. The boxer has one job this summer and it is to stay out of trouble. Miriam can't secure Alexis a visa, but she knows enough to know there will be no visa if the missing license of a missing person is ever found on him.

For once, the bad thing hasn't happened yet. She can stop it. She *will* stop it.

Three hundred and fifty days spent looking inward, trying to figure out how to be. A life spent looking inward. What if this whole time all she had to do was look out?

Alexis has left the door unlocked, done as he's told.

He is not expecting her in uniform, but he has no complaints. Miriam stands over the bedside. He is sitting up, lower half under the covers. "License and registration," she says in a voice that isn't her voice. A voice that is.

Alexis grins up at her, scratches his chest. "Sorry, Officer," he says. "What'd I do?"

"I said, license and registration." She is serious, so he gets serious, too, nods to his wallet on the nightstand. She picks it up, rifles through. A bank card. A Target card. And there it is.

She does not gasp at the shock of it, or tremble. She does not let on in any way. Miriam Lopez has gone elsewhere. Officer Lopez pulls out the license. Name: Rothstein, Nathaniel Joshua. DOB: 10/27/81. The photo is a chunky white face. Thick black freckles. Vacant eyes. Of the millions of teenagers who surely looked nothing like Alexis Cepeda as a teenager, this kid must be at the top of the list.

"Sir," says Officer Lopez, "I'm going to need you to step out of your vehicle."

Alexis peeks under the covers. "I'm, uh, not sure that would be appropriate, ma'am."

"Does it sound like I'm asking?"

"It does not," says Alexis. He pulls off the covers, impressed at his own big reveal.

Officer Lopez doesn't look. "Up against the wall," she says.

Alexis makes no attempt to cover himself, keeps his eyes on Miriam as he swaggers toward the dresser. His hair is messy, his grin suppressed.

Once his back is to her, Officer Lopez tells him to brace his hands against the dresser. She pockets the license, tosses the rest of the wallet back onto the nightstand, begins her approach.

She won't destroy it, this she knows. She likes the idea that it might eventually be found. Scrubbed of prints, scrubbed of Alexis. The missing boy, now a missing man, will probably remain missing forever, but there are parts of his case that still don't make sense to Miriam, his presence at Hippie Hollow chief among them. Maybe a new piece of evidence will lead to renewed interest, a proper re-opening of the case. Bob Alexander deserves that, at least.

When she's within touching distance, Alexis whirls around to face her. He's scrunched his shoulders inward, scrunched his face. "This is bullshit!" he rasps. He is no longer Alexis Cepeda; all he's missing is the beanie.

They both stay in character as he unfastens her duty belt, as she unholsters her weapon and puts it on the nightstand. "Make a face long enough and it might become your face," warns Officer Lopez, pressing into him.

"You always had it out for me, fool!" he cries as they struggle into bed.

There's a strange moment after she climbs on top of him when she sees Alexis re-emerge: the face unscrunches, the time for joking passed. He is one man, then another. That's when it comes to her. She thinks about the license, in her pants, on the floor. How had she not thought of it before? The perfect solution. Elegant. A little wicked.

Since the eighth grade, Alexis Cepeda has been Nathaniel Rothstein, at least according to the license in his wallet. Now it's someone else's turn.

Never trust a cop.

Kuchizi

CARLOS ORTEGA ROAMING AFRICA was a ridiculous proposition, which was why everyone who heard the idea savored its deliciousness. For all his forty-two years, Carlos had prowled the same mangy patch of North Austin, and to conceive of him elsewhere seemed impossible to those who knew him. At Terry Tucker's Boxing Gym, where Carlos spent most days, folks had long been urging their leader to give Ortega the boot. Terry always refused, confident his onetime fighter would burn down the place in retribution. He instead warned newcomers to treat Carlos like a grizzly bear: regard him from a distance and never make eye contact. "Ortega's not all bad but he always goes too far," Terry would explain. "He's an acquired taste no one's yet acquired."

Carlos had fought on and off into his thirties, a journeyman who built up a respectable record inside the Texas Triangle. In retirement, he'd become increasingly isolated, boxing his one true talent. Without it, he was left skulking around the gym at all hours, forever trying to shoot the shit with the old-timers, who did their best to ignore him.

Their disdain was moderate compared with the young Black fighters, whose contempt for the man came from his use of the n-word, which he employed as both salutation and slur, and which everyone, from Terry on down, had pleaded with him to erase from his vocabulary. The other Mexicans were more forgiving. They'd shake their heads when they saw him but would at least pretend to listen to his suggestions. Carlos himself was especially interested in the college boys, mostly white guys in bright running shoes who could jog and do pull-ups but tripped over themselves trying to pivot around a heavy bag.

"Let me see what you got," Carlos would rasp, stroking his chin and circling as they shadowboxed or skipped rope. "Wasting your money here, fool," he'd offer after a minute. "You hear me?" he'd add, punctuating the question with his favored racial epithet.

Carlos's journey to Kenya was the result of a favor Terry called in for Felix Barrowman. Once a gifted middleweight, Felix's career hadn't played out as he'd planned. His signature defeat came in January 1999, a third-round TKO at Torwar Hall in Warsaw. Since that fateful night, he'd been as unable to give up as he was to break through. "Boxing makes you stupid," was his ex-wife Kiara's take, the *you* in this context not all people who chose to make a living getting whacked in the head, but Felix in particular.

It was true. For a couple years, he'd been the young phenom. He'd traveled with Terry to places neither of them had been; fought on HBO and ESPN; had some money coming in. Felix wasn't a star, but he could taste it. And then it didn't happen. Not because he didn't work hard, or train right. It just . . . didn't. He got outboxed in Mexico City. A bad break on a split decision. Another TKO.

By then, Felix had put so much into it, he couldn't imagine doing anything else. So he kept chasing that taste he'd had in his early twenties, and it did make him stupid. He made dumb investments, spent money he didn't have.

He'd also, until recently, been engaged in a heavy flirtation with functional alcoholism. With each passing bout, Felix made less and drank more. Maybe, he sometimes mused, it would've been easier to move on if his downfall had happened overnight. His was a crueler kind of losing, interrupted by the occasional, always fleeting, win. Felix Barrowman hadn't nosedived straight from champ to chump. He'd descended like a Plinko chip, zigging and zagging to the bottom.

At a bout in Boston the year before, he'd finally reached his nadir. A clover-tatted up-and-comer named Mad Dog McDermott knocked

Felix through the ropes, out of the ring, and onto the judge's table two rounds in. The fight received some coverage, mostly because of the pathetic visual, but also because of the whiteness of the crowd, whose sneering triumphalism at a Black man's humiliation led to a brief round of "How Far Have We Actually Come?" on a smattering of sports blogs.

"Shit," Carlos bellowed the first time Felix appeared at the gym after the fight. "Mad Dog fucked you up." The Boston incident, Carlos knew, riled Felix. Now thirty-five, the fighter was seven months sober but suffering an existential hangover, and nearly broke. It didn't help to find Carlos standing below the ropes whenever he sparred, yelling "Don't fall on me!" in mock horror.

The fight Terry arranged for Felix at the Malindi Grand was an exhibition, entertainment for the guests and little more. The payday wasn't extravagant—$5,000, win or lose—but Felix wouldn't have to squander his earnings on the support staff a sanctioned match required. All he needed was someone to stop the bleeding, and while Carlos wasn't a trained cut man, he'd watched enough of them attend to his own wounds through the years to play the part. Plus, Terry was already giddily imagining the respite to come: five days Ortega-free.

"I get my own room?" asked Carlos, when Terry proposed the gig.

"That's Felix's only requirement," said Terry. "We have a deal?"

In the month leading up to his departure, Carlos Ortega wondered if he'd made the wrong decision. He imagined missing major gym news, say a sparring session that devolved into an actual fight, and worried about being forgotten entirely. As the weeks passed, Carlos began to hope that the expedited visa Terry Tucker was paying for would not be expedited enough, that his first-ever passport might get lost in the mail.

And then the day was upon him, and before Carlos quite knew what was happening, Terry was dropping the fighters off curbside, helping to unload their duffels from the bed of his truck. Carlos kept waiting for Terry to tell him that the plans had changed, that they needed him back at the gym, but the older man just wished Felix luck and gave Ortega a goodbye whack on the shoulder. "Don't forget me, you piece of shit," Carlos called out hopefully as the truck sputtered off.

It wasn't until they were seated at the gate that Carlos, legs spread wide, pulled out his wallet, double-checking to make sure that the license he'd tucked behind his license was still there. At the very least, Africa would force him to steer clear of that cop for a bit.

Some nuts on her, that Miriam Lopez. A couple days earlier, she'd approached Carlos at the gym, gone in for an awkward side-hug to wish him "safe travels." She wasn't near as crafty as she thought she was; he'd felt her doing it as she did it. Even so: planting a missing kid's license in the back pocket of his shorts? Extremely fucked up. He had to respect it.

How'd she get her hands on it? Carlos wondered. Or even know who the kid was? All these years later, Carlos had never given the disappearance much thought. Bob's nephew had arrived in Austin a dumpy loser and seemed like less of one when it was time to go home. Why go back? If Carlos had been Nathaniel Rothstein, he probably would've run away, too.

I can't believe Alexis is fucking a cop, thought Carlos, which was one of two places his mind always ended up after thinking about Miriam long enough. (*What would it be like to fuck a cop?* the obvious other).

Seven months before, Carlos had pretended to mug Miriam; now Miriam had planted evidence on him. As Carlos saw it, they were tied. He'd find a way to retake the lead when he returned. By then, Nathaniel's license would be long gone. No point ditching it in his home city, covered in prints, if he could dispose of it 9,000 miles away. For all that cop's clever scheming, did she miss the part of the story where Carlos Ortega was going to *Africa*?

On all three flights, Carlos was assigned the aisle and Felix the window, with one unfortunate passenger or another stuck between them. From

Austin to Dallas the men didn't speak at all, the music from Felix's headphones so loud that Carlos could have sung along if he knew the lyrics. On the flight to London, Carlos, knees bobbing, could stand the silence no longer. He began unfastening his food tray, catching it mid-fall, and then repeating the process again and again until Felix leaned over the elderly woman in the center seat and fastened the tray himself.

"I'm not fucking around anymore, Ortega," said Felix as they walked through Heathrow to their next gate. The two made an unusual pair. Carlos was gaunt and watchful, his face scrunched into an expression of bewilderment and suspicion. In his jean shorts and beanie, a small backpack slung over his shoulder, he looked almost deformed next to Felix, whose red-and-white tracksuit accentuated his muscle. Broad and handsome, Felix's drinking and fighting had flattened his good looks but not erased them entirely, his hazel eyes sunken yet still striking, a once-delicate nose now crooked and compressed.

"The loudmouth managers, the shit contracts, the guys like you. I've been around guys like you my whole life." Felix stopped beside a water fountain. "We're gonna make our money and leave. No silly stuff."

"You know your problem, man," said Carlos. He tapped his forehead. "You think too much."

"I drink too much," said Felix, walking again. "And this whole fucked-up world leads me to it."

"Bullshit," called Carlos from behind. "I don't drink, I don't smoke, I don't think. You know why?" Carlos threw up his arms, presenting himself to all who passed. "Carlos Ortega don't give a *shit*."

"And look how it's turned out for you," said Felix, putting his headphones back on.

Carlos nodded. "And look how it's turned out for me."

If any Kenyan city were designed for the seamy spectacle of boxing, Malindi was it. Forty-six years after independence, a visitor to one of the seaside resorts there would be forgiven for assuming the British had simply transferred their power south to the Italians, who ran the tourism industry with the sort of wink-wink malfeasance that the Sicilian Mafia would appreciate, and probably did. At the Malindi Grand, the marble-floored guesthouses were designed to look like thatch-roofed huts, and tiki lamps outnumbered people. In the restaurant, bright and airy, the masks lining the walls came from Benin and Togo, or so claimed the maître d', who was also responsible for destroying the boxes they arrived in, stamped *Fragile* and *Handle with Care* in Chinese.

The moneymakers themselves were rarely on-site, outsourcing the day-to-day management of the Grand to Malindi locals, who donned gold metal nameplates engraved with Italian pseudonyms. Urbano Abbascia was the head chef. Giovanni Cracchiolo waited tables. For years and without fanfare, Donatella Versace managed housekeeping, each morning filling heavy-duty garbage bags with half-eaten pizzas and used condoms, curled and slick.

As for the guests, their interactions were confined to short, flirty back-and-forths with muscled men in puka shell necklaces who trolled the lobby and the pool area, offering massages and short lessons in Swahili, windsurfing instruction, and, on Thursday nights, a beachside African dance class that included a tutorial in the Electric Slide.

"The great champion has arrived," said Marco Giordano, the hotel manager, when Carlos and Felix entered the lobby. Marco was a short, pudgy Kenyan in pinstripe, an unlit cigar dangling between his fingers. "There is Las Vegas, there is Macao, there is Malindi," said Marco, his hand on Felix's shoulder. "What does it feel like to be home, my African brother?"

"Yeah, my African brother," snickered Carlos. "What's it feel like?"

As Marco led Felix around the hotel grounds, Carlos dallied a few steps behind, poking his head down hallways, plucking a mint from an abandoned housekeeping cart. Occupancy was high in August, and Carlos observed the largely Italian clientele with the thoroughness of an anthropologist. It was an older crowd at the Grand, and on the rare occasion a young woman passed, bikini-clad and flip-flopping here or there, Carlos bowed slightly, trying to contain a smile.

More frequent sightings included hairy potbellies dripping over tiny nylon swim briefs, so ghoulish an image that Carlos found himself tucking his chin into his chest whenever one passed, his cheeks tingling with shame and glee. Standing over the saltwater pool, Carlos could contain himself no longer, aghast at the pink, gelatinous creatures basking in the sun. "You fuckin' seeing this?" he asked Felix, who shook his head, signaling for Carlos to be quiet as Marco fastened gold plastic bracelets around their wrists and explained the colored bands all guests wore on the property: bronze if they'd paid for food and drink but not alcohol, silver for food and well drinks only, gold for the highest level of inclusivity.

"What's blue?" asked Carlos.

"Our blue guests pay for everything à la carte," said Marco. "Mostly Germans."

The fight was scheduled for the next evening against a Kenyan opponent whom Terry had referenced only as The Butcher. Marco led the men down a stone path to the oceanfront guest huts, set back from the water and semicircled around an expansive shore. "This is your new residence," he said proudly. He continued toward the shoreline, Carlos and Felix following behind. As they zigzagged between lounge chairs, shoes kicking up sand, Marco explained that they'd construct the ring here, just far enough from the ocean that the waves wouldn't reach the canvas.

"I suspect it is not a night any of us will soon forget," said Marco, before suggesting the men settle into their rooms. "Hakuna matata, arrivederci, and have a most wonderful day," he added, and marched back toward the hotel, leaving Carlos and Felix gazing at a just-departed snorkel cruise zipping out to sea.

In the afternoon, Carlos and Felix were scheduled to train at the facilities of The Butcher. On the ride downtown, the men the sole passengers in a twelve-seat van, Felix relaxed into his headphone-protected daze. Carlos, meanwhile, felt as if he'd been plunged into an especially pleasing hallucination. He lay across his row of seats, playing with his wristband, as they sped along the newly paved road that separated the hotel from town. A mile in, the road gave way to pockmarked highway, and soon they were chugging past mud-flecked trucks and minibuses crammed with wizened men in white skullcaps, women wrapped in black cloth. The minibuses—matatus, said the driver, a genial pug of a man called Luigi—were themed, which was how, during a spell of traffic, Carlos found himself parallel to one with a Wu-Tang Clan decal splashed across its windows, stickers featuring the larger-than-life-size heads of RZA and Method Man covering the sliding door.

Malindi was not the Africa that Carlos had anticipated. The city consisted of a few overcrowded blocks of Kobil gas stations and internet cafés, advertisements for Coke and Bayer Aspirin hand-painted onto the sides of dirt-smudged apartment buildings. The roads were noisy with traffic, horns blaring from Peugeot 504s, the tailpipes of Isuzu pickups hiccupping exhaust. Conductors hung off the sides of their matatus, hawking cheap rides to Marereni or Mombasa, and from the mosques, competing muezzins blared the call to prayer through loudspeakers mounted on minarets.

Carlos had expected dark women with baskets on their heads, their breasts substantial and uncovered. The women here were lighter and wore buibuis—black robes with head coverings—only their hands and faces exposed.

"Al-Qaeda!" Carlos exclaimed as they drove down a narrow road, two slender women in oversized sunglasses with plastic Nakumatt grocery bags brushing past.

"No, no," assured Luigi. "Swahili, Swahili."

"Swahili," repeated Carlos, shaking his head and smiling. *How stupid do I look?*

Luigi parked down a puddle-smeared side street and nodded toward a small concrete building that tilted ever so slightly to one side, as if it had been constructed during a mild windstorm. Outside the van, it was hot but not Texas hot, heavier, balmier, and as the boxers entered the gym, the familiar stench of sweat and leather mixed with the smells of the city: newly butchered marlin, charcoal from the seaside vendors, wet cement.

Inside, men in track pants and tank tops jabbed at real opponents and shadowboxed imagined ones. Turned fists thwacked speed bags, jump ropes cracked against concrete. Carlos recognized the hangers-on immediately: so-called managers with loud voices and no clients, would-be champions who expended more energy acting exhausted than moving their feet. In the back corner across from the ring, a round woman in a buibui slouched in a chair, head down, possibly asleep.

"Look at *this* fuckin' place," said Carlos approvingly. He patted at the front pocket of his workout shorts, gave Nathaniel's license a little making-sure-you're-still-there rub with his thumb. Carlos had resolved to bring the license everywhere he went in Malindi, worried a snooping maid might find it if he left it lying around, sure he'd know where to get rid of it when the opportunity presented itself. Back in a recognizable world after a day of foreign travel, Carlos felt a strange surge of affection toward the license, as if, these many years later, he was finally returning the boy to his rightful home: the gym. "This is where it's *at*, right, boss?"

"This'll do the job," Felix agreed, sliding onto a bench near the entryway, tossing his bag down next to him. Back when he was still a cocky upstart, Felix had once given a pep talk to a bunch of kids visiting Terry Tucker's from juvenile detention. He'd told them that in every city in the country, in most countries in the world, there was a boxing gym like this one, a place anyone would be accepted, if they were willing to put in the work. Felix no longer believed a lot of the things he did in his twenties, but he still believed that. "Good to be back in the office," he said.

The gym was ostensibly run by three twentysomethings: Omari, Kadara, and George. All elbows and knees, they rambled about the room, slapping backs, collecting dues, and offering guidance.

Carlos spotted Omari first, squeezed between two double-end bags, playing hacky sack with a coiled hand wrap as flyweights threw jabs on each side of him. A few others looked on, and when Omari saw the Americans, he kicked the wrap high enough for one of the spectators to catch it, straightened his back like a child playing grown-up, and strode over. Kadara, droopy-eyed with a pointed goatee, soon followed, just ahead of George, a jaunty power-walker whose swinging forearms did little to mask a pronounced limp. Soon, all three Kenyans were huddled around the guests. A trio of long men in mismatched outfits, they looked as if they'd been given thirty seconds to choose their wardrobes for the day and had thus ended up in camouflage pants and a Celtics jersey, or a plaid sarong and a tie-dye T-shirt from United Way.

"Karibu, karibu," said Omari solemnly. He bowed toward Felix, his glasses sliding down his nose as he took the fighter's hands.

"It is wonderful to have you here," said Kadara, clasping Felix's shoulder.

"Your presence means more to us than you can know," said George, hanging his arm around Carlos, completing the circle. Carlos recoiled from the stranger's touch, his squint now so vigorous it looked like he was experiencing daylight for the first time in months.

"Thanks for having us, guys," said Felix.

"What might we do to help you get started?" asked Omari, pushing his glasses back into place.

"We good," said Carlos, puffing out his chest. He leaned into Omari. "You know," he added, not unkindly, "this fool could fuck up everyone in this joint."

The Kenyans exchanged quizzical glances.

"I'm all set," said Felix, ignoring the cut man.

"You ready to throw some mitts, boss?" said Carlos, stretching his elbow behind his head.

Felix unzipped his gym bag and started rifling through it. Getting lost in a workout was one of his few remaining pleasures, and he wasn't going to let Carlos ruin it. "Hey, Ortega," he said. "It look like I'm bleeding?"

Carlos wrinkled his forehead. "You're not bleeding."

"That's right," said Felix. "I'm not bleeding. And I don't plan on bleeding today. So unless I trip and cut myself, you best find something else to do."

As Felix loosened up, Omari led Carlos past the rope-skippers, through the heavy bags that swung across the gym's midsection, and to the back, where The Butcher, Hassan Hassa, was practicing combinations in the ring.

At the hotel, Carlos had noticed a chrome signboard advertising the fight, *The Rumble in OUR Jungle*, underneath an old photograph of Felix, shirtless and fists up. Watching Hassan train, however, did not exactly call to mind Kinshasa 1974. Six foot something, 250 pounds of bulging, veiny muscle, head shaved and beard patchy, The Butcher had the bearing of one of those matatus, and about as much finesse. His sparring partner, wearing focus mitts, called out combinations for The Butcher to throw, and whenever the big man made a mistake—dropping his hands or jabbing when he'd been instructed to cross—he'd knock his glove against his face, a self-deprecating move that also looked brain damaging. The partner, short and squat, was swathed in protective gear, a necessary precaution, and held the mitts high above his head like he was being taken hostage.

From behind the ropes, the men watched Hassan lumber drunkenly around the canvas.

"*That's* The Butcher?" asked Carlos.

"This is The Butcher," said Omari, poker-faced, glasses clinging to the tip of his nose.

Entranced by the spectacle of the plodding fighter, Carlos began bouncing lightly on his toes, suppressing the urge to offer Felix's opponent instruction from the sidelines. With a minute left, each of The Butcher's punches wilder than the one before, the cut man couldn't stop himself. "You should be hitting here!" Carlos yelled, punching at an invisible body. "Here! Here! Here! Here!"

Omari, unstirred, kept his eyes on the action until the end of the round, then hopped onto the floor.

"You gotta hit *here*!" Carlos cried from behind the ropes, poking himself in the jaw as the sparring partner stood on tiptoes, emptying a water bottle into the mouth of the crouching Butcher. "You hear me, fool?"

Hassan offered an unconvincing nod and kept drinking.

Vaulting back up the steps to the ring, Omari called Hassan over, whispering instructions to his wheezing fighter.

"I got you, I got you," Hassan told Omari, his voice high and singsong. The Butcher clumped back to the center of the canvas.

"What's his problem anyway?" asked Carlos.

"He has lost his job selling meats and needs money badly," said Omari.

"Selling meats?"

"A butcher, yes." Two months before, Omari explained, Hassan Hassa had answered an advertisement in a local paper looking for a fighter to star in tonight's exhibition. Desperate for money and looking the part, he secured the job, then showed up at their gym asking to learn how to box. "Have you encountered this type in America?" Omari asked.

"Welcome to my fuckin' life, man," said Carlos.

As the rounds wore on, Carlos noticed a curious pattern: each time Omari left the ring, he'd seek out Kadara and whisper in his ear. Kadara would nod and find George, *whisper whisper*, and then George would hobble over to the corner across from the ring, to confer with the woman slumped in the wooden chair, a few feet removed from the action. Then they'd reverse course, the woman sending George a message, who fed it to Kadara, who passed it to Omari and back to Hassan.

The woman, the only one in the building, was unusual-looking, with a head wrapped to enormity and a lazy right eye that pointed up, as if it had seen enough of the world and was trying to seek refuge behind her head. Her flowing buibui did little to hide her girth, and with legs spread and back hunched, her pose and expression reminded Carlos of the veteran coaches who slouched their way through Texas State Golden Gloves.

"Who she?" Carlos finally asked Omari, after witnessing four rounds of this peculiar charade. Across the room, the woman scratched at the start of her hairline, as if her buibui was wrapped too tight.

Omari tilted his head toward her, glasses sliding. "Ah, Mama Aisha," he said casually. "Kuchizi." He tapped his forehead. "Not right in the brain."

"Why she here, then?"

"Maybe she feels more comfortable around so many who have been hit in the head."

"Maybe," said Carlos, but he had his suspicions. "Listen," he said, testing his hypothesis. "You tell that woman your butcher's right foot needs to turn in, OK?" Carlos got into position, the gold wristband he'd been given at the resort sliding down his arm. "Like this, you hear?"

Omari didn't seem to be listening, but the next time he jumped off the canvas to consult with Kadara he repeated Carlos's motion with his right foot. Kadara imitated the motion for George, and on it went until Omari was back in the ring, instructing The Butcher to turn his right foot in.

"Motherfucker," said Carlos, clapping triumphantly, happy to have cracked the code. "Now listen," he said, unable to mask his exuberance. He poked Omari in the chest, then once on each side. "Here! Here! Here!" he instructed. "That's the key."

And so it went for two rounds, three rounds: Carlos relaxing Hassan's shoulders, bending his knees, adjusting his right foot this way or that, all without laying a finger on the panting butcher. Once, he looked back to Felix, worried that his defection might be revealed, but the boxer was circling a heavy bag, throwing combinations with such velocity that a few of the younger fighters had gathered around to watch.

Carlos continued on.

He liked how Omari furrowed his brow when taking advice, the way the others imitated his motions with precision. In Mama Aisha he seemed to have met a worthy match. Carlos had never figured out how to talk to women. Pretending to rob them or instructing them to light their clothing on fire was his clumsy version of *I'm interested in knowing more*. A vanished teenager's license dropped into his shorts was the closest he'd ever come to being passed a note in the hall. The circuitous way he communicated with Mama Aisha, then, suited him well. Sometimes, Mama Aisha would veto Carlos's instructions, waving George away dismissively. Others, she'd tweak them, or accept them outright. In the end, talking to a woman was easy for Carlos, so long as he had three more temperate personalities serving as a buffer between them.

Hassan wasn't improving, exactly, but Carlos felt the rush of the old days, when he could lose himself in the nitty-gritty of strategy and the drama of the fight, when his enthusiasm for battle seemed justified, necessary. Anyone who knew Carlos knew he was always punching, but the man made more sense when he was actually in a ring.

"Hey," said Carlos, motioning to Omari. "How 'bout I spar him?"

"*You* want to spar Hassan Hassa?" asked Omari.

"Just show him what's what," said Carlos, already shadowboxing in place.

"Do you think that's a good idea?"

"A good idea?" repeated Carlos, amused. "You think any of this is a good idea?"

Omari tapped his forehead as he had when describing Mama Aisha. "Kuchizi."

"Kufuckinchizi," agreed Carlos.

With a push of his glasses, Omari approached Kadara, who stalked over to George, who limped over to Mama Aisha, who scowled and seemed to laugh, and soon enough the three men surrounded Carlos, helping him climb into a body cup, Velcroing his head gear, wrapping his hands, and tying on a pair of gloves. Kadara held up a mouthguard.

"It used?" asked Carlos, before opening wide.

"Open palms," said Kadara sternly. He inserted the mouthguard. "No fists."

Hassan Hassa, a foot above the cut man, looked down on him wearily as they tapped gloves to start the round. At first, Carlos did as promised. He stuck with a jab to the chin, over and over until Hassan remembered to keep his glove up. Next, he moved to a hook, forcing Hassan to protect himself with his elbow.

The Butcher was stronger than Carlos but too slow, and for much of the second round Ortega dodged punches without throwing any of his own, leading Hassan into the corner before ducking out of it. He went back to the chin, tapping, just tapping, The Butcher still dropping his left, opening himself up, then tried his cross, his glove, palm wide, landing just under the other man's throat.

Thwap! It was a harder hit than Carlos intended and throwing it electrified him: that startling smack, the stick of moisture pooling under his headgear, the sound of his own breath, urgent, steady, a ventilator only he could hear. Carlos slapped his gloves together and side-skipped around Hassan, then swooped back in, jab! jab! hook! jab!

The warrior in Carlos now fully re-awakened, he clenched his fists and, with thirty seconds on the clock, forgot his mission entirely and began punching in earnest: a few swift uppercuts, a left hook to the body that caused Hassan to groan and buckle.

From the sidelines, Omari yelled, "Enough, enough!"

Carlos couldn't stop himself, could barely hear Omari, had to keep going until the bell sounded.

When it did, he looked to Omari's corner of the ring, sure that Mama Aisha's intermediaries would be impressed with his performance. Instead, he saw Felix, gloved hands on his hips, staring at Hassan Hassa, who was curled in pain on the canvas. The middleweight seemed gloomy, serious, like a man awaiting an execution, though whether Felix was to be hangman or hanged, Carlos couldn't say.

"Am I a boxer or a hit man?" asked Felix from the back of the van.

"Or a hooker?" said Carlos, splayed out over the front row of seats. "You gotta admit I still got it, boss," he added, hoping to cheer his fighter.

Felix ignored him. "I've made mistakes. No denying it. But this . . . It isn't *sport*. I could kill that man."

"You sore at me for working with him?" asked Carlos.

Felix grabbed his headphones from his bag. "I can get my ass kicked for money but this . . ." he said, voice fading. "You watch, Ortega: They'll cheer me when I'm beating him to death and yell *How could you?* once he's dead."

Back at the Grand, a bevy of hotel staffers had taken over the beach to assemble the ring. Shirtless workers slung thick red and white ropes around their shoulders, men hammered boards and posts. The green canvas was spread out near a cluster of guest huts, its edges held down with cinder blocks. A woman with a broom stood at its center, brushing off stray sand.

"You've got to be kidding me," muttered Felix. "Doesn't this all look a little close to the water?"

Carlos had to admit they were building the platform quite near the shoreline. "Maybe they know something about the tides," he said, hopeful, but Felix wasn't having it.

"You trying to see how many people we can humiliate in one night?" Felix yelled to the bemused workers, who shook their heads and kept hammering.

The Rumble in OUR Jungle fell apart the next morning. Marco Giordano, the hotel manager, interrupted the boxers' breakfast—neat rolls of prosciutto, balls of mozzarella, and a gray slab of meat labeled Venetian sow—to announce it was time for Felix's fitting. Unclear on the meaning of this order, the men followed Marco to his office, heavy on the mahogany and adorned with both a stuffed zebra head and a portrait of Sophia Loren, where a diminutive tailor with the unlikely name of Leonardo Mazzafaro took measurements.

The costume featured a loincloth and actual shackles. "For high, high drama," Marco declared, tossing Carlos the key.

"I'm not wearing this," said Felix, examining the loincloth.

"You'll try it on and then decide," said Marco, smiling.

"It's not happening," said Felix.

As the two went back and forth, the hotel manager reminded the Americans of the money involved, and Felix grew more incensed at the idea he could be bought so easily. Marco became increasingly agitated, too, rubbing his neck, unsure where to look, working hard to keep the officious glimmer in his voice.

"A slave? You want me to go out there as a slave?" said Felix.

"You must admit, five thousand dollars is an extremely generous offer," said Marco. "Especially considering your Gold Membership."

"You think I'll just do anything for money?"

"We believe five thousand is more than fair," said Marco, with a final-offer stiffness to his posture.

This was enough for Felix. "You call Terry Tucker, call whoever," he said, brushing past the tailor and heading for the door. "The fight is off. C'mon, Ortega, let's bounce."

Under normal circumstances, the outburst would've amused Carlos, but there was a certainty to Felix's tone that suggested this time it was best to go along with the younger man, and he did.

The corporate chieftains in Naples were not happy with Felix's breach of contract, and within an hour they'd dispatched three block-shouldered men in Hawaiian shirts, earpiece wires snaking down their backs, to escort the Americans back to Malindi Airport.

One guard stood on the porch of each hut, urging the men to gather their belongings, while the third made Carlos offer up his wrist and snipped off the cut man's gold band with a small pair of scissors.

It would've gone on like this until their departure were it not for the scene Carlos observed through the window as he packed his bag. On the blustery beach, trotting toward them, were the three men from the boxing gym: Omari pushing at the bridge of his glasses so they wouldn't fall off; Kadara taking exaggerated steps, like a kid trying to avoid the cracks on the sidewalk; George in front, in a baggy suit, holding a fedora in place atop his head.

Carlos expected the men to seek out Felix, but they came to his hut instead, each bowing to the sentry more grandly than the one before, Omari last, leaning so far forward that his glasses almost touched the ground.

"Bwana Carlos," said George, winded, shambling through the open door, "it is urgent that we speak with you."

The others followed, spreading out across the room, as Carlos sat on the bed, unsure what to make of his visitors.

"As you have seen," said Kadara, running his fingers along a bamboo armoire, "Hassan Hassa is a terrible boxer. Do you know what rivals his terribleness?"

Omari was inspecting the bookshelf. He turned toward Carlos, a frayed paperback open in his hand. "His persistence."

Hassan Hassa, it seemed, would not take no for an answer. "He has threatened to continue his training until a new opponent emerges," said George.

"It is absolutely essential that the match occurs," said Omari. "The Butcher takes up too much of our time and too much of our space."

"He is a drain on our resources," said Kadara with a slight smile.

"Where's the woman if it's so important?" asked Carlos, skeptical.

Kadara raised an eyebrow. "The woman?" He glanced at George.

"What woman?" said George.

"Kuchizi, kuchizi," said Omari knowingly, and the three laughed.

"Ah, yes, the *woman*," said George. "Do you think the prestigious Malindi Grand Resort and Hotel allows the insane onto their property?"

"A crazy woman in a prayer shawl," said Kadara.

"Allahu akbar!" called Omari, hands raised in praise.

Carlos glared at him. "So fuck you want from me, then?"

"Plainly," said Kadara, "you like to fight. Which is why . . ." He hesitated, turned to George.

The suited man smiled. "We have a proposition."

This was how it came to pass that on a windy Friday evening in Malindi, Kenya, fighting out of the red corner, at 147 pounds, all the way from Austin, Texas, USA, came Carlos Ortega, in shackles and a loincloth, once-taut skin now loose with age, wrists wrapped and gloves tied. Underneath the loincloth, Carlos had tucked Nathaniel Rothstein's driver's license into his black compression shorts, the boy's slightly agape lips kissing the boxer's literal ass. At Carlos's side stood Felix Barrowman, fanny pack filled with cotton swabs and Vaseline.

Some two hundred onlookers surrounded three sides of the ring, under speakers blasting what sounded like tribal music gone electronica: conga drums and heavy bass, scratching turntables and ululations.

The Butcher entered first, throwing light punches at the incoming sea breeze as he ambled down the sandy aisle, still a little swollen from the beating Carlos had given him the day before, his handlers moving in concert close behind.

Carlos followed, fully in his element. He bopped his shoulders awkwardly to the music, delighting in the thrum of the crowd. They were a roaring, drunken throng, a pulsating mass of pink skin. Spider veins crawled across shrieking cheeks; ogre hands pawed at the breasts and asses of much-younger women, the few actual wives present compensating with faces lifted so far back their eyes were almost at their temples, makeup thick as football paint.

"You sure you want to do this?" called Felix over the din.

Carlos raised his shackles above his head, basking in the horde's boozy warmth, declaring victory before the fight had even started.

Once Carlos ascended the steps to the ring, Felix followed, unlocking the fighter's shackles and slinging them over the ropes. As the crowd rose for the Italian national anthem, a wave broke behind them and a few flecks of salt water tickled Carlos's thighs. Felix shot him a look: *I told you so.*

The referee, whom Carlos recognized as one of the bartenders from the pool, reminded both fighters of the rules and introduced the judges, seated in front of the ring at a folding table in the sand. They included the hotel manager, Marco Giordano, who waved to the crowd in the style of a pageant contestant.

Just as Carlos and Hassan tapped gloves, it started to drizzle.

So unexpected was this trickle of moisture that as the first drops stained the canvas, both boxers fell out of fighting position and looked up.

"It's raining," yelled Carlos, befuddled. His loincloth flew up in the breeze and he nudged it back into place over his compression shorts.

"Mvua," agreed Hassan.

"Fight!" yelled the spectators. "Dai, combattete!"

Both men raised their gloves.

It didn't take long for Carlos to see that Hassan had heeded his advice: The Butcher's stance was not too squared up, not too wide, and he kept his hands up, blocking Carlos's jabs, even fending off a hook with his forearm. Hassan was boxing, really boxing, and Carlos enjoyed testing the bigger man, one! two!, seeing how well The Butcher could protect himself.

For all his improvement, The Butcher was still slow, and each time he swung at Carlos, the smaller man slid past. It didn't take long for the crowd to become restless. They booed each time Hassan lunged for Carlos, annoyed that the beast that was The Butcher wasn't clobbering this defiant slave. *Send him back to Mexico!* cried a voice in stilted English. *Kill him!* shrieked another.

During the break, Hassan's handlers bounded up to his corner, wiping the rain from his forehead and pantomiming vigorously, reminding The Butcher to keep his hands up, his elbows in, to stay calm.

"What you think?" Carlos asked Felix, who'd leaped onto the canvas but saw no need to unzip his fanny pack.

"I think it's wet up here and I want to go home," said the new cut man as the bell sounded for the next round, the drizzle turning to downpour.

A minute into the second, the winds picked up and a wave broke against the platform, sending a sheet of salt water cascading across the canvas. Both men stumbled and had to catch themselves against the ropes, the ring now slick, their gloves heavy. As the deluge continued, the crowd covered their heads with anything they could find but stayed on the beach, screaming for a knockout, a knockdown, anything, e rapido!

Carlos, energized from the whoops of the crowd, punched with abandon, his hair matted against his forehead, the rain so torrential it was becoming hard to see. The physical challenge of the storm exhilarated Carlos, and he yelled for The Butcher to keep going. Hassan, unsettled, began gunning for a knockout, his crosses morphing into windmills and hooks into attempted haymakers, anything to make contact.

Bam! A wild cross struck Carlos in the gut, sending him skidding into the corner. He ducked a left hook as a second wave arced over the ropes. "That's what I'm talking about!" he yelled, encouraging The Butcher to fight on. He slammed together his sopping gloves in exclamation.

A thick gust of wind caused the spectators to finally retreat. They ran toward the stone path as water flooded the beach. Marco and the other judges followed suit, and though Felix wanted to stay put, the water was at his shins, so he fled too, calling for Carlos to jump down to safety. Omari and Kadara put George between their shoulders and went with the crowd, yelling for Hassan.

Carlos kept throwing jabs and hooks as a third wave, then a fourth, glided over the ring, past his hips, his chest. He kept going, at Hassan's head, at his belly, at first not even realizing when The Butcher tumbled into the water and began crawling toward the shore.

The absence of an opponent didn't dampen Carlos's bellicosity. He kept at it, slashing at water, uppercutting air.

As the cinder blocks that had once secured the canvas tumbled past him, Carlos paid no mind. He was focused only on the rhythm of his feet, the rotation of his hips, the familiar sense of feverish possibility that coursed through him every time he jab-jab-jabbed, never more comfortable in his own body than he was now, in the center of the canvas, in the center of the fight.

From halfway up the beach, Felix could make out the stooped silhouette of his former cut man, now fighting the ocean itself. "What you doing, man?" Felix called above the mayhem.

Carlos never faltered, punching punching with such ferocity that he almost seemed to be dancing, electric and alive, as the current pulled the ring into the sea.

The next morning, fishermen a half mile northeast of the hotel reported that the remains of a boxing ring had washed up on the shore. The padding had fallen off the posts, the canvas was salt-stained and torn, and, most curious of all, someone had double-knotted a set of shackles around the wilted ropes.

With Luigi, the driver, Felix spent the morning interviewing locals, hunching his back and scrunching his face into Carlos's likeness. No one had seen him.

At Hassan's gym, they hadn't seen him either, and when Felix asked to speak with Mama Aisha, Omari told the boxer he must be mistaken. The woman was not only crazy but mute and had been since birth. She shrugged when Felix approached and mouthed "Sijui"—*I don't know*—before motioning George over and whispering instructions into his ear.

Their flight was to leave that afternoon and Marco Giordano made it clear to Felix that they would not be extending his reservation. "If you'd like to contact home first, we do offer phone cards in the gift shop," said Marco. Out of options and money, Felix climbed aboard the van and departed for Malindi Airport. He figured Carlos would turn up one way or another, or that he'd drowned.

Back at Terry Tucker's Boxing Gym, Felix recounted the details of the storm to anyone who asked. "He just kept going," he'd say solemnly, wrapping his hands as the others leaned in, heads shaking. Some wondered if it was all a complicated prank, if Carlos might pop out from behind the bathroom door once they'd stopped paying attention. But as days became weeks, and the reality of Carlos's disappearance set in, a wary nostalgia took hold. Hearsay about what had become of the missing cut man dominated the gossip between rounds.

To all who knew him, the rumors were strangely plausible: Carlos had fallen in with Somali pirates and was patrolling the Indian Ocean in a ramshackle speedboat; Carlos was hunting Joseph Kony in Uganda with a motley crew of mercenaries and renegade Peace Corps volunteers; Carlos had befriended an octogenarian carpenter on the island of Lamu and spent his days as an apprentice, carving intricate designs into the backs of expensive wooden chairs.

The closest to hard evidence came in the form of an anonymous postcard that arrived at the gym a few months later, in the late fall of 2009, from Lake Nakuru National Park: a photograph of a lion lunging after a gazelle with SAFARI TIME! in bright red script across the top. In pen, someone had drawn little droppings underneath the lion. There was no message and no return address.

Terry Tucker tacked the postcard to the wall behind his desk and inspected it on occasion. No one would argue Carlos was missed, exactly, but no one could deny he was a topic of conversation: a "person of interest," as Terry might say. Newcomers who asked about the postcard were given Carlos's entire history, as told by whatever assemblage of regulars happened to be around at the time, and as the months passed, it became impossible for gymgoers to conceive of Carlos Ortega anywhere but Africa, laughable to think that anyone had ever believed a few blocks or a single city could contain him.

Coyote Revisited

IN NOVEMBER 2010, FIFTEEN months after Carlos Ortega left for Africa, a second piece of mail arrived in Austin, Texas, from that faraway place. It came in a battered airmail envelope postmarked Mombasa, and rested, after its twelve-day journey, first in the dark of a residential mailbox and, later, on a butcher block countertop, sandwiched between circulars, as Bob Alexander made his lunch.

At seventy, Bob no longer ate proper meals before dinner, instead subsisting off pimento-stuffed olives and sun-dried tomatoes and any other item that made its home in thick oils or briny juices. 11:30 a.m. meant Wheat Thins dipped in red pepper hummus, a swig of diet ginger ale, a decisive sorting of the mail. Recycle this, tear that. This was the professor in retirement, the professor on the day that his long-missing nephew would re-center himself in Bob's life.

Retirement, it should be said, did not suit Bob Alexander. A popular presence on the UT campus, Bob could've taught American history until he *was* American history. These were coveted positions, and he had known professors who'd held on till they were institutionalized, or interred. One of his colleagues showed up to Garrison Hall each morning wearing a nasal cannula connected to an oxygen tank. Of the five historians of Texas on faculty, only two still had their original teeth.

Why *had* Bob retired? To spend more time with Marlene? "Nooooo," his wife would say if anyone suggested it, her pitch low as a ghost's. To pursue hobbies? He played tennis twice a week and went to the boxing gym most mornings, but he'd done those things *before* retirement. He had not spent his life in a chicken plant. He was an endowed chair at a major university: he'd been halfway retired for years.

His reasons were a mystery to everyone, even to himself. If he'd had to sum up how he felt in those final few semesters, *bored* would be the obvious choice, but that wasn't quite right. Bob had felt a sense that there was supposed to be more to his life than his life had been, and yet he had enough agemates enduring similar crises to know that this sensation was the very stuff of life itself.

If he'd really *gone there*—and, in 2010, this was not his way—Bob might've connected this malaise to his missing nephew. There were details from Nathaniel's disappearance that Bob had never told anyone. Not the police. Not even his wife. Embarrassing details about his nephew's behavior. About his own. Details he'd tried not to dwell on in the twelve years since the boy disappeared.

It wasn't always like this. After Nathaniel vanished, Bob had entertained a far-flung theory about what befell him. Well, theory would be too generous a description. More like a *notion*, a vague and out-there inkling, based on what happened right before Nathaniel left. What happened right after.

In the late summer of 1998, Bob became quietly preoccupied with his half-baked hypothesis. Back then, he was grateful for the distraction. Though he downplayed it to anyone who asked, the first weeks following the disappearance were a mess. After an initial burst of police and press, the Alexanders were left with nothing: no nephew, no attention, no clues.

Like most couples, Bob and Marlene had always had their schtick: he the ornery raconteur, she responsible for rolling her eyes, for reining him in. After Nathaniel disappeared, the act turned too real. More than once, Bob shouted at Marlene to shut up. More than once, Marlene told Bob to fuck off. They'd never talked like that to each other in their lives. Back in Boston, Bob's sister—Nathaniel's mother—was practically catatonic.

Whenever Bob checked in with the police, their line was that Nathaniel would turn up somewhere. There was no evidence of foul play; suburban white boys didn't just vanish into thin air. The summer became fall, and as the weeks passed it became easier for Bob to just believe them. The important thing, Bob knew, was to get their lives back on track. To get his family back on track. No one needed him secretly obsessing over cockamamie theories.

So Bob Alexander did what most people do when a terrible thing happens. He got through each day as best he could. Nathaniel was never forgotten, but life continued on. Losing a nephew, Bob assured himself, wasn't the same as losing a son.

Bob had moved to Austin, with Marlene, back in '69 for the job at UT. He'd always been an easy fit for the city. Irascible, sure, but not uppity in the way of his northeastern forebears. After-class pitchers of Shiner at Scholz Garten, swim briefs to Barton Springs. A connoisseur of cutting through bullshit, of finely rolled spliffs.

Were it not for the disappearance, Bob might've submitted his whole self to his Be Free side in late middle age. The man seemed destined to sport a long beaded necklace or a small hoop earring, to dive deep into Eastern religion and hallucinogens. But when the tornado that was the summer of 1998 passed, Bob learned that some of his crinkly insouciance had blown away with it.

He could still turn out a lively lecture, might take a couple sucks on a doobie to fall asleep. But now there was a tempered quality to the looseness. A loving wife, a sensible son: before Nathaniel, Bob could get pretty baked on a random afternoon and no one was the worse for wear. A fragile family coming to grips with a tragedy that happened under his watch: now the professor needed to feel the ground beneath his feet.

The timing of Bob's closing-off felt especially unfortunate, since even his more prudish acquaintances seemed eager to experiment in empty nest–hood. Parents who'd practically Munchausen-by-proxied their children into peanut allergies and celiac disease were now trying their hands at homemade edibles. Once, at Half Price Books, Bob spied the most fretful of their parent cohort, a frumpish woman who'd spent her forties in a tizzy over the MPAA ratings of the movies screened at sleepovers, buying *The Art of Kama Sutra* on used DVD. Lee Gorbinski (he of the Vaselined nipples) and his wife even gave a go at swinging. For years, Bob had been the one baring his bony ass at Hippie Hollow. In a cruel reversal, he became unwilling to cede control of his body, of his mind, at the very moment everyone around him was finally beginning to tug off their dowdy jeans.

The old Bob might've confronted his nephew's disappearance like a historical puzzle, marveling at the kaleidoscopic weirdness of the country and its people as he pieced together clues. This new Bob refused to see any magic in the mystery. Imagining felt like a good way to get snookered. Safer to see the world for the gray place it was.

Or *mostly* was, for try as he might to extinguish his wilier self, it watched from a distance, that gonzo spirit exiled from his body, rebuffed anytime it swirled too close to his lanky frame.

Indeed, in the years ahead, this was the pattern whenever Bob learned of strange tips or wild leads. Ransom notes, deemed counterfeit, in '99 and '03. Alleged sightings in '01 and '05. On an otherwise unremarkable Tuesday in August 2008, ten years after the disappearance: a note left on Bob's windshield, Nathaniel's birthdate written in a childlike scrawl.

Each time, Bob would remember his own silly ideas, then try to put them out of his mind: there and gone in seconds but never fully vanquished, either, lingering like a coyote's howl as it faded into the dark.

That coyote. What a sight. Early one morning in 2008, some twenty-four hours after Bob found the note on his windshield, he'd driven past Ed Hooley on his bicycle, a coyote wrapped around Ed like a stole. Bob had never been able to make sense of the image.

He'd never asked Ed about it, either. *Did I see you riding down North Lamar Boulevard with a coyote wrapped around your neck?* At the time, Bob told himself Ed couldn't handle a question like that.

He'd seen Ed riled over less, the mellowest of confrontations enough to send his left eye twitching.

In hindsight, Bob wondered if he didn't ask Ed for other reasons. The professor was only a few months retired when it happened. "Next stop Meadowbridge," he'd told Marlene at his going-away party, a reference to the kosher-friendly nursing facility popular among demented Jews that the Alexanders had begun to joke/worry about ending up in.

He'd been so *sure* of what he'd seen. In the intervening years, Bob had begun to doubt the memory. Begun to doubt his motivations for never bringing it up with Ed Hooley. If he'd asked and Ed said it *hadn't* happened, what would it say about Bob Alexander?

Please let her be real.

Bob had always subscribed to Occam's razor. The simpler answer was, unfortunately, usually the answer. He was old. He'd been confused, misremembered.

And yet, and yet, still that spirit swirls . . .

How to account for the occasional impossible thing?

November 2010. Fingers slippery, a little splotch of hummus on one side of Bob Alexander's lip. The mail: a *Costco Connection* magazine, coupons for H-E-B. Read and rip and recycle. Then: *What is this?* An airmail envelope, striking as the stamp crookedly affixed to its upper-right corner: a drawing of a red-and-purple-plumed touraco, mid-flight, above the words REPUBLIC OF KENYA.

"*Ortega?*" said Bob to the envelope, as if Carlos might be inside. Bob wiped his hands on a paper towel, tore the seal.

A single piece of beige loose-leaf paper so thin it felt to Bob as if it were from another time, folded three ways. Wrapped inside: an expired driver's license, once stiff and shiny, now aged enough that the ink had started, ever so slightly, to fade.

This was not some useless, anonymous note. This was *the* license, gone, like Nathaniel, these last twelve years.

Bob held the license up to the light. It was strange to see his nephew in this way: unchanged by time, unchanged, even, by that transformative summer of 1998. This was Nathaniel in his original form. Nathaniel the lemon. *A schlemiel of the first order*.

So transfixed was Bob by the sight that he didn't, at first, even notice the curious note written in pencil, in all caps, on the paper into which the license had been folded:

NEVER TRUST A COP

Bob knew his wife was out running errands. "Hey, Mar?" he called anyway, just to make sure. For so long, Bob had done his best to resist re-opening wounds that never had the chance to properly heal in the first place. Now, though, he felt a lightness about him, a lightness he hadn't experienced in years. The lightness that comes from progress. From *action*.

Until now, Bob had always seen it as his duty to report any tip, no matter how outlandish, to APD headquarters. There was something fatiguing to him about that blah brown building and its unsmiling inhabitants, all of whom acted as if they'd seen it all before. *If you've already seen everything,* Bob always wanted to ask, *is it possible you've stopped seeing anything?*

This time Bob felt no such duty to follow the rules. The note accompanying the license gave Bob license of his own. *Never trust a cop*, Carlos warned. Was he suggesting an officer was in on the disappearance? Why was he only speaking up now? And how had Carlos, of all people, acquired the ID?

What Bob needed was someone with access he *could* trust. A younger officer, perhaps, someone who wasn't on the force when Nathaniel disappeared, who *couldn't* have been a part of any conspiracy because they weren't around yet. Or maybe someone who knew Carlos Ortega?

Bob felt a sudden urge to get high, or strip down. To do the things that used to accompany his most electrifying epiphanies.

Was it possible he knew someone who matched *all* these criteria?

Bob found his cell phone farther down the butcher block, didn't search his contacts but instead dialed the number the old-fashioned way, from memory.

"Terry Tucker motherfucker," he said, the phone light in his hand. "I'm trying to get in touch with one of your habitués." Bob raised his bushy brows high. "You have a number for *Miriam Lopez*?"

From a window booth facing the parking lot of Magnolia Cafe, Bob Alexander watched the police officer exit her cruiser in the fading light of the late afternoon.

Was *this* the same person he'd met outside APD headquarters on a Tuesday morning almost two and a half years before? Same runner's body, same black hair tied tight into a bun. Yet even from a distance, Bob could see this was a different Miriam Lopez.

In the months after their first encounter, Miriam and Bob had exchanged pleasantries at the gym a handful of times. She'd always seemed so . . . passive. So . . . *civilian*. Now she wore dark aviators and the slight frown of police the world over. Now she moved the way cops move. Looked left, then right, as if trouble might come from any angle.

Inside, Miriam slid into the booth across from Bob. "It's been a while," she said warmly. Miriam had taken on a new role within the department, she explained, her schedule no longer conducive to the gym. "But it's good to see you, man. You're looking fit!"

"What have you done with Miriam Lopez?" joked Bob.

"Do I seem different?" said Miriam.

"You seem like you know what you're doing," said Bob, "which is more than I can say for most of us." Bob had never enjoyed dealing with cops, but if that was what Miriam wanted to be, it was nice to see she was figuring out how. "You look good, kid."

"So, what's this top-secret business you wanted to talk to me about?" Miriam asked.

"Do you remember," said Bob, "when I told you about my nephew, Nathaniel?"

Miriam glanced at the menu, turned it over in her hands. "A little, yeah. You didn't tell me much."

"I needed to show this to an officer I could trust." From the back pocket of his jeans, Bob took out the airmail envelope, placed it on the table, and pushed it Miriam's way. "Arrived this morning. From *Kenya*."

Miriam opened the envelope. She inspected the license, the note. She looked out toward the parking lot.

Through the window's reflection, Bob watched her hard stare. He assumed Miriam was contemplating the mess he'd just handed her, had no way of knowing that the only person these clues would ever lead to was already sitting across from him.

"What do you think?" asked Bob.

Fucking Carlos, thought Miriam.

In the first weeks after Carlos Ortega left, Miriam had found his absence disconcerting. She didn't *think* he knew she'd been the one to plant the license on him, but his silence rankled. A silent Carlos couldn't mean anything good.

Fifteen months later, she'd assumed their perverse horseplay had ended in a draw, Carlos and the license gone forever. When Bob called and asked to see her, Miriam knew it might be about his nephew. She wondered if the old man had received another clue, like the note on his windshield. Wondered if she might put some of her secret knowledge of the case to use.

Now Miriam wished she'd found an excuse not to meet Bob Alexander. Shivving Carlos was one thing, giving Bob false hope another. Miriam wanted no part of it. Staring out onto the parking lot, she thought about the night she stole the license. She thought about the real reason she'd stopped going to the gym.

Once, Alexis Cepeda had shown Miriam how he masked fear with his face. Furrowing his brow, jutting his chin. It had made sense to Miriam in the abstract, but it took stealing the license off him to put her own version into practice. The vague grimace, the inscrutable stare. The bland stoicism her field training officer had encouraged from the beginning. It had always seemed so corny. Something she could never pull off. But when protecting Alexis became the most important thing, Miriam Lopez made it work.

It worked at the substation, worked on the streets. Miriam spoke with a new resoluteness when she wore that foreign face. Strode firmer, walked taller. Liked the feeling so much she began wearing it to hide other emotions. Revulsion and anger. Disappointment and the hope that precedes it. By the end of her tenure in Leonard District, Miriam was wearing the mask so often she had trouble taking it off.

She wore it home, and to the gym. She wore it to his fights. To theirs. "Why would you be with someone if you don't like their face?" she asked him, near the end. "I don't like *that* face," he said. He missed the light way they'd had together. "It's one thing being with a cop. But a *cop* cop?"

Alexis could never understand what it was like to be her, out there. What it was like to get into the ring not for twenty minutes a few times a year but four times a week, ten hours a time. A girl as socially maladroit as Miriam? Sometimes it felt as if she'd been getting into the ring every day, all day, her entire life.

So she wore the face that wasn't her face, and used the voice that wasn't her voice, and moved in a way she'd never moved, and she did these things long enough that the face became her face, the voice her voice, the body her body, and it made being with him harder and the job easier, and she got promoted and that was that.

And now, in a booth at what had been her and Alexis's spot, she stared her inscrutable stare out the window and, in the reflection, Bob Alexander stared back, sure that what he was seeing was an earnest young cop figuring out what to do next.

Miriam Lopez already knew.

"I'll be honest, Bob," she said, returning to him. "I doubt an officer was involved in all this. It's *possible*, but to keep it hidden all this time? What would the motive be?"

Bob admitted he had no idea. "None of it makes sense. How did he even get the license?" Carlos's name had never come up in the investigation. Should it have? "Don't you find it all a bit . . . *weird*?"

"It's weird," agreed Miriam. "But people are weird." The best course of action, in her view, was to let her submit it as evidence to APD. "Most of the cops from back then, they're retired. And who knows about Carlos. If there's anything there, we'll find it. But we gotta play this by the book. Some big conspiracy? That's just in the movies."

Bob felt a flash of irritation. *My nephew's license miraculously arrives in the mail from* <u>*Africa*</u> *twelve years after he disappears and* <u>*this*</u> *is your reaction?*

He took a sip of ice water, told himself to be reasonable. How was the girl supposed to react? Was he expecting her to hide evidence, maybe risk her career, for *him*? Bob couldn't fault her for keeping cool in the face of somebody else's drama. Wasn't that sort of the job?

"So what's your new position?" Bob asked.

"Public Information," said Miriam. Media relations, stuff like that. On Thursday evenings, she taught a "Citizen Police Academy" course to educate Austinites about "how the department operates." They had a new class starting up after the holidays. "You and your wife are more than welcome."

"Sounds interesting," said Bob, "but I'm afraid Marlene's evenings are consumed with UT extension courses. In her dotage, she's become enamored with early Jewish history."

"She might fit right in," said Miriam. "Seems like every session a few nice Jewish ladies enroll. We advertise at the JCC." Miriam checked her phone, stood up. "I need to head out, Bob, but I'll get this taken care of," she said, pocketing the envelope.

Bob's eyes lingered on the empty spot where it had been. "You'll let me know when you find something?"

Should there be developments, Miriam assured him, someone would get in touch.

On the drive home, Bob Alexander went over each moment of their exchange: Miriam's apparent lack of surprise at encountering a missing person's long-missing license, the way she'd swept the evidence into her pocket without so much as snapping on some latex gloves.

In Miriam's presence, Bob had been careful to keep his post-Nathaniel persona intact. He hadn't wanted to seem pushy, or paranoid. Alone in the car, questions percolated. Had he erred in giving up the license so easily? Wasn't her take on the case a tad naïve? It had felt so good to *act* for once. Now he'd ended up where he always did after approaching the police: waiting for a phone call that would never come.

Bob thought about the last time he spoke to Nathaniel. He thought about his former friend David. He thought about spending his next twelve years as he'd spent his past twelve years, trying to put his nephew's disappearance behind him.

He'd be eighty-two then, if he were still kicking. Twelve years after that? Kaput for sure.

Would there be any harm in channeling his nimbler former self a bit longer? In poking around some on his own? It's not like he'd be impeding the investigation. Miriam had the license. Everything else from the summer of 1998 was locked in the evidence room in the basement of APD headquarters.

Well, not *everything*, remembered Bob.

After their investigation, the police had let the Alexanders keep many of Nathaniel's possessions. Years later, Bob donated all of them to a person in need. He'd never thought of the stuff he'd given Ed Hooley as evidence. But if he had to start somewhere . . . Was there a chance that among those dated leftovers lay another clue?

Don't get out over your skis, Bob told himself. *You're not a detective. You're an old man.*

Bob said these things half-heartedly and too late, for by then he had bypassed his own home and was turning into the gravel lot outside Terry Tucker's Boxing Gym.

If that hesitant young woman could figure out how to be a cop, why not Bob Alexander?

A little past 5:45 p.m., almost dark.

Bob never came to the gym at this bustling hour, didn't know the after-work regulars, a separate cast from his First Thing crew. It was the first cold night of the season, the crisp air a natural toxicant against the usual backseat boxers and man-spreading yentas who provided commentary from their seats. Tonight, everyone was up. In the ring: atop foam mats, a dozen patrons sat on their heels in child's pose, sweaty worshippers prostrated before their poker-faced god. On the floor, gymgoers stretched and jumped and threw.

Into the scrum plunged Bob Alexander, creaky and alive. He radiated purpose. Bob would explain the license to Ed Hooley, ask to look around the man's makeshift bedroom. *Take action.*

He felt as he had when he first saw the license that morning: a shimmer of his brash old self returning. Diving into a plan that made only nominal sense, *going for it* even if he wasn't sure what *it* was: Bob hadn't allowed his displaced spirit to reclaim control of his body, but he could feel it swirling ever closer, trying to find its way back inside.

Bob spotted Ed in the crowded weight room. A stout white woman in a long-sleeved Jazzercise T-shirt was exiting as Bob entered, a shaggy golden retriever following close behind. "See ya, Barbara-Ann Jaffee," Ed called. "See ya, Frisco Jaffee."

The woman sidestepped Bob, making room, as the passing golden retriever enveloped Bob's jeaned leg in fluff. "Serious hips on that thing," declared Bob. He pointed a finger-pistol Ed's way. "Can I borrow you?"

In the five-plus years Ed had lived at the gym, Bob had never ventured into his private space. Surveying Ed in his habitat, Bob realized why he'd avoided it.

Evidence of Nathaniel was everywhere. In the near-empty bottle of ancient cologne that sat on an old wooden dresser, alongside a lava lamp and a deck of Uno cards, like some weird shrine to a suburban childhood Ed had never experienced. On the small garment rack from which hung a couple pairs of Nathaniel's carpenter jeans and some flannel shirts: a Gap display from a previous decade. Ed stood uneasily in front of his cot, biting his lower lip. He wore the Patriots hoodie and beanie, also relics from the summer of '98. If Bob made his eyes go blurry, he could even *see* Nathaniel in Ed, the shapelessness of the era's clothing heightening the illusion.

All day, Bob's airy former self had egged on the stiffer, newer model. Goaded him to meet Miriam. Goaded him here. Now, face-to-face with a man dressed like Nathaniel, surrounded by Nathaniel's things, he tried to access the Bob of Before who'd taken him this far. He found the spirit was nowhere to be found, the past crashing into the present with such unexpected, dizzying force that for a moment the old professor forgot why he was even here.

Bob glanced back at the shut door behind him. Bob looked to Ed Hooley.

"I in some kinda trouble?" asked Ed, his left eye already watery.

"Trouble?" said Bob, distracted. "No, of course not . . ."

No matter where Bob turned, Nathaniel loomed. Underneath the cot: the worn UT gym bag he'd once bequeathed his nephew. On top of a stool masquerading as Ed's nightstand: a Velcro wallet, electric blue.

"It's peculiar," confessed Bob. "Seeing all my nephew's old things."

"Is that what you wanted to talk about?" asked Ed. "You can have it all back if you want—"

"This stuff wasn't a loan," said Bob. "It's yours. I—"

"It's helped me out a lot, Bob," said Ed. "I shoulda told you that a long time ago."

From the other side of the door: party noises, the fratty theater of a rowdy weight room.

Bob blurred his eyes again, made them clear. He had seen Ed in the Patriots ensemble many times before, but never, until now, in this bizarro museum of his missing nephew's life, had he allowed himself to consider—to remember—what it meant that all of Nathaniel's belongings were here.

Here meant *not there*. Not with Nathaniel. Here meant that wherever his nephew had gone, he'd gone without a way to wash his face, his teeth, without a change of clothes, without so much as a sweatshirt to protect against the cold.

Bob tried to think back to Ed's arrival in 2005. What was he wearing when he showed up to the gym? What did he wear in that in-between time, before the First Thingers assembled their donations? What had he worn before finding this place, when he lived in the wild, on the streets?

Bob had never thought to ask Ed about before. Now questions spawned questions. What did you eat? Where did you go to the bathroom? Was it possible to ever truly sleep?

How long did you last out there, Ed Hooley?

How long *could* a person last out there?

Could you make it twelve years?

Bob knew he couldn't ask these questions of Ed, knew in asking them he was really asking something else, of some*one* else. And because these were questions Ed could never answer, Bob instead blurted a different question, one he hadn't even realized he'd wanted to ask.

"Did I see you bicycling down North Lamar Boulevard with a coyote wrapped around your neck?"

Ed turned his head as if Bob might be talking to someone behind him. As if Ed hoped he were. "What you say?"

Bob tried to keep his voice even. "A couple years ago, I'm driving here. To the gym. Early, like I do. And I see—I *thought* I saw—you, well, *transporting* a coyote."

Bob knew it sounded crazy. Was this the real reason he'd never asked Ed about the coyote? The real reason he'd allowed Nathaniel's case to go cold in his mind? Aging brains got confused in the dark; troubled kids ran away. The simpler answer *was* the answer. "What I'm asking is, *Did I see what I thought I saw?*"

Ed shifted his gaze to the ground. His left eye twitched. In Ed's experience, *what happened* was supposed to be the purview of other people. The sallow caseworkers of the varied government agencies tasked with determining if Ed could live independently and what resources were available to him, their decisions based on whether his sense of reality comported with their own. *What happened* was what a judge said happened. What a cop said happened. Fifty-four years and Ed had rarely been trusted as the narrator of his own reality. Now he was supposed to arbitrate someone else's?

He couldn't imagine why Bob would care about that coyote all this time later, why he'd never asked about her before. But he knew all too well how all-consuming it was to doubt what you'd seen with your own eyes. To think you might have reason to doubt.

Did I see what I thought I saw?

Ed glanced at the back of his right hand. In the soft tissue between his thumb and his index finger: two small and faded pink circles, parallel scars. *You know what happened. You got the proof. Tell him.*

Once, before Ed's mama left him, she'd told him and his brother that it wasn't about being together that makes a family. *It's about looking out for each other from wherever we are.* In times of trouble, Ed treated that mantra like a security blanket, an assurance that even if his mama and his brother, Larry, weren't in front of him, still they were with him. They were here.

Ed could never admit that those words were meaningless. Admitting that would mean accepting that first his mama and later his own twin had deserted him, that living inside a boxing gym at the mercy of people who came and went, as gymgoers do, was not an incredible stroke of good fortune but an indication of how little fortune Ed had ever known.

He might never reckon with his mama's betrayal or his brother's abandonment, but this hadn't stopped Ed Hooley from suffering their consequences. He knew the moral of the story, even if he couldn't admit the story was his own.

People need their people. That's what Ed would've told Bob Alexander if he'd been able to articulate what he was feeling. That coyote wasn't supposed to be sick under a boxing ring. She belonged with her family. Needed her family. Ed Hooley took her home.

For a time before the gym, Ed had slept a few miles southwest, in a pocket of wooded parkland alongside Shoal Creek, whose once-rushing waters had, by the time he knew them, been reduced to an inconsistent stream. Late at night, Ed would walk the rocky creek bed, searching for pools to wash in. Sometimes, he heard howls on those lonely late-night wanders. When he found the coyote, Ed figured there was as good a chance as any that she'd come from there.

Ed didn't know how to explain all that to Bob. Instead, he approached the old professor and held up the back of his jittery right hand. "Got me good," said Ed. "Found her underneath the ring. Girl was all turned around."

Bob bent down to get a better look, daring himself to take Ed's hand in his own. He examined the traces of bite mark. "My goodness," Bob murmured. From his lowered position, he looked up at Ed Hooley. "Do you think she's still alive?"

In the middle of the wild, in the middle of the city, the men stand on a low footbridge and wait for the coyote.

Bob and Ed arrived at seven to this lush patch of park, the creek snaking down its center. Bob has never been here after dark. In daylight, it's as enchanted as a fairy-tale forest. Live oak trees shade the gently sloping dirt path down to the creek bed, their knobby branches grasping for the sun. Cross the bridge and find a short stretch of running trail abutting a craggy limestone wall known to sweat spring water.

During the day, it's trademark Austin nature, exuding seclusion despite the city all around it. Follow the dirt path back out of the park and wind up at the medical complex where Bob receives his annual colonoscopy. Beyond the craggy wall is a psychiatric center. The closest Bank of America is 0.2 miles away.

In the winter dark, the encroaching city is more evident. Bob studies the surrounding litter with a flashlight he found in his trunk. Around the creek bed lie the usual suspects: a foam Whataburger cup; a plastic bag wrapped around some brush. The bridge is a concrete slab with no railing, a thin flow of water underneath. On a dry spot off to one side, a sign of more permanent life: a filthy blue tarp, neatly folded.

"You shouldn't be called a transient if you live here," proclaims Bob, clicking off the flashlight. "*I'm* the transient."

Since learning of the coyote, Bob has been letting loose with these off-kilter epiphanies like a stoned fortune cookie. He is hyperattuned to his surroundings, picking up the clipped croaks of grackles, critters crunching over dead leaves. "You feel me, Hooley?"

"'Course, Bob," murmurs Ed. He has no idea what Bob is talking about, only vaguely understands why they're here. He doubts they'll see any coyotes. But Bob had insisted, and now they've been out here for what feels like forever (an hour? three?), peering into the dark, Ed shivering in his hoodie, Bob only in a light jacket, oblivious to the chill.

Ed hadn't wanted to come here, doesn't like to remember the urban wilds where he once lived. He doesn't like to remember the green slatted steel trash cans whose hard bonnet lids meant he couldn't look for scraps, instead had to stick an arm deep into the abyss. Doesn't like to remember the eerie quiet, nor the fear that the quiet wouldn't last through the night.

But he is loyal to his friends. Bob has always been good to him. Good from a distance. *Will you take me there?* Bob had asked back in the bedroom, holding his hand. Ed doesn't want to let slip this rare chance to be good back.

So the men stare into the dark, listening to far-off traffic, and Ed prays for a coyote he doubts will ever come, because unlike Bob, who feels an illicit thrill being in the park after hours, Ed finds no novelty here.

There is no explaining this to the old professor, however, for Ed can see that he is locked in, so focused on the task at hand that even when Bob speaks, he keeps his eyes on the creek.

The Bob Alexander who existed prior to 1998 was not an adherent to mysticism in the traditional sense. He was never up for Tarot or down with crystals. Bob's was a thornier inquisitiveness, the agnosticism of the truly curious. Now he feels that cosmic openness returning to him.

Are you out there, coyote?

For twelve years, Bob has kept his distance. From the investigation into Nathaniel's disappearance. From poking too hard at his own inner self. He has clung to his title as uncle. Uncles are steady. Uncles are detached. *Uncle!* What we cry when we've had enough.

But Bob is tired of living life from that remove. All day, since receiving the license, he's flirted with playing detective, with reexamining the theories he'd discarded long ago. Bob understands that were he to continue down this path, he'd need to shed the staider skin he's inhabited these last years.

He'd have to keep his inquiry secret, for starters. From his wife, who is too grounded for goose chases. From the police. The learning curve would be steep. Bob already suspects he surrendered the license too quickly. A rookie mistake he'd have to make up for somehow.

Still, maybe there is a way. This afternoon, Miriam Lopez told him she taught a course for the public on "how the department operates." Might he enroll and use the knowledge he gleans to make headway on his own investigation? At the very least, it'd be a good way to remain on Miriam's radar, to make sure she follows through. Some nice

Jewish ladies sign up each semester, she'd told him. Why not a nice-enough Jewish man?

Bob knows it sounds nuts, and that's the appealing part. He has acted responsibly for twelve long years. At seventy, he's ready to go a little nuts.

Please, coyote, show me a sign!

Here's a dirty secret: you can always find a way to give yourself permission. A dream portends a breakup; a just-averted car wreck augurs the start of something new. The truth is, you were prepared before your head hit the pillow, before you slammed on the brakes: to end it all, to fall in love. A sign from the universe isn't an answer. It's an excuse. To do the thing you were already ready to do.

Ed hears it first. A rustling down the creek bed. He nudges Bob, points a meaty finger toward the sound.

Parallel to the footbridge, some scattered slabs of raised limestone form a bridge of their own. It is here that they emerge.

Five rangy silhouettes in crooked single file. Snouts low and sniffing or else in the air, bushy tails down. They trot briskly on long legs. A jaunty quintet.

The coyotes canter across the rocks one after the other. The caboose, Bob sees, keeps looking behind, as if to make sure they aren't being followed. In a line of elegant swindlers, she's a scrappier gangster than the rest. Slight hobble, chary eyes.

It's you, Bob thinks, his lips opening in astonishment. It is only then that he feels the spirit of his previous self finally return.

Between his teeth and down his throat the spirit goes, with such force it's as if all the drugs Bob hasn't taken over the last twelve years come rushing into his system at once. It burrows into his chest and expands, until the wraithlike essence extends to the tips of his fingers, to the top of his head, until that trickster spirit *is* Bob, again, and the soberer iteration of the man is the one that's cast out, tossed from his body and left there like a plastic bag, wrapped around some gnarled brush.

Do something, Bob! *Tell* someone, Bob! Bring the past to the present and figure out what happened to your nephew. Find a way to make it right.

Bob is so enraptured by this sensation that he doesn't notice how the shabbiest member of this passing family has provoked something in Ed Hooley, too. Doesn't see how Ed's face, once a rictus of discomfort, has rearranged itself into an expression softer but no less strained. Is it longing? *Take me with you.*

In the middle of the rocks, where the stream is at its strongest, this last coyote stops. She cranes her neck, brings her eyes to the men. Now it's her turn to be amazed. She stares and they stare back and then she cocks her head slightly, as if to say, *Is what I'm seeing real?*

Bob turns to Ed Hooley, as awestruck as he is. Bob looks back to the coyote. He wears the feral face of a supplicant in the presence of a faith healer. There are tears in his eyes. Bob cups his hands around his mouth, and, speaking the coyote's language, tells her to believe.

Awoooooooooo!

Citizen Police Academy

WE MET BOB ALEXANDER in February 2013, on the first night of Citizen Police Academy.

The course was not what we ladies expected. It was fourteen weeks, four hours each Thursday evening all spring in the conference room at Austin Police Department headquarters. If we followed the rules, the uniformed officer behind the podium assured us, we would have a "productive" experience.

There was no sewing during Citizen Police Academy. Crocheting, embroidery. "No needles, no sticks." A student who missed a class would receive a *marked absence*, which would disqualify him or her from entrance into the *perfect attendance lottery*. The winner of the *perfect attendance lottery* would be entitled to a ride-along on an APD helicopter with the Air Support unit for an entire shift. Any student prone to motion sickness was asked to *self-select out*. "Once they're up," the officer said, "they're up."

"Most importantly," she concluded, "please remember you are not training to be the police." Occasionally this message had not gotten through, which was why she was repeating it now. The purpose of the program was to give the citizenry a "working knowledge" of how the department operated and—"given recent events"—to open a dialogue between the public and the police. "You're the public," said the officer. "I'm the police."

The officer was called PIO Lopez. Public Information Officer Miriam Lopez. She was neither fair- nor dark-skinned, had black hair she hid away in a bun. If it weren't for the clue of her surname, her ethnicity would've remained a mystery. She could've been part Greek, part Indian, part Italian, part Black. She was less multiracial than all-racial. If one was *every* race, were they any race at all?

If she belonged to any obvious demographic, it was Police Officer. This was her race and sexuality, her ethnicity and gender. All the officers, we would come to learn, were more or less the same. They looked Police, spoke Police. Their language was weirdly proper, technical in a way that somehow obscured. There was no *I* in Police, no *police* in Police, either. Passive voice had disappeared them from their own narratives. Suspects were *taken in* for questioning, perpetrators *had been* apprehended. By whom? No one ever said.

We were not in the majority. For starters, this was not a Jewish group of people. "A few years back, Rich and I drove through Coeur d'Alene," whispered Barbara-Ann as we huddled together at the first break. "Had no idea it was the *skinhead capital of America*. Coeur d'Alene? More Jewish than this."

"Bergen-Belsen was more Jewish than this," said Eileen.

"I hate to break it to you," said Barbara-Ann, "but Bergen-Belsen was pretty Jewish."

Michelle snorted. "You guys are bad."

We'd assumed, coming in, that our classmates would be like we were. Jews? No. Eager for dialogue? Wasn't that the point?

To be clear: we weren't flamethrowers. We didn't *hate* the police. The police were mostly not part of our lives, infrequent if memorable guest stars from the occasional speeding ticket, from our kids' D.A.R.E. classes twenty years before.

Still, we knew the stories. One year earlier, we'd followed the terrible tragedy of the African American boy who'd been killed in Florida, deemed "suspicious" for the crime of being a teenager, for walking alone at night. We'd watched in horror as the police took their sweet time in arresting the killer. Worse, we understood this wasn't an isolated incident. Racial profiling, shootings of the unarmed. We'd read the news stories, remembered the names.

The previous fall, when we'd "applied" to be "Citizens" in this, the "53rd Class," we'd assumed that since the purpose of this project was to "start a conversation," there would be a large Black population in attendance. We imagined serving as intermediaries of some sort, using our skin color to give us credibility in "dialoguing" with the police. Maybe, finally, six decades in, we'd even make some Black friends.

But if we'd come to Citizen Police Academy because of Trayvon Martin, once inside we found George Zimmerman instead. George Zimmerman*s*: joyless Neighborhood Watchpeople in workout shirts, in yoga pants, gin-breathed Texas busybodies who'd eased into a life of permanent athleisure.

This was the largest bloc of Citizens: the ones for whom the reminder that we were not law enforcement was no doubt directed. We should've known what we were getting the moment we pulled into the garage that first night, nestling our Lexus, our RAV4, our Fit in between Jeep Grand Cherokees and Explorers and a Toyota Tundra with COME AND TAKE IT bumper-stickered to its foreboding rear. While we sat in our cluster off to the side, they made up the room's innards: thrilled to be there, eager to please.

During breaks, we eavesdropped as they complained to each other about rising violent crime (*here?*), about how President Obama was "ruining" their lives. (That Toyota Tundra? *$30,000.* We googled it. If that's a ruined life, please, Mr. President, ruin ours!) An epidemic of "political correctness" was allegedly raging out of control. "You can't *say* anything anymore," they'd gripe. *If you can't say anything,* we wanted to retort, *why are we always hearing the sound of your voice?*

The agendas of the few non-white participants were more difficult to parse. Most obvious was Harold Lafontaine, Sr., the ebullient owner of Lafontaine's Diner on Burnet Road. A complimentary buffet-style dinner was offered at the start of each session, provided by Harold, as Harold let us know. An Indian woman came in jeans and work boots; a Middle Eastern–looking guy showed up in a smart T-shirt/blazer combo. In the last row, an older Black woman in a houndstooth suit quietly took notes.

The format of the class was straightforward. Each week, officers from a different division would come to educate us about what they did. Child Abuse. S.W.A.T. "Homicide," said PIO Lopez. In front of us, someone *ooh*-ed.

Our speaker that night was the jolly Hispanic woman who headed up the Citizen Police Academy Alumni Society. She had the harried bearing of a parent leading a bake sale, the level of urgency with which she performed her tasks incommensurate with the stakes. Successful graduates of Citizen Police Academy were permitted to volunteer for APD training exercises. Last year, thirty-five graduates signed up to play the victims of a mass shooting.

"Some of us were assigned living and some of us were assigned dead and the officers had to figure out which was which," she explained. "They don't use ketchup, either. It's real fake blood." The biggest thing to remember: wear loose-fitting clothing. "You may be handled roughly," she said hopefully. "You may be dragged up to thirty feet." Around us, hands shot up with excited questions.

It was only at class's end, when PIO Lopez announced it was time for a "go-around," that we noticed Bob Alexander. We were to state our names, why we were here. Why *were* we here? "To show our support," said several of the men. "To learn how to protect what's mine," said an old crone called Pat Spackleman.

"Just here to learn," said Barbara-Ann, when her turn finally arrived.

"Same," said Eileen. "Educating ourselves."

"Learning," said Michelle.

"My name?" came a voice from the row behind us. "Officer Lopez here already knows me, but for the peanut gallery: I'm Bob Alexander."

We didn't even need to look to know. The rhetorical question, *the peanut gallery*. "Maybe it *is* more Jewish here than Coeur d'Alene," said Barbara-Ann.

How had we not sensed him before? In fairness, in a sea of old white men, it was easy to miss an old white man. He dressed as if he'd just stepped off the court: rumpled white windbreaker, white hair wonky. His one exotic trait was a small hoop earring, like Harrison Ford. "Now *why am I here* is a story," said Bob.

"Oh boy," whispered Michelle. "Here we go," said Eileen. "It's the Ghost of Husbands Future," said Barbara-Ann, and we had to bite our lower lips to keep from laughing. He was over seventy, a generation ahead, but there was no denying he looked like an amalgamation of our husbands, aged. Bony shoulders, bushy eyebrows, long legs. Part Rich part Jeff part Steve.

"I'm afraid this is not my first experience with the Austin Police Department," said Bob Alexander. In August 1998, he explained, his sixteen-year-old nephew went missing. The kid had been staying with Bob and his wife for the summer. "Went out for a drive one night and never came back."

Fifteen years later and there'd never been a single credible sighting of the boy. "He'd be thirty-one now. If, you know . . ." Bob let the silence sit heavy.

"My word," said a man in the crowd. "Terrible," said a woman.

"Mr. Alexander is an old friend of Citizen Police Academy," said PIO Lopez. "He's one of the only students to have enrolled more than once."

"Fourth time's the charm, right?" said Bob. "I know it's *unusual*, but I find it comforting, somehow, to come here. Plus, I like to remind these guys"—he pointed a chummy finger PIO Lopez's way, trying for merriment—"we're still around. Still looking."

"As are we," said PIO Lopez, a bit curtly. "So tell us, Mr. Alexander, is there anything you're hoping to learn this time you haven't previously?"

"I'm always interested," said Bob, "in how you do what you do."

At this, he turned to our trio, raised his bushy eyebrows as if daring us to speak, and, when we didn't accept, returned to his seat. We exchanged puzzled glances. Did we know this person?

"Sorry for your loss," tried Michelle, who was closest to him.

Bob Alexander offered a shrug/grimace familiar to Jews the world over. We'd seen it from Rich, from Jeff, from Steve. From each other, too. It said, *What can you do?*

We'd moved to Texas in the early-middle aughts in our mid-middle age. Forty-six, forty-nine, fifty-two.

We came from White Plains, from Chappaqua, from Needham. Around all those other Jews, we weren't all that Jewish. We enjoyed pork in our lo mein, crab legs as much as whitefish. From the pupu platter of our own parents' Reform-at-best traditions, we picked and chose as we saw fit: taking the kids to feed the ducks on Yom Kippur, each crumble of stale multigrain representing a sin they were casting away; a match to the menorah and a spin of the dreidel before the great unveiling of the Nintendo 64.

First generation we weren't. Our parents had survived the Holocaust from their parents' homes on Long Island, in Brooklyn. We were raised to know it could happen again, even here, but we didn't feel it like they did. To our husbands, World War II was a more visceral affront, an insult to their own masculinity. Though they never said it aloud, we suspected they fantasized about going back in time and enlisting to fight Nazis. Their killing-Hitler fetish manifested itself in 750-page hardcover histories of D-Day, of Kristallnacht, which they'd tear through from beach towels in Boca or deck chairs on the Cape. A black-and-white documentary about Treblinka at the local art house and off they'd go, a nice cooldown after Sunday morning softball. Aren't you a little Holocausted out? we'd ask. We preferred *As Good as It Gets*.

Each of us had moved west due to job upgrades for our other halves. We'd been full-time moms and part-time other things: market researcher, therapist, grant writer. *Texas?* We were skeptical. But we fell in love with Austin.

For starters, our husbands were happy. Oh, were they happy! They were making the most money of their lives in the most affordable city we'd ever lived in. On weekend trips around our new state, they'd turn into scavenging hawks, their prey the obscure Jewish connections to wherever we happened to be staying. *Who would've thought*, they'd exclaim, marveling at the remains of a long-shuttered synagogue here, a tiny Jewish museum there. How did they find these places? *Why* did they find these places? "Next time you take me to a Jewish cemetery," we wanted to tell them, "I'm bringing a shovel and I'm leaving alone."

Best of all, a new openness overtook our husbands in this winterless land. Freed of salting, sanding, scraping, Rich discovered flip-flops, Jeff rock-climbing, Steve Cosmopolitans.

We, meanwhile, found each other, via the Shapiro-Stern Institute's Jewish Women's Book Group at the JCC. We were the three newest transplants, and we knew each other as soon as we saw each other, knew each other so well that at first we wondered if we *did* know each other. *What camp did you go to? Where'd you send your kids?*

We started walking on Tuesday mornings, going to Zumba on Friday afternoons. For years, our children had criticized us for the grave offense of keeping them up to date on the lives of their childhood friends, whose parents were still our friends back east. They apparently didn't want to know that Aaron Rosenberg got the kids a Goldendoodle, that Julie Stein was engaged. But *we* wanted to know, wanted to know about each other's friends' children. Over time we developed an almost-sister language, the vast web of characters central to each of our stories uniting into one web, one story. Our friend circle in Austin was as tight as any we'd ever had.

We also, strangely, started to pride ourselves on our Texanness. As our East Coast friends downsized to condos in suburbs neighboring the ones they used to live in or retired to the same couple of states in the southeast, it felt good, somehow, to know we'd gone west instead. A lifetime of doing more or less what was expected of us and suddenly we were pioneers.

"It's not like in the movies," we'd assure old friends when they called concerned about the nutty gun laws, or whatever fanatical congressman had made the news that day. "We're a blueberry in the tomato soup," we'd tell them, adopting a maxim we'd heard from like-minded women at the J. Their worrying sounded provincial. Times and people and places change.

The re-election of our nation's first African American president affirmed our sense that our country was evolving for the better. *We are the change we've been waiting for*, our president liked to say, and we, in our own little way, felt part of that progress.

On matters of race, however, we knew we were out of our depth. After the tragedy in Florida, the only Black woman Barbara-Ann had worked with over fifteen years in market research wrote an eloquent Facebook post about the difficulty of being "the only one" at her job. Barbara-Ann commented that as a Jew in Texas, she knew just what her old co-worker meant. "This actually isn't about you," the ex-colleague had responded.

Over the years, each of us had proven equally clumsy in similar situations. Yet even if we never knew exactly what to do or say, we got the basics. We really did. Minorities in our own country did not feel safe around the police.

This was what led us to Citizen Police Academy. We wanted to be part of the solution, wanted to *be the change*, only we didn't know how. It was Bob Alexander who promised to show us.

Strange to say, but in those first weeks we didn't give him much thought.

Sure, we googled his nephew's case. Nathaniel Rothstein was from Newton, of all places, a Boston suburb each of us knew. But 1998 was before everything was online, and aside from an old article in the *Statesman* commemorating the ten-year anniversary of the disappearance, little information was available.

Looking back, maybe it's not a surprise Bob chose us. We were, we can admit, not always discreet. Were our husbands to describe our behavior, *running commentary* is a phrase that might've been used. In those first sessions, we were known to exchange glances, to display our aggravation through what we believed at the time were low-volume scoffs and clucks.

In fairness, we weren't *us* in APD headquarters. A mere mile away? We were sunny, funny women. We cooked, we laughed. Oh, did we laugh! That place drained our batteries.

The building wasn't bright or dark, dirty or clean. It was tired more than anything, the air heavy with fatigue. More than once on our journey through the metal detectors, up the elevator, and to the fourth floor, we posited we'd gone back in time. Through office windows we could see chunky desktops, fax machines. It was a world without Apple, or Google. Sometimes, we'd hear the static screech of a bygone printer, a page with perforated edges making its bumpy descent. "What do you think that *smell* is?" Eileen asked the second night, as we entered the conference room. "The seventies," said Barbara-Ann.

The conference room was newer: blue industrial carpeting and four rows of long, curved tables. The fluorescent lighting did no one any favors.

On a folding table in the back, Harold Lafontaine, Sr., would set up his buffet before we arrived. "Enjoy enjoy," he'd say, handing out paper plates. "Thank you much."

Though we never ate, we knew the menu intimately, for PIO Lopez would send it to us before class. She had peculiar email habits, a tumultuous relationship with capitalization. We'd *best come hungry for Bacon-wrapped chicken and Hushpuppies*. She hoped we'd join her in *saving room for a Banana Pudding Dessert*.

"What is this?" Barbara-Ann asked, peering at her iPhone, as we waited for that second class to begin. "*The Canterbury Tales*?"

Back then, PIO Lopez was our special preoccupation. She was in her mid-twenties and attractive, always tastefully made up, an alluring enough presence that it was her visage on billboards above the interstate reminding commuters not to drink and drive. PIO Lopez never deviated from her script, her inflection always neutral, though perhaps because of her age and gender we each sensed there was a living, breathing person somewhere inside her crisply pressed blues.

The woman was liberal with her adjectives, highly attuned to the weather. PIO Lopez hoped everyone had made it safely through the heavy rain, the moderate winds, the light hail. At the start of each class, she'd offer a Greatest Hits update on criminal activity from the previous week, always preceding her litany with *You may have heard.*

You may have heard about the incident of vehicular homicide on the 400 block of Rundberg Lane, the suspected arsonist targeting warehouses around Montopolis, the public defecator inside the Walgreens at 354 North Pleasant Valley Road.

We had never heard of any of these things. Sometimes we got the sense that PIO Lopez lived in a different city, a city of permanent catastrophe, which, in a way, she did.

Though we'd never heard, the goyim had. Oh, had they heard! On the local news, which they seemed to watch at five, at six, at ten, at eleven. On Nextdoor and Facebook. On a circular that sat atop the counters of convenience stores, a little newspaper of mug shots called *GOT YA!* that featured the bedraggled faces of the captured alongside the details of what they'd done.

GOT YA! sold for $1.50 and the gentiles of Citizen Police Academy paid up. With actual money! With actual cards! After Pete Wilbur—a retired SCUBA instructor who'd traded out his flippers for socks and shower shoes—learned of our unfamiliarity, he brought extras to the next class. "Never know who you'll find in there!"

The course was structured so that the least-controversial material was presented at the start. One week, we ventured to the first level of the parking garage to feed carrots to the horses of the Mounted Patrol. Another, PIO Lopez dimmed the lights for a slide presentation by the Nuisance Abatement Unit on the scourge of extreme hoarding.

Even the juicy-sounding stuff proved a bit of a snooze. A visit to the evidence room in the basement involved standing in front of a locked security cage, staring at rows and rows of cardboard boxes.

As for the presenters, they spoke in the same tone we'd experienced those rare times we'd been pulled over, the dry and aggravated *ma'am* we'd heard after unsteadily rolling down our windows expanded to encompass their every syllable.

With each other, during breaks, they joshed and joked. They treated the members of Citizen Police Academy closer to suspects than colleagues, which seemed, oddly, to please much of the Citizenry, the older white men especially, who spoke to the officers with a needy reverence, their every question, comment, comment-masked-as-question, offered like a too-firm handshake.

It took us little time to become attuned to our classmates' other annoying qualities. Bernice Ramos, who owned a small power-washing company, was the Forrest Gump of minor crime, having borne witness to seemingly any offense a visiting officer described. Bernice had observed a purse-snatching in the Costco parking lot; at the central library, she'd seen another woman get flashed. Her sister, a bank teller, was once attacked by a wild dog in Dick Nichols Park and had, "in '97 or thereabouts" been forced to move after learning a registered sex offender lived next door, only to learn a registered sex offender lived next to her new house, too. "You know the craziest part, though?" said Bernice, at the end of this O. Henry–like tale. "She's never been held up!"

As was true with many of Bernice's counterparts, the purpose of her contributions to Citizen Police Academy was mysterious. Whenever an officer "opened up the floor" for questions, Bernice was usually the first to step onto it, but the questions never came. A phrase that might've concluded any of Bernice's stories: *Just thought you should know*. Once, Bernice entered the 7-Eleven on East Ben White at the exact moment a knife-wielding man in a balaclava was exiting. "Did you get his plates?" asked that day's presenter, an officer from Robbery. "On foot," she said, shaking her head. "You can only do what you can do," said the officer, which in the case of Bernice Ramos was apparently nothing.

If Bernice was ridiculous, at least she was benign. The real idiotheads tended to emerge at the end of class, when PIO Lopez asked if there were any topics of interest we hadn't yet discussed. Chip Coons, forever swathed in Under Armour like some knight from the kingdom of Academy Sports, was endlessly braying about "securing operational control" of the border. ("Isn't he an *endodontist*?" whispered Michelle.) Garrett Feeney was a fiend for acronyms. "How long after an ADW would an APB go out, rough estimate?" ("I want to tell him to STFU," said Barbara-Ann.)

To our surprise, the only quiet white man in the student body turned out to be Bob Alexander. But as the weeks went on, we did start to pay him more mind. A ramp at the front of APD headquarters led down to a separate basement entryway, inaccessible to the public. One evening, as we exited the building, we found Bob coming up it with a large catering tray, which he proceeded to load into the trunk of a minivan, its hazard lights on.

Bob shut the trunk and started toward us. "Forget the evidence room. They've got a whole industrial kitchen down there!" he said, as if we knew him. Then, without turning back to the van: "Great meal tonight, Harold!" Bob raised a thumb high in the air; through the rolled-down driver's side window, Harold Lafontaine, Sr., countered with a thumbs-up of his own. "Thank you much," Harold called.

It stuck with us—those two had never so much as passed words in our presence and now they were best friends?—but men were like this sometimes. It wasn't that out of the ordinary.

Nor, really, was the other reason we'd begun considering Bob Alexander: because he seemed to be considering us. Bob always sat one row behind, and we could often feel his squinty eyes on our backs, like a gnat who never came quite close enough for us to shoo away. Whenever we turned to see if he was looking at us, Bob Alexander would stare right back, bushy brows raised.

Still, it seemed explainable. We were chatty Jewish women, he a solitary Jewish man. If we were him, we reasoned, we'd be interested in whatever we were saying, too.

So, it didn't seem especially peculiar, during the fifth meeting of Citizen Police Academy, when he said he had a matter to discuss with us and asked if we might grab a cocktail after class.

If nothing else it would be a story, and after four hours with that crew, who wouldn't want a drink (after, of course, we used the john)?

We each drove separately to the bar on 11th Street.

It turned out to be a small gay bar. A multicolored disco ball spun over an empty dance floor; the mustachioed bartender wore a T-shirt that read DADDY. Bob insisted on buying our Chardonnays. "Do you do *Cosmopolitans*?" he asked the bartender.

At a table by the front window, we sipped our drinks awkwardly, waiting for Bob to explain himself. "Do you come here a lot?" asked Michelle, trying to break the ice.

"I wanted to find a place where *they* wouldn't be," said Bob.

"Who is *they*?" said Michelle.

"Yelp calls this a *bear bar*," said Bob, ignoring the question. "Couple Thanksgivings ago, my son Max's partner, Peter, gave me a tutorial on *gay taxonomy*. I used to think *twink* meant *small woman*. I thought Katie Couric was a twink! Peter and I, we went a little heavy on the peace pipe after dinner and he walked me through the nomenclature. It's a real trip, getting older. Don't you think?"

We exchanged glances: the ice was broken, melting, rising to our knees.

"Are you married?" tried Barbara-Ann.

"Forty-nine years," said Bob. "*Marlene*. She's over at a wine-and-cheese celebrating the halfway point of her UT extension course on Talmudic studies." He rolled his eyes with his face.

"I've always heard the Talmud is very beautiful," said Eileen.

"Not you, too," said Bob. "Marlene loves pontificating on the beauty of the Talmud. I said to her, 'Can you recite a single *line* from the Talmud? What *is* the Talmud?'"

"Marlene isn't interested in Citizen Police Academy?" ventured Michelle.

Bob winced: *I don't think so*. He took a swig of Cosmo. "I'm seventy-three, and do you know what I've learned in my *advanced age*?" The more he leaned in, the more we leaned back. "Bob Alexander"—he paused for effect—"is a coward."

"You're a coward?" said Eileen.

"I frequently do the wrong thing," said Bob, "and it's not because I don't know what the right thing is."

"I'm sure you're not a—" started Barbara-Ann.

"Hit seventy and you start to assess yourself as you *actually* are. I mean, look: My prostate is the size of the Hindenburg. I haven't had leg hair since Y2K. *If not now, when*, right? Are your kids religious?"

We'll admit: this little monologue, a question about our own lives . . . a half-glass of wine in and we felt our first tingle of warmth toward the guy. "My daughter-in-law is a *Reconstructionist rabbi*," said Barbara-Ann. "Puts the orange on the seder plate. A little hippy-dippy for my tastes. But . . ." *What can you do?*

Bob nodded in appreciation. "My son doesn't care, which, good, but it means after I'm *incinerated* I'll probably end up, where? His attic in San Diego? Faced with that, you start to think, What have I done on this earth? And you know what the answer is? *I've moved food around the plate*."

"I'm sure you've done more than that," said Eileen.

"Not me and not you, either," said Bob.

"You don't know anything about us!" said Barbara-Ann.

"Look, I watch you ladies," said Bob. "Every week. You know this class is horseshit. But *knowing*? What does that get you? What does it get anyone?"

"I'm not sure I follow," said Michelle.

"I'm planning something before I zip out of this place that I *know* will be of tangible and long-lasting consequence," said Bob. "And I'd like you to join me."

Now it was our turn to lean in. *Tangible. Long-lasting*. What do you have in mind? we asked.

"We'll get there," said Bob Alexander. He took a final gulp of Cosmo. "But first I need to tell you what happened to my nephew."

He sounded like children our children had known, children we'd known through our children. Thick freckles, thighs, belly, bosom. "*Nipples like milk saucers*," said Bob Alexander.

Our kids had always brimmed with brio, but we knew this other breed of Ashkenazi adolescent, too. He was the kid we'd scold our kids for complaining about but who, truth be told, we didn't care for either, that meh child we always found ourselves ferrying in the rear-facing seats of our station wagons to day camp, to Hebrew school, no car pool complete without one cautionary tale (about only children, or older parents), the names still stuck in our heads like gum under a desk. *Ari Hershkovitz. Ian Lichtenberg. Anna Finger-Klein.*

Perhaps because we'd known our own Nathaniel Rothsteins, his story resonated with us. Even more because, in an only-in-Austin coincidence, Nathaniel had spent much of his time at the same boxing gym Barbara-Ann used to visit. "2007 to 2010. *Evening person*," she told Bob. "Sciatica got in the way."

"I thought you looked familiar," said Bob. "Did you have a dog with *child-bearing hips*?"

"We prefer to say Frisco has an *hourglass figure*," said Barbara-Ann.

For an hour we sat rapt as Bob described his nephew's Austin evolution: how he discovered boxing, the disappearance of his thighs, belly, bosom. Bob attributed these changes mostly to the influence of Nathaniel's boss at the nursing home where he was volunteering. This was Bob's friend, David, a man Bob spoke of with such reverence and regret that we wondered if he'd died. "He was so *good* for Nathaniel. At least at the start."

Bob's storytelling style was digressive—any real emotions buried beneath a mountain of little asides—but his delivery was no match for his M&M-sized eyes, watery and ablaze with purpose, which he kept fixed on some distant point between our heads, a meager attempt to hide his pain. There was no fooling us, we wanted to say. A mother always knows.

At first, Nathaniel's story had us thinking about our own children, now chasing their big dreams on one coast or the other, happy and themselves. He'd been on the cusp of figuring out who he was, who he'd like to be. To lose a kid at that unformed age. How cruel.

But as we learned of Nathaniel and David's deepening bond—as they began to meet nightly at the gym—each of us went from pitying Bob's bashful nephew to feeling something else. Envy would be too strong a word. More like a tiny twinge of yearning deep inside ourselves.

The truth was, Nathaniel's friendship with David made us want to be friends with David, too. He was so tender, so understanding. And, yes, we'll say it: *he was Black*.

We know, we know. Trust us, our kids have let us know. It's not an acceptable reason to want to be friends with someone. But nor is being white a reason, and for much of our lives who we'd interacted with—at school, at work, in our neighborhoods—was determined by this even more than by the normal factors that should go into deciding who becomes a friend.

How many times had each of us had a warm encounter with a Black woman—in line at Whole Foods, a seatmate on the plane—and wished she were part of our circle? They'd put up with so much nonsense in their lives! Yet always so confident, didn't tolerate a lot of BS. Was it so wrong to long to connect?

We weren't like those numbskulls over at Citizen Police Academy, so sure that the changing world was passing them by. We worried there was *another* world, a *better* world, to which we had no access.

So it didn't surprise us to hear how much Nathaniel looked up to David, how he copied his scent, his walk, adopted his catchphrases. Nor did we even think much of it when Bob said his nephew, as the summer progressed, had started to tan.

Bob went to refresh our drinks, and when he returned, he launched in before even setting down our glasses, picking up the story in the way of Rich, of Jeff, of Steve: as if there'd been no pause.

Bob had been so proud of his nephew, he told us, but for weeks one thing had given him pause. A strange murmuring he'd heard coming from Nathaniel's bedroom early in the mornings and late at night. When he'd asked Nathaniel, the boy said his uncle had misheard.

"I knew he was hiding something, but he'd undergone a genuine de-putzification that summer. I didn't want to hector him. Whatever he was up to, how bad could it be?"

The night Nathaniel disappeared, Bob went to the boy's bedroom. "The next morning—that would've been Saturday, August 8—he was supposed to get into the ring to spar for the first time. It was a big deal for him and David. So I bought him a pair of boxing shoes, for good luck. Well, I go to give them to him, and I hear that murmuring—"

He knocks lightly on the door. No answer. He goes into the bedroom, sees the boy is in the en suite bathroom. Knocks on that. "And then I—"

"You *didn't*!" said Barbara-Ann.

"Oh, Bob," said Eileen. "Privacy is so important at that age."

"What if he was taking a BM?" said Michelle.

"If only," said Bob. Inside, he found his newly svelte nephew fully nude. "He had his cell phone in one hand," said Bob ominously, "and was *pleasuring himself* with the other."

That wasn't the half of it. "All summer, Nathaniel had been getting a lot of sun, but I had no idea the extent," said Bob. The boy's skin was weirdly inconsistent. "He looked like a car made from junkyard parts. He was a patchwork of earth tones. *A human L.L. Bean*."

"This is not where I thought you were going," admitted Barbara-Ann.

"Honey," said Bob Alexander, "we're just pulling out of the driveway."

In the fifteen-second window between opening and shutting the bathroom door, Bob also learned the source of those mysterious sounds. His nephew was engaging in the filthiest talk imaginable, and not the generic kind. "I'll spare you a re-enactment but Nathaniel, he was . . . *pretending to be Black*."

Thirty years with sons, with husbands: we knew stained sheets as well as we knew the dishwasher. Pretending to be Black? This wasn't covered in the *What's Happening to My Body Book for Boys*.

"Why would he do such a thing?" asked Eileen.

"I had no idea!" said Bob. "I mean, we all have *proclivities*. Was it a *fetish*? I didn't know what to say. What to do. I'd seen him and he'd seen me—"

When Nathaniel emerged from the bathroom, he was wrapped in a towel, teary-eyed. He begged his uncle not to tell David what he'd done. "That's when it started to make some sense to me," said Bob. "David, he was a very confident guy. I think Nathaniel was trying to harness some of that."

"Did you find out who he was talking to?" asked Eileen.

"He tells me it's his *girlfriend*," said Bob.

"From Newton?" asked Michelle.

"Says he's never actually *met* her," said Bob.

"And this is how he talks to the girlfriend he's never actually met?" said Barbara-Ann.

"Apparently," Bob told us, "this 'girlfriend' thinks Nathaniel *is* Black. I say to him, 'With that skin, I hope you never *plan* on meeting her!' He looks, I don't know . . . khaki? He looks insane. Well, that does it: waterworks. I mean, he really loses it. I didn't know what I'd said!"

We'd had so many fights with our kids when they were teenagers: we could perfectly picture the plaid sheets on the unmade bed, the piping hot tears. When Bob told us he'd pointed at the full-length mirror affixed to the closed bedroom door in front of them, not only did we envision uncle and nephew regarding each other's reflection wearily, we could see ourselves, too, all of us in a huddle surrounding the boy.

"After I leave this room," Bob told him as we looked on, disappointed, "I want you to examine yourself. What you've *done* to yourself. And I want you to ask yourself: *Is the person staring back at you the person you want to be?*"

An hour later, Nathaniel was gone.

"I heard the Volvo pulling out of the driveway, but I didn't think much of it," Bob told us. "All summer he'd come and gone as he pleased."

The next morning, Bob went to wake Nathaniel for sparring, but he was nowhere to be found. "His bedroom looked as it had looked all summer. As far as I could tell he hadn't even packed a bag."

It was only when Bob went to search the en suite bathroom that he found something unusual. A prescription bottle on the sink top. "Methoxsalen?" he said, reading aloud from its label. "Who is *G. Abruzzi*?" Bob unscrewed the bottle, but there was nothing left inside.

"So I drive to the gym."

Bob was in it now. Tone: confessional. Tense: present. "I pull into the parking lot, and there's David, leaning against the hood of his Civic," said Bob. "He's invested so much time in this kid. But I can tell by that far-off look in his eyes that Nathaniel hasn't shown."

It felt wrong to tell David what had happened, but more wrong to let him think Nathaniel had blown him off. So out it came: Nathaniel's bizarre behavior on the phone; those mysterious pills; the boy not coming home.

"I told him, 'Look, man, this kid sees so much *power* in you,'" said Bob. "I wanted him to know Nathaniel had no ill intent."

Bob was so relieved to have the truth out that at first he didn't notice David still had that far-off look. "And then David tells me: *I knew about the pills*."

"He *knew*?" said Barbara-Ann.

"Tells me he *might've had something to do with Nathaniel acquiring them*."

Nooooo, we said in unison.

"'*You knew about the pills*? You knew?' I can't believe it. 'What do they *do*?'"

The methoxsalen, when combined with exposure to the sun, would *darken a person's skin*. Turned out, not only had David known Nathaniel was imitating him, he'd *approved*. "From David's point of view, it was working," said Bob. "Nathaniel, he was becoming a different kid. A better kid!" He'd left the pills in Nathaniel's locker at work the day before. They were, as far as Bob could tell, David's way of saying, *Keep it up*.

"I don't think he thought Nathaniel would *take* them," said Bob. "Or all of them. David keeps telling me it isn't *about* the pills. 'Who knows what that boy could become if we encourage him? Maybe a fighter, even!' A *fighter*? I say, 'David, that boy's gonna become a psychiatric patient if he keeps taking other people's meds.'"

"Did he really think your nephew had potential as a boxer?" asked Eileen.

"'Crazier things have happened,' he tells me," said Bob. "And I'm getting agitated. We brought Nathaniel to Austin to become *less* of a fuck-up, and now he's embroiled in this? I tell him, 'David, this kid has enough going against him without also trying to make himself over as a Black man in the United States.'

"Well, that did it. I'd never seen him so mad. Says my problem is I just can't imagine anyone aspiring to be him. 'Who could ever possibly want to be David Dalice?'"

"I don't think that's what you were saying," said Eileen.

"Then he gets right in my face," said Bob. "'*At least your nephew owns it*.'"

"Owns what?" said Michelle.

"I had no idea," said Bob. "'Are you training for Senior Golden Gloves, Dr. Alexander?' This is what David asks me. Says in all the time he's known me I've never come to the gym for *boxing*. No, I'm there to bump fists with the *brothers*. To shoot the shit with him. 'All these young Black fighters trying to make something of themselves, and here's Bob Alexander, the professor, *in the mix*.'"

"That seems unduly harsh," said Barbara-Ann.

"He says I see this whole boxing thing, this whole *David* thing, as a means to an end for Nathaniel. Did I ever consider it might be a worthy end in itself?"

Now Bob Alexander's face went grim. "I should've left it there. It's not as if he knew where Nathaniel was. But I was angry."

Understandably, we assured him. It didn't seem an especially ambiguous case: David had acted out of line.

"What I did next, though . . . I told myself I was doing it to *protect* people, but I didn't believe that. It's not like I thought David was a high-level trafficker of psoriasis medication! It's just, there was some truth to what he said that day. More than I could admit back then. And, boy oh boy, that pissed me off."

So what did you do? we wanted to know.

"I called the nursing home where David worked and told them he'd been stealing pills."

The first lead in the investigation into Nathaniel's disappearance came after a petty thief was picked up with a bag of goods he'd stolen off sunbathers at Hippie Hollow. This was Austin's only nude beach, a place Rich, Jeff, and Steve had each, at one point or another, suggested "checking out," no doubt because they thought beautiful women would be luxuriating on the rocks there instead of who *we* knew would be: other Riches, Jeffs, and Steves.

Among the items found on the thief: Nathaniel's Velcro wallet, the only thing in it an appointment card with the boy's name. Even his license was gone. According to the police, IDs were purchased on the "black market" all the time. To identity thieves, even people smugglers. "These cops. *Illusions of grandeur*, right?" said Bob. "What, some Mexican guy is gonna sneak across the border pretending to be a teenager named *Nathaniel Rothstein*?"

The police determined the thief had no connection to the disappearance, and soon ruled out foul play altogether. When Bob first reported Nathaniel missing, he'd told the detective assigned to the case that they'd had an argument the night before. "*Teenager stuff*," Bob told him, and left it at that. All indications, the detective concluded, suggested Nathaniel had run away.

At Bob's request, the detective did half-heartedly investigate whom Nathaniel had been talking to the night he vanished. "Figures out it was a forty-one-year-old *phone sex operator*," said Bob, "who was also, bizarrely, the detective's longtime hairdresser." The hairdresser swore she had no idea about any of this. "Detective tells me if it was embezzlement, she'd have made a good suspect," said Bob. "But sex with a minor? 'That ain't Belinda's *bag*.'"

So Nathaniel had deluded himself into believing his "girlfriend" was a lady on a 900 number? It was all perfectly in character for Bob's friendless nephew, and sad.

But why'd he go to the nude beach?

"Don't you think it's obvious?" said Bob. At the library, Bob had learned methoxsalen was the same medication the writer John Howard Griffin had used to "change" his race in *Black Like Me*, a book we remembered from our childhoods. Griffin had done it over a few days with a UV lamp; could Nathaniel, upping the dosage and lying under the Texas sun, have done it in one?

With that skin, I hope you never <u>*plan*</u> *on meeting her!* Bob had yelled at Nathaniel the night he disappeared. In Bob's view, he'd inadvertently goaded the boy into taking those pills. "My nephew went to Hippie Hollow to *even himself out*."

This, Bob believed, was why they never found Nathaniel. "We'd been obsessing over a missing white boy when we should've been searching for a Black one."

Till now each detail of this strange story had made a modicum of sense, but taken altogether and, well, *nuttier than a fruitcake* was a phrase that came to mind. We responded as politely as we could—"An interesting hypothesis, Bob!"—all the while employing our secret eye language, a series of highly subtle glances we'd honed over years of friendship. They said, *Is this guy a loon?*

"I never shared any of this with the authorities, of course," said

Bob, oblivious to our code. "I knew *they'd* never believe me." He also knew if the cops ever learned about the pills, it would lead them to David, so he threw the empty bottle in the trash compactor. "A week after the disappearance, I heard through the gym grapevine that David had been let go from his job. *Downsizing* was what he was telling people. I figured that was punishment enough."

"Oh, Bob," said Eileen. As the therapist of our group, she was the most invested in keeping the conversation tethered to planet Earth. "This all must've been so hard."

"All the race stuff," said Bob, "it was embarrassing to talk about, and I knew it sounded ridiculous. So I just—I let it go."

And twelve years passed.

Bob's sleuthing began in earnest in late 2010, after the mysterious re-emergence of Nathaniel's license.

"So PIO Lopez went to the boxing gym, too?" asked Michelle, after Bob explained he'd handed the license off to her. Was there anyone in Austin *not* connected to this place?

Bob began spending hours in his home office, ostensibly working on a new book, but really re-creating the timeline of Nathaniel's disappearance. He enrolled in his first Citizen Police Academy to better understand how the police had investigated the case.

News articles Bob would've read with mild interest back when he'd convinced himself his theory was irrational now took on new meaning. One day, he heard an NPR piece about Black parents sitting their teens down with instructions on what to do if they ever got pulled over: *always keep your hands on the wheel, never argue with the police*. "The Talk, the reporter called it," said Bob.

Soon he was monitoring stories across the country: of false arrests, of "officer-involved" shootings. He signed up for one of those "Google alerts" for the phrase *unarmed Black man*. "I'm getting multiple notifications a *day*."

He began to entertain dark thoughts about what had happened to Nathaniel. What if he'd wound up in jail, or worse? "He had no ID. No sense of how he'd be perceived in that skin."

Bob felt guilty for not thoroughly investigating his theory when it would've mattered. He felt guilty for how he'd thought about these cases up until now: as *cases*, not as *lives*.

"I was way more up on this stuff than plenty of white folks. But what did I ever *do*? Nothing. I read the story, I moved on." For the first time all night, he looked right at us. "But when it's the kid *you're* responsible for . . . When it's *your* kid . . ."

One morning, Bob searched the internet for stories about arrests in Austin from around the time his nephew disappeared. As we knew from our own googling of Nathaniel, there wasn't much. But in the *Statesman*'s archives, he came upon a since-discontinued column called Police Beat, which featured little summaries of that week's notable arrests.

Seventeen "offenders" were mentioned in the Police Beat from the second week of August 1998. Over a couple months, Bob figured out what had become of each of them.

Of the seventeen, fifteen were alive. Of the fifteen, eleven were Black. Of the eleven, nine were still incarcerated. "I wrote to every one of them, asking if I could visit." Of the nine, seven wrote back.

So off Bob went. To the Connally Unit south of San Antonio and the Roach Unit, almost in Oklahoma. To the Duncan Geriatric Facility in Diboll, wherever that was. "This guy's been locked up on and off since *1964*. Guard tells me he's running late because he's *emptying his catheter*." In dingy waiting rooms or from behind smudged glass, Bob explained he thought that his nephew had been arrested in Austin around the same time they'd been in 1998.

No one had heard of Nathaniel Rothstein. "These guys, they'd been convicted of some horrific stuff. But back in '98? Most of them were kids. And their initial offenses? Small ball."

One man managed to rack up two felonies before the age of nineteen, both times for possession of under a gram of cocaine. If he'd lived in one of our hoity-toity neighborhoods, it might've resulted in rehab, not a year behind bars. "Ten months after getting out the second time, he's hopped up on god-knows-what, steals a car. Doesn't realize there's a four-year-old in the back." He was arrested for aggravated kidnapping. "*Fifty years*," said Bob.

The whole thing disturbed Bob so much he even went to see the man's family. Dad owned a small restaurant, mom was a retired teacher. Like Bob, had only the one son. "The spread this man lays out! A missing nephew was almost worth it for that creamed spinach. But after the chitchat? What was there to say? I know what it's like when you lose a kid. There's no coming back from that."

We sat in silence then, pretending to imagine our own children locked away, though really what flashed inside our minds were images of the last Black man each of us had seen, imprisoned. The handsome teller at the Bank of America; the studious undergraduate from the "Genius Bar" at the Domain. A couple false moves, some experimentation with substances: How far had any of these promising young people been from suffering a similar, horrible fate?

We remembered Bob's words from the start of the night. *Tangible. Long-lasting.*

"So this plan of yours . . ." said Barbara-Ann. "What do you have in mind?"

By the spring of 2011, Bob told us, he'd already begun spinning his wheels. His first foray into Citizen Police Academy was ending, and he'd gleaned no new insight into solving his nephew's case.

"Then, on the final day of class, PIO Lopez is giving her farewell spiel," said Bob, "and she tells us that the department is always on the lookout for *constructive ideas* to make our city a better place. 'My hope is these last fourteen weeks will inspire you to come up with one.'"

At the "bear bar" on 11th Street, Bob Alexander raised his empty martini glass. "And you know what, ladies?" he said. "*It did.*"

All week, as we power-walked around each other's neighborhoods, arms swinging high, our encounter with Bob Alexander remained at the forefront of our minds.

None of us had left the "bear bar" remotely convinced of Bob's wacky theory. But even if Bob's hypothesis was cuckoo for Cocoa Puffs, we'd be lying if we said his cryptic call to action didn't excite us. He'd remained aggravatingly vague about his "plan," telling us he'd reveal the details only in "due time." Left to cogitate, we let our imaginations run wild.

Our speculations were, we can admit, grand and highly specific. We envisioned using the communications skills we'd honed in our previous professions to create a gut-wrenching presentation about the inequities in the system, telling the awful story of the restaurant owner's fifty-years-imprisoned son in a way only mothers could, our words aimed at other white people. Perhaps we'd end up testifying before Congress, raising our right hands to take the oath in unison, our passion and rage so palpable it would galvanize the country, leading to nationwide reform.

To our annoyance, Bob told us he'd get into the plan's specifics only once we'd proven we were "ready for confrontation," and though, amongst ourselves, we scoffed all week at the idea of our unpreparedness ("Until five minutes ago he didn't know us from Adam!"), we knew our irritation stemmed from the fact that he did have a point.

Get us going among the like-minded and we had no problem piping up. But despite our disdain for the people in that conference room, we'd been too timid to ever challenge them face-to-face.

We got our first chance during the following week's *You may have heard*, when, after PIO Lopez apprised us of a spate of auto thefts, dreary Pat Spackleman chimed in that since "everyone" thought cops were such terrible people, maybe the police should turn off 911 for a day, "see how that goes."

"Absurd," declared Barbara-Ann (replacing the *s* with a *z* as she was wont to do).

"There's nothing ab*z*urd about it!" sneered Pat Spackleman.

"So anyone should just walk off their job the second they have to show some accountability for their actions?" countered Barbara-Ann.

"Ladies," said PIO Lopez, "let's stay on track."

What track? we should've said. Wasn't *this* the track? But whether it was due to the shock of being chided by PIO Lopez or simply because we hadn't had enough practice engaging in so heated an exchange, we couldn't gather ourselves with the speed necessary to respond. The obvious follow-ups seemed obvious only once the moment had passed.

After class, we met Bob on the sidewalk outside headquarters. "C for effort tonight, hon," he said to Barbara-Ann, and began striding across the street toward the parking garage.

"I should've said more," admitted Barbara-Ann, trying to keep pace.

"I wouldn't worry about it," said Bob. "Warren Buffett is too Jewy for this crowd. You think *Barbara-Ann Jaffee* is going to have much impact?"

"Wait a minute," said Michelle. "Weren't you just telling us we needed to *do* something?"

"If you don't do *something*, you'll never realize there's nothing you can do," said Bob, to our bafflement, as we reached the bottom of the stairwell. "You gals on two?"

Offered in a single eight-day span, Bob's twin pronouncements—that we were useless and that trying *not* to be useless was also useless—mystified us. If futility was inevitable, why have a plan for anything?

"What if I told you it was all part of the plan?" said Bob, starting up the stairs.

From the bottom of the steps (we'd parked on ground level) we asked what *it* meant. "Us speaking out?" said Barbara-Ann. "Us being ignored?" said Eileen. "Us being confused?" said Michelle.

"Part of the plan," said Bob, and he disappeared into the lot.

Two days later, police in Cincinnati "mistook" a Black jogger for a robbery suspect, shooting and killing him. The story made national news.

We arrived the following class to find a new officer standing behind the lectern. He was tall and thin with a salt-and-pepper mustache, like a cop from TV. Off to the side, PIO Lopez explained that her boss, "Sergeant Gary D'Angelo," had "asked to address" the Citizenry about "last week's tragedy."

The presentation was unlike any we'd seen at Citizen Police Academy before. For fifteen minutes, the sergeant explained everything that had gone wrong in Cincinnati, the policies that had been ignored, what APD was doing to make sure nothing like that could happen here. When thin-lipped Pete Wilbur asked why the sergeant was taking responsibility for some other cop's screwup, D'Angelo stopped him. "It's important we get this stuff right, Mr. Wilbur. Don't you think?" For the first time in seven weeks, it seemed someone interested in actual accountability had arrived on the scene.

Heartened to finally have a good-faith actor in the room, Eileen raised her hand. "I appreciate this presentation, I do," she said. "But given how many times a case like this makes the news, given that some similar things have even occurred in our city, I'd like to know why you think it keeps happening?"

"Well said," said Michelle.

"*Nice*," said Barbara-Ann.

Eileen shot Bob a look: *Take that*.

Sergeant D'Angelo explained that for legal reasons he couldn't address anything specific to Austin. "But I will say this . . ."

Just then, Eileen, sitting in the middle of our threesome, felt a tap on her shoulder. It was Bob, who passed her a little folded-up note, which she opened for all of us to see. We read Bob's handwritten words as Sergeant D'Angelo was saying the exact same ones:

"We can't be responsible for the actions of others, but we CAN be responsible for our own actions."

"I had an inkling of an idea after I enrolled in this thing the first time," Bob told us on the way back to the garage that night. "And I had time to burn. So I took it again. And again. *And again.*"

Every time, he said, a tragedy like the one in Cincinnati had unfolded at some point during the semester. Every time, Sergeant D'Angelo had "asked to speak" to the class. The subtle shutting-down of a noxious classmate; "that meaningless final line": Bob had seen it all before.

"Nothing ever changes," said Bob. "They don't *want* change. They want the illusion of change to keep everything the goddamn same."

As we drove home that night, this last line of Bob's stuck with us. Each of us *had* been captivated by D'Angelo's presentation. We imagined returning home to tell our husbands how forthright the sergeant had been about the incident, how he'd countered miserable Pete Wilbur. We imagined how, after, we'd do what Bob had told us he'd done so many times before, what *we'd* always done: moved on.

The murder in Cincinnati came as the course was beginning to orient itself around the "issues of the day." Still in the dark about Bob's "plan," we continued to try inserting ourselves into the conversation, only now we became students of our own attempts, increasingly cognizant of the tactics the cops used to short-circuit real debate.

Statements like D'Angelo's were repeated so many times they started to sound like conventional wisdom. The fact that no officer wanted, or deserved, to be killed was frequently invoked as a defense for officers killing others. "None of us came here to sign our own death warrants," more than one officer proclaimed, as if that settled it.

On the single occasion an entire session was dedicated to race—a three-hour presentation called "Diverse Viewpoints on Racial Profiling"—information was provided in colossal chunks, and we were told to hold our questions to the end, as if after a ninety-six-slide PowerPoint and a couple cups of decaf we could even remember what it was we wanted to ask in the first place.

Perhaps most bizarrely, the more we outed ourselves as rabble-rousers, the more solicitous of our comments the presenters became. *What do you think, Mrs. Jaffee?* Or: *That's an interesting point Mrs. Weiss raises*. But our thoughts and points were never actually addressed. Instead, we were allowed to pontificate freely, the silence of our interlocutors compelling us to push harder. Sentences were garbled, voices raised. We knew how it looked to our classmates. An agitated Jewish lady isn't a rabble-rouser; she's a nut.

If we were waiting for any of the people of color to back us up, we should've packed pillows. The Black woman kept to her notes; Harold Lafontaine, Sr., to his food. The Indian in the work boots was aligned with the reactionaries; the Middle Easterner in the T-shirt/blazer had enrolled only to recruit people, during the breaks, to a "social networking" site he'd created to "connect Americans across the ideological divide." ("You think he's a con artist?" asked Eileen. "I think he's a moron," said Barbara-Ann.)

As for the rest of the Citizenry, their adulation for law enforcement only seemed to grow stronger with each passing class. One evening, we walked a few blocks from APD headquarters to the county jail, where a baby-faced guard—Alfred E. Neuman with a baton—led us on a tour. The purpose, he explained, was to show what happens to the just-arrested from the moment they enter the facility, the prospect of "playing" prisoner in this way electrifying to our classmates.

In a darkened hallway, we sat on parallel backless benches among actual suspects, who were handcuffed and waiting to be processed. A Charles Manson–like fellow talked softly to no one; a Black man in an Astros cap stayed focused on his lap. Pete Wilbur had conveniently chosen to sit across from a skeletal white prostitute in a knit miniskirt the width of a potholder, her legs uncrossed. "It's neat to be able to experience this," Bernice Ramos told our guide. "Wouldn't it be more realistic if we were cuffed?"

For the next hour, we moved through the processing process, passing from lobby to nurse's station and on toward the cells, each stop a slightly reconfigured tableau of the same haggard people. Unlike in the movies, the cells had doors, so all we saw of their inhabitants was what we could make out through the tall, narrow windows above the food slots. According to Alfred E., prior Citizens had been so disappointed by this that, in our honor, the powers-that-be had emptied a few cells at the end of a long, wide block, giving us free rein to "make ourselves at home."

There was something gross about it, a bunch of well-off mostly white people treating jail like it was the zoo. We sat on the bottom bunk in the last cell on the block, purses in our laps, repelled by our classmates, who made jokes about what the green vinyl mattresses had been through, about the lidless toilets. We thought about the bank teller, the Apple "Genius." There was nothing funny about anyone ending up in this sad, cold place.

Our only ally remained Bob, who, traveling back with us to the garage each evening, seemed pleased by our ever more pointed observations. In class he remained silent, though sometimes we'd turn to find him mouthing along to an officer's presentation, a never-ending karaoke to the dullest song in the world.

Only once, during our twelfth session, did Bob speak, and then it was only a single word. On that night, a muscley officer from Gang Suppression gave a gruesome presentation on the violent criminal syndicates that allegedly (and unbeknownst to us and literally everyone we knew) controlled entire blocks of our city. On the screen behind him, he showed mug shots of various gang leaders.

"How do you stop yourselves from just smashing these guys' heads in?" asked Chip Coons, the endodontist, as we stared at a stony-eyed Hispanic man, his face covered in tattoos.

"Use of force is *always* a last resort," said the officer. "But look, none of us came here to sign our own death warrants, right?"

"You know," said Michelle, "it's not as if that jogger in Cincinnati wanted to sign *his* own death warrant, either."

"What part of this is so difficult to understand?" said Pete Wilbur. He pointed to the officer. "*He* can only be responsible for *his own* actions."

We'd never believed in "trickle-down" economics. But trickle-down obfuscation? We slowly turned to gauge Bob Alexander's reaction.

"Yup," said Bob.

"The Simulation" occurred the second-to-last Citizen Police Academy.

To give us an understanding of what officers experience "day-to-day," PIO Lopez told us, we'd use the APD's "state-of-the-art" training simulator, just like cadets in the real police academy. Outfitted with a "simulated handgun," we'd participate in a series of "real-life scenarios" projected onto a screen, interacting with "real-life" perpetrators whose responses would be controlled by an officer via laptop. We'd be forced to decide, "in real time," whether to pull the trigger.

As The Simulation could accommodate only one Citizen at a time, we were invited, before and after our turns, to "take advantage" of the perfect spring evening on the roof, where Harold Lafontaine, Sr., had set up that night's buffet. There, PIO Lopez told us, we could "celebrate" the "hard work" we'd "accomplished so far."

The Simulation itself took place behind an unmarked door on the top floor of APD headquarters in what looked like a grade-school classroom after the final bell had rung for the day. Linoleum flooring, lights low. A projection screen pulled down at the front of the room.

From a folding table in back, an officer brusquely Velcroed us into a "tactical vest," buckled a "duty belt" around our waists, stripped of its normal accoutrements but "weighted" to simulate "real life." We learned these facts courtesy of a male voice, a Police voice, who introduced himself as our instructor and sat behind the folding table, his face obscured behind a large computer monitor.

The belt was awkward and heavy, the vest too big. Could they be adjusted? "Please ask us questions" was not the vibe in the room. We felt as we did before zip-lining in Costa Rica, before the high ropes course at family camp in Mohonk, which was to say: not good.

For the first time in our lives, we held an actual handgun, its insides subbed out for "laser technology" that would allow us to see what we hit when we fired our weapon. It was heavy, that gun, and though we knew it wasn't "real," the bullets replaced with CO_2 cartridges like we used in our SodaStreams, still when the silhouette of a man appeared on the screen in front of us, a target across his black torso, our arms quivered as we ready, aimed, fired at the instructor's command.

The pulling of the trigger shocked us. The recoil shocked us. We didn't hit the target. We didn't hit the man. Of course we didn't. When we turned back, the officer who'd given us our gear had disappeared.

"Go again," ordered our instructor from behind his monitor. "I need a second," each of us said. "There is no second," said the instructor. "Go again."

We were grown women, almost two hundred years on this earth between us. We knew if we wanted a second, we could take a second, knew this wasn't real. But when we were in it, it didn't feel as if there was a choice, and we went again, and aimed and fired.

Then the man with the target on his torso disappeared, and we found ourselves in a city park in broad daylight, soccer fields in the distance. Frozen in front of us was a young white man in sweatpants and an undershirt, a hand behind his back as if he might be holding a weapon.

"You're responding to a call of a man threatening residents in a neighborhood park," said the instructor. "Right now, he's twenty-one feet away. Ready?"

Before we could reply, the man unfroze and began running toward us. "Stop!" we called. "Police!" He didn't stop. Barbara-Ann shot air; Eileen, a tree. Michelle shot nothing, the sight too unsettling to move. The man kept coming. Just as it appeared as if he were going to burst through the screen, he froze, a blade in hand pointed our way. "You're dead," said the instructor. "Again."

And on it went. We shot, we missed. We froze, we died. On our third effort, a young Black woman in leggings and pushing a stroller showed up in the distance just as each of us was pulling the trigger. Had she been there before?

"Oh god," said Eileen, lowering her weapon.

"You're dead," said the instructor.

"Oh god," said Michelle, who kept it raised but didn't fire.

"You're dead," said the instructor.

Barbara-Ann didn't notice in time. The mother went down, shot in the ankle. Actually went down, as if Barbara-Ann had really shot her. "No," said Barbara-Ann. "No no no." The stroller rolled slowly on.

"You're dead," said the instructor. "Again."

On our fifth attempt, Eileen shot the man in the head. "Did I get him?" she asked, though by then he'd fallen backward and was lying faceup on the ground, his hands open. "Wait a second, he had a . . . What happened to his . . .?" Where, before, there'd been a knife, now Eileen saw he held a cell phone.

When it was over we felt as if we'd just landed after the most turbulent plane ride of our lives. "Not so easy, was it?" said the instructor as we shakily unbuckled and unstrapped.

In the ladies' room we thought about what we'd done—though we hadn't done anything, had we?—thought about all of those officers we'd met over thirteen weeks, all of those officers who had somehow become one officer. What would it feel like to be twenty-one or twenty-two, and have none of the life experiences we'd had, and to be told, *There is no second. Go again again again*?

We found Bob leaning against the railing on the roof of APD headquarters, far from the others, looking out toward the grounds of the Capitol a few blocks away. "That was horrible," said Barbara-Ann, joining him on one side. "Awful," said Eileen, and she and Michelle joined him on the other.

What had, thirteen weeks earlier, seemed merely like a total waste of our time we now suspected was more sinister, a way to control the narrative. Every Pete Wilbur and Pat Spackleman would leave Citizen Police Academy with a new set of talking points to hector their neighbors with, to post in never-ending Facebook threads, these arguments, and the knowledge of how to present them, more sophisticated than anything they'd come up with on their own.

We'd enrolled in the course assuming that the killing of innocents was a problem the police wanted to solve. That manipulative simulation suggested they viewed the killing of innocents as acceptable collateral to keep themselves safe. And if those innocents were disproportionately all one race, well . . . These situations were complicated, the officers under impossible stress. No one becomes a cop to sign their own death warrant, right?

On the rooftop of APD headquarters, Bob told us that soon after his first Citizen Police Academy class ended, he'd returned to this very building to see if any progress had been made with the evidence he'd given PIO Lopez. "And you know what they told me? They had *no record* of Nathaniel's license." He didn't think PIO Lopez was to blame; Bob believed that whatever happened to that license happened well above her pay grade.

"Four times I've done that simulated training, and you know what it's taught me?" said Bob, staring ahead. "They killed him. I don't know why or when or where. But they killed him and then couldn't figure out who he was. Or they could and covered it up. I'm sure of it. *And I let it happen*."

"Oh, Bob," we said, turning to him. The lids around his eyes were a terrible red. For the first time since we'd met, he looked every one of his seventy-three years. "We're so sorry."

The jokes, the crazy story: none of it could hide the fact that Bob had lost his nephew. And though we didn't believe what Bob thought happened to Nathaniel, it didn't change the fact that it did happen to kids in this country, their families' hearts as broken as Bob's.

"Nathaniel's never coming back," said Bob plainly. "But we can help others."

"Tell us the plan," said Barbara-Ann.

"We're ready," said Eileen.

"Anything," said Michelle.

"We're going to break into the evidence room in the basement," said Bob. "And then we're going to burn it to the ground."

The orange jumpsuits had been washed before, they claimed, but we'll admit we had our doubts.

"It's very flattering on you, ladies," said Barbara-Ann, trying for levity.

"Now *this* is not a Jewish group of people," said Eileen.

"How did we end up here?" said Michelle, surveying the glum scene.

A few months earlier, on the rooftop after The Simulation, Bob had gone over the details of his long-awaited plan. At the end of our next and final class, we were to leave as usual, but once outside Barbara-Ann would announce she'd forgotten her scarf. Instead of returning through the front, we'd go down the ramp that led to the basement entrance. The door would be magically unlocked.

Once inside, we'd proceed down the hallway, past the kitchen, to the evidence room. There, we'd find a knapsack containing three ski masks, three extra-long lighters, a gallon of gasoline.

Four times Bob had enrolled in Citizen Police Academy, each time using his access to the building to fine-tune his plan. The second time he'd taken the course, a Citizen had experienced chest pains while visiting the evidence room; Bob had watched the officer normally posted there escort the ailing Citizen to a break room off to the side, leaving the caged boxes of evidence unattended. Before we entered the basement, Bob would already be down there, helping the caterer move his trays. "I'm seventy-three, so I shouldn't have a problem faking a minor cardiac event," Bob said.

He knew it sounded kooky. But if Nathaniel's license had been disappeared so easily, wasn't it likely other evidence had been also? And if they could disappear evidence, who's to say they couldn't plant it, too?

In Bob's view, the system was corrupt and racist, so keeping people of color out of it should be priority one. "*No evidence, no prison time*," he said. "You want to create *lasting change*?" This was the most effective way Bob could think to do it.

"But if it's too much of a risk for you, I understand," he said. If we came to that final class next week, he'd know we were in.

Bob bid us adieu then, and we were left on the roof to consider this wild idea.

"What if it led to someone really bad getting out?" asked Michelle.

"What if it led to someone innocent not going in?" said Eileen.

"Do you think it could *work*?" said Barbara-Ann.

It was only alone in the elevator down to the lobby that we considered a hole in Bob's plan. Between Bob's departure and our arrival, who would drop off the knapsack of supplies?

Later, at home, we each googled *"four-year-old" + kidnapping + "Austin 1998" + "fifty years"* but by then we already understood that Bob had a co-conspirator. How had we not figured it out earlier? "A restaurant owner's son"?

We knew it as soon as we walked out of the building and saw the caterer coming up the basement ramp with one of his big trays. If you're a Senior it meant there was a Junior out there. Harold Lafontaine didn't smile when he saw us. "Ladies," he said. "Thank you much."

That night, we each lay awake imagining ourselves doing it.

We thought of Bob's nephew, of Harold's son. The more we considered the last thirteen weeks, the angrier we became: at our country, at ourselves. The whole system *was* rotten, and we'd never done anything to make it better. Burning evidence wasn't who we were, but we liked the idea that it was who we could be. What if *this* was the change we'd been waiting for? It was crazy, we knew, but wasn't imprisoning a twenty-year-old kid for *half a century* crazy too?

That night, The Simulation and Bob's red-rimmed eyes so fresh in our minds, each of us resolved to go through with it. Why couldn't we be the ones to do something really and truly big?

Maybe, we'd think later, we'd have done it if we'd done it that night, if we hadn't awoken the next morning to our husbands and our houses and our happy Austin lives. *Burning the evidence room?* What seemed so reasonable when the sun was down was obviously ludicrous once it had come up. A nice thing to imagine, maybe, but it wasn't us. We'd keep brainstorming, keep fighting. Surely there were other ways.

On our walks that week, we talked little of Bob, a bit embarrassed how into his idea each of us had briefly become. Nine days after our rooftop rendezvous, we received an email message from PIO Lopez. Despite our "admirable dedication to the Program," we had made it to only thirteen of fourteen meetings, thereby disqualifying us from entry into the perfect attendance lottery. We never saw Bob Alexander again.

Occasionally, scrolling on our iPads while waiting for a prescription, or in the bath, we'd find ourselves searching up Nathaniel, or trying to locate his mentor, David. We didn't have so much as a last name to go on, but it didn't stop us from thinking about him.

What would happen, each of us wondered, if we ever ran into him? Would we tell him the story Bob had told us? *What do <u>you</u> think happened to Nathaniel?* we wanted to ask. *What happened to you, dear David, after you were fired from your job?*

We imagined jogging David's memory, together uncovering a clue. We imagined becoming good friends.

None of it would come to pass. Nor, regretfully, would our hopes of becoming players in the movement to reform the police. In the beginning, we stayed up on it: sharing articles, making Facebook posts of our own.

But this was 2013: a time of hope! We had another four years of Obama, thank G-d; even the new pope, of all people, seemed like a decent guy. 2013 was the year Barbara-Ann planned her daughter's wedding, Eileen's son got engaged, Michelle welcomed her first grandchild.

Everything really does feel different when it's your kid.

And then, three months after the end of the course, we received another email, this one from Margarita Muñoz, president of the Citizen Police Academy Alumni Society. As "successful graduates" of the

53rd Class, we were now entitled to participate in APD training exercises. The next one was only a few weeks away.

We met early on a Saturday morning in a gymnasium on the east side. At the check-in—forty-some Pete Wilburs and Pat Spacklemans and also, to our irritation, Pete Wilbur and Pat Spackleman—we were each given big manila envelopes with our roles and our costumes.

The scenario was straight out of the movies. A prison bus had collided with a school bus on the highway. There were fatalities, but there was also the risk that prisoners had escaped or were playing dead.

It was incumbent we didn't accidentally reveal our status, and so only once we were all in position would Margarita come around with index cards. "A green dot means you're alive," she announced through a bullhorn. "Yellow? Pretending to be dead. Red dot? RIP." Anyone "still breathing," said Margarita, should be prepared to be slung over shoulders, carried like babies, dragged up to thirty feet.

As we zipped our jumpsuits over our clothing, we thought back to those moments when Bob's Nathaniel felt like *our* Nathaniel, Bob's sadness our sadness, his rage our rage.

Why had we come back here? We didn't like the citizens of Citizen Police Academy. We didn't like the police. But it had been nice to feel so committed to ending this bullshit that we'd imagined ourselves doing the unimaginable. Had been nice to feel like we—we of all people!—might get so sick of the wrongs in this world that we'd burn down a building to make it right.

We lay on the ground and hoped we'd be identified as living. Maybe if they dragged us long enough, we'd feel it all again.

The Other Rothstein

August 8, 1998

DAVID DALICE STARTED TOWARD the Shady Creek Condominiums at 8:24 p.m.

What was he *doing* exactly? *I created this mess, so I should be the one to end it*, he told himself, though as was often the case with David, there was more to it than that. In the gravel lot outside Terry Tucker's Boxing Gym that morning, David had waited for Nathaniel to show for his first Saturday sparring session. Instead, he'd had it out with Bob Alexander. Nathaniel, Bob said, hadn't come home the night before.

David should've told Bob about the Post-it then. He'd seen it in Nathaniel's locker when he left him those stupid pills: a date and time and address. Tonight at 9, Shady Creek. David wasn't sure what he expected to find there, or if Nathaniel would even show. Still, it was surely useful intel, and David would've shared it with Bob at the gym if both men hadn't stormed off.

In the hours following the blow-up, neither had called the other to apologize. Running errands that afternoon, David began to feel guilty, decided to give Bob a ring. He pulled his mobile from his jeans pocket and that's when he saw the missed call and voice message. It was not from Bob but from David's boss at Shoal Creek Rehab. "A troubling report," she said. "We need to talk."

He was being fired, this he knew. He'd told Bob he'd stolen those pills, and Bob had told Shoal Creek, and now the executive director had called his mobile on a Saturday. Soon, David would have to confess to his wife. What would Ramona say? Would there be charges? What had he done?

He'd returned the phone to his pocket without calling his old friend.

David knew of the Shady Creek Condos because of the Whataburger across the street. He hadn't been in probably twenty years. Now, dinner with Ramona finished, that's where he headed. Off for groceries, he'd claimed ("Feel like getting out of the house for a bit"), and south he went, an A.1. Thick & Hearty burger a sensible second course, given the circumstances, to the beef bourguignon he'd eaten with his wife.

At the drive-thru window he found a jovial-seeming Black man, fast-careening toward middle age, whose strained, smiling face relaxed as soon as he saw David.

"How goes it this fine evening?" David asked.

"It's going, man," he said matter-of-factly, filling up David's soda cup. "Going, going—" He raised his eyebrows as he handed off the Coke. "Gone."

David took his food and drove into the Shady Creek lot across the street. Dead at this hour: 9:01 p.m. Still, he drove slowly. David wanted to stay covert, to see what the boy might be up to before confronting him. Maybe, if he brought Nathaniel back to Bob, he could start to smooth things over. Maybe Bob would even contact David's boss at the nursing home, walk back what he'd said.

After finding the right building, David put the car in reverse, parking five spots away from the stairwell that led up to the apartment listed on the Post-it: #2E. David shut off the engine, killed his lights.

He ate and waited and pretended he was a detective on a stakeout. And as David did these things, he began to imagine what would befall him after he was fired from Shoal Creek. He thought of the contorting face of the man at the Whataburger and of the name tag on the man's uniform, and saw, with perfect clarity, himself leaning out of that steamy drive-thru window, all forty-eight years of him, pits so wet they'd made his inner arms slick, saw his own chest and belly, too tight against the bright orange collared shirt.

DAVID

PROUDLY SERVING *YOU* SINCE 1998

A car door slammed. David put the food on the passenger seat, turned toward the noise, and saw Nathaniel, who must've parked directly below #2E, begin to approach the stairwell, keys and cell phone in hand.

Or was it Nathaniel? A security lamp illuminated the lane between cars and building, the rest of the lot dark. The boy wore jeans, a black hoodie, hood up. Outside the lamplight, the boy's back to David, it was hard to say who he was.

No sooner did maybe-Nathaniel start up the stairs when both the boy and the man surveilling him heard someone yell, "Hey!"

The yeller was a gangly white boy, jogging over from near the entrance to the lot. Dockers, dress shirt, a bouquet of tulips in one hand.

Maybe-Nathaniel returned to ground level to talk to this newcomer, who now blocked David's view.

At first it seemed like the gangly kid might be asking for directions. David heard him say his name was Jesse. "What are you doing here exactly?" said Jesse. "And you're sure *2E*?" More back-and-forth.

"Fuck," said Jesse after a while, turning away from the stairs. He stepped into the brightly lit lane, as if he were performing a one-man show, leaving maybe-Nathaniel the sole audience member, in the shadows.

"Why would she tell me to come here?" he said to no one. He ran a hand through his hair. "What the fuck." Still holding the tulips, Jesse braced his hands against his knees. He looked like he was going to be sick. He looked like he was going to burst into tears. And then Jesse's face stiffened.

David understood what was about to transpire, had been around enough guys like this in his life, guys who couldn't differentiate grief from lust from even love, recognized it all as fury.

Jesse turned back to maybe-Nathaniel, dropped the tulips, and got in his face. "Are you fucking in on this?"

"What—?"

"I mean, who even are you?"

"I'm . . ." Maybe-Nathaniel hesitated.

"Who the fuck are you?"

"I'm her boyfriend." His voice was indisputably Rothstein's.

"That's great," yelled Jesse, a nasty edge developing. "Just great. You know she has a dick, right?" He puffed up his chest so it was touching Nathaniel's and started toward the steps, forcing them to trade places. Nathaniel was now lit, his back again to David.

"She said her ex was crazy," said Nathaniel.

"So you gonna suck it?" said Jesse.

"Screw you," said Nathaniel.

Jesse shoved Nathaniel, sending the boy's keys and cell phone from his hand. "What was that?"

"Why would you talk about her like that?"

"You gonna suck my girlfriend's cock?" Another shove, driving Nathaniel, his back still to David, deeper into the light.

"Shut up," said Nathaniel.

"You shut up."

"I said *shut up*," said Nathaniel. He shoved Jesse back. "You want me to beat you up?" Nathaniel raised his hands.

Jesse lifted his palms, then shut them into fists, two Venus flytraps catching dinner. He was unsure what to do with his feet, kept them parallel with his shoulders. "So you gonna come at me or what?" said Jesse.

This was how Nathaniel Rothstein's sparring match, set for that morning, was rescheduled to the night, the square of light from the security lamp forming an impromptu boxing ring, the boys, like moths, sticking to it.

Did either of them know exactly why they were fighting? A lover spurned, slurs leveled. Because one had pushed the other. It made sense in the way of all fistfights, which was to say, not much.

Jesse threw the first punch, not a one or a two, not an anything, a tomahawk chop on the diagonal that was intended to create distance, not make contact. Nathaniel fought the air in kind, jab jab cross, a signal to his competitor that he knew what he was doing.

Even watching him from behind, David could see Nathaniel was looser than usual. Shoulders down, jabbing in short snaps, *pa-pa pa-pa*, as David had taught him. The dance wasn't graceful, but he moved with precision, intention. This other boy was fighting, but David's boy, David's boy was boxing.

Jesse tried for a hook. Nathaniel protected his body with his elbow. Jesse tried a jab. Nathaniel swatted it away. Desperate, Jesse went for a haymaker, a single knockout blow, aiming straight at Nathaniel's face.

How many times had David and Nathaniel practiced for this moment? How many times had Nathaniel botched it? But this time Nathaniel saw it coming, swerved his head past his lead leg. The perfect slip.

Now the boy pivoted around Jesse, *pa-pa pa-pa*, and under the security lamp in the parking lot of the Shady Creek Condominiums, David saw the new Nathaniel Rothstein in the front, in the face, for the first time.

My god. This couldn't be real.

How many of those pills had he taken?

No longer was Nathaniel a faded David, David's son from a mother of a different color. Now he was a copy of the original, not son of David but younger David. The buzzed head, the youthful swagger. That *skin*. *His* skin.

David saw in the boy the might-be-a-businessman, the could-be-a-lawyer, the maybe-one-day-a-boxer, the growing David who'd flown to this growing city almost twenty-eight years before. David saw in the boy not a goofy imitation of himself but himself. *Him*self. Except.

There comes a moment in every young fighter's life when he stops thinking about boxing long enough to box.

For Nathaniel Rothstein, that moment came on August 8, 1998, at the Shady Creek Condominiums, thirty-five seconds in.

Everything over the past twenty-four hours had gone right. Late the night before, he'd snuck into Hippie Hollow, got what sleep he could, and woke up with the sun. For the ten hours that followed, Nathaniel had baked naked on an isolated boulder at that rocky beach's end, hoping Dr. Abruzzi's pills would work their magic. They did, and somehow, *somehow*, he'd left Hippie Hollow as the person he told Sasha he'd been all along.

Nathaniel was sore and sun-poisoned, but didn't feel either, the rush too great from bursting out of one skin and into another. Even the fact his wallet had been stolen seemed a little serendipitous, a final goodbye to the old Nathaniel. In its place, the boy carried the Haitian passport David had given him the day before, a good luck charm tucked into the back pocket of his jeans.

Standing before Sasha's psycho ex-boyfriend in that bright light, it felt to Nathaniel like the entire summer had been building to this moment, his entire life had been building to this moment, his courageous David self melding with his actual self, his actual self ready to act. Ready to fight.

He slipped, he pivoted, he let loose with everything he had. A barrage of jabs and crosses, a right hook to the kidney and a left hook to the chin, or at least approximations of those punches to approximations of those places. To most spectators it would've looked sloppy. To Nathaniel it seemed like he'd figured out the key to the universe.

Humans are never more cartoon-like than when they're passing out, and, at first, it seemed like Jesse might be pretending. Down he went, his knees hitting the concrete, then over to his side, out cold.

Now Nathaniel circled, circled, consistent as a carousel, as if, in his circling, he could will the other boy to stay down. Around and around

Nathaniel went, and David, who hadn't, it seemed, moved since the fight began, now found that he couldn't even had he wanted to, hypnotized by the swirl of the circling Rothstein.

David was there and also not there, in his Honda Civic and also in a boxing ring in Alvarado, 1973; in a dorm room in Austin, 1970; on his first-ever plane ride, fingering the front pocket of his dress shirt to make sure his passport hadn't gone anywhere as he flew out of Port-au-Prince and into that anything's-still-possible world.

Around and around the boy went, and out of this entrancing swirl emerged in David's mind first this vision of his past, and out of that vision a second vision, suddenly, all at once, whole—

See the boy at sixteen and ten months.

Backpack strap slung over his shoulder as he ambles down the hall, this first day of junior year. He's tan and loose, lighter than the last time he was here. Somehow there being less of him has resulted in the people noticing him more.

Nathaniel's not an A-lister overnight. He is not on the receiving end of palm-reddening high fives nor (praise Jesus) the elaborate greetings on offer from the theater kids (jazz squares and short tap numbers; melodramatic faints, as if they've come down with a case of the vapors). But he isn't invisible like before. Now he is the beneficiary of half-salutations—three-finger quick-waves and abashed smiles—from the half-people of Newton South High School: the treasurers and secretaries of sundry off-brand clubs; heavily breasted Madrigals.

None of his fellow students know about Nathaniel's foray into blackface. He ended up staying an extra five days in Austin, confined to the Alexander home. He'd confessed everything to Bob, who'd been baffled, horrified, ultimately forgiving. By the time Linda Rothstein, aware of her son's transgressions, picked him up at Logan, his summer skin had begun to fade and peel. Thank god.

At lunch, in the cafeteria, Nathaniel returns to his Lunch Bunch. They're just as he left them, this unfortunate congregation of white boys (plus Edgar Chang and Ryan Lai) whose cystic acne and chronic discomfiture oft render them red.

The Lunch Bunch fetes Nathaniel's homecoming, clinking their Surges in celebration. After, breaths hot with the Domino's pizza the school buys and resells, with candy purchased from the members of the improv group, the chorus, who ramble the halls like ballpark vendors hawking king-size Caramellos to fund their varied ventures, the members of the Lunch Bunch, eyes glazed, lips chapped, lean in.

Tell us.

Tell us everything.

Tell us about her.

There was a her, right?

Had to be. How else to explain the easy gait? The snugger jeans? That just-been-f'd glow?

There was a her, and the members of the Lunch Bunch, they want, they need, to know.

What were her tits like? How did her snatch smell? Did they do it face-to-face or did he slam her from behind?

Nathaniel recognizes this talk, has spoken this way about girls in the past, as if a kiss, a touch, a date were his birthright, as if the boys at that table were virgins because of every girl's narrow-mindedness, and not their own.

He knows the Lunch Bunch will not understand his summer of Sasha Semyonova. After the fight, he'd wanted to call her, to explain why he never showed up. Why he didn't want Sasha to see that darkened version of himself. Where would he even start, though? It was too weird to explain.

The tan, the pills, Hippie Hollow: he'd done it all to convince her that he was someone else. But in the parking lot at Shady Creek, it was Nathaniel who'd known what to do and how to do it. He'd owned his punches. Owned his body in a way he never had before.

This was the lesson he learned in that summer of 1998, the summer he left his own skin.

Later, he'll credit Sasha for this education, he'll credit Bob and

Marlene, and his mother, too. Mostly, he'll credit David, who he'd tried to become, for it was in this misbegotten attempt at becoming that Nathaniel Rothstein finally came into his own.

After a while, the Lunch Bunch can feel themselves losing him. Nathaniel is there but not there, looking past the nerd herd, through them. Two tables down, his victim sits alone. The other kid he'd beaten the crap out of that year, the reason he'd been sent to Austin in the first place. A broken jaw? What had he been thinking?

Unlike the other members of the Lunch Bunch, anonymous to the masses, Elliott Glomb-Golden has long been a known personality in the cafeteria. Manic, reviled. Before Nathaniel beat him up, one of his signature moves had been to take a dump in the boys' room, not flush, and hang around the sinks, giggling maniacally as the next guy went in.

After the incident with Nathaniel, Elliott missed the rest of sophomore year to recover. None of the Lunch Bunch called him over summer break to check in. They were too busy rejoicing over, re-enacting the beatdown: in Ryan Lai's basement and Bryan Hillman's den.

At the cafeteria table, they credit Nathaniel for taking Elliott Glomb-Golden down a peg. Ryan Lai has A-block chemistry with Elliott and claims he didn't say a word all period. If Nathaniel hadn't done what he did, Ryan tells the others, Elliott would be carrying on in front of them right this second, bragging about how he'd stolen Mr. Norman's mole puppet and was using it as a Fleshlight. "Fuck that Ritalin-hungry beeyotch," says Ryan.

Nathaniel excuses himself, tosses his plate in the trash. The beeyotch is nibbling at the top of a Kit Kat. He's pulled its red one-piece down past its chocolate ankles, holds it by the hips in both hands, as if someone might try to take it otherwise. He is guarded, goblin-like. A Gollum in sweats.

Nathaniel can feel the eyes of the cafeteria on him as he approaches. *Kill him*, thinks the vengeful Lunch Bunch. The same campus aide who headlocked Nathaniel four months prior shifts his weight from one foot to the other. A few tables from the action, the flanneled jock boys and their yearbook-editor girlfriends don't take sides. They're the Roman aristocracy of Newton South High School, this their Colosseum, and slaves are slaves are slaves. They turn on the plastic molded stools that are their thrones, hungry for bloodshed.

"Hey," says Nathaniel. "Can we talk?"

Elliott keeps his eyes on his plate, assents without assenting.

"Look, I was in a bad place when school ended," Nathaniel explains. "I shouldn't have done what I did. I'm really sorry, man." (Does Nathaniel say *man* now?) He puts out his hand.

Elliott Glomb-Golden can feel the eyes of the cafeteria on him, too. He knows that to not shake would invite endless opprobrium from his classmates and his teachers, and he craves it, this disdain, he wants it, because them hating him is better than them not seeing him at all . . .

He wants it, and yet the summer of 1998 has also changed Elliott Glomb-Golden. It wasn't the reality of his broken face that did him in—his lower jaw wired to the teeth of his upper for two whole weeks—but the silence after, from Nathaniel, from the others.

He always knew they didn't like him, that they were his school friends, not his friend friends, but at home, with his mom and dad, he talked about them constantly, about Bryan Hillman did this and Edgar Chang did that, and whenever the Glomb and Golden grandparents came to visit, from Short Hills, from Great Neck, it was those names they'd fixate on, those names the evidence that their offspring's off offspring would be all right.

After this summer of applesauce and egg noodles, this summer of silence, the secret is out.

Nathaniel Rothstein has indeed taken Elliott down a peg.

He shakes Nathaniel's hand.

See the boy at seventeen, eighteen.

That fall of junior year, Nathaniel starts skipping rope in the basement after school. For his birthday, Linda buys him the full setup: a heavy bag and a speed bag and a bench press, a Terry Tucker's for one in the cellar they don't otherwise use.

One night, Linda returns home from work to find Nathaniel lying on the couch in the living room, TV off, floor lamp on, *Hamlet* and highlighter in hand. "It really is easier if you just do the reading," he tells her, as if she hasn't said this a zillion times before.

Nathaniel's low C's become high C's become B–'s, occasionally +'s. The musical that spring is *A Chorus Line*, and Nathaniel applies to be the head prop master, gets the job.

Ryan Lai's twin sister, Jasmine, operates the light board. There are 346 lighting cues and seventeen props, all canes. "I wouldn't want to inconvenience you," says burly Mr. Oliver, the first day of tech rehearsal, when he comes across Nathaniel sitting on a wooden block in the wing, all of his canes on stage, in use, "but why not head up to the light booth to see if you can, you know, *do something*?"

Nathaniel knocks on the door to the booth and, when no one answers, opens it a quarter of the way, knocks again. "This isn't, like, my bedroom," says Jasmine Lai, mystified as to why Nathaniel is just standing there. "Why are all my brother's friends like this?"

"Like what?" says Nathaniel.

"Like *meek*," says Jasmine. "It's extremely irritating. Could you come in and shut the door?"

Jasmine exudes a terrifying competence. She works the light board like a blind savant, maneuvering the controls without glancing at board or script, mouthing along to the actors' dialogue. ("*And on a scale of ten they gave me / For dance, ten, for looks, three.*") There's a casual slovenliness to the girl that appeals to Nathaniel: she wears holey black jeans, her hair in a sloppy bun.

That first day, he is bumbling in his old way, never able to fill the silence between them. This is the residual Nathanielness left over from his pre-David days, and it irks Jasmine Lai. "Do you want to learn to do this or what?" she asks. All Nathaniel can manage is a feeble *yuh*.

"I'm not, like, some studious Chinese quiet girl, if you couldn't tell," says Jasmine. "Are you?"

"Am I a studious Chinese quiet girl?" says Nathaniel.

"You're *such* a Ryan person. You want to know what I am?" Jasmine leans in so close her lips are almost touching Nathaniel's ear: "I'm a total bitch."

In the week that follows, Jasmine teaches Nathaniel about cold and warm washes, backlighting, how to illuminate an actor's face while keeping the rest of the stage dark. "Hey, Ryan's friend," she says on their third afternoon together. They're rehearsing the Act II opener and, on stage, the entire company is attempting a kick line, none of the boys able to get their legs higher than their waists. "Did you knock on Monday because you thought I was in here *flicking the bean*?"

"Flicking the bean?" says Nathaniel.

"You know," says Jasmine. "*Finger painting*." She turns her index finger into a hook and makes a lascivious scooping motion above the fly of her jeans.

"Gross," says Nathaniel. "No, I— "

"Have you ever even kissed a girl?"

The old Nathaniel would've said nothing, gone hot, and hoped the moment would pass. "Not yet."

Nathaniel's legs grow hairy, his shoulders broaden. He was never fated to be skinny. "If we got you a Nordic sweater," Jasmine tells him one Saturday night, as they make out on the inflatable love seat in her bedroom, "you'd be, like, Santa's quietly hot grandson."

On the evening of the Senior Scavenger Hunt, Nathaniel and Jasmine stay in and watch a movie instead. The hunt is a school tradition in which teams of rising seniors maraud across the city, completing a series of ever-more-horrifying tasks. In the popular imagination, this is an event by and for the highest castes, but in truth it is always the second-tiers, hoping to ascend, who humiliate themselves the most profoundly, a fate the newly confident Nathaniel has narrowly avoided. The next day, the word on the street is that chin-warted Lindsay Faber fingered herself for an audience on Jared Weston's basement pool table, and stringy-haired Danny Gladstone jizzed on top of a sundae and ate the whole thing. The cops were involved only once this year: the chunky Hobson twins, Alex and Eric, were arrested for attempting to steal the giant, glowing V off the storefront of the Newton Centre CVS.

Two weeks later, Linda sends Nathaniel to get double-A batteries at that same CVS. "You'll never believe who was picking up a prescription," says Nathaniel, genuinely stunned, when he returns home. "*Eric Hobson*. I mean, can you believe it?"

Linda is unfazed. "What's he gonna do? Get his acne meds in Framingham?" She is cleaning out the junk drawer in the kitchen. "Teenagers do stupid crap all the time. *As you well know*. They learn. They move on. It's life."

At the start of summer break, Linda goes on a work trip, and Nathaniel invites Jasmine over to spend the night.

In Nathaniel's bedroom, they strip down to their underwear, fool around. Nathaniel is so nervous about getting the condom on right that he excuses himself to the bathroom to get situated. They have sex above the covers, him on top. Nathaniel doesn't speak to Jasmine as David spoke to Sasha. For the entire ninety seconds, they are silent, eyes locked. After, each senses that there's more to it than this, that they've had sex in the sense that they have now done it, but have not yet *done it* done it, va-va-va-vroom *done it*, have not gone to the places they go when they're alone.

For Nathaniel Rothstein and Jasmine Lai it isn't about sex, not really. It isn't about sex but about having had sex, crossing SEX off the list. Jasmine excuses herself to the bathroom, stays in there for a long time. "So," she says when she returns, easing back into the bed. "We're no longer virgins."

"No longer virgins," says Nathaniel, smiling crookedly at the ceiling, dazed.

With his little right toe he toasts her little left.

Thank god thank god thank god.

Even with his better grades, Nathaniel's GPA can't recover from its freshman-sophomore shellacking. The essay prompt on the common app is *Recount an event that sparked in you an increased empathy for others*. Per the advice of his mother, he decides to write about his summer at Shoal Creek, about his friend David, who came from a country Nathaniel had barely heard of, who called Nathaniel his brother and taught him what it means to be a man.

Nathaniel leaves out the part where he remakes himself in David's literal image to meet the Russian phone sex operator he's fallen in love with. Still, there is truth in his words, and as he writes the banal version of his story it becomes the story.

Nathaniel applies early to Bates, where Linda went, but so-so grades and a 1250 SAT from Newton, Mass., do not a Bobcat make. He's rejected from BU, Brandeis, Clark. His only out-of-state application is to UT Austin. It's a moonshot: only the top 10 percent of Texas kids are guaranteed admission there, and here, in Newton, Nathaniel is ranked 170th in his three-hundred-person class.

One night, over take-out Chinese, Linda announces she's spoken to her brother. "It *turns out*," she says, emphasizing seemingly random words, "that your uncle *Bob* has a *friend* who has donated *substantial sums* to the *university*."

"Why are you talking like that?" asks Nathaniel.

"He'd like to *meet* you." Linda says *meet* as if it's code for *fuck*.

That fall, Bob and Marlene help Nathaniel move into his dorm in the Jester Center at UT. He has plans to start back up at the gym, to call David once he's settled, but there's always a reason not to: free pizza in the student center; he doesn't have a car and hasn't learned the bus system. In truth, Nathaniel is embarrassed about what happened, feels guilty that David lost his job.

Besides, he's a different person than he was in high school. Still a nerd, but a nerd ambassador, a nerd accessible to civilians. *A-dorkable*, his new girlfriend, Julia, calls him: the slightly embarrassed grin, the Dad dress (cargo shorts and Tevas and still with the safari hat but it's different now, it's part of his look).

Julia is vice president of a campus club that takes underprivileged kids on outdoor adventures. She wears hunter-green Chakos and keeps a Nalgene bottle carabinered to her backpack. Sometimes, on weekends, the couple drives out to the Hill Country to hike. This is not Nathaniel's natural habitat and he is always fighting to keep up, taking giant steps forward, as if he were playing Mother May I?

The August after their sophomore year, a big group of them go to Hippie Hollow. At first, Nathaniel isn't sure about getting naked in front of everyone, but among the shaggy high-ropes enthusiasts and farmer's-tanned rock climbers who make up his Julia-fied friend circle, exposed private parts during an outdoor activity are as commonplace as B.O.

Nathaniel floats on his stomach, on his back. The water feels most thrilling in those places it isn't supposed to be, under and between. Only after, while the others lie out on the rocks, do the memories of the darkening return to him.

This is how it goes with Nathaniel: the mistakes and humiliations from that seminal summer struck from his memory except when he is at his most vulnerable. While pulling off a condom or wiping his ass. His face goes flush when it happens, his mother's words the cool washcloth he needs to get right again. *Teenagers do stupid crap all the time. They learn. They move on*, he'll tell himself, tossing the rubber into the wastebasket, flushing the soiled paper down the bowl.

See the man at twenty-three, at twenty-five.

Nathaniel and Julia start out in a dingy apartment complex off Dean Keeton. Wasps' nests latch like barnacles on to the paint-peeled railing on their balcony. They can't leave dirty dishes in the sink, lest those everything-really-is-bigger-in-Texas roaches emerge, antennae first, from the drain.

"All part of the adventure," says Marlene cheerily, the first and only time she and Bob come to visit.

"It's only an adventure," Bob tells her, "since they know it will end."

Indeed, all parties understand the situation is temporary, a test home for the young couple's post-grad relationship, their post-grad lives, and as Nathaniel and Julia spray the wasps' nests with Raid and wrap the shoe-beaten roaches in their paper towel tombs, they can already imagine telling their future kids about their grimy first apartment way back when.

Their classmates in the deepest debt have tried for jobs at consulting firms or doubled down and gone straight to law or medical school. Nathaniel and Julia can afford softer landings courtesy of cushions stuffed and sewn prior to their births. Linda's salary has always been good, Julia's father's better, but neither's is the special sauce that has kept them all "comfortable," its recipe known only to and kept secret by the money-managed among us: "good investments."

Years before, a former president of Julia's urban adventure club at UT founded a nonprofit version, now almost exclusively staffed with alumni of the original program. Julia is brought on as "communications coordinator": no health insurance, but twice yearly she gets to tag along on trips to Big Bend or Palo Duro with a digital camera.

Nathaniel has not considered his future with the same intention. He majored in psychology with no ambition of becoming a therapist. Mostly, he worked stage crew for UT shows and hung out with his girlfriend, and marveled that he was the kind of guy who had a girlfriend to hang out with. He takes the first job he's offered, in the customer service department of a company that makes healthy pre-made meals in reusable plastic cases.

Nathaniel's twenties aren't a boozy mess like those of his single friends. Still. He is disorganized, a well-meaning slob. He puts his boxers on top of the wicker hamper instead of in it, forgets (?) to close drawers once he's done with them. Sometimes Julia will enter the kitchen after he's exited and it will look as if a poltergeist has been there: every cabinet door mysteriously open.

Their friends from college have largely moved away. The replacements are new colleagues, new neighbors. These people are like the cast of *Saved by the Bell: The New Class*: updated, lesser versions of the original players. Of the old crew only the dregs remain: a pear-shaped fellow, prematurely bald, who invites Nathaniel on long, silent bike rides; a well-meaning evangelical woman, perpetually "struggling" with the politics of "the church."

That first April, Nathaniel and Julia spend an entire weekend on the phone with her dad and his mom, trying to navigate TurboTax. Each new question is annotated with paragraph-long definitions of terms they don't know: *dependent*, *exemption*, *1099*. The prompts that appear at the start of each successive TurboTax section provoke a tingle of existential dread: *Now let's talk a bit about your life.*

There is a liquescence to their lives in these years, a feeling of permanent impermanence. Nathaniel and Julia need something to hold on to, and so they hold on to each other. Their friends who marry later will serve short ribs on urban farms, register not for gifts but for "experiences." At twenty-five, Nathaniel and Julia are content to let her parents do the planning. They wed at the Four Seasons in Dallas, a venue large enough to accommodate all her dad's business associates. To Nathaniel's utter indifference and to various withering comments from Bob, they are married by Julia's family's Episcopal priest.

See the man at twenty-seven, thirty-seven, forty.

The $6.99 magnums of Yellowtail that the Rothsteins used to bring to friends' parties slim to standard-size bottles of $11.99 pinot noir. Tevas become Rainbows become toe-covered sandals. Julia's ponytail dissolves into a pixie.

Nathaniel bounces from one meaningless corporate job to the next. Nate@GoodGrub begets Nate@Dell, @Nvidia. In the spring of her husband's thirtieth year, Julia sees through a community listserv that McCallum High School is in search of a new technical director for its theater department. It will be a pay cut, but Julia's the executive director of her nonprofit now, and every October and April her father gifts them each a $6,500 check—a penny more and he'd have to report it on his tax return. "Everyone deserves the chance to do something they love," Julia tells Nathaniel.

Four thousand dollars for a "lateral certification" program, which allows him to teach and get certified at the same time, and Nathaniel Rothstein becomes Mr. R. Among the general population, Mr. R is as invisible as he is during a production, that bearded, burly guy in the black jeans and black polo who hangs out in the theater wing. Among the stage crew kids he's revered. They love him for his competence, and for the gentle way he passes that competence on. He speaks their languages—Elvish and alienated—knows that teaching a kid to operate a spotlight or a soundboard is another way of saying, *I see you. I'm here.*

Mostly, Mr. R understands the transformational effects of transforming others: the thrill of sitting in a darkened lighting booth or standing in the wings and using your hands, your mind, to turn an unsure theater kid into an old man into a knight, to make a swatch of stage a dungeon, a tavern, somewhere, anywhere, other than where you actually are.

If there's a connection between Nathaniel's return to high school and his return to boxing, it's not one he consciously makes. That first fall, he resolves to get back into shape. He could go to Gold's or to the Y, but he suspects it wouldn't be the same. *It feels good to smack the shit out of things, doesn't it?* And so he drives up North Lamar Boulevard, turns when he sees the corroded gas tank, parks in the gravel lot.

The place is just as Nathaniel remembered it, and because it was grubby then and is grubby now, it is as if Nathaniel has never left. Terry Tucker fourteen years later is a craggier version of his 1998 self. "Rothstein," he says when Nathaniel enters the cramped front office. Nathaniel can't believe he remembers him. "Don't know where my glasses are half the time but names? Names I know."

Terry is exactly as surprised at Nathaniel's return as he would be if he never saw him again. People come, people go. Sometimes they come back. It's a gym.

"What kind of aboveboard operation you think I'm running here?" Terry says, when Nathaniel tries to hand him a credit card. "Bring cash next time, you're good for it." He points to the clipboard at the front of his desk. "And don't forget to sign in."

Nathaniel starts coming every few days after school. He loves it for the same reasons he loved it then. For the sweat he works up. For the people. He loves it because it feels real.

One afternoon, taking a break from the heavy bag, Nathaniel wanders into the weight room when he hears another familiar voice.

"The great fighter goes another round!" David sits on an old recumbent bike in the corner, a towel draped over his shoulders. He has reconfigured his body in the way heavy men with resources and an interest in staying alive sometimes do. Given up red meat, eased up on the beer. At sixty-two, he has the loose skin and Scooby-Doo jowls of a vegan-era Bill Clinton.

"David," says Nathaniel. For fourteen years, he's avoided his old boss altogether. He hadn't known what to say to the man who'd gone from star of Shoal Creek to "Paint Associate" at the Home Depot on MoPac and Braker. (David's Whataburger prophecy hadn't been quite right.)

In those years, what Nathaniel learned of David he learned from his uncle Bob. Their friendship had never fully recovered, Bob and David's. Still, they ran in the same circles, and, when they did see each other, bantered in the equal-parts-leery-and-chummy way of a divorced couple years after the cutthroat custody battle and well into successful-on-the-surface take-twos.

What made David so charming to the residents at Shoal Creek, according to Bob, was less appealing to the pre-dawn paint buyers at the Home Depot. They were contractors rushing to beat the sun, or else retirees on a mission: "grouchy white men in Columbia-brand fishing shirts," Bob once told Nathaniel over backyard Mexican martinis.

It was not a tragedy. This was what Bob relayed to Nathaniel. If anything, David got off easy. He was fired, had to sign an NDA. But Shoal Creek Rehab was not about to open itself up to a lawsuit from the family of the nearly dead woman whose non-narcotic pills he stole. To Shoal Creek's executive director, the situation didn't even make sense. A prank gone wrong? Under REASON FOR TERMINATION, she'd listed POOR WORK PERFORMANCE, called it a day.

No, it was not a tragedy to have a fine if boring Home Depot job, to go home to a nice house and a loving wife. On the weekends, David and Ramona tried new restaurants; in the summer, they went on trips. It was not a tragedy, compared to all the other tragedies out there, that the life he'd worked for didn't end up his life. It was not a tragedy: it *was* life.

Nathaniel had always assumed when, if, they met again, the moment would be loaded: a Bob-style blow-up or a somber heart-to-heart. This revealed his fundamental misunderstanding of David and of himself and of the time they'd spent together, and also of adulthood, whose most successful graduates know that the primary objective is to get through the day in one piece.

David points to the chest hair protruding from Nathaniel's sweaty A-shirt. "The boy has become a man. And the man has become an old man." After David threw out his back, bag work became a no-go. He still sits on the bike now and then, likes to keep tabs on who is lurking around the place. "Maybe I'm still holding out hope to find that diamond in the rough."

They don't see each other often, once every couple months. But when they do, they always make time to trade updates out in the gravel lot. Nathaniel feels like a kid again in David's presence. He lets him do most of the talking, feels a weird sense of triumph every time he asks David a question and David answers.

They never discuss what happened. To Nathaniel, this talking-without-talking signals if not absolution then resolution: teenagers do stupid crap, every thing need not be a Thing, the past really is past.

Will they ever meet outside the gym? Each makes vague overtures to the other. Nathaniel and his "young lady" should come over for dinner. Has David been to Casa Colombia? The house special is *really* good. "We should go sometime. The four of us." Neither ever follows through.

Hannah Grace is born just after Nathaniel turns thirty-two. Arnie comes twenty months later.

The children allow them to make allowances they never thought they'd make. Austin's public schools are hit-and-miss, and Nathaniel wants for his kids the same opportunity afforded him: the chance to be whoever they want to be. Nathaniel and Julia don't consider themselves "private school people," set up an interview instead at an "independent" school with a "Montessori foundation."

The kids are shepherded away to sit in with their respective classes while the Rothsteins meet with the admissions officer, a frog-like woman with bulging eyes and the skittish countenance of a hyperthyroidic Mr. Bean. "A little about us," she tootles, handing each of them a glossy school brochure. On the cover: a Black girl holding a papier-mâché globe high above her head. OUR STUDENTS HAVE THE WHOLE WORLD IN THEIR HANDS!

On the tour that follows, they see this same girl taking a math test in the fourth-grade classroom. She is, as far as they can tell, the only one. It unsettles them, her only-oneness. "Isn't it kind of, like, *tacky*?" says Nathaniel, after the admissions officer leaves them in the courtyard to grab a key to the multipurpose room. "To put the one Black kid on the brochure?"

For all the talk of inclusivity, the only other "students of color" appear to be a smattering of East and South Asian kids: the same ethnicities that lend the Rothsteins' own street in Hyde Park its "diversity," though somehow—Nathaniel never articulates this, but he knows it, knows it when he uploads candid photos from the neighborhood block parties to his Facebook—this diversity isn't *true* diversity, the Lees and the Singhs don't "count" as much as they would if they were Washingtons or Rodriguezes.

"Am I correct in saying that the student body is overwhelmingly white?" says Julia when the admissions officer returns, wagging the key above her head with a vigor that overestimates the enthusiasm the Rothsteins have for seeing the multipurpose room.

"That *is* a problem," says the admissions officer. "And one the school is taking significant steps to address." Enrichment programs focus on "inclusion." A scholarship fund is being developed. The entire humanities curriculum has been rewritten to encompass the "full breadth" of the American experience: in an ideal world, the admissions officer explains, there'd be no need to celebrate Black History Month at all, because Black history is integral to understanding American history, *is* American history. ("Though we do celebrate it," she adds with an anxious titter.)

Not ideal. Still, the Rothsteins like the emphasis on "place-based learning," how every child is taught Spanish. That night in bed, they brainstorm ways to "bridge the gap." In the summers, Hannah and Arnie can join their mom on one of her camping trips, where they'll share tents with kids from the east side of town. Both parents will explain to their children how their school world isn't representative of the "actual world."

Three weeks later, they sign the first-year contract and pay the first semester's tuition (or, rather, forward Julia's parents the form to pay it). And as they gain admission into this not-actual world, it's almost as if they aren't *actually* doing it, almost as if by acknowledging the structural problem they've exempted themselves from the structure, from the problem.

Besides, what else is there to *do*, really? It's one thing when it's all academic—of course every child in America, every child in the world, should have these opportunities—but when it's your kid, *your kid* . . .

What Nathaniel will do is vote for the right candidates and donate to the right causes and teach his kids to respect and accept people who aren't in their schools, on their block, in their lives. And two Thursdays before the children's first day, when Nathaniel sees David at Terry Tucker's Boxing Gym, he will, not fully conscious of why he's doing it and without asking Julia first, invite the Dalice-Stews over for a cookout. "It's crazy you've never met the kids. We'd love to have you."

The Rothsteins go all out: steak and chicken sausage, shrimp for shrimp cocktail. Because David "was good to your dad," Julia tells the kids. David was there when he needed him. The story Julia knows is the same story Nathaniel wrote in his college essay two decades before. He's never corrected the record.

They arrive at 4 the next Sunday, David bearing coloring books, a Slinky. Ramona, now deep into her seventies, has never met the man who helped her husband lose his job. Nathaniel can't tell if she has residual resentment or if this is just Ramona. Noting the pile of shoes in the front hall, she takes off her own, despite Julia's protestations. "I believe in respecting the culture of a place," says Ramona. Then, to Arnie, half hiding behind his mom: "It's why I wear sensible flats." Later, alone with Nathaniel in the kitchen, Ramona peers at his FEMINIST DAD T-shirt, which his daughter "gave" him the year before. "Isn't it odd that your wife called *me* with the address?" Ramona asks.

"You mean I should've called David?"

"Just an observation," says Ramona.

Still, thanks to David, the evening is a success. In retirement, he's begun wearing colorful guayaberas: not an homage to his Caribbean heritage so much as the costume of choice among his aging band of Austin boomers. David has a seemingly endless supply of hard candies in the pocket of his slacks, which he "secretly" hands off to Hannah and Arnie when they think no one is watching. He charms Julia with his easy way around the kids, his orgasmic reaction to her (store-bought) peach cobbler.

At twilight, David and Nathaniel sit on the front porch, beers in hand. The elderly couple from the end of the block passes on their evening stroll, and later, Mike Huggins from next door, taking the dog out. Both times, the neighbors wave. Both times, they linger a beat too long. Are they curious who David is? Hopeful for an introduction? Nathaniel doesn't oblige. He hates that this is atypical, that having a Black man here is atypical.

And so he resolves not to treat it that way. Both times, he waves back, returns to their conversation. Both times, Nathaniel Rothstein feels a surge of pride.

Once Nathaniel's kids are older, they'll have a vague recollection of David's presence: at that cookout; from a single photograph taken at Hannah's bat mitzvah party some years later, in a tent in the backyard. David wears a too-big suit, Ramona's in her Austin formalwear: turquoise jewelry, something shawlish. The kids will know them in the way kids know all the adults who swirl around the periphery of their lives. As names, mostly, names to pester their parents with on long car rides or instead of doing homework. Adolescents are detectives, forever putting together the pieces of lives they only half remember living. Those names are clues.

Remember Simona, the cleaning lady?

The landscapers, first Juan and then his Vietnamese successor, Tran? Why'd we fire Juan? Tran? Even if *we're just not using them anymore*, isn't that still, like, getting fired?

Whatever happened to Great-Uncle Bob's weird friend Lee Gorbinski? Wasn't he a *widower*?

Remember David and Ramona? What was up with them?

Add them all to the great list of names, kids. In the meantime: Hannah's middle school graduation and Arnie's bar mitzvah and Arnie's middle school graduation. A Portuguese water dog is adopted, buried. First dates and wet dreams. *Joseph*, *Gypsy*, *Fiddler*. PSATs, SATs, prom.

At sixteen, Nathaniel Rothstein never could've imagined this life. Now, an alternative history, without Julia and the kids, is just as unimaginable. They're the Rothsteins, as solid, as inevitable, as the dishes in the sink.

Forty-five becomes forty-six, forty-seven, and even through the hardships, cancer scares or even not-scares, the death of Nathaniel's mother or his uncle or his aunt, tragedies no one can foresee, Nathaniel will be steady, because he'll know deep in his bones those things he's always been told, those things his own life has proven: that everything happens for a reason, that everything will turn out OK.

See the man at forty-eight.

From his Honda Civic at the Shady Creek Condominiums, David can see Nathaniel's future so clearly. He might not be able to foretell every detail, but he knows the thrust, and he knows this: that the boy will do things he doesn't believe in or doesn't care about or doesn't think about because at twenty-two, at twenty-six, at thirty-six, it will seem to him that doing these things isn't *actually* doing them, that this is a trial run and not the real thing. And before Nathaniel knows it, this life that is practice for his life will *become* his life, the chasm between who Nathaniel understands himself to be and who he is so vast as to seem unimaginable, which is why he won't imagine it.

Lucky, comfortable, fortunate. He will never see the secret machinery that shapes sixteen-year-old Nathaniel into the Nathaniel he'll become. He won't see it because it's not secret, it's out in the open—that's the trick, don't hide something and no one will bother looking for it—and since he doesn't realize how this machinery has built him in the first place he won't realize, either, when he's handed the controls.

Yes, David can make out the contours of Nathaniel's next thirty years, just like that, and can see his own, his last, thirty years, too. He sees himself at that cookout over at the Rothsteins'. How, alone on the deck with Nathaniel—the younger man flipping meat in his World's Best Dad apron—there will come a moment when David *could* say something, about the fact that it actually hasn't been fun giving up a career he was good at to help cranky old assholes pick out paint, and how he knows he'll make a joke instead, or stand in uneasy silence until the moment passes. How he'll *want* to say something but also won't want to give Nathaniel the impression he's been *dwelling* on it, which is true, he hasn't, Nathaniel Rothstein is not his sun and stars, primary or secondary or tertiary source of his hope, of his joy, of his pain, it would just be nice to acknowledge what happened. How it had turned out for each man.

David sees himself at the daughter's bat mitzvah. How, aside from a couple of cater-waiters, maybe the dreadlocked lead singer, if there's a band, he'll be the only one, and this only-oneness will provoke, in the other guests, an oversolicitousness.

At some point, the band will veer toward hip-hop. Or maybe a DJ will play an expletive-bleeped version of a popular rap song. David can see the kids jumping up and down, masking their lack of rhythm by making themselves big: doing the running man, the shopping cart, the worm. No one will acknowledge those dancing children are making fun, not of the songs themselves, but of the dissonance between the suburban white kids they are and the streetwise Black tough guys they imagine the rappers to be.

David can see himself and Ramona on the car ride home after the bat mitzvah party. They won't speak for a few minutes, both tired, irritable. "Well, that was lovely," Ramona will say, finally, and turn up the radio, ending the conversation.

He sees himself at his own funeral, in the casket, Nathaniel, decades of life left in him, standing over, paying his respects. How will Nathaniel remember his old mentor? Like all of David's past volunteers do, or at least the ones who haven't lessened him to court jester or forgotten him altogether. He was a shepherd, guiding them on their own journeys, David's overarching purpose to help them figure out themselves.

The fight is over. Nathaniel can't find the car keys and cell phone that Jesse knocked out of his hand. The fallen boy is stirring, and Nathaniel has the sense to keep moving, toward the entrance to Shady Creek. He'll return in a few minutes. For now, he'll give his opponent a chance to slink away; better than risking another confrontation.

David knows it's time to go, too, but he doesn't. His mind is too deep into his own past and the boy's future. He watches as Nathaniel passes his car.

At first it seems Nathaniel's missed him, not all that strange when the car is a Civic, every car's a Civic, when the lot is dark and David's headlights and engine are off. At first it seems he's missed him, but then he turns back, once, a fleeting glance, probably to make sure the other boy is still down, that a sneak attack isn't imminent.

Except. Nathaniel holds his stare. A single beat. Does the boy see him? David isn't sure. "Nathaniel." David says his name, but by the time it's out—the windows are up, it's not like he could hear him anyway—Nathaniel's turned away. Away from David and toward his old life, his new life, and in this turning, David can see the boy of right now and of tomorrow, can see himself as he was and as he is and as he'll be.

In this moment, the man who always said it isn't his country knows of course it is—he's always known it—the man who always said it was a joke doesn't find it funny—he never has—and before David can rationalize what he's doing, he has his own mobile phone in his hand.

Later, David will tell himself he just wanted to see what would happen. And in fairness, as he dials, there are things he doesn't know. He doesn't know that when Jesse comes to, he'll be eye level with Nathaniel's keys and cell phone, which in the scuffle ended up underneath a car. He doesn't know how Jesse, humiliated and with no one to take his anger out on, will take it out on that cell phone, on those keys, and throw them in the dumpster on his way out of Shady Creek. He doesn't know that the only identification on the now-Black Nathaniel Rothstein, fists wet with blood, is an expired Haitian passport.

Yes, there are things David Dalice does not know. But as he makes that call he does know this: that the boy who was once Nathaniel Rothstein will be seen without being seen, heard without being heard, that the boy who was once Nathaniel Rothstein, to the men who arrive on the scene, won't be a boy at all.

"Hello, yes," David Dalice hears himself saying. He starts the car. "There's been an assault . . . Shady Creek . . . The attacker is running away. Please, yes, come quick . . ."

SATURDAY

THE AFTERNOON BEFORE ALEXIS Cepeda was to fight to become the super lightweight champion of the world, a stranger arrived at Terry Tucker's Boxing Gym.

This was at 5:46 on a Saturday, an hour before the longtime denizens of that place were set to congregate to watch the match. It was May of 2014, the gym's thirtieth year. The stranger, a woman, would not have guessed she was two years older, for even at thirty-two it still felt hard to believe she was older than anything. And yet she was older than a lot of things, older in the scope of all human history than most things maybe. Older, somehow, than here.

Here weathered fight posters were stapled over more weathered fight posters, clippings taped atop clippings. In the small front office, she noticed a thumbtacked postcard of a lunging lion, droppings penned in underneath him. On the desk: newspapers in ominous, Pisa-like stacks; a sign-in sheet on a clipboard. Behind it: a man who looked too big for his surroundings, as if he'd found himself stuffed into an especially dumpy dollhouse.

The man was filling out paperwork. He wore a red track jacket, rectangular readers. "What can I do you for?" he asked without looking up.

"I'm here on the strict orders of my therapist," said the woman.

"It's a good way to work stuff out, definitely."

"Oh, I'm not here to fight."

The man looked up, gave the stranger the once-over. She wore dark jeans, a black T-shirt, the vaguely amused expression of a person who might fit in here. "I don't know," he said. "You got good height. Could probably do some damage, if you trained."

"My mama always told me I needed to learn to fuck some folks up."

"Sounds like a smart lady."

"What's that phrase? *She was a crazy bitch but she was my crazy bitch*? Anyway. I never fucked anyone up in my life."

The man introduced himself as Felix Barrowman.

"Sasha," said Sasha.

This was the third boxing gym Sasha had been to that day, and the last one on her list.

"You think it's actually worth trying to find him?" she'd asked Eileen the week before.

"It's a pivotal episode from your life!" insisted Eileen.

"It was just so long ago. Like, at some point, who cares?"

"Ah, yes, *let's not think about the past*. What every therapist loves to hear. Listen, you don't want to do it, say I made you. Blame me. I'm used to it; I'm a Jewish mother. My kids do it all the time."

Sasha had started seeing Eileen the previous fall, after her own mama was first diagnosed. Breast cancer. Back then, Sasha's fear hadn't been that her mama would die, but that she wouldn't. "I don't want her to, like, drop dead tomorrow," she'd told Eileen. "But you ever fight with my mama you learn quick: she can go on a while." It had taken Sasha years to build a life apart from the woman who raised her. She didn't want to get drawn back in.

Six months later, Belinda St. James was gone. Uncharacteristic, since even in her final days, Belinda had remained Belinda. "These titties were my start," she'd taken to saying, "so seems fitting they'd be the end of me, too." The day she died she told Sasha she was beautiful. "You're the best thing I ever did in this stupid world." Even then, she couldn't bring herself to call her daughter by her name.

Now, freed of her mama's complicated love, Sasha Markham was preparing to leave. The mortgage processing company where she worked had a Phoenix office. Sasha would transfer there after the Memorial Day weekend.

She had no connections out west, hadn't saved enough, really. But she was tired of living in the place she grew up. No matter how big Austin was becoming, it would never be big enough for her. Something else Belinda said on the day she died: "Sometimes you just gotta get moving."

And so she'd begun to pack and say her goodbyes. "Not to be too therapisty," Eileen had told her the week before, "but there is such a thing as closure."

According to Google, three boxing gyms existed in Austin in 1998 that were still around today. At neither the one on the southside, nor the one on the east, had anyone heard of a "David from Haiti."

"Now, that's not a name I've heard in a minute," said Felix Barrowman, leaning back in his too-small swivel chair.

"You know him?" asked Sasha.

"Oh, yeah. He's known Terry since . . ." Felix realized he didn't know how long the men had known each other.

The gym was normally closed at this hour, Felix said, but they were having a little get-together in honor of the fight. He was happy to see if David would like to join. "Assuming he's still alive," said Felix.

Sasha gave him a closed smile. *Weird joke*, she thought.

Felix picked his iPhone up off the desk. "Will he know who you are?"

"We'll see."

She'd told Eileen the whole mortifying story the week before: how back when she was in high school, she'd started up a phone romance with a boy named David. She even invited him over once, knowing full well that the Sasha he was expecting would not be the one he found.

Around the time David was supposed to show up at Shady Creek, Sasha heard yelling in the parking lot outside. "A fight," she'd told

Eileen. "I knew the whole thing was dicey to begin with, and I just got freaked out—like, what if *that* was David?—so I took the phone into the bathroom and called my best friend, Margaret Clanahan." *Just calling to see if you remembered the Depends for Old Lorraine.*

By the time Sasha had hung up, whatever had been going on in the parking lot was over. "I'd convinced myself I'd have my answer that night. He'd love me or he'd kill me. And then he didn't show."

That night in 1998, she'd called David's phone a dozen times. Each time, it went straight to voicemail, one of those automated messages: *You've reached 617 . . .*

Then, a week later, Margaret Clanahan reported seeing Jesse Filkins at Barton Creek Mall, said it looked like someone had beaten him up. Was that from the fight in the parking lot? Could David have done it? "I started to imagine he was my guardian angel, which, let's be honest, is probably not what happened. Think I just told myself that so I'd be less embarrassed about the whole thing." Her only chance to figure out the truth was to ask Jesse, but on the first day of junior year he was nowhere to be found. Rumor was his parents had moved the family out of state. She never saw him again.

"I had so many of those experiences growing up," Sasha told Eileen. "Something would happen, and it wouldn't even make sense, and I'd end up feeling bad. But the thing with David, it had been fun. Not the getting-stood-up part. But trusting the world, you know? Like, why would I *ever* think something like that would work out? It made me feel brave. Once you feel that, well, you want to feel it again. You want to *be* that again." She peered at Eileen. "Why you look like you've seen a ghost?"

"This is my *interested* face," said Eileen. "It's a highly interesting story." Eileen said she believed it was pivotal Sasha try to find David before her departure. "There might be some answers waiting for you. *And* I want you to promise me you'll report back next session."

Sasha asked Eileen why she cared so much.

"*My therapist cares too much*. Poor you. Let me ask you this, hon: If you manage to track this David down, what will you tell him?"

"That whole thing, it was the start of something important. It's part of my story, so I guess I just want to know what happened. And also to say fuck you for ditching me."

So this is where you were hanging out that summer, huh? thought Sasha, stepping into the gym proper while Felix made the call.

As a rule, Sasha didn't like old places. Folks in old places were obsessed with what was. Her mama had been wrong about a lot of stuff, but she'd been right about that. No bigger grift in America than nostalgia: convincing people who didn't have it good yesterday to be grateful because tomorrow would be worse.

This old place felt different. This old place was filled with new things. A half dozen guys worked around worn-out bags swathed in fresh duct tape. These were not the real fighters. Not yet. They were skinny boys and chunky boys, high school boys who—judging from the bacne creeping out the tops of their tanks—heard the gym was open on a Saturday night and felt relief. No one acknowledged Sasha as she passed, the work a good excuse to pretend a woman wasn't on the scene.

A darkened weight room, its mirrored walls newly Windexed. Past it, strange pink light emanated from a small room in the back.

"Excuse me," came a voice. Sasha turned to find Felix in the entrance to the weight room. "He says he doesn't know you."

"I see," said Sasha. Probably for the best: no weirdness *and* she could still tell herself (and Eileen) that she tried. "Well, I won't take any more of your time."

"No trouble," said Felix, heading back toward the office. "I think he's happy to have a mystery to solve. He'll be here in an hour." Felix told Sasha she was free to hang out till then. "We even got cable now," he said, gesturing toward the ring.

In the center of the canvas, a big-screen television. The ropes in front of it had been removed. To its left: a life-size cardboard cutout of a small Latino guy, shirtless, gloved hands on hips. Big, goofy grin.

"David's good people," said Felix, Sasha following. "Maybe he'll be able to help you find what you're looking for." At the entrance to the office, he turned to face her. "Just don't take him too literal, OK? That man likes a story."

* * *

Would you even recognize it now?

From the outside, smushed between matching condominiums, the gym looks almost like a novelty, authentic as Frontierland. This is the way of Austin now, old things replaced by new things made to look old, ancient dive bars bought by restaurant groups and rebranded with the same names.

The condominiums had been developed by a real estate company called OneATX. They'd tried to buy Terry out: he'd scoffed at their initial offer and they'd declined his counter, reasoning the gym could be used to their advantage, a nod to The Way Things Used to Be.

This was why they'd christened the buildings Left and Right. Left has a first-floor coffee shop called Southpaw; Right features Ringside, a rooftop bar. Terry had thought he might get some business from the tenants, but he'd gotten more walk-ins when the Burger King was next door. Left and Right have gyms of their own.

The condominiums aren't all that's changed since 1998. So much from that summer is no longer around. DreamSkinz Tan & Spa became a Chipotle. Drive to the Frisco, where you and David once shared lunch, and find a Walgreens. The Shady Creek Condominiums are no more either, replaced by a mixed-use "urban village."

Eight hundred and twenty-two Saturdays have passed between that fateful night in 1998 and this one. Eight hundred and twenty-two Saturdays since the old you disappeared.

August 8, 1998. 9:12 p.m.

Do you remember what it felt like, in the parking lot at Shady Creek, after you'd left that writhing body behind?

You'd turned back once, wondering what had become of your stuff. But you had time then. So much time! Time to return for your keys, your phone. Your first fight: won. Soon: your first kiss.

What was ten minutes to let everyone cool down?

At sixteen you had all the time in the world.

Here's something that hasn't changed: the Whataburger across the street. It's still there now. If the parking lot has been repaved since then, it doesn't look it: same potholed land of the famished and the full.

Can you remember the heady walk out of that dimly lit condo complex sixteen years ago, toward those fluorescent orange lights?

Shoulders hunched, bloody hands bunched in the pockets of your jeans. There's a madness to that place after dark, the drive-thru line so long that a Chevy Tahoe is backed up into the street, its roided-out driver, an Ed Hardy mannequin come to life, halfway out the window, daring the traffic he's blocking to beep.

In the parking lot proper, rowdy crews come and go. Mostly carbo-loading before a night on the town: well-oiled Westlake kids home from college or during-the-week squares, from Round Rock, from Georgetown, who bitch about those tatted Austin pinkos but, on the weekends, will still drive the thirty minutes to get sloshed on Dirty Sixth. No better way to acclimate their suburban selves to the city than a franchise.

You float above and between. Once you would've done anything to avoid this scene. Too untamed. Too free. Now you breathe it in. You're high off the reality of what you've done, off the possibility of what's to come. Somehow, living in another man's skin, you finally feel comfortable in your own. Around you, chaos swirls.

Make way for flirting couples, fighting couples, couples that aren't couples because one just wants to be friends.

Make way for done-up brown girls and spaghetti-strapped white girls, make way for a working girl, a working *woman*, you realize when you make eye contact: she's older than your mom, face slack as a melting candle. "Only knob job left tonight is for Mr. Pibb," she says, misinterpreting your lingering glance. You know to look away, but don't. "You deaf? I said, *Kitchen's closed*."

Make way for a bachelorette party, girls in pink boas holding up their blotto bride-to-be, who seems to have twisted her ankle earlier in the night. She wears a tiara, Single Tonight sash. "We're in a this-bitch-needs-a-burger situation," one of her handlers announces into an invisible walkie-talkie. A chubby girl on the end is making siren noises: "eeee oooo eeee oooo!"

When the chubby girl sees you staring at her she breaks away from her friends, gets in your face. "BWEEP," she deadpans, like a patrol car in traffic. "Bip bip BWEEEEEP." She hurries off to join the others.

"Hey," you call after her. The siren girl has dropped a pair of pink plastic sunglasses and you pick them up. Printed on the inside of one arm: ERIN'S BACHELORETTE '98. "Your— " It's too late. She's gone inside.

On a bench outside the restaurant a leathery drunkard lolls. Harley T-shirt tucked into Wranglers wrapped around Lincoln-thin legs, Texas-shaped belt buckle, Texas-sized. "How can a chopper go down like that? I mean, how does it *happen*? I ask, see, 'cause I was *personal friends* with Stevie Ray Vaughan . . ."

You have no money, no wallet, nowhere to be, so when the man beckons for you to join him, you sit. "Nice shades," he says. "You mind?"

You hand them over.

"These are badass," he says, trying them on. "Now, let me ask you something, brother . . ." But before he can say more: a coughing fit, and soon his head's between his knees. He's throwing up, a dry, bronchial heaving. On the sidewalk below: a wad of bloody phlegm.

"Are you OK?" you ask. The man raises a bony claw, stays down there.

The drunkard is so skinny you can see his spine through his shirt. You think you should get help, let someone know this man is vomiting blood. Except you don't know who to tell, and the man's still at it, and because you own your body now, you do what you'd never normally allow that body to do: you place your palm in the middle of his back. His breathing steadies.

Your whole life you've been so timid. So afraid. Of what? Of *this*?

"You'll be OK," you tell the drunkard. "It'll be OK."

And then you hear it.

Eee ooo eee ooo eee ooo.

Someone must've seen this poor man, the blood, and called.

The sirens are here, and this time they're real.

* * *

May 17, 2014. 6:25 p.m. Back room of a boxing gym.

"We call this the Ed Hooley Memorial Reading Room," said Terry Tucker as he led Sasha inside. Felix had surrendered his duties as tour guide to set up some folding tables for food, leaving Sasha in the older man's charge. The crooked stacks on the desk in the front office had metastasized here in back, cardboard boxes and whole newspapers piled halfway to the ceiling, the path between them so narrow Sasha had to follow Terry single file.

Squint and she could see the bedroom this once was. In the far corner: a cot, undressed. On top of it, someone had arranged clothing in the shape of a man. White tube socks where the feet would go, denim shorts for legs, a Patriots hoodie chest. A small wooden dresser near the door was the only other area free of clutter. On it: a beat-up Velcro wallet, electric blue; a lava lamp, its pink boluses doing their psychedelic boogie.

Terry was sixty, short and muscular, in jeans and a ringer tee, tucked in. When he'd pulled up in his truck a few minutes earlier, Sasha was putting out her cigarette and he'd been on her about it since.

"I always tell my fighters," he said now, unstacking a tall pile of boxes, "enough things in this world can kill you even if you play your cards *right*. Best not to volunteer for more."

"Like boxing?" said Sasha.

"David's in this one here," said Terry, squatting down to open the bottom box.

Sasha surveyed the mountain of newspapers closest to her. At its peak: an old copy of the *Statesman*, below-the-fold side up, date obscured. The largest headline: *Ten years later, still no sign of missing teen*. "How do you know where anything is in here?" she asked.

Terry pulled a single sheet of wrinkled computer paper from deep inside the box. He stood, handed it to Sasha. "I'm an adherent to a philosophy I call *disorganized organization*."

This room Terry knew. This place he knew.

The forgetting had started a couple years before. "You're probably losing your mind," his longtime internist, crinkly Dr. Walls, had joked with him at his annual physical when he'd first reported it. Turned out he was. The diagnosis: *mild cognitive impairment*. Not enough to interfere with Terry's daily routine, but "let's just say if I knew this'd be the outcome," said Dr. Walls, "I might've laid off the one-liners."

"So it's not Alzheimer's?" asked Terry.

"I'd think of it as more of an appetizer."

In the ensuing months, everyone played their roles. Terry's ex-wife, long remarried, offered to fly out from Denver. When he demurred, she sent a care package: a Trojan horse for the going-bonkers set, its CLIF Bars and salted almonds just a cover for the "key bracelet" and *Jumbo Book of Brainteasers* his ex knew he'd never buy himself. Terry's loyal early-morning crew—the First Thingers—offered to start a "meal train" so he wouldn't have to worry about dinner as he acclimated to his new life. Alexis Cepeda vowed to stick with him to the end.

Terry threw the word searches in the recycling bin, told the First Thingers that he wasn't riding their meal train, had no intention of suffering "death by casserole." Alexis's offer was particularly half-assed. In 2010, he'd signed with one of the few remaining big-time management companies, and they'd had their own ideas about who should be in his corner. Alexis worked out with Terry when he was in town, passed on a small cut of his earnings. But Terry's dreams of trainer glory had died years before his diagnosis. "I expect you to be exactly as helpful as you've always been," Terry told him.

And so the old man had what he'd always had: Terry Tucker's Boxing Gym. He missed appointments, sometimes lost his keys, which he never wore on a bracelet. He asked Felix, who'd stepped in to help with the management of the place, to make sure the books stayed balanced. But he knew where every scrap of paper was in the old garage, knew which posters were where and the posters underneath them. Terry never forgot that *one* was jab and *two* cross, and he worked the mitts with his private clients same as he always had. Some things were too ingrained to fall to *mild cognitive impairment.*

No credit cards, no hidden fees.

Something rips, put some tape on it.

Hit the speed bag and it always comes back.

Sasha inspected the wrinkled paper. It was a transcription of an article, dated December 9, 1973. Top center: a single pinprick, a thumbtack scar. *Newcomer Rasta Dalice gives hometown hero Bandit Bengochea a run for his money!* "This is David from Haiti?" she asked.

"David Dalice," said Terry.

A full-grown man in 1973? It didn't make sense. "If you don't mind my asking," said Sasha, "did David have a son?"

* * *

Will Terry think of you before he dies? Will your former face float through his addled mind?

Unlikely. Yours is but one story from Terry Tucker's Boxing Gym. It's a good one, sure, but 2,933 people signed that sign-in sheet over these three decades, and even before Terry had started to lose it, you'd all begun to blend together, a blob of humanity.

Strangely, had Terry's sentient self ever been told your story, he wouldn't have found it *that* strange. Terry didn't think of himself as a great brain, but the one maxim he'd always stuck by had proven true: you never knew. Who'd grow, who wouldn't. Who'd learn, who wouldn't.

He knew it from his own life, from the lives of those 2,933 bodies who'd walked into his cramped front office. People don't go to boxing gyms to stay the same. We are not static. This world is not static.

Stories that start as one thing sometimes become another.

August 8, 1998. 9:21 p.m.

The patrol cars come one after another—one, two, three—surrounding the bench outside the Whataburger. One cop per car, and soon they're upon you.

"Sounds like you've had quite a night, my man," says the first, short and bullnecked. "What you think, Officer D'Angelo? This him?"

"Looks like it, Hernandez." D'Angelo is in his early twenties, tall and thin, his shirt so loose he could be playing dress-up.

The third man says nothing. He's forty-something and moon-faced, acne scars deep enough they've rendered him moon-featured.

You want to tell them that the drunkard's been coughing blood, to get an ambulance, but they speak in a way that suggests you're not supposed to speak back.

"You get into some trouble at Shady Creek tonight?" says the bullneck, Hernandez.

How would they know about Shady Creek? You try to see past the officers. Where did everyone go? The lot is like a cuckoo clock five seconds after the hour, its wild birds disappeared. The revelers have scattered: into the restaurant, into their cars. Through the window behind you, you glimpse the working woman, weathered hand bringing a fry to lined lips, engrossed in a paperback copy of *Primary Colors*.

"Someone was assaulted in that lot back there," says D'Angelo, nodding across the street. "You know anything about that?"

There's been a misunderstanding. The other boy attacked you. It was self-defense. And also: this guy next to you needs help. He's sick. These are the things you intend to say, things you know they'll understand, if you can just get them out, except the fact of the cops, of their guns, has reverted you back to original Rothstein, except they won't stop talking—

"Officer D'Angelo," says the moon-faced man. You read the brass nameplate pinned onto his uniform: BENNINGTON. "Did you just ask this gentleman if he knew about an assault in the lot across the street?"

"Yeah," says D'Angelo. "I asked him."

"You deaf?" Hernandez asks you. He nods to D'Angelo. "You think he deaf, Officer D'Angelo?"

"Doesn't look deaf," says D'Angelo.

"Doesn't *look* deaf?" says Bennington. "Does he smell deaf, D'Angelo? Sir, stand up."

"I just meant he's not, like, *signing*," says D'Angelo.

"I'll be sure to include that astute observation if you're ever up for detective," says Bennington. "Sir, stand the fuck up."

Till now, the drunkard has remained stock-still and stone-faced, a statue in pink sunglasses. This last instruction has agitated him. He grumbles, curses under his breath.

"'Scuse me, brother," he says finally, reluctantly. He leans in close, like he's telling you a secret. There's blood still trickling down his chin. "I think they're talking to you."

First you can't speak, then you can't stop. You were visiting a friend, out of nowhere this guy attacked you, except the officers aren't listening, it's like you're telling yourself the story, and even though *you* know it's true, their silence makes you push harder—*He's an ex-boyfriend or something, he threw the first punch*—and this only makes it sound more made up.

D'Angelo has turned himself into a one-man perimeter, keeping the comers and goers at a distance, while Hernandez pats you down against his cruiser.

He pushes between your rib bones, presses hard against your inner thighs. He slides his hand over the back of your jeans, deep between your ass cheeks, and this prompts you to stop talking, bite your lower lip.

You did pretend (are pretending?) to be Black. You did beat up a stranger. You did abandon David. You did do all those things. But somehow the officer feeling inside you, *him* doing it, is the first time all night you've felt like *you* did something wrong.

When he finds the passport—the only ID on you—in the back pocket of your jeans, he clicks his tongue.

"What you got there, Hernandez?" asks Bennington.

Hernandez tosses the passport to Bennington, who, based on the fact that he's been watching this whole time without doing anything, you assume is in charge.

According to Bennington, you're a "Haitian national." According to Bennington, your visa expired six years ago. According to Bennington, fourteen minutes ago a witness called 911 to report an assailant matching your exact description coming this way.

You start to protest: you don't understand, I'm—

Bennington lifts a finger to shush you. "You seen any other average height, average weight Black males with expired identification out here tonight, now would be a good time to fill me in."

You don't look anything like the man in the photograph. You don't sound Haitian. You're sixteen.

—Look at the passport, you manage. Just look one more time . . .

Bennington turns to Hernandez: "My wife tells me I don't listen. I listen!" He flips through the booklet, squints down, taps the page. "Expired in '92," he says, and turns the visa your way.

—Not that, the . . .

"It was me, six years past my expiration date, I'd lay off the fisticuffs. But— " He hands Hernandez back the passport. "You're not me, are you?"

You don't understand, you keep saying, until Bennington says, "That's enough, you hear me? Enough," and signals again to Hernandez.

Now your arms are twisted behind your back. Now the cuffs, scraping against your wrists. You've seen enough cop shows to know how this will play out—a ride to the station, a phone call—except Hernandez escorts you not into the patrol car but instead back to the bench from which you came, the drunkard nowhere to be found.

—Please, you try again, unable to keep from panicking, please, if you'll just listen—

This time Hernandez crouches down, gets right in your face. "What did he just say to you, bro? *Enough*." He says it so softly you know he's not messing around.

The people begin, again, to linger. Glances snuck from the just-finished, the about-to-eat. Always looking away the second you look back. "C'mon, keep it moving," says D'Angelo. "Nothing to see here."

He seems to believe this—nothing to see here—all the cops do, the handcuffed person on the bench, their literal purpose for being in this place, almost incidental to the proceedings. They stand in a semicircle, backs to you.

If these officers know why you're all stuck in the parking lot of a Whataburger on a Saturday night, they don't let on. They chat about everything but what's happening, their sentences punctuated with deep crotch scratches, hocked loogies.

According to Bennington, 99 percent of a man's problems can be solved by Gold Bond. According to D'Angelo, if you pause *The Little Mermaid* during the wedding scene, the bishop has a full-on boner. According to Hernandez, the best place to drop a deuce on patrol is the lobby of the Red Roof Inn: "5999 South I-35."

"Fuckin' ridiculous," says Bennington. "There's a Hyatt less than a mile from there."

"So what?" says Hernandez.

"So you don't pass up a steakhouse to take a dump at Mickey D's."

Sometimes, a new patrol car will pull up parallel to the three officers. Once, a police SUV. When this happens, Bennington leans into the window, trades intel with the driver, sends the car away with a few pounds on the roof.

Through these interactions, you begin to discern the reasons for the hold up. There is ambiguity about whether you're to be read your rights. There is ambiguity about where to take you.

"A criminal alien carrying around *proof* of his undocumentation," announces Bennington, after one of these tête-à-têtes. He says this to the other officers, to the assorted lingerers. "Not exactly D. B. Cooper over here. Not Lucky Luciano. Stay in school, ladies and gents. That's the moral of this tale of woe."

The Whataburger lot is like the deepest recesses of Chuck E. Cheese: a place without time. How long has it been?

D'Angelo wants to know if the others have given much thought to the term *old lady*. "Isn't it kind of weird that it could mean your girlfriend *or* your mom?"

Hernandez asks for the craziest thing each of them has pulled off a perp.

"I got one," says Bennington. Bennington came to Austin '89 from Hartford PD. Has always worked patrol. *Loves* patrol. First month on the job, he's working Raymond District, gets a call 2 a.m., some hophead is running bowlegged down Ed Bluestein Boulevard, screaming his nuts off.

This banter is recognizable: from David, from the gym. They're funny, these guys, the way they see the world. With their backs to you, inserting yourself into the conversation feels possible—

—My name's Nathaniel. I'm from Newton. It's west of Boston?

"We drive out there, this schmo's hoofing it like he's got a bar between his legs."

—My uncle is a professor at UT. You can check.

"I'm thinking he's body packing, right?"

—I'm an American citizen, I swear—

"What's body packing?" asks D'Angelo.

"C'mon, bro," says Hernandez. "*Body packing*."

—I don't even know where Haiti is. *Please*.

"*Body packing*," says Hernandez, "is when a perp's converted his *shitter* into a *pharmacy*."

"You mean you thought he had drugs in his ass?" says D'Angelo.

—I know it sounds weird, but this is all a mistake—

"Ding ding ding," says Bennington. "Eight-ball up the wazoo."

—I was just being an idiot. I—

"First honest thing this one's said all night," says Bennington, acknowledging your idiocy without turning back. "Anyway, we strip search this guy. Upshot is this: we had it all wrong. *Other end*, if you can believe it. He's got a Bic pen shoved up his urethra!"

"Fuck," says Hernandez. "Gross."

—Please. *Listen to me*.

"That's his pisshole, D'Angelo," says Bennington, "if you didn't know."

"Why'd he put it there?" says D'Angelo.

"Never forgot that one," says Bennington. "Bic pen up the urethra. I mean, this fuckin' world, right?"

When it's finally time, D'Angelo is assigned to take you wherever it is you're supposed to go.

You aren't used to strangers touching you, to anyone touching you. At sixteen, your body barely belonged to you in the first place, and now it doesn't belong to you at all. Outside D'Angelo's cruiser, Hernandez ushers you roughly into the backseat.

Your T-shirt has ridden up your belly. You want to pull at the front of the shirt—you do this often when you're sitting, it hides the flab—but you can't, you're cuffed, and this mild roll of exposed flesh is what you'll remember most vividly when you think back to this time in the patrol car.

The officers say their farewells. Bennington's going inside for a soda; Hernandez is off to "do some serious damage" at the Red Roof Inn. No one has read you your rights.

On the road, you can feel D'Angelo soften. He taps the steering wheel to a song only he can hear, lets his face, once strained as a Guy Fawkes mask, relax. "You OK back there?"

—I have to pee.

"We'll be there soon."

—I get a phone call, right?

You'd like it to be David. He'll require the least context, won't respond with the theatrical indignation of a blood relative. You're not 100 percent sure of his number is the only thing. If you get it wrong, do you get a second try?

D'Angelo tells you to sit tight. "I'm the low man on the totem pole, if you haven't noticed."

—Honestly, it was self-defense. You have to believe me . . .

"Just save your breath, man. It's all INS now."

—INS?

"Immigration. Same guys you dealt with on the way in."

He doesn't seem as jaded as those other cops. He's probably not that many years older than you. If you can get D'Angelo to look you in the eye, really *look*, you're pretty sure he'll see what's obvious.

—Please. This is crazy. There's no way I can be that guy. Do I look like I'm in my *twenties*?

D'Angelo keeps his focus on the road. It's quiet on Congress at this hour. You cross the bridge, pass through downtown, the low-slung buildings festooned with signage from bygone eras: the vertical letters off the pink stucco side of a shuttered Yarings department store; outside the Paramount Theater, an old-timey marquee. At the end of the wide street, the Capitol looms.

And then he does it. Through his mirror, Officer D'Angelo looks you square in the eye. He looks, and you look back, and you swear he sees it, sees *something*, something isn't right, and just as you're sure he's about to pull the car over, to check your face against the face inside the passport, he returns his eyes to the road and slams the brakes and turns the wheel, because only feet ahead a man has stopped in the middle of the street.

"Fuck!" yells D'Angelo. "*Fuck.*" You've missed him, no one was hurt, but D'Angelo's shaken, you're shaken. D'Angelo keeps driving, turns his head to see who's back there, and as he does, you do, too—

It's your drunkard, pink sunglasses still on. He gives a little wave, a *My bad* shrug.

"Goddamn it," says D'Angelo.

Facing forward again, you want to pick up where you left off: *I'm not who you think I am, remember?* Except D'Angelo's face has rearranged itself back into its furrow of Authority.

You keep your eyes planted on his rearview, hoping he'll meet your gaze again. And though he does, just as you'd hoped, now there's no *something's wrong*, no *something's there*, now there is only the look and look away, like you yourself have done all those times: to kids at school you wanted to be friends with but didn't know how; to the patrons of Terry Tucker's during your first days there; to people asking for money on the side of the road.

How many times this summer has that happened, on the Drag or at 45th and Lamar on the way home from the gym? A glance, at the asker, at the spare change in your console, a tickle of conscience, and then: the cold resolve to keep plowing forward, as if, were you to give this one change you might have to give them all change, as if, were you to recognize their humanity, you might reveal too much of your own.

* * *

May 17, 2014. 7:23 p.m.

From the far wall facing the television, Sasha watched as the main room filled. The gymgoers were not accustomed to seeing each other in going-out clothes, and the novelty of it meant they'd dressed to impress. A trio of tightly packaged Latino fighters wore khakis and stretch-fit dress shirts, and arrived trailing much taller dates, who looked Strip-ready in leggy minidresses covered in shimmery metallic discs. Two handsome Black women wore matching tuxedos. A couple of white girls rocked boho crop tops and fedoras as if they'd been headed to Coachella and taken a wrong turn. The less fancy were still spiffed up in their own ways: hair gelled; Terry with his tucked-in tee. The young boxers who'd been working the bags an hour before remained in gym clothes, though someone had thought to bring them clip-on bow ties. Even the older patrons had made some effort, a small army of aging Seinfelds in their button-downs, sneakers, and jeans.

"Now, *this* is Austin, Texas," one of them was saying to her now, his bushy eyebrows raised. "You an *evening lady*?"

"An *evening lady*?" said Sasha. "That like a *woman of the night*?" (*Lord*, she thought, *nothing gets me sounding more like my mama than an old white guy in need of a neck trim.*)

"It's like a lady who *comes in the evenings*," said the man. "I'm a *morning guy*. A First Thinger?"

"Actually," confessed Sasha, now a little embarrassed, "I'm a no-time person. Just waiting for a friend."

The man introduced himself as Bob Alexander. "You know much about this fool sport?"

Sasha confessed she didn't.

Bob warned of multiple anthems from multiple nations, a robust undercard. "There's more throat-clearing in boxing than at Dr. Petrossian's office." When Sasha didn't respond, he raised his eyebrows again: "My ENT."

The bout was in Atlanta, Bob explained, a title shot for Alexis Cepeda, who'd once trained here. Alexis was twenty-seven. "The kid," said Bob, had traveled farther and longer than almost anyone else from the gym. Since going pro in '08—six years before—he'd sometimes even appeared in the Top 15 rankings of the various bodies that sanctioned fights. The World Boxing Consortium, under whose auspices this fight was occurring, currently had him ninth.

Tonight, the reigning super lightweight champ, a Haitian named Mozart "Socka Doc" Chevalier, had been expected to fight the second-ranked in the division, Ezekiel Small. But a torn ACL had sidelined Small, allowing Chevalier, per WBC regulations, to select any challenger from the top fifteen in his weight class.

"The honorable move would be to choose to fight the *third*-ranked, not the ninth," Bob continued, undeterred by the fact that Sasha hadn't asked for this—or any—level of detail. "A lot of those top guys are more seasoned than Alexis, so I'm guessing Chevalier likes that our man is a little green, at least on the national stage. Going with a lesser-known talent, it probably didn't make the television execs too happy. But at least it got us watching, right?"

"So you from around here?" asked Sasha, already boxing-ed out.

"Been here forty-five years," said Bob. "You?"

"Born and raised," said Sasha. "I'm leaving soon, though."

Bob looked up to the ceiling. "Me too, probably. Y'know, if this was a couple decades ago, I'd do the whole who-do-we-know-in-common game. But now?" A whistle. "Now our little town is all grown up. Not like it used to be, is it?"

Usually this was when Sasha would say, *Sure was nice to meet you*. Bob-looking men longing for a bygone Austin had defined huge swaths of her childhood, *the way things used to be* a favorite of those who'd taken a turn under her mama's salon cape. The way things used to be hadn't worked for Sasha. She had little appetite for pretending that they had.

But the way Bob said it, she had to agree. "My mama always said this place was for dropouts and dreamers."

"And which was she?" said Bob.

"Miss Belinda was *in it*," said Sasha. "Only dropped out when she died."

"That's a shame," said Bob.

"It's fine," Sasha assured him. "She was . . . a lot."

"That's just what we say to make it hurt less," said Bob. "It's hard when people go away."

They both went quiet, and Bob nodded toward the weight room. "You know, a man used to live in the back of this place. Homeless fellow, little *off*. Showed up one morning and just . . . stayed. For years! Ed, he was a weird guy. Everyone was cordial with him, but you know: *tolerance was limited*. Then one day he left and . . ." Bob grimaced.

"You miss him, huh?" said Sasha.

"I barely knew him!" said Bob. "He was a minor presence in my life. Miss him? How could I miss him? But I'll tell you, honey: *I do*."

What had happened to Ed Hooley?

Probably nothing good, Bob figured. He'd been gone eleven months without a word. In recent years, Ed had begun to talk with increasing frequency about tracking down his twin brother, Larry, who allegedly lived in Galveston. No "Larry Hooley" had ever shown his face at the gym, and Ed was not exactly known for his reliable narration. Still, the number 2 carved into Ed's neck did suggest that somewhere out there was a #1. When Bob and the other First Thingers arrived one morning to find no trace of Ed but for some old clothes and the blue Velcro wallet, they assumed it was to Galveston he'd attempted to go.

Had Bob been a closer observer of Ed's ways, he might've noticed that it was soon after their adventure together, in the wilds of Shoal Creek, that Ed's fixation with finding his twin took hold. But though Bob was grateful for the role Ed had played in his own spiritual re-awakening, it never occurred to him that their encounter with that passing family of coyotes had altered anyone's trajectory but his own. Afterward, Bob became too obsessed with his nephew's case to mull the inner workings of Ed Hooley, and the men had returned to the pleasant but distant acquaintanceship they'd had before.

It wasn't as if Ed's departure was especially shocking. He was not the first "off" person to enter through the garage doors, nor the first to exit them. If anything, the shocking part was how long he'd lasted. Bob and the other First Thingers had done their best to keep an eye on him, but they weren't therapists, or social workers. Nor was this a hospital, a prison. It was a gym. People came and went as they pleased.

Those last few months, Bob could sense a deterioration. Ed was nearing sixty, but a sixty from an earlier era, the sixty of a man who'd spent much of his life on the streets. His left eye, which twitched when he was agitated, began to do so with increased intensity. He spent more time in his room, in dialogue with himself, and invoked his brother with ever-greater regularity. "People need their people," he'd taken to saying. One day, Ed went to the 7-Eleven for a Slurpee and didn't come back for three hours. Another, he disappeared overnight.

"You trying to get to Galveston?" Bob asked when Ed rode in the next morning on his bicycle, stinking and disheveled. "Listen, man, it's a four-hour drive. It's nothing. *I'll* take you."

"Naw, that's all right," said Ed. "Think I'd like to bike."

Two weeks later, Ed Hooley was gone.

Ed left soon after Bob's fourth—and final—graduation from Citizen Police Academy. In his later years, Bob had tried to do some big things and tried to do some little ones. Ed's departure was a final confirmation that he'd failed at all of them. He did not burn down APD headquarters. Ed Hooley wound up same as the last person Bob had attempted to help house and clothe and feed: vanished. The case of Nathaniel Rothstein would remain forever cold.

At seventy-four, Bob couldn't quit the notion that there was more out there than we allowed ourselves to conceive, that even an imagination as fertile as his was no match for the vast peculiarities of this world. But if his failure to convert the Jewish ladies of the 53rd Class of Citizen Police Academy to his cause had taught him anything, it was that maybe it was better to hold those ideas close, to protect that fragile part of himself that still believed in the occasional impossible thing.

It was for this reason that Bob Alexander never told anyone that a few months after Ed disappeared, he spotted the man helping himself to a free hot dog from the vat at the entrance to Ginny's Little Longhorn Saloon, where, on Sunday afternoons, folks crowded around a giant plywood bingo board to take bets on which numbered square the bar's resident chicken would take a shit.

"Hey, Hooley!" Bob had called from across the packed room. The man made panicked eye contact and exited without answering. By the time Bob maneuvered his way outside and adjusted to the light, this ghost of Ed Hooley was nowhere to be seen.

It probably wasn't him anyway, Bob told himself. He'd seen no eye twitch, and Ed combed his hair forward, whereas this man's hair was combed back. Mostly, Bob chalked up "seeing" Ed to wanting to see Ed. Their city, Bob knew, was changing. He didn't like to think they'd allowed Ed Hooley to get lost in the change. Even so, it sure had looked a lot like him . . .

At Terry Tucker's Boxing Gym, a small gaggle now encircled Sasha, Hooley talk like chum, causing gymgoers to cluster. Bob introduced them as "The First Thingers," a graying group of gossips who, Sasha noticed, all wore orthotics, each on a different body part than the others.

"It just doesn't feel the same without him," said a squat redhead, a knee brace pulled over her jeans.

"If there's no room for a Hooley in this town, where is there room?" said a reedy man in a stained running shirt, who wore support straps with inflatable pads banded beneath both elbows, like pool floaties.

Maybe, they speculated, the city's tolerance for weird had always been overstated. Still, another frequently homeless Austinite, Leslie Cochran, who often walked 6th Street in a thong and heels, had mounted three serious mayoral campaigns here. His issues were gentrification and police accountability, and one time he'd finished in second place. The Leslies had given Austin its weirdness, but to newcomers, a whiff of quirkiness was more appealing than the stink that comes from actually having nowhere to bathe. Turned out real eccentricity was kind of a pain in the ass.

Like Ed Hooley, Leslie was now gone, though dress-up magnets of him and his outfits were available in area gift shops, alongside tie-dye T-shirts exhorting passersby to Keep Austin Weird, a slogan that was less city creed than savvy marketing, and whose provenance was the subject of endless litigation.

* * *

August 9, 1998. 12:26 a.m. Travis County Central Booking.

A thin hall; a long, backless bench. The just-arrested sit in their street clothes, handcuffed. Eyes shut, eyes half shut, bloodshot eyes pressing on the scuffed linoleum; necks surrendering to heavy heads, necks leaning back or all the way forward.

You're in the latter group, thus you meet your neighbors via their footwear: chunky basketball sneaks connected to skinny brown ankles; fat toes stuffed into pink platform jellies; new New Balances, their tongues hidden beneath the cuffs of khakis; a tapping, stockinged foot inside a high heel, taps so vigorous the heel is off the ground.

The heel belongs to the neighbor on your right. You glance up to see a white woman in a business suit, mascara streaming down her face. "Don't look at me!" she hisses. "Don't you dare look at me!"

—Sorry, you murmur, return your gaze to the floor.

To get here, you were passed from one cop to another. Down hallways, down an elevator, each time protesting that they didn't understand, you weren't who they thought you were. In a few days your skin would be totally different!

You didn't think twice about saying this last part in front of the officers—so far all white—but on this bench is a darker demographic, and here it would feel weird.

Shoes shuffle out, shuffle in. When the name on the inside of the passport is called, an officer escorts you to what looks like an especially shitty airport terminal. In the seating area, the listless and the blitzed sprawl on blue vinyl chairs bolted to the floor. These people are without handcuffs, yet stripped of the simple tools we all use to tamp down, to cover up—rubber bands and hair elastics, button-downs over undershirts—the congregated boast the unmoored look of all the world's institutionalized.

A wide aisle separates the men from the women—a half dozen or so on either side—and this is the plank down which you walk, the glassy eyes of the people focused on their hands or the floor or the television overhead, on anything but you or each other. You recognize a single pair of shoes from the other room: the new New Balances, now shorn of laces. Their owner, a swoop-haired white kid, bites his nails, pretends to watch TV: a muted Nancy Grace sounding off above closed captioning.

At the front of the room, a buff and buzz-cut Asian cop, hands covered in blue latex gloves, stands next to a folding table. Sitting behind it: a middle-aged Black officer looks down at her clipboard, pen at the ready.

The most prominent Black women in your life thus far have been your second-grade teacher and Roz, the bailiff on *Night Court*. These women look and sound nothing alike, though in your conception of them each is especially uncharmed by bullshit (Mrs. Price would, in fact, "move on" at the end of your second-grade year, her clipped style "not a good fit" for the parent body). This knowledge gives you hope: you are positive that neither Mrs. Price nor Roz would believe you are a fully grown Haitian man.

Behind the officers, on the tiled wall, two metal placards: NURSE'S STATION above an arrow pointing right, CELL BLOCK above an arrow left.

As you approach the desk you hear, from the direction of the nurse's station, a woman—"There isn't any need for that"—followed by the demon voice of a man possessed: "Let Jesus fuck you! Let Jesus fuck you! Lick me! Lick me!"

"Mr. Espinoza, what did I—"

A third voice: "That's just *The Exorcist*, ma'am. Movie buff, for real, ma'am. I'm just playin'. Won't do it again, cross my heart. I'm playin'."

The Black officer speaks without looking up. "Mr."— she says your new last name—"tell me: Any suicidal thoughts today?"

You start to speak and stop yourself. If you say nothing, she'll meet your eye, and when she does, she'll see what those white officers couldn't see, what your fellow inmates might've noticed on the backless bench if you'd dared let them look at you.

"Let's try this again, sir: *Any suicidal thoughts today*?"

You stay silent. This time, it works. She looks up, and so you start in on your now-perfected song and dance: *Nathaniel Rothstein, American citizen . . .*

From the nurse's station, the incubus returns. "Your mother's in here, Karras!" he screams, before once more being exorcised. "Naw, ma'am, I'm just playin', trust me, dawg, trust me."

—Look at me, please, just look at me, you say, and wait for that something's-wrong recognition.

The officer only raises her eyebrows. "I'm going to ask you one last time, sir: *Do you feel suicidal*?"

You are suddenly overcome with the same acute drowsiness you've felt on the most interminable of errands with your mom—Honda Village, Best Buy—the perpetual waiting designed, according to her, to wear you down. Now what about insurance? Extended warranty? Yes, please, whatever, just let me out.

The officer knocks her head toward the NURSE'S STATION sign. "We need to get you checked out?"

—No, you say, returning to yourself. No, I don't feel suicidal.

"That's good, that's progress. And have you ever felt suicidal?"

—No.

"Any history of suicide in your family?"

—No. I mean, I don't think so—

History of mental illness. Mental illness in your family. History of drug abuse.

—No. No. No.

"He's all yours," the Black officer tells the man in the blue latex gloves, who asks you to rest your palms on the folding table, begins to pat you down again.

—What happens next? you ask the Black officer.

"What happens next?" She's already returned to her clipboard. "Tea and crumpets, of course. You're at the county jail. What do you think happens?"

You're moved to a single-occupancy bathroom off the lobby. *You're moved*, passive, because you're no longer tracking who moved you. At first you could distinguish between them. Hernandez, D'Angelo, Bennington. Now, despite their varied races, genders, body types, they've all begun to bleed together: Police.

The officer goes into the bathroom with you, props one of his black shoes, thick-soled as Dr. Abruzzi's, in the jamb to prevent the door from closing.

There's only a toilet, which means you'll have to do it without the privacy a urinal's siding provides. And because Nathaniel Rothstein, even this new Nathaniel, can't take his dick out in front of a police officer and pee freely, literally would not be able to pee, and because you must pee—this is nonnegotiable—the only option is to not be Nathaniel Rothstein.

Thus, as you unzip your fly, you feel yourself, your actual self, moving outside your body, above your body, observing what you left behind.

You are Nathaniel Rothstein and this is happening to the man from the passport photograph, and it is this dissonance that allows a piss so lengthy you half-expect the officer to make a joke, but he doesn't, he's seen a thousand men piss and jiggle and flush.

Yes, this is all happening to the man in the passport, which is why after the officer instructs you to remove your clothes, you do: sweatshirt and T-shirt and braided belt and sneakers and socks and jeans, all in a pile on the floor.

"All the way, please," he says when you're down to your boxers, and because this is happening to someone other than Nathaniel Rothstein, you step out of those, too.

Who cares if he sees this dick that isn't your dick?

Except he isn't looking there, isn't looking anywhere, or at least isn't *seeing*, his face as expressionless as before you'd undressed, before you'd pissed, his face the face of workers the world over engaging in the mundanity of daily life: standing over a Xerox machine, waiting for the coffeepot to fill.

Into a pair of pale green boxers, into a black-and-white striped jumpsuit. Plastic sandals so big that each time you step you have to curl your toes to keep them on.

Back in the lobby, a man has come to fetch the guy in the New Balances. You know this man. The high white socks pulled up unevenly; the tennis shorts and ratty Longhorns tee; eyes squinched in disbelief, horseshoe hair askew. He could be your uncle Bob, one of Bob's friends: a dad, rolled out of bed.

As you pass, you hear the Black officer telling New Balances to sign here, sign here. "You know what *your own recognizance* means, Mr. Bloom?"

"It means you got lucky this time," says the dad. "You know that, right? We thought when he turned eighteen we'd be done. It never ends, does it? Thank you, Officer. His mother thanks you. I thank you. You hear that, Martin? Twenty-two years old and your father is apologizing on your behalf. My apologies, officer. *Thank you.*"

It's so familiar, this performative scolding, not that the dad isn't angry, he's angry, but there's a little give to the anger, a wink, because this is, more than anything, a waste of resources (financial, time), it's a headache, no more or less.

It's so familiar that for a second you've returned to Nathaniel again, because when this is all over, that's who you'll be, *you'll never believe what my meshuggeneh nephew did this time, boy oh boy*, a little sweetness to the *boy oh boy*, because you did kick that other kid's ass.

You're Nathaniel and then you're gone again, because there's no Rothsteinian dawdling permitted on this brief journey out of the lobby. "Keep it moving, keep it moving": down another wall-tiled, fluorescent-bright hall, around a corner, and through two sets of heavy green doors that lock behind you with a click.

* * *

May 17, 2014. 8:42 p.m.

At the exact moment David Dalice, sixty-three, pulled into the gravel lot, a communal gasp could be heard inside Terry Tucker's Boxing Gym.

The undercard was underway, and the assembled had gathered in tailgateish bunches: on barber's seats poached from long-folded salons and brought-from-home chairs varied as the Village People (camping, beach, plastic Adirondack), on the floor. Between bouts: glimpses into the dressing rooms of tonight's stars. Each time they showed Alexis Cepeda—getting his hands wrapped, shadowboxing in the mirror—the crowd at Terry Tucker's cheered.

From her post along the back wall, Sasha pretended to follow the action. Why was she still there? It had been hours, no David in sight. And yet each time she thought about leaving, something compelled her to stay. A newspaper clipping; a chatty old man. A gasp that started on one end of the room and, like the wave, cascaded to the other.

The impetus for the gasp was something happening on the television. The scene: Alexis Cepeda's dressing room. Alexis had maintained his dopey good looks, the thick eyebrows and *who me?* grin. But he was a man now, broad and muscled, the tight fade of his youth grown out into a full head of black hair. He projected the airy determination of the underdog that he was, throwing loose combinations in front of a row of lockers.

Alexis's corner had presumably decided to give their fighter space, except for one man who stood at the other end of the lockers. He was a squat older fellow with a sizable gut. Jean shorts, black T-shirt with CEPEDA TOUGH in white block letters. Thin graying hair combed forward. The man appeared almost stage-frightened, as if he hadn't meant to be caught on film but didn't know how to exit gracefully.

Bob Alexander noticed him first. "Holy crow," said Bob, rising halfway out of his collapsible chair. Other exclamations soon followed: "My god—" "What the heck?"

And then, as if the cameraperson could hear the questions inside Terry Tucker's Boxing Gym and wanted to provide an answer: a three-second close-up of the man. He stared directly at the camera, mouth agape. One second, two seconds. A gasp inside the boxing gym as, on the television, his left eye twitched.

A truth about Alexis Cepeda:

He was not a gym person. Not like the others. Gym people were mordant, paranoid. Gym people treated tsuris like a sauna, enjoyed a good schvitz in their own regrets.

Not Alexis. Sure, as a boy he'd flirted with the sorts of dramas that defined gym personhood, the storm clouds that roiled his young soul usually the result of excess moisture off the sea of love. The entire start of his career could, in fact, be traced back to failed entanglements: the diminishing affection of one woman, the thumb of another.

But angst-ridden had never been his natural state. Step into the maze of your own interiority, Alexis knew, and you only end up lost. This was what had doomed his relationship with Miriam Lopez. It got too serious. *She* got too serious. She'd always wanted to be more like the cop she'd been hired to be. At some point—Alexis wasn't sure exactly when or how—she made it happen. Make a face long enough and it becomes your face. Alexis couldn't do that kind of heavy.

To win, he needed to do what he did best: keep it light. Keep it loose. Looseness in life translated to looseness in the ring and back to life. Looseness begat looseness. Like the centenarian who credits her longevity to chocolate and sherry, his breezy way of being was not an impediment to his success but rather its cause.

No, Alexis Cepeda was not a gym person, for he believed the troubles of the world were not meant to be contemplated, obsessed over, engaged with. They were meant to be avoided.

And so, when, forty-three minutes before The Gasp, Alexis, hopeful for a final breath of not especially fresh air before the biggest fight of his life, poked his head through the one open overhead door in the vacant loading area behind the State Farm Arena in Atlanta and found Ed Hooley, of all people, leaning against a dumpster, his first thought was not *Where has this person been and why is here now?* It was *Turn before he sees you.*

Except Ed did see him; Ed had been waiting for him. "Have I got a story for you, boy," bellowed Ed, and though it had been some time since Alexis had last encountered him, he knew that Ed did not *bellow*, Ed did not *got a story* for anyone, Ed would never call him *boy*.

The dumpster was a few yards away, the interloper cast in shadow. Alexis squinted. "That you, Hooley?"

"It is indeed."

What's different about him? wondered Alexis. The man had Ed's face but not Ed's face, his guileless eyes gone cold. Alexis approached warily. "How you doing, Ed?"

"Never said I was that," said the man. "As much as I wish it was otherwise, I must admit my dear number two's whereabouts are a mystery even to me." He craned his neck so Alexis could get a clear view. "You dealing with number one."

A simple fact that Larry Hooley had overlooked in presenting himself here: Alexis had met him only in a wig and whiteface. He'd never seen Larry in the (actual) flesh, never put together that Ed's brother and the man who'd conned him in Reynosa were the same. "I'm The Clown," said Larry, by way of explanation.

"You seem like a clown," Alexis agreed.

"Not *a* clown," said Larry. "The Clown. *Your* clown."

"*My clown?*" said Alexis. "I don't have a cl—" He peered at Larry, looked up to the sky. "No way." He looked back to Larry. "No fuckin' way." Alexis scrunched his face. "Are you kidding me right now?"

"Clowns don't kid."

"You're my *clown* clown?"

Larry Hooley flashed his big clown grin. "Tell me, Rothstein: How you been?"

How had Alexis never connected Lucky Larry to his brother? He did remember The Clown talking about a twin. Had he said his name was *Ed Hooley*?

"What the fuck are you doing here?" said Alexis. "You know, I'd tell girls about you. On dates. They'd ask how I got to Texas and I'd tell them. And you know what? *No one believed me.*" Miriam had thought he was messing with her when he told her that seemingly far-fetched story. Most of her successors figured the same, except the white girls, who always assumed he was deflecting, a goofy anecdote to redirect from some horror of which he couldn't speak.

"So how *did* you get across?" asked Larry.

"I *walked*," said Alexis.

"On *stilts*?" said Larry.

"That bartender helped me off them. And I *still* broke a toe on the way down. You know you left me *nine miles* from the border? Hobbled *all day* to get there. I could've *died*."

"You go clowned up?"

"Had no choice. It took me *two days* to get that shit off."

"And?"

"And here I am, man." The border agent had barely even glanced at Nathaniel Rothstein's license. "You're the second one today," the agent had told Alexis, then asked how long the circus would be in town. He was thinking about taking his son. "Y'all got one of them little guys they stuff into the cannon?"

"You telling me it *worked*?" Larry asked Alexis.

"I told him I *was* the little guy," said Alexis.

Larry suggested they not obsess over the past. "We have some here-and-now to settle."

At this, a bald and burly figure in a sports jacket appeared in the overhead door frame. "You good, boss?" he called.

"Just an old friend," Alexis called back, waving the security guard off. He turned back to Larry. "You got two minutes, clown. So *spill*."

He'd seen better days was the gist.

The previous century had been fertile ground for the crooked of the state, but by 2014 Larry's particular style of Lone Star fraudster was few and far between. Addiction had done a number on some; prison on others. A few had leveled up, exploiting their shady pasts to give credibility to their allegedly aboveboard new lives, pastoring second-tier megachurches or as right-wing gabbers on satellite radio. Of course, the luckiest of the cohort had never engaged in the penny-ante crap in the first place. They'd learned how to put their corrupt natures to use not under boardwalks playing three-card monte, like Larry, but in law and B-school classrooms. The A-list flimflam men of modern-day Texas didn't run shell games atop cardboard boxes; they ran the state government.

Larry, meanwhile, stayed forever Hooley, a pen-and-paper grifter unwilling, unable to adapt to the digital world. He'd never tried Google, didn't have email. With each passing year, the list of cons available to him got shorter. After 9/11, border shenanigans became a no-go. The advent of Craigslist ended Larry's side gig as a bootlegger of allegedly top-dollar loudspeakers; his homemade "dietary supplements" were no match for the goods on offer from the multilevel-marketing moms of Katy and Fort Worth. The Great Recession killed his few legitimate ventures: even Cutco cut him off. Debts accrued: to cartel-adjacent strongmen and prison gang consiglieres, 8K and counting to the Aryan Brotherhood of Texas.

By 2014, Larry spent his days drinking cheap beer at coastal dives—his actual schnoz almost as red as his foam one—telling anyone who would listen tales that quickly descended into bibulous lunacy. "Yes, Lucky Larry's Clown Spectacular. Beaucoup bucks and a near-perfect batting average!"

The Cepeda scheme was a last-gasp effort, a far cry from the razzle-dazzle of his big-top days. To understand it, Larry told Alexis, required "a tale of three news stories." Back in '08, Larry had come across a newspaper article commemorating the anniversary of the disappearance of a boy with a familiar name. *Nathaniel Rothstein*. Larry had acquired the license in the late nineties, but teenage boys had never been The Clown's typical clientele, and he'd sat on it a few years, waiting for the perfect clownling to use it on. Sat on it, literally: Larry had the thing in his own wallet so long, he could still picture Rothstein's face, even knew the kid's date of birth.

After the '08 article came out, Larry had tried to get some money off the boy's uncle, who'd been quoted in the story. He found the man's address in the phone book and, in the middle of the night, left a note on his windshield with Nathaniel's birthdate: *10/27/81*. Larry's plan had been to follow the uncle around the next day and, when the opportunity arose, corner him and offer what he knew about his nephew's whereabouts in exchange for a few shekels. But lo and behold, when Larry started tailing him before sunup, the uncle had driven straight to Terry Tucker's Boxing Gym, the same gym where Larry had stashed his twin. "Little too much of a co-inky-dink for Larry Hooley," he told Alexis now, which was why he'd abandoned the whole thing.

"Wait," said Alexis, "are you saying *Nathaniel Rothstein* is a *missing person? From the gym*?" Alexis wasn't sure when it happened or how, but at some point he'd lost his good luck license, had always felt bad about it. Now he felt a surge of relief. The last thing he'd needed as he built up his career was to be carrying around the ID of some missing kid.

"Try to keep up," said Larry. "*Story number two*." Some months after the Rothstein article appeared, Larry was watching the local news and a syndicated story out of Austin came on. It was a fluff piece, "feel-good crap," about a young boxer named Alexis Cepeda who never got into the ring without first giving a fellow in his corner a lucky fake punch to the belly. "Proudest moment of my life seeing my brother on the TV."

"Where are you going with all this?" asked Alexis.

"About a month ago, my debts finally caught up with me," said Larry. More specifically, a biker-bearded Brobdingnagian—his leather vest embroidered with SS bolts and the othala rune—cornered Larry at 3 a.m. in a Port Aransas alleyway. Said his name was The Owl.

"Guessing that moniker ain't on account of a Rice graduation," Larry told the man.

The Owl was unamused. "Owls eat weasels," he'd said, jabbing a Sig Sauer Mosquito into Larry's belly. Larry had thirty days to pay off his 8K loan, with significant interest. If not: "dinnertime," said The Owl. His final words as he disappeared into the darkness: "Hoot hoot."

The next morning, Larry said, he went to Restaurant Cozumel, a two-table joint with a floor tacky as flypaper, where he ordered a chilaquiles plate with extra jalapeños and two Modelos. He planned to keep the grog coming until he ended up in the clink or dead, an exploded liver preferable to The Owl determining how many licks it took to get to the center of Larry Hooley.

A fiend for heat, Larry plucked the jalapeños into his mouth barehanded as he ate, then retired to the trash-riddled unisex restroom to take a leak, forgetting first to wash his peppered fingertips. Soon he had his pants around his ankles and was straddling the can, cursing loudly while attempting to dunk his scorching sack into the toilet water. Larry didn't have the muscle for that particular maneuver, but it was from this position that he noticed what he'd later dub "notable litter from a previous sitter": a single page of the sports section from the *Port Aransas South Jetty*. The top headline: TEXAN CEPEDA TAPPED TO BATTLE CHEVALIER IN ATLANTA. "*Story number three*," said Larry. "And that's when it came to me. Like Moses, I'd found God courtesy of a burning bush!"

At this Alexis said to Larry Hooley eight words that Larry had heard many times before. "Dude. *I have no idea what you're talking about.*"

"Which part?" said Larry.

"I don't understand the words coming out of your mouth."

On the unmade bed in the Port Aransas beach motel where he'd been staying, Larry had left a suicide note, bidding farewell to his beloved identical twin, and wishing him luck on his career in Alexis's corner. He assumed The Owl would find it when he came looking for his money.

"I've been told if I don't pay, that will be the end of Larry Hooley," said Larry Hooley. "And so it was written." The end of Larry and the rebirth of Ed. The #1 becomes #2. "A Hooley switcheroo."

"You want me to help you hide out as your brother?" said Alexis. "And why would I do that?"

Larry dropped the grin. "Because if you don't," he snarled, "I'll tell everyone you ain't here legal."

In Alexis's memory, The Clown had possessed near-supernatural power. Now Alexis considered the purple bags under the man's eyes, the tattletale delivery of this pathetic threat. Like some good-old-boy legislator who'd missed the memo that he could no longer spit out the n-word on the floor of the Senate, Larry's failure to adapt had extended to his demagoguery, which was no longer in step with the times. A lover of euphemism, he somehow didn't know the dog whistles of the day, *Black-on-Black crime* and *long-form birth certificate* as foreign to his vocabulary as *skilled worker visa.*

"Good effort, clown," said Alexis. "But I'm about to have the biggest fight of my life, so I should probably, like, *warm up*."

"Wait," said Larry, a new desperation overtaking him. "I'll pay you. When I get back on my feet. Four K."

"No can do, man."

"Five if I can muster it. These guys, they'll *kill me*. Do you want Hooley blood on those hands?"

"The only one with Hooley blood on his hands," said Alexis, "is you." He started to go, realized he had more to say. "Did you even check on him? After you left him there?"

"I did," said Larry, pleading. "I swear. That's why I'd come to Austin in the first place. Least once or twice a year." Larry would park across the road from the gym, wait to spot Ed before driving away. "He'd always come out, my brother. Doing some chore. And then one day, about a year ago, he didn't."

"So you just gave up?"

"I looked for him best I knew how. Every few months. I went all over town looking. Eventually, I moved on. Ed was better off without me anyway. Always had been."

"Better off abandoned?" said Alexis with a smirk. "You know your problem, man? You're a *liar*. Your brother was weird as fuck, but Ed was *nice*. And he told the truth. In all this time, I don't think you've told me one true thing."

"A brother's love is nothing to be trifled with."

"Yeah, whatever," said Alexis. "You didn't give a single shit about Ed."

"Now, that ain't true—"

"You left him and didn't look back—"

"That's just not the way it went down—" said Larry, louder.

"You think it's OK just to leave people like that? And what'd you get in return? Nothing. *Nothing*. You're just a drunk old loser."

It came out angrier than Alexis intended, angrier than Alexis realized he was, the wobbly fury of a child made sturdy in the body of a man. He always *had* presented the clown thing as funny; even though it was a true story, maybe he'd been deflecting, too.

Larry licked his lips, determined not to show he'd been wounded. "Well, son, it was worth a shot, right?"

"Sure, clown."

Larry turned to go, hesitated, turned back. "I just thought it'd be bigger is all," he said. Then, softer, "I thought I'd be bigger."

Alexis went to speak, stopped himself. He tried again. Nothing. He may not have been a gym person, but like all gym people, maybe like all people, Alexis Cepeda understood wanting more. You get one life, one chance. Larry Hooley had used his up.

In part he did it because Alexis didn't do baggage, and having a dead man on his conscience, even this man, was more weight than he wanted to carry. In part, he did it because Larry forced to live as his brother seemed like an elegant punishment for his crimes. Mostly, he did it because in a strange way it felt simpler than not doing it. Terry Tucker may not have been his trainer any longer, but Alexis had never had a better tutor in the art of strategic nonchalance. The boxer could expend energy fighting the specter of a vengeful Hooley or he could let Larry expend that energy pretending to be Ed.

"You want to do it, you gotta *do* it, OK?" said Alexis. "You want to be Ed in my corner, you're Ed out of my corner." The twitching eye, the gentle spirit. "No more playing-the-clown shit. You're playing a good person now. *Twenty-four seven*."

"What about my neck?" said Larry.

Alexis told him they had Band-Aids inside. He started back toward the loading area.

"So you think I can pull it off?" asked Larry, not yet following behind.

"I doubt it," said Alexis without turning around. "Now c'mon."

* * *

Later, years later, on stretches of the internet that do not yet exist, you'll learn you were not the first.

Ricardo Reyes of Topeka, Kansas, mistaken for Ricardo Reyes of Toledo, Ohio. Syed Ibrahim, three DUIs, and Syed Ibrahim, one DDS: swapped. Ten years after your disappearance, a white American man with an olive complexion and a slew of intellectual disabilities will be arrested for assault in Louisiana and, courtesy of a sloppy intake clerk at a medium-security prison, be listed as another man with another name and deported to interior Mexico. He'll roam that land for years, lost and destitute, staggering south through Central American towns whose names he can't pronounce, eating garbage in Ojojona, in Sensuntepeque, saved from dying a vagrant only due to a chance encounter on a microbus in San Salvador with an earnest intern from the U.S. embassy there. Eventually, the man will be returned to his original name, his original country, though not the country he thought he'd come from, not after something like that.

The story is so unbelievable that, had you been sixteen when you'd heard it, you wouldn't have believed it. The story is not as unbelievable as yours.

If they'd thought you were from Cuba or Canada, Costa Rica or Chile, you'd have remained in the Travis County jail a few days or more, your skin paling, until a judge considered the strange, bronzed creature before her, the one who'd told seven different officers his name was Rothstein, until she or they or someone in the courtroom put that fact together with the UT professor they'd seen on the local news the Tuesday after your disappearance: a lanky fellow, hand over brow to block the sun. "If he's watching this? I'd tell him my sister is gonna kill me if he doesn't get his butt back here." Then, serious: "Come on, kid. Come home."

But Haiti is the country on your passport, which means the U.S. immigration laws that are supposed to apply to everyone but don't apply to everyone especially don't apply to you. The courts may not be known for their swiftness, but there are ways to get things moving when they're eager to bid someone adieu. (Or not adieu. Rarely adieu. Adios, kwaheri. Orevwa!)

You are used to keeping things inside, used to, when confronted with conflict or discomfort or something you don't understand, simply taking your batteries out, and this is how you manage the first evening and following day, how you cope with your high-on-something bottom bunkmate, who gabbles all night in the oddly formal syntax of the oft-incarcerated—"You know what I need? A *female*. Damn!"—before falling asleep in time with a sunrise neither of you can see.

In brief moments of inspiration, you try to reason with passing guards. A couple times, you give them your uncle's name—*please, just call him*—point out that it's his Volvo still parked at the scene of the fight. But no one is listening to what you have to say, and by the time the police *do* start looking for the Volvo, it will already have fallen victim to Shady Creek's resident buttinsky, a cocker rescue volunteer named Dot Meese who, having noticed a doesn't-belong-here vehicle a few nights running, will report it to the property manager, who will call the towing company, a notoriously sketchy South Austin operation whose owner will wait six of the required thirty days a car must be impounded before selling it part by part.

No, no one is listening to what you have to say, but you're sixteen: until this summer, no one has ever listened to what you have to say. So you keep your batteries out, comforted by the knowledge that your aunt and uncle must be looking for you, that your skin will soon lighten. Comforted by the one assurance you've been given all your life. *Everything will turn out OK.*

And so, when a woman who has the same tweed jacket and tired eyes of many of your high school teachers, who wears the same lanyard of credentials and carries her files in the same bulky rollaboard, when this sigh of a woman meets you in a bare room with a metal desk bolted to the floor and tells you there is no need to be scared, she knows the truth, and that if you initial here and sign here and date here then you can go home, you do.

The fact that the name you sign—NATHANIEL ROTHSTEIN—and the name on the document are not the same name will go unnoticed, by this woman and by everyone else. To notice is to care, and there are no diplomats in Washington whose interests are entangled with the immigration service getting this one right. You haven't paid close attention to the document either, which is why you assume *home* is Austin, or Newton. Why you assume this is the end of the story and not its beginning.

Dinner passes, lights-out passes. You fall asleep, are woken up. Cuffed again. More tile-walled halls, bright fluorescents. A stairwell draped in coin vinyl flooring. Through a metal door and into the hot garbage smell of another Austin summer night.

A loading dock behind the building. An unmarked white van. Outside it, two beefy, bearded men in ball caps, one auburn-haired, one blond, their badges clipped to the front pockets of their tactical pants. A silver star encircling the words UNITED STATES MARSHAL.

You have begun to acclimate to law enforcement. The line between captor and captive is thin, the caustic humor and quickness to anger as common among officers as inmates. The key to surviving is to never acknowledge this kinship. As the marshals and the cops joke—"So we meet again," "Good to see you assholes too"—you don't make eye contact, know that a smile or a shake of the head, any indication that you're listening, that you're part of it, will lead to trouble.

Was I talking to him? Was I talking to you? What could I have possibly said that gave you the impression I was talking to you?

They're the new officers, same as the old officers, as impenetrable as the black lenses in their wraparound sunglasses, which wait for dawn on the brims of their ball caps.

You have already been trained to comply without complaint, know there is safety in silence, which is why, though you've been promised freedom, you say nothing during the exchange of handcuffs: off with APD's, on with the marshals'. Why you say nothing as a belly chain is wrapped around your waist, the cuffs fastened to it so you can't raise your hands, as leg locks are shackled over your ankles.

The blond officer slides open the van door, takes a step stool out, and places it on the ground with a controlled ire that lets you know he's following a procedure he doesn't care for.

Up you go. Out of downtown, onto the interstate headed north.

Bars separate you from the marshals up front. You don't bother attempting eye contact, remain focused on the passing exits.

Georgetown. Temple. Bruceville-Eddy.

Thirty minutes pass, an hour. Why didn't they just let Bob pick you up, like the dad did for the kid with the New Balances? Or, at worst, put you on a plane back to Massachusetts? You try to ignore these questions.

Talk to no one, look at no one. Follow the instructions and you can go home.

* * *

May 17, 2014. 8:43 p.m.

They didn't see him.

Not Bob Alexander, nor Terry Tucker. Not any of the people he didn't know, either, which, by then, was most people. Perhaps, metaphorically, no one at the gym had ever really seen David Dalice. Now they literally didn't see him, either. They were too fixated on the television, on a close-up of—what was *he* doing there?—Ed Hooley.

Only Felix Barrowman, leaning against the far wall, noticed the tall, lumbering figure lingering in the doorway. Felix was on the phone, checking in with his fiancée, who'd opted to pass on the night's proceedings. A lot had happened in Felix's life since he'd returned from Malindi without Carlos Ortega five years earlier. It would be too much to say he came back a changed man: the change, in fact, had started before he journeyed to coastal Kenya and continued well after. Still, he did say it.

"Things are gonna be different now," he'd told Terry, upon returning. The Felix of that second was, of course, the product of every single second of life leading up to it, but he wanted to make clear to his old trainer—wanted to make clear to himself—that before was before and after was after. Felix told Terry that the night of the storm, the night Carlos Ortega blew away, he'd watched a man wholly in his element. "That guy," he'd said, "was doing exactly what he was meant to be doing."

Felix had long known that he, on the other hand, had not been. "It's the thing I'm very best at and I'm not good enough" was what he believed, though it was too painful to say. Instead, Felix told Terry a different truth: in Kenya he'd discovered that maybe he didn't need to get out of boxing. Maybe what he needed was to get out of the ring.

"Sounds familiar," said Terry. Terry offered one-on-one sessions for $50 a pop, and soon he was handing clients off to Felix, whose professional background made him a bigger draw than the eponymous gym owner. The dynamics that had always been at play at the boxing gym—mostly white just-for-fun-ers willing to pay up for an "authentic" experience—were supersized with a handsome Black ex-contender now available for private lessons. With Terry's blessing, Felix upped his hourly rate to $65.

Even if the Malindi epiphany hadn't occurred exclusively in Malindi, it did change Felix Barrowman. He officially hung up his gloves, began dating one of his few Black clients, Monica Hidalgo-Grant, the morning anchor on KXAN's weekend show. "Why aren't any of you TV people named something simple, like Joan Smith?" he'd asked after she introduced herself. On their first date, Monica took him to Fonda San Miguel for dinner. "I'm not paid by the hour and I have excellent benefits, so it's my treat," she'd said on the ride over. At the maître d' stand, she greeted the hostess warmly. "It's under Joan Smith," she said.

As a trainer, Felix took on a few amateurs, then a couple of pros. Slow progress interspersed with setbacks, small but genuine improvement: this was a language Felix understood. He prized consistency and told his clients that if they could give him that, they'd find this work rewarding. He liked being around people who got down to it. The boxing gym had always been his place.

After Terry's diagnosis, Felix started taking on administrative duties, welcoming folks in. That work, he was surprised to find, suited him, too. He remembered names, faces. Felix Barrowman saw his people. He saw David Dalice.

The trainer saluted his old friend with his free hand, then pointed to the woman standing a few feet away. *Sasha*, Felix mouthed. David nodded, headed her way.

* * *

August 11, 1998. 4:39 a.m. Love Field, Dallas.

A puddle-jumper, as your mom would say, so small you can see into the cockpit. In addition to the marshals behind you, there are two Black men chained in the same restraints you are. The one next to you is skeletal, dreaded; the other pudgy, mustached. Both wear bright orange jumpsuits. On the tarmac, a Benneton ad of patrol cars: DPD, DPS, Customs Service, Department of Aviation.

You keep your eyes out the window as the pilot reverses and the cars start to disperse. If you dared to turn back you would see that the marshals have put on their sunglasses. Over their polos, they now wear bulletproof vests.

* * *

May 17, 2014. 8:45 p.m.

David didn't think he'd seen Sasha before. Nor had Sasha ever seen him. Slacks, khaki golf cap, pink guayabera. Gray mustache, gray brows. An old man.

He took off his hat, introduced himself.

"I know this is weird," said Sasha. "Should we maybe go somewhere a little less—"

"Please," said David, leading the way.

In the darkened weight room, they settled onto two utility benches parked parallel to each other, David sighing a little as he went down. "You get to be my age, it gets difficult to sit. Difficult to hear." He chuckled. "Difficult." He surveyed their surroundings: weights racked, machines unplugged. "Don't know if I've ever seen this room so empty. I haven't been here in a few years."

"It different than the last time?" asked Sasha.

"Oh, this place doesn't change," said David. "The older I get, the less I think anything changes."

"Some things change," said Sasha. "I hope you didn't have to come too far."

"Not every day I'm told a mysterious stranger is hot on my trail." He peered at her. "You are a stranger, right?"

"I think so," said Sasha. "I— " She hesitated.

"You're making me nervous," said David.

"Oh lord, well— " An apologetic wince. There was no way to say it but to say it. "Back when I was in high school, I made a friend with your name. I know David is a common name, but this person, he was in Austin, and he was of your, well, nationality. He was Haitian. And he said he went to a boxing gym."

"*Sounds* like me. Did he *look* like me?"

"Well, that's the thing. We never met. We had a sort of telephone romance, I guess, and . . . well, the details don't really matter. But it was . . . *formative*."

"A romance?" said David, his tone hardening.

"It wasn't the *classiest* moment of my life, but— "

"Miss, I'm sixty-three years old. Are you asking me if I had some sort of relationship with a young student when I was a grown man?"

"Oh gosh, no, I'm— "

"Because respectfully, I don't think I've seen or spoken to you ever in my life."

David inspected his hands, took a deep breath. Neither of them had expected this flash of anger. "I was asking for this one," he said, regaining his composure. "Every few years I come by this place and it's always something. My wife, she always tells me, 'David, do not go to the boxing gym!' She thinks it stirs up too much inside me. I always tell her, 'Ramona, the past is past,' you know?"

"I didn't mean to imply—" started Sasha. "I'm not trying to accuse you of—"

"But I had good friends here. Good memories." He jabbed the air. "You ever tried it?"

Sasha said she hadn't.

"When you're inside the ring, it's a wonderful thing! Even if everyone thinks they know you, thinks they know what you're all about, when you're throwing those punches, none of it matters. In there, you're how *you* see you." David shook his head. "But then the bell rings, and you walk down those metal steps, and you're back. You're here. And here it is always some bullshit." He stood to go. "I'm too old to keep coming back to this place. So I wish you luck, madam, but I am not your David."

He started to shuffle off. "Wait," said Sasha, rising. "I'm so sorry to have upset you. This David, my David, he was my age. Or just about. As soon as I realized you weren't that, I should've had Felix call you—"

David turned back. "Then why didn't you? Is my time not worth anything?"

"No it's not that," said Sasha. "I guess I thought you might have some link to it. Some idea who this person was. All I know is that summer of '98 was such a turning point for me. My life *did* change, is the thing. *I* changed it, and for the better. I—"

David squinted. "Did you say the summer of *1998*?"

"'98, yeah. We started talking that June and he was supposed to come over one night in August, never showed," said Sasha. "August 8, 1998. Sixteen years later and I still remember it."

"August 8, 1998," repeated David.

"That's the date," said Sasha. "It mean anything to you?"

* * *

The houses are built into the hills, cinder-block houses painted azure, salmon, lime.

Focus on them and maybe you won't throw up: from the unceasing traffic, diesel fumes forever sputtering out of passing dump trucks;

from the road itself, the potholes long and wide as dug graves. You've been in the backseat of the lieutenant's car for almost an hour, but only in the last few minutes has your breath settled, has the worst of your body odor, which had begun to travel, returned to your pits.

This isn't like any place you've been before. Here there are roads too narrow to accommodate two-way traffic that somehow still do, and roads wider than any back home, bustling with painted minibuses and motorcycles.

A few stretches are barren. Others teem with vendors who hawk their wares from woven baskets or wheelbarrows, from underneath umbrellas or in their hands. Here everything is for sale. A long-limbed confectioner stands watch over a folding table, his goods laid out like artifacts: a miniature Krackle, a warped 100 Grand. Here people sell things you've known were bought but have never seen sold: live chickens, coal.

The afternoon is sweltering, yet in this place the sweat stains and matted hair of an Austin August are nowhere to be found. Down one side street, you spy two little girls in matching dresses chasing each other, their socks a startling white. For a whole city block, the lieutenant drives parallel to a man carrying a refrigerator strapped to his back. The refrigerator man chats amiably with his fellow pedestrians, points and waves like the strongest politician in the world.

You're pretty sure this is a poor place but you've also passed outdoor cafés and bars and a shopping mall, passed a red, white, and blue symbol so familiar you turned back to make sure you'd seen it correctly, the only sign you recognize from home. Domino's.

There's so much happening it feels as if each street is its own city, yet none of the streets seem like they'd belong to any other city, the only appropriate city for these disparate cities right here.

Here, no one is white.

Up front, the lieutenant listens to a radio program. He is portly, dispassionate, breathes like a purring cat. He has barely spoken during this long drive, has not mentioned where you are going or what his intentions are. He has not told you how you ended up in the back of his car.

Every now and again, the lieutenant observes you through the rearview mirror, and each time he does he says, with a nostalgia you have never associated with these two words: "Newton, Mass."

This is what you remember.

An airport police station. Grimy, bustling. Officers dressed as if they're playing cops for Halloween: ostentatious yellow stripes down the side seams of their pants, old-fashioned police hats. The others you flew in with—the dreaded man, the pudgy man—beside you on a bench, hands zip-tied behind your backs. The U.S. marshals nowhere on the scene.

The dreaded man is stoic. The pudgy man: a blubbering mess. He wails, weeps, begs in a language you don't recognize. Most of the officers tune him out, attend to paperwork. One keeps looking up. The crying man cries on, the officer rises. He smacks him across the face with his baton, returns to his desk.

Unlike the others, the lieutenant wears a suit. He gives quiet instructions to his subordinates; they take the dreaded man one way, the pudgy man another. To you, he offers a short command and, when you don't know how to respond, signals with his index finger for you to stand.

An intense dizziness. The wild heat that precedes throwing up. All you can think to do is that same old song and dance. It's desperate this time, embarrassing. You can barely get it out.

—Please please. You stifle a dry heave, say your birth name. Say your home city, home state.

There is no need to hit you with a baton.

—America, you manage, and then you're on the ground.

A sleepy street far from the hustle-bustle of downtown.

The lieutenant pulls up to a small blue house. There is a Wild West vibe to this place: a scraggly dog trots down the dusty road; across the way, two men sit in plastic lawn chairs playing dominoes, the table between them a legless piece of plywood they balance on their knees.

From the driver's seat, the lieutenant explains he knows the place you say you've come from well. A few years prior, the government here disbanded the military and placed the police force under civilian control. Several select up-and-comers were chosen to receive training in the States. "MS in criminal justice from Boston College," he says. "Newton, Mass."

As you have not been charged with any crime, were not wanted in this country for any crime, the lieutenant assures you that you're free to go. But after you passed out, he did take the liberty of examining your file. Given that you look nothing like the man in your passport photograph, given that there's no way you're the age of that man, given that you appear to speak only English and seem to have no idea where you are or why, he's inclined to believe this is a case of mistaken identity. "I've dealt with those marshals before," he says. "We all look alike to them, right?"

Tonight you will stay with a friend of his. Tomorrow, he will call your family. If you're telling the truth, you will need a bureaucratic in-fighter on your side to get it all straightened. "And resources," he adds. "But where you come from that should be no problem." You are old enough to understand the threat implicit in his delivery.

The lieutenant is not a bad man. He has never quasi-kidnapped anyone before, has only a vague sense of how to pull it off. If you were white, he'd never have risked it; the lieutenant has no intention of starring in an international incident. But for forty-four years he has played by the rules while watching his most unscrupulous colleagues rise and rise. Of the select up-and-comers, the others run their own divisions. The lieutenant spends his days at the airport.

He did not seek you out. But before you fainted you said, "Newton, Mass.," and this was a coincidence too rich to ignore. What were the chances?

A woman lives in the small blue house. She wears a roomy white shirt and long black skirt, her hair wrapped in a black scarf. She is neither friendly nor unfriendly, shows you to a beige love seat in the modest living room. Once, this woman was indebted to the lieutenant, and though she is not in a position to refuse the young prisoner he has requested she stash here, their relationship is well-worn enough that she does not have to hide her displeasure at the ask.

The lieutenant departs. The woman retreats to the adjacent kitchen, starts the kettle. You are afraid of the lieutenant, but she is not, and this makes you not afraid of her. By the time she returns with a cup of tea, you're asleep.

In two hours, you will wake. What will happen then is beyond your imagination. But given that already this summer you've seduced a Russian phone sex operator by pretending to be Haitian and gotten deported in the process, perhaps this says more about your imagination than it does about the world.

It's still light when you hear it.

That noise.

How could it be? You wonder if it is an aural mirage, the still-warm leftovers from a just-ended dream. Except it keeps going, this unexpected wake-up call, keeps going as you remember where and who you are.

The woman sits on a love seat opposite you, reading a magazine. You look to the front door, look to her. She shrugs: *Come, go, not my problem*. She knows you will not wander far.

Out of the little blue house and into the street. Before this summer, you never would've done something so bold as venture out alone into this unknown land. But you know that noise, trust it. Past the other houses, past the scraggly dog curled up in the middle of the road.

Round a corner and the neighborhood gives way to a vast field. Dead grass, dirt. In the middle, as promised, it stands.

You've been here before, to this place you've been told you can find in every city in the country, in most countries in the world. Down an alley and up a creaky staircase in Tokyo; in church basements in Belfast and Boston; through the unmarked doors of crumbling buildings in Philadelphia and Fortaleza, Rawalpindi and Rome. On east sides and outskirts. In a moldering ex-theater in Sarajevo where the stage plays the ring, and in the smoldering back room of a butchery in the Sudanese town of Umm Dam, where the *Rocky*-loving proprietor-cum-trainer has substituted gaunt goats hanging from meat hooks for Sly's thick sides of beef. In rec centers and strip malls. An old mechanic's garage.

It may not be much to look at, this place, preferably it isn't: the other patrons can joke about the pool on the second floor, but it's just a joke, if the place is legitimate, there is no pool, there is no second floor, just leather against flesh, flesh against bone, rope slapping concrete, slapping earth, that machine-gun fire of sideways fists against speed bag.

Badada badada badada badada.

You can hear it in Manila and Malindi, Managua and Montreal.

You can hear it from a little blue house on a sleepy street in Port-au-Prince, around the corner from a boxing gym that seems to have sprung whole out of a field.

An unfinished building. Three cinder-block walls, one side open, like a diorama, the action facing you. This place is not the same as your place, but even from a distance you can see it is—

Same junkyard of old equipment spread around the periphery, a post-apocalyptic Gold's: an overturned truck tire; a bench of rusted metal, long ago stripped of its leather and foam; a rowing machine, its cord plugged into nothing, a coiled tail.

Same coterie of movers and sitters. You know the three jabbering men sitting atop upside-down paint buckets outside, men expressive as ASL interpreters, legs wide. Rawboned men in ragged cuffed khakis and A-shirts, less in conversation with each other than engaged in overlapping monologues, arguing politics or sports or boasting about sex, high off their own umbrage, men whose eyes never veer far from what's happening inside, and in their watching reveal a second conversation each is having with himself: about what was, what could've been. What should have been.

The inside men are different. The inside men are punching toward the future. Your Pied Piper is a rangy dude in a striped tank top, his flute his speed bag, which hasn't stopped ping-ponging between backboard and bare fists since you awakened to the sound. Elsewhere is the regular hodgepodge of slim, sinewy, shredded; tenderfoot and warhorse; agile and less so. The brawniest among them groans his way through a set on a rusted pull-up bar. The scrawniest skips rope in the dead grass.

It isn't an exact replica. No garage doors. No beer guts, either. No one much past forty. In the center, in the ring: a small fighter, packed tight. Red trunks, black racerback tank. She ducks and slides across the canvas, the fastest one there. *Pa! Pa-pa!*

The noise begins to fade. The singsong patter from the paint bucket crew, the *badada* of the speed bag, the *pa pa pa* of the woman in the center of the ring. They stop, one after the other, stop and turn, turn and squint, a dozen sailors peering through their telescopes out to sea.

You are a sight coming at them. The striped prison jumpsuit. Too-big sandals flip-flopping in the dirt.

They stop and you stop, and you turn too, turn back, once, toward the road from which you came.

"Vini la!" One of the paint bucket men half-stands, hands braced on knees. The others shush him, scold him. *You don't know who that boy is. Why are you inviting over a prisoner?* He brushes them off, beckons.

Now the gym's dialed-down audio knob is turned clockwise once more. Cross-talk. Muttered interjections. Incoming fire: questions shouted, good-natured (?) ribbing. The woman is skeptical. A ropy redhead by a heavy bag is more curious. *Let's see what he can do.*

The paint bucket man—craggy-faced, mustache full as a nineties Newton dad's—holds out his arm as if you've fallen overboard. *Come to me*, those arms are saying, and you do. "Bon, bon." He slaps at your upper arms, squeezes a bicep. Satisfied, he grabs your wrist.

* * *

May 17, 2014. 9:12 p.m.

What happened to Nathaniel Rothstein?

In the weight room at Terry Tucker's Boxing Gym, David admits he doesn't know. He does not tell Sasha about the pills or the tanning or the fight outside Shady Creek. He does not tell her about calling the police. Nor does he confess that the next afternoon, no Nathaniel in sight, he called APD himself, worried that he was the cause of the vanishing. They assured him no one with that name had been arrested in the previous twenty-four hours. Eventually, the case went cold. Nathaniel's car and keys and cell phone would never be recovered.

Instead, David Dalice tells a different truth: about a boy who came to Austin as one thing and slowly became another. "He was a shy guy," says David. "But there was a bolder version of him. Waiting to break out. And he started to, right here. With me."

Sometimes, David still imagines what would've happened if the boy had stuck with boxing, if David had developed his own little squad of fighters. "Don't get me wrong. He was no natural talent. But he wanted something, you know? I don't even know if he knew what it was. But *something*. I always liked that about him."

"Maybe that's what I liked about him too," says Sasha. "He was lucky to have you."

"Oh, I don't know about that." David asks Sasha if she met the old man with the eyebrows. "Bob was his uncle."

"Wait . . ." says Sasha. "So my David, your Nathaniel, he was *white*?"

David and Sasha will meet only once, on this Saturday night. There is too much neither would consider telling the other for them to get anywhere close to what happened sixteen years before. They instead spend forty-five minutes talking around their mutual acquaintance.

These are stories they haven't considered in years. "She was a real Italian, that woman. No use for timidity. And she couldn't stand that boy!" "The Days Inn off I-35: not exactly the Four Seasons, right? But that night? I thought it was so fancy."

Next month, Sasha Markham will make her move to Phoenix. It is there she'll marry, settle. By the end of her life, she'll have spent more years in Arizona than she did in Texas. But sometimes, after a bad day or an especially good one, she'll become wistful for the city of her birth. She'll miss not a place but a feeling, a feeling she can't explain in words but only in moments. The only-in-high-school exhilaration of making a not-from-childhood best friend. After a shift working the stuffy drive-thru at the Whataburger, the relief of walking home surrounded by all that air. Encountering a stranger at a boxing gym, a man different from her in almost every way, in whom she still found a little of herself.

At 9:50, Felix pops his head into the weight room. The fight is starting, if they're interested.

David and Sasha return to the main room, to the television, just as Alexis Cepeda enters the arena in his blue satin robe, his corner following in their CEPEDA TOUGH T-shirts and jeans. In the ring, Alexis doffs his robe, and then, as he's done so many times before, gives Ed Hooley a jab in the gut. The shock of seeing Ed is such that, for the second time that night, no one at the gym notices the two Band-Aids on their old friend's neck.

Nor does anyone at the gym think what happens next is especially unusual, as Mozart "Socka Doc" Chevalier's impressive entourage begins its journey to the ring.

No one, that is, except David Dalice.

On the screen: a dozen shirtless Black men outfitted in knee-high boots and fitted white britches and tight-fitting military jackets that stop at their midriffs, like some lunatic offshoot of Napoleon's Grande Armée.

Theirs is a mischievous, manic energy. They boost themselves up on each other's shoulders, raise their hands to hype the crowd, their gold epaulettes shaking like the grass dresses of hula girls. Amid these shenanigans, the man bringing up the rear—the fighter himself—is almost an afterthought. He wears the Haitian flag like a cape.

Halfway up the aisle, the whole crew begins doing a peculiar sort of jig. *This can't be*, thinks David. He looks to Felix, chatting with a couple of clients, only half paying attention to the television. He looks to Terry, who watches unperturbed, his mind no longer capable, perhaps, of recognizing the meaning of the movements on the screen.

In single file, each member of Mozart's crew takes two steps forward, one hop back. And *clap*! They do this all the way up the aisle, a little army so devoted to their crisp performance that it's difficult to pay attention to any one man, too much pizzazz to focus on the details.

* * *

You never know.

A little blue house starts as a prison and morphs into a refuge. Strip a filling station of all its pumps but one and suddenly it's an homage to a filling station, then an homage to the homage. Cities grow, or they die. People die, or they don't. Put a confused kid in the ring as one thing and twelve rounds later he's another.

Your uncle came closest. He knew you'd tried to change your skin. In his version, your old race was your privilege and your new race your punishment.

But that isn't your story, Mozart Chevalier. It's just the only one that your uncle could imagine.

Your real story starts on an August day in 1998, when you come upon a boxing gym off a sleepy side street in a city you'd never even heard of three months before.

Bob Alexander will never figure out exactly what happened to you, or why, but the answer to this moment is right in front of him.

It's in front of all the denizens of Terry Tucker's Boxing Gym every time they pull into the gravel lot, sign the sign-in sheet, go down the step. It's in front of them now, on a big-screen television in the center of the ring.

As your self-appointed trainer—the paint bucket man—leads you deeper into the gym, the long man returns to his speed bag and the brawny man to his pull-ups and the woman in the ring flicks her wrist—*enough with you*—and gets back to work.

The ropy redhead has returned to his heavy bag, but now the paint bucket man barks at him to move out of the way. The redhead does, and your new trainer braces himself against the back of the bag.

Later, you will return to the country that you vanished from that fateful summer of 1998. Later, you will return with your new name and your new skin and your tangled reasons for keeping both.

But that is a story for a different day.

Today, right now, there is only you and this heavy bag, so much duct tape that it seems like it might only be duct tape, wrapped and wrapped and wrapped.

Today, right now, there is only one way you can go.

On the television at Terry Tucker's Boxing Gym, the referee gives his instructions. David leans in. This is a feeling he knows well, that moment just before whatever is to happen happens, when anything still can.

"Goumen, pitit!" calls the trainer, in this language you don't speak. In this language you do.

On the television, the boxers tap gloves.

Hands up, elbows in.

"Goumen! Goumen!"

Fight, my child.

Fight!

Acknowledgments

Anyone who believes the canard that "editors don't edit" has never worked with Tim O'Connell. Tim's sense of what this book needed and how to make it happen proved, over and over, infuriatingly correct. One thing I've learned from Tim about writing fiction is that sometimes what seems like a detour isn't a detour—it's the route. Thank you not only for your guidance but also for giving me the time and the freedom to chart my own zigzagging course.

Thanks, too, to everyone at Simon & Schuster who worked on *The Slip*: Samantha Hoback, Sara Kitchen, Martha Langford, John McGhee, Maria Mendez, Lewelin Polanco, Danielle Prielipp, and Jack Smyth. Special thanks to Anna Hauser for guiding this first-time novelist through the ins and outs of the editorial process.

Thank you to my agent, Christopher Schelling. If there were a field of medicine dedicated to making worried writers maintain their confidence and sanity in the fickle face of the publishing industry, Christopher would have a Nobel Prize in Medicine. Your faith in this project allowed me to keep the faith, too, even in those moments when success felt far away.

The Slip was written with crucial support from the Studios of Key West, the Vermont Studio Center, and the Wellstone Center in the Redwoods. I'm grateful, too, to the fellow artists I learned from in those places (especially my Key West co-conspirator, Jean Fineberg, and Liz Arnold and Liz Latty in Vermont).

Thank you to the Corsicana Artist and Writer Residency for two highly productive stints in your city. Thanks to Kyle Hobratschk, Nancy Rebal, David Searcy, Wayne Hall, Amanda Valdez, and everyone else who made those experiences so special. Thanks also to Gwen

Chance and the GW Jackson Multicultural Society for their generous support of my time there.

Parts of *The Slip* were workshopped under the singular guidance of Joy Williams at the Juniper Summer Writing Institute and at the Cuttyhunk Island Writers' Residency with Hernan Diaz, whose keen observations about a pivotal chapter transformed my approach to revision.

Thank you to the literary magazines that have allowed characters from *The Slip* into their pages, and to the editors who helped bring those characters to life. A special shout-out to Patrick Ryan at *One Story* for treating my work and the work of so many debut writers with such tremendous care. Thank you to J. W. McCormack at *The Baffler*, Bobby Rea and Mary Klein at *Southwest Review*, Laura Spence-Ash at *CRAFT*, and Jake Wolff at *The Florida Review*.

While any factual errors in the novel are my own, I'm grateful to those who helped me avoid making more of them, especially Taisia Kitaiskaia and Ben Philippe for guidance on translation, and Rachel Guberman, who (whom?) I have been debating literature and grammar with since Mr. Jampol's ninth-grade English class. Thanks to Holly Holmes for putting up with my many questions about boxing terminology and choreography, and for years of friendship. Thank you, Jordan Pollock, who answered so many highly specific hypotheticals about immigration law that I'm confident she could provide effective counsel to multiple characters who appear in these pages.

Many books and articles informed various aspects of *The Slip*. On the subject of immigration, William Finnegan's "The Deportation Machine," published in the April 29, 2013 issue of *The New Yorker*, provided particularly useful context.

I am indebted to the New Writers Project at the University of Texas at Austin, and especially to Oscar Cásares, Alexander Chee, Cristina García, and to my fellow Newtonite Elizabeth McCracken, in whose transformational workshop this project was born.

Thanks also to my brilliant 2015 New Writers fiction cohort: Scott

Guild, Cassandra Powers, and Parini Shroff, who read a few of these chapters more than any human should.

I am grateful to the late Larry Goodwyn for believing in me as a writer before I was doing all that much writing. When I was floundering some post-college, Larry suggested I might find what I was looking for in his former city of Austin. He was right.

Thank you to the friends who offered necessary feedback on various drafts over the years: Anna Cox, Malika Jacobs, Rachel Kondo, Antoinette Perez, and Dan Sheehan. Thank you, Mary Adkins, with whom I've been proudly plotting on the page and in life since she was in a neck brace and I was in the closet (a lot happened between 2000 and 2001). Thanks to the Austin literary community, especially Lauren Hough, Maya Perez, Jackie Rangel, Leila Sales, and Shanteka Sigers. Thank you to Téa Obreht and Steph Opitz for your consistent encouragement. Thank you, Adam Wilson, for good advice on publishing and nineties Newton fashion. Thank you Blair, Dylan, Emily, Erin, Joseph, Laz, Leila, Riddhi, Sara, Sarah, Suz, and Will, for many different things, but mostly for being good friends.

I would not have been able to write this book without the support of my family. Thank you to my parents, Mark and Elizabeth Schaefer, who always encouraged me to follow this path and who, if they were at all concerned over the many years it appeared their son was not succeeding, never let on. Thanks to my brother, Evan Schaefer, and to the Abram, Arthur, Distler, Marshall, Tannenbaum, and Wilson clans.

Finally, thank you to my husband, Greg Marshall. What is there to say, babe? We did it together. The next chapter awaits.

About the Type

The body of this text is set in Times Ten Linotype Standard, a font whose origin dates to the original design for Times New Roman in 1931. This font was commissioned by *The Times of London* after Stanley Morison published an article accusing *The Times* of being typographically archaic and poorly printed. With Plantin, an older typeface, as his inspiration, Morison himself updated the type's readability and, as a nod to *The Times*'s previous typeface, Times Old Roman, called his revision "Times New Roman." The Times font family has enjoyed global success and popularity since then. Times Ten Linotype is designed for use with smaller text sizes, and its neat, sharp serifs continue to make it a highly legible choice.

The display font is Trade Gothic Next Linotype Pro, part of the Trade Gothic family originally designed by Jackson Burke in 1948. As is typical of many gothic, pre-digital fonts, this typeface is known for its irregularities. In opposition to later, neater sans serif fonts such as Helvetica and Univers, Trade Gothic's inconsistencies lend personality to the text.